BOX OF HEARTS

NIKKI ASHTON

This book is dedicated to all you daddy's girls out there

.

Please note that some of the words in this book, are written using the US English spelling

PROLOGUE

♥

MILLIE

"Well, this is it," my brother sighed. "You're going to walk down that aisle and throw your life away on Rick the Prick. Are you sure that's what you want?"

I smiled and cupped his face in my hands. "Javi, it's going to be okay. Dean loves me, he's good to me. And stop calling him Rick the Prick. Ricks is going to be my surname in less than an hour, are you going to call me that, too?"

"No!" Javi scoffed. "You're not a prick for a start. He is."

My younger brother, Javier, did not like my fiancé one little bit. It wasn't that Dean was a prick, he was far from it. He was my best friend; we shopped together, he had a great eye for shoes and bags, his understanding of what suited my body shape was second to none – which I should point out is a big voluptuous bum, inherited from my Spanish mother, a trim waist, which is all mine, and much more than a handful of boobage, thanks to my grandmother, who I also happen to be named after. Dean also loved a rom-com, so what more could I want? Well, there *was* more that I could want – good old, down and dirty sex from time to time. That was the only fly in my beautiful relationship ointment; Dean's desire to wait until we were married before we indulged. Okay, it wasn't something I was happy about, what twenty-six-year-old woman in her prime wants to rely on her vibrator and a dirty book? Not me that's for sure. Nothing is the same as having a man's hands on you, but I had to respect Dean's wishes.

"Javi," I pleaded. "Just be happy for me."

He looked down at his highly polished shoes and kicked at the cork matting in my mum's hallway.

"Okay, but if he ever hurts you I will kill him, I swear."

I laughed, trying to make light of my brother's words, but what a visionary he turned out to be.

***

"Mierda," my mother cried, returning to her mother tongue as she always did when she was cursing, despite having never lived there. "How could he do that to you, Armalita?"

While my mum screamed and cursed, I tried to shut out the noise and huddled into the corner of the sofa, clutching one of my mum's throw cushions as if it was the lifebelt that would stop me from drowning. And at that point it truly was. I was numb from the heart down, unable to comprehend what had happened to me. It had to all be some sick joke, or maybe I'd been having a nightmare. Every bride has nightmares leading up to their wedding day; mine just wasn't about me arriving at church wearing jeans and a ratty t-shirt.

I had stood at the altar next to a handsome man, who swore he loved me, only for that moment to happen that usually only occurs in films.

"Does anyone know of any just reason why these two should not be joined in matrimony?" will forever be the phrase that gives me nightmares.

At that moment, while I laughed at the stupidity of such a question, a booming voice echoed around the church that was packed with almost one hundred people.

"I do!"

We all swivelled around to see which of the local nutters had been let in, only to let out an en masse gasp as Dean's bearded, tattooed, man-mountain friend, Ambrose, stood there clutching at his normally perfectly styled hair.

"Armalita," my mother cried. "What have you done?"

Javier snorted like a donkey. "I don't think it's Millie."

I snapped my gaze to my brother. "You don't think *what* is me?"

He didn't say anything but pointed towards Ambrose.

"Ambrose," Dean groaned. "Not now."

"Baby," Ambrose whispered. "We have to tell her."

I quickly looked back to Dean, who had tears in his eyes and was fanning his face with a perfectly manicured hand. It was that exact moment that it hit me, right smack between the eyes. The great fashion sense, the love of shoe shopping, his huge collection of Diana Ross CDs, and most importantly, the sex ban; he was just one big cliché.

"You're having an affair...with Ambrose," I whimpered.

"Millie." He took a step towards me, his hand outstretched. "Sweetheart."

"Do not touch me," I hissed, and turned to look at Ambrose who was now walking down the aisle towards us. "I want the truth, Ambrose."

He stopped a few feet away and, despite his humongous size, looked absolutely petrified that I was going to punch him; which I would have done had I not needed a box to stand on to reach him.

"We love each other, Mill. I'm so sorry."

My breath hitched violently as I felt my champagne breakfast rear its ugly head. Slapping one hand to my mouth, I hitched up my dress with the other and ran as fast as I could along the plush purple carpet and out of the huge double doors. With half of Rickeby watching me in amazement, I ran and ran, only stopping when I reached my mother's front door. It was then that I realized I had no key, so I collapsed down on to the step and sobbed, waiting for her and Javi to come home.

And so here we were, almost an hour later, me in a bedraggled white dress, and my mother and brother at opposite ends of the emotional scale; mum in tears and devastated for me, while my brother, while still consoling me, was trying to hide his happiness that I wasn't marrying Rick the Prick.

CHAPTER 1

♥

JESSE

"Momma, I don't give a damn whether she's travelled here from Mars. I have work to do and don't have time to meet a damn babysitter."

"Your dad's gone. I need your help, Jesse."

"You should have thought of that before you hired her. Why the hell did you hire someone from England anyway?"

"Ms. Braithwaite isn't just a babysitter. She'll teach your daughter things that I can't. Addy's a bright child and needs more schooling than I can give her."

"Whatever, I've got cattle to see to."

"Well, are you actually going to come for dinner tonight, or spend time with your daughter today?"

"Nope. Told you, I'm busy. I'll pick your woman up for you, but that's it. Tell Addy I'll see her tomorrow."

CHAPTER 2

♥

MILLIE

As I stepped into the cool air of the arrivals lounge, I took a huge breath and sent a silent prayer to Grandma Armalita, asking her to make this work for me. After my debacle of a wedding, there was no way I could stay around Rickeby, so I gave notice at my job as a nursery school teacher, rented out my house, and packed my bags.

Summer, my cousin, saw an advert in the paper for an agency that specialized in oversees appointments of nannies and pre-school teachers, and while I was having dinner with her and her hot as hell husband, Roman, one night, she persuaded me to contact them. Mum had an absolute fit when, only three weeks later, the agency called to say they had an ideal position for me in a town called Bridge Vale in the United States. At first I wasn't sure; the job itself seemed okay, it was for a four-year-old girl that needed care during the day and would also benefit from some basic lessons because she was bright for her age. However, when I looked the town up on line, I was swayed and became determined that it was the right job for me.

The town of Bridge Vale consisted of one bar, a bank, a library, a diner, a grocery store, a hardware store and a small department store, amongst a smattering of other small shops and businesses. It was quiet, thirty miles from the next town and, most importantly, no one would know that I had been dumped at the altar for another man.

And so, here I was. Mrs. Connor, the lady who was employing me, had said someone would meet me at the airport, probably her son, but the problem with that was that I had no idea what he looked like and no one was holding up one of those signs with my name on it. Not that I could see, anyway. The only thing to do was to wander down the line as though picking out a felon. I searched the crowd for an older teenager, or young man, but the line of people was mainly made up of older, ruddy faced men wearing cowboy hats. She may have sent her husband I supposed, but these men all looked as though they'd be too old to be the father of a four-year-old.

I was almost at the bottom of the line when I spotted him. I had never believed in love at first sight; it was a myth for fairy tales and girls who believed in bloody unicorns, not me. That was until I saw Jesse Connor waiting with my name scrawled onto a piece of paper, one arm folded across his chest, his dirty blond hair dishevelled and his hard, broad chest and slim waist filling out his white t-shirt and Levi jeans to absolute perfection. His hand went up to run through his hair, causing his t-shirt to ride up, giving me a glimpse of a tanned stomach. I licked my lips, pretty sure that I had drooled. He did not dress like the cowboys I'd seen when Googling 'ranching'.

When I was standing a mere two feet away from him, my reaction intensified. I couldn't help but stare as his piercing blue eyes narrowed their gaze onto me. My breath was literally whisked from my lungs and my heart was beating so fast I could practically feel it thumping against my t-shirt.

"You Millie or are you just staring at me for no reason?" he snapped.

7

"I'm Millie," I croaked as I swallowed the huge lump in my throat. "You must be Mr. Connor."

The disappointment hit me like a punch to the stomach. He was Mrs. Connor's husband, and I would be working for him and *his* wife. His bloody *wife*. This was going to be a nightmare. He was my boss and I had never felt such an immediate and deep attraction like this to anyone before. I couldn't possibly work for a woman whose husband I was crushing on; I was practically panting for the man. The affect that he was having on me was both exhilarating and scary at the same time. Never mind butterflies flying around my stomach, it felt as though there were a couple of Pterodactyls having a fight in there.

"Mr. Connor is my father, I'm Jesse, but call me whatever you please."

"Oh, so you're not Addy's father then?" I asked, trying to hide my excitement.

"Yes, I am," was his short reply before he took my suitcase from my hand and stormed out of the airport building.

***

The drive to the ranch was not only silent, but uncomfortable, too. Jesse's pickup truck was old and battered, the dark red leather seats were worn and torn, with the horsehair padding bidding for freedom. With every bump in the road, I shot in the air, almost hitting my head on the ceiling of the cab.

As we moved along the open road I coughed nervously and turned to Jesse.

"So, tell me about Addy."

"You'll find out soon enough," Jesse replied, his eyes remaining firmly on the road.

"Oh, okay."

A hint, if ever I'd heard one, that no further conversation would be required. I therefore spent the journey to the ranch sneaking glances at Jesse's profile and staring at his arms. They were tanned and strong, with corded veins, and as I watched them rest on the steering wheel, I had to keep reminding myself to breathe.

His profile was almost as beautiful as the front view of him. He had a strong, square jaw and his nose had a tiny bump in it, and I wondered whether he'd broken it at some time. At one point, I had to sit on my hands to stop myself from running them through his hair; it looked so damn sexy in an 'I've just had amazing sex' kind of way. Shit, only an hour in this man's company and I was a goner – how could I feel like this when, at this very moment, I should be settling into married life with my new husband? Evidently, the lack of sex over the last year and a half was taking its toll.

Finally, we drove under a wooden arch made from thick timber posts. On both sides of the arch was a white stone wall and hanging above was a huge sign, crafted from wrought iron that said, 'Connor Ranch'.

Although the driveway that we were travelling down was brown dust, on either side were thick, lush trees that met above our heads, their leaves dappling the ground as the sun shone through the branches. It was like a magical tunnel that was leading to a new life for me.

We rounded a bend and the ranch house came into view and I almost danced in my seat. I wasn't sure what I was expecting, but the sight before me caused me to gasp. As far as the eye could see was green, flat land. In the distance, beyond a wooded area, was a range of hills and mountains, and that along with the beautiful cloudless, blue skies were the perfect backdrop to the most gorgeous house I'd ever seen.

"Wow," I whispered.

"We just remodeled, last year," Jesse muttered.

"It's stunning."

The house was huge, with a grey slate roof that sloped down on all sides. The walls were all a lighter grey with the upper floor creating a slight overhang to the ground floor, and all the windows were white, a bright contrast against the grey. Because the ground at the front of the house sloped downwards, there was a set of white, wooden steps up to a columned entry with an arched roof that lead onto a white fenced wraparound porch.

Stunning didn't really cover it.

"Taken two years of hard work, but the old house was in real bad shape," Jesse explained as he pulled the truck up in front of the house.

This was the most that he'd spoken since we'd been in the truck, so I simply stared at him in shock.

"You okay?" he asked, pushing open his door that screamed with old age.

"Oh yeah, sorry. The house, it's just so pretty."

Jesse paused and lowered his head back into the cab and stared at me with a lip curl.

"It's a house, houses aren't pretty."

With that he was gone and before I could even get my door open, he was running up the steps to the house carrying my suitcase. Although I was getting the majority of my stuff shipped over, the case was still bloody heavy as I had packed enough clothes for at least a month, just in case a problem arose with my shipment. I almost groaned with desire. Jesse's strong arms picked the case up as easily as if it were a shopping bag. Shit, what the hell was happening to me? I was like a bloody bitch in heat.

Pushing the truck door shut, I hooked my bag over my shoulder and made my way to the house. As I reached the top of the steps, the door swung open and a woman dressed in jeans and t-shirt came rushing out, wiping her hands on a towel.

"Millie, oh goodness, it's so good to meet you, honey. I'm Bonnie, Bonnie Connor, we corresponded via email."

She held out her hand to me and I let out a long sigh.

"Oh, it's so good to finally meet you." And it was. The relief at finally being there, finally seeing a friendly face, was immense. I hadn't realized how tense Jesse's demeanour had made me.

"I thought you were Jesse's wife," I blurted out.

Her pretty face broke into a grin as she flicked her blonde ponytail over her shoulder. "No honey, I'm his momma. Addy is my granddaughter. Didn't I say that in my email?"

I shook my head. "No you didn't."

"Seesh, I'm getting forgetful in my old age. I'm just used to everyone knowing my business I guess. Well, you come inside and I'll get you some nice, cold lemonade," she said enthusiastically. "My husband, Ted, is out of town, but he'll be back in a couple of days, you'll meet him then."

"Okay, I look forward to it," I replied, following her onto the porch.

"Here," Bonnie said turning to face me. "Let me take your purse."

I furrowed my brow but with an internal shrug, I fished around in my handbag and found my purse. I smiled and passed it to Bonnie.

"Erm, what...?" She held my purse in her open palm, looked at it and then started to laugh. "Sorry honey, your bag, I mean your bag, not your wallet," she explained handing me back my purse.

"Oh, God!" I cried. "I'm so stupid, I'd looked up on the internet the different words that you use, but totally forgot that one. You must think I'm an idiot."

Bonnie shook her head and opened the door. "Don't be silly. There'll be lots of things we'll both have to learn."

As we stepped inside, my heart somersaulted as the most beautiful, blonde haired child came running towards me and wrapped her arms around my legs.

"You're here," she cried. "I've been waiting, haven't I Granma?"

"Yes, sugar, you have. Now let Millie take a seat so I can get her some lemonade." Bonnie gently pried Addy from my legs and led her over to the sofa, picked her up, and plonked her down on it.

As I placed my bag next to my suitcase, which Jesse appeared to have dumped as soon as he got through the front door, I took a quick look around the room. It was just as gorgeous inside as it was on the outside. The space was huge and sectioned off into different areas by white wooden shelves filled with not only books, but lots of different colored glassware and silver photograph frames of various shapes and sizes. We were in the lounge area where the grey and white of the outside was continued. A four-seater, dark grey sofa dominated the space and was placed opposite a grey stone fireplace. Next to the sofa was a huge teal colored armchair that was partially reclined, and was positioned in exactly the right position to see the large TV that sat in the corner.

"Your home is lovely, Bonnie," I said as she turned towards me.

"Oh, thank you. It's all Jesse's work, he and Melody had a vision of how they wanted it when Ted signed the house over to him. Me, I prefer things a little bit more rustic, shall we say, but Jesse was adamant we stuck to what Melody wanted."

"Melody?"

"That's my momma," Addy cried. "She's dead."

My eyes shot to Addy and then back to Bonnie. "Oh God, I'm so sorry."

Bonnie waved her hand at me. "Don't worry about it. How could you have known? Something else I forgot to put in my email. I'm sorry honey, everything has just been so hectic around here. We're in calving season, so you can imagine how busy we've been."

I couldn't really; the only thing I knew from Bonnie's email was that we were on a fourth generation cattle ranch with six-hundred pairs of cattle. I'd meant to research the Connor's ranch on the internet, but my leaving had been a last-minute decision and so I'd been really busy preparing to come here.

"That's why you're here," Addy added from her seat in the middle of the sofa. "Granma is getting too old to look after me *and* help on the ranch, so we needed you."

I laughed softly and shook my head. "You sure she's only four?" I asked. "Her vocabulary is brilliant."

"She is definitely four, and three months. That three months is real important, hey Addy," she replied, ruffling Addy's hair. "But you're right, she seems older. That's why we need you, too. She could go to pre-school, but to be truthful, the local one isn't so great and," she said on a sigh. "I had a falling out with the teacher when she told me that Addy had behavioral problems and should be tested for ADHD."

"Really, anyone can see she's bright and it's probably boredom."

"I know, exactly, so you can imagine how Jesse took that when I told him. He told me to pull her out of there and said she'd learn more on the ranch than anything that 'mean-spirited old witch could teach her'." Bonnie did air quotes with her fingers to indicate that they were Jesse's words.

"Could she not start school a little earlier?"

"I tried, honey, but the principle is the husband of the pre-school teacher, so he listened to her. Told me that unless I got Addy tested to prove otherwise, he'd have to accept that she was a badly behaved child and would not be allowed in school until the law required. So, that's where you come in. Our cook left, and Jesse has struggled to get a replacement; everyone's already settled into a contract. We have four hands living in the bunk house who need feeding. This means that Monday through Saturday the cooking and packing of lunches for seven men, and the family, is down to me, so I don't have time to teach her, and," she said with a glance at her granddaughter, "a bored Addy is a mischievous Addy."

Addy grinned up at her grandmother and then at me.

"Well, I'm here to help now, and we'll make sure you have plenty to do. Won't we, Addy?"

"Yep, we sure will."

"Okay, Millie," Bonnie said. "Let me get you that lemonade while you make yourself comfy. Take a seat, honey. Then once you've cooled down some, I'll show you around. But, while you're here, I want you to treat this as your home. As for caring for Addy, well she's still a little girl, so I don't want anything too routine. Make it nice and relaxed, just see what the days bring. The main thing is she won't be sitting around here trying to amuse herself when I'm busy, and I won't be run ragged trying to amuse her."

"Sounds perfect," I replied, and it did. The money wasn't brilliant, but I hadn't taken the job for the money. A year on this ranch was just what I needed.

As I moved over to sit next to Addy, I heard a door open followed by a pair of heavy boots stomping across the room. I looked towards the back of the house as Jesse appeared from what I thought was the kitchen as I could see the edge of a countertop from behind the shelves. He was now wearing a plaid shirt tucked into his jeans and a black Stetson that was pulled down so you could hardly see his eyes.

Jesse stopped, looked at me, and then turned to Addy.

"Hey, Daddy," she cried, her eyes lighting up at the sight of her father.

"Addy, I'll see you tomorrow. Be a good girl for Granma."

"Okay, Daddy."

I couldn't help but notice that Jesse barely looked at her as he moved past the three of us to the door. It also struck me that Bonnie had been the one to deal with getting a pre-school teacher. I also couldn't help but notice that Addy's eyes were shining and her bottom lip had a little tremble to it.

Once the front door slammed shut, Bonnie bent down and kissed the top of Addy's head.

"Daddy's real busy today, sugar."

"I know. Can I go and play in my room, please?"

"Don't you want to stay and get to know Millie?" Bonnie asked.

Addy shook her head. "Not just yet, thank you ma'am."

"It's okay, Addy," I interjected. "You go and play, we can have a talk later."

With a little nod she climbed down from the sofa and ran to the stairs that were off to the right.

"I'm sorry," Bonnie sighed. "It's been hard for her. She's a bright child, but she's still *a child* and doesn't always understand how hard Jesse has to work."

"It's okay, Bonnie, I understand." Actually, I wasn't sure I did. Jesse seemed to be totally blind to how his behaviour was upsetting his daughter.

Bonnie studied me carefully before flopping down onto the arm of the sofa.

"He's not been himself since Melody died."

"Well that's understandable. How long ago was it?" I asked, thinking it would be a few months.

"It's been almost two years since she died. It was a car accident."

I gasped and felt my heart break for the little girl who so wanted to be seen by her daddy.

"God, this is too much for you. You haven't even been here an hour yet."

"No, it's fine," I whispered. "But, poor Addy."

"I know. He's shut us all out to be honest. All he does is work and got to Rowdy's, when he's not falling asleep on his feet."

That I did know about; Rowdy's was the only bar in town.

"So you see, honey, there's lots of things you can do for Addy, not just teach her math and English, but don't worry about that just yet. Maybe take a week to settle in, get to know her, and then think about some lessons."

I smiled and nodded, knowing that this job was probably going to break my heart more than being ditched at the altar.

CHAPTER 3

♥

JESSE

As Rowdy's came into view, I thought about Angie, my latest fuck buddy, waiting inside for me. She was always waiting for me, even when I didn't want her to be. I'd never promised her anything, told her from the start all it would ever be was sex, nothing else, but fuck if she didn't keep trying.

Then the damn English woman's face flashed before my eyes. Those fucking sexy lips and that hair that I'd love to grip hold of while I made her forget her own name.

Shaking my head to erase the images, I pushed open the truck door and went into the bar.

CHAPTER 4

♥

MILLIE

It was the day after my arrival, and I had not once seen Jesse since he'd left the house. The sad part about that was it meant that Addy hadn't seen him either.

Thankfully though, by dinner time, after her tearful retreat to her room, Addy seemed to have recovered from her disappointment and played happily with me, showing me around the ranch while Bonnie was busy in the kitchen cooking up a storm, making cakes and pies for the house and bunk house. All of which were especially welcoming now, because it was calving and they were all out with the cattle for long hours.

With Bonnie still busy, Addy and I had made lunch and taken it outside to eat in the pasture opposite the house, under a massive old oak tree for shade.

"Grandpa gets home today," Addy said excitedly. "I missed him."

"Where's he been, somewhere nice?" I asked.

"He's been to the city to see Uncle Garratt."

"Oh right, okay." I hadn't heard about any uncle. "Is Uncle Garratt mommy's brother?"

Addy screwed up her face. "No silly. Uncle Garratt is Daddy's brother. He's at college but Grandpa says he keeps screwing up."

"Addy!" I exclaimed. "You shouldn't say things like that."

"But that's what Grandpa said," she replied indignantly.

"Well, maybe so, but you shouldn't. Okay?"

With a big sigh and heave of her tiny shoulders, she nodded her head and began tucking into her sandwich. Once we had eaten our lunch, I got out one of the reading books that I had brought with me. It was really for age's six to seven, but I was fairly confident that she would be able to make progress with it. She'd amazed me at how bright she actually was. I'd done some basic arithmetic, or math as she'd called it, with her the night before, not to start teaching, but just to gauge what level of lessons I'd have to give her. She'd flown through it, so I knew that I'd have to keep her constantly engaged with learning. I'd already decided to go online and find some lesson plans, realising that caring for Addy would need far more input than the basic reading, writing and arithmetic that Bonnie had expected. It wouldn't be a problem for me, I had a teaching degree, but teaching hadn't been for me and I'd much preferred being a nursery school teacher, but now it would help me to help Addy.

We had been reading for few minutes when a truck rumbled up the track to the house and pulled up where Jesse had parked his truck the day before. This truck, however, was a huge shiny black one, with sparkling wheels, nothing at all like Jesse's decrepit old girl.

"Grandpa!" Addy cried, and with her book forgotten, she ran as fast as her little legs would take her to her grandfather.

"Sugar pie," a tall, sandy haired man called, and swept Addy into his arms, swinging her around, making her giggle.

I walked over to them and stopped to watch their happy reunion. When he finally placed her carefully on her feet, laying a hand on her head, I took a step forward.

"You must be Millie," he said, thrusting out his hand. "Ted

Connor, it's great to meet you."

I took his proffered hand and shook it. "Hi, Mr. Connor, lovely to meet you, too."

"Ted, please, Mr. Connor is my dad, God rest his soul."

I let out a laugh. "That's exactly what Jesse said when he picked me up at the airport."

Ted frowned. "Jesse picked you up?"

"Yes." Was my succinct reply. What else could I say? 'Yes, he picked me up and acted like an ignorant idiot the whole time'?

"Wow, his mother must have bribed him with something." As he saw me raise my eyebrows, Ted laughed. "No offense to you, but Jesse doesn't exactly do anything except work as a rule."

"So I gather. Anyway, I know one little girl who is glad you're back." I nodded down at Addy who was gazing up at her grandfather.

"Oh, hey sweetie pie, I have a surprise for you in the back seat of the truck. I already opened the door for you."

"Yay," Addy squealed as she skipped off to the truck.

"Wait for it." Ted grimaced and put his fingers in his ears, just as a piercing scream of excitement filled the air.

"Uncle Garratt is here, too!" Addy cried excitedly. "Millie, come see, it's Uncle Garratt."

"I brought my youngest home, he was sleeping on the back seat. I figured it was time he woke up."

As we both turned, a pair of black converse appeared out of the truck and planted themselves on the dirt. Long legs clad in dark jeans followed, and then finally, a lithe body in a white t-shirt. The head that appeared was almost as gorgeous as his elder brother's but he was darker and his features were still slightly boyish, not yet those of a man. The potential was there though and Garratt Connor was definitely going to be a heart breaker, if he wasn't already.

"Hey beautiful," he crooned, bending down to pick Addy up. "You miss me?"

Addy rubbed her nose against Garratt's and then threw her chubby little arms around his neck.

19

"Yep, I guess you did." Garratt turned to me. "Hey, Garratt Connor, the prodigal son."

"Hi, Garratt," I replied, instantly liking the boy/man standing in front of me. "Millie Braithwaite."

"The nanny, right?"

I nodded. "Although I like to think of myself as Addy's new friend."

Garratt grinned widely and snuggled his face into Addy's neck, appearing to breathe her in. "I've missed you so much, beautiful."

"Are you staying home now, Uncle Garratt?"

Garratt's eyes shifted towards his father and then snapped back to Addy. "I think so, for now."

Ted let out a breath and moved back towards the truck. "Okay, Garratt let's get your bags inside and let your mom know you're home."

Garratt put Addy down on the ground and followed Ted to the covered flatbed of the truck. A few seconds later they both appeared again, carrying various bags.

"Is there anything that I can bring in?" I asked.

"There are some boxes," Ted said. "If you could bring one of those it would help."

"Me too," Addy cried, jumping up and down.

"Okay, sweetie, let's see what we have." I peered into the truck and saw about four or five boxes of various sizes. I found the smallest for Addy and placed it in her outstretched arms. Luckily she was still able to see over the top, just about. "Go carefully."

"I will. Come on, Millie, let's go and see Uncle Garratt."

I smiled, glad that Addy seemed truly happy that her uncle was home. Even if her father had no interest in her, at least Garratt appeared to. I picked up a box and followed them inside, and bizarrely felt a little pleased myself that Garratt was home.

***

Addy was taking a little afternoon nap, and Ted and Bonnie were 'having a chat' in the office; a chat that I guessed was about their youngest son. I didn't know much, but what I had gleaned from Bonnie's words when he first got home was that he'd been in trouble at college, but for what I wasn't sure.

With both of us at a loose end, I suggested that we sit on the porch with some of Bonnie's lemonade. Garratt agreed with a grin, and a warning from his mother to behave.

"So," he said as we sat on the swing on the porch. "What on earth brings a beautiful woman like you to Bridge Vale? Most can't wait to leave, believe me."

I took a deep breath and wondered whether to lie, or just be out there about my humiliation. I'd only known Garratt a couple of hours, but he seemed a genuine, fun loving sort of guy, and it really didn't worry me about telling him the truth. I didn't expect him to judge me.

"Long story short, I got dumped at the altar by my gay fiancé."

Garratt almost choked on the lemonade that he'd taken a swig of. "You're kidding, right?"

"No, unfortunately, I'm not."

"A sexy Chiquita like you and he prefers dick?"

I burst out laughing at his bluntness. "Firstly, I'm half Spanish not Mexican, and secondly, I'm not sure that statement about Dean's sexual preference is actually politically correct."

"I knew it," he cried. "Those eyes, the black hair, the sexy Jennifer Lopez booty, you had to be a Latino. As for Dean, well, however you wanna dress it up, the guy is a prick!"

I started to giggle. "That's exactly what my brother calls him. I think you'd get along with Javi, you evidently have the same sense of humor."

"Yeah, maybe," Garratt mused. "So, you decided Bridge Vale was the best place to mend your heart?"

"I don't know about that," I sighed, thinking about the brooding and handsome eldest Connor son. "But, at least no one here knows what happened. Well, of course you do now."

"Yeah but you can trust me not to tell."

"Okay," I said. "I've told you something, so now you tell me something about yourself."

Garratt tilted his head to one side. "Let me see," he mused. "Okay, I just got thrown out of college for running an escort agency."

My eyes widened in surprise. Getting thrown out of college was major, no wonder Bonnie and Ted needed privacy to talk about it. But an escort agency? That was practically being a pimp!

"Seriously?"

"Yep," Garratt replied solemnly.

"You really pimped out women?" I asked in total shock.

"Ah, you see, Millie, that's exactly the same mistake the college and my dad made. No, I did not pimp out women."

"Well, what other sort of escort agency is there?"

"The sort where the popular girls in college can earn more in one night than they can waiting tables in an on-campus diner. And, I should stress, without having sex. Sex is totally not allowed. If they liked a guy and wanted to sleep with him, then it was when they were off duty."

"How on earth can you stop that happening?" I pulled my legs up and turned in my seat, totally engrossed.

"Because they escort the guys to functions, frat parties, football games, that sort of thing. Places where the guy just wants to be seen with a cute, popular girl. The guys who needed my services were usually the ones who struggled to get dates, so sex wasn't generally on the agenda anyway."

"Just because you're shy, or not good looking, doesn't mean you don't want sex," I scoffed. "And I've read about your frat parties, don't tell me that there isn't opportunity for sex there."

"Yep there is, but each girl has one of my guys watching over her, so first sign that they're gonna disappear somewhere alone, my guy steps in. Besides, the guys that pay for the dates don't tend to know what a vagina looks like, unless it's tattooed with computer code."

"Blimey, you really had it worked out, didn't you?"

Garratt started to laugh. "Say that again. Blimey," he repeated with a passable English accent.

"Not bad, a little iffy but we'll make a Brit out of you yet."

22

"I am a man of many talents; businessman being the best of them. Plus, I know someone from England." Garratt looked into the distance, a shadow passing over his boyish handsome features.

"How were you found out?" I asked.

"Ah well, that would be my so called best friend, Tyler. Let's just say we fell for the same girl and when she chose me, well, Tyler wasn't happy. He reported me to the Dean and the rest, as they say, is history." Garratt chewed on his bottom lip and rubbed at his temple.

I could see that he was hurting and wanted to give him a comforting hug, but didn't know how he'd react. We hadn't known each other long, despite the details that we had both imparted.

"What about the girl?" I asked quietly. "Is she still yours?"

Garratt shrugged. "Don't know. She's an overseas student, from England, like you. The day before I was called into the Dean she got a call to say her sister was sick so she had to fly home. I tried calling her cell, but she's not answering, so I sent a text and an email explaining everything."

"You like her a lot," I surmised.

Garratt smiled, a soft one full of memories. "Yep, she's really cool. But, we've only been together for a month, so I can't really expect her to wanna do the long distance thing."

"The city is only four hours away, that's nothing for you American's," I said with humor.

Garratt gave me a stunning smile and poked me in the shoulder. "I'm gonna like having you around, Millie. It'll be like having a hot, big sister. I can see all my friends are gonna wanna visit, a lot, when they find out I'm back and that you live here."

"Big sister, hey?" I grinned and poked him back. "I think I like that. So in the last couple of days, I've gained another baby brother and a new best friend in Addy."

"Sounds like a perfect deal to me, sis."

We both laughed and took sips of our drink, enjoying the summer breeze that had lifted.

"What happens now?" I asked after a few minutes. "I mean, do you apply for another college, or will you work here, with Jesse?"

Garratt shrugged. "Not sure. I didn't really enjoy school anyway. I had no idea what I wanted to do when I finished, so I'm no worse off. But you've met Jesse, right?" I nodded. "Well, you'll guess that working with him probably isn't gonna be the easiest job in the world."

"But you won't have a degree, surely that will hinder your future."

Garratt shrugged as he took a swig of his lemonade. "I'm a genius with numbers, it's where Addy gets it from. I'll find something."

He appeared to be so nonchalant and confident that I had to agree he probably would find something.

As we sat in silence, Jesse suddenly appeared from around the side of the house. He pulled off his gloves and, pushing his Stetson back, he wiped his forehead with the back of his hand. He looked so damn good I felt a shiver run through me and stop firmly between my legs. I quickly pushed my thighs together and took a huge swallow.

"Hey, big brother," Garratt called, jumping up from the swing. "How you doing?"

"Garratt." A small smile flashed over Jesse's face as he strode towards us. "When did you get back?"

Jesse's gaze moved to me and then back to Garratt, and a look of confusion furrowed his brow.

"We were just getting to know each other," I explained. "Addy's taking a nap, but she's probably due to wake up if you want to go up and see her."

Jesse turned to look out to the horizon before staring at the floor, with his hands fisted on his hips. "Leave her be. I'll call in before bedtime."

I opened my mouth to protest, but Garratt beat me to it.

"Still like that, is it?"

"Garratt!" Jesse warned. "I've told you before, this has nothing to do with you."

"But it does; she's my niece."

"And she's *my* daughter, and I'll raise her how I see fit."

"That's the thing though, Jess. It's everybody else that's raising her, not you."

Jesse removed his hat and pointed it at Garratt. "Addy is perfectly fine with how we do things around here, so drop it, once and for all."

"Whatever," Garratt grumbled. "But you're the one missing out, not us."

With that, he swivelled around and stormed into the house, slamming the door behind him. I sat perfectly still, watching Jesse as he looked up to the sky and cursed under his breath. Part of me wanted to tell him that Garratt was right, he *was* missing out, but I got the feeling that he already knew that and he was struggling with his actions, but had no idea what else to do. I just didn't understand why he would be like that; why couldn't he simply give his daughter the time that she deserved?

"You got something to add?" he asked. "I mean you've been here the sum total of twenty-four hours so you must have an opinion."

I shook my head. "No, not really. I just think Addy is a beautiful little girl who loves her daddy."

Jesse took a step forward and then stopped. "Ah, fuck this," he muttered and disappeared in the direction that he'd come from.

I stayed on the porch for a few more minutes, just in case Jesse came back, but he didn't, so I finished off my lemonade before going in to wake Addy.

CHAPTER 5

♥

JESSE

"Fucking Garratt," I muttered as I stormed back to the bunk house. "Sticking his damn nose into my business."

"Woah, steady on there, Jess."

Brandon Reed, my best friend, caught hold of my shoulders just in time to stop me from barrelling into him. He helped out on the ranch during calving and the rest of the time helped his parents run their guest ranch, ten miles down the road.

"What's bitten your ass?"

"Nothing," I snapped and moved to walk around him.

"Jess, I've known you for over twenty years, so I know when something is troubling you."

"Garratt is home," I replied, hoping that would quieten his questions.

"Why?"

I pinched the bridge of my nose. With all the talk of Addy, I hadn't even asked my little brother why he was back on the ranch. A few days ago, I'd heard Dad mention something about him being in trouble with the Dean of his college, but that was all I took in.

"Some trouble at college," I replied evasively. "What happened to that calf?"

Brandon shook his head. "Didn't make it."

"Okay," I sighed. "Let's get back out there."

"Why don't you stay here, go have dinner with your family? You've been out there for fourteen hours straight. I don't know," he said with a grin. "Maybe spend some time getting to know Addy's new nanny. I saw her this morning and she's hot man. That ass is something else."

My eyes narrowed on Brandon. "Just get Drake to saddle me up a fresh horse, Brandon."

I stormed off, not wanting to hear any more thoughts that Brandon had on Millie fucking Braithwaite.

CHAPTER 6

♥

MILLIE

I had only been at the ranch for four days and could already see why Bonnie needed help with Addy. Normal play just wasn't stimulating enough for her, well not for long anyway. After a few hours, she would start to get bored and, as Bonnie said on my first day, get mischievous. Only yesterday I found her drawing on the wall in the office, at the back of the house. It was where Ted did all the paperwork for the ranch. He couldn't ride for any great length of time any more, due to a problem with his knee, so he ran the business side of things while Jesse ran the practical side.

The scolding that Addy had received for writing on the wall obviously didn't worry her, because I was now watching her fill Garratt's trainers with soil from the garden at the back of the house.

"Addy," I scolded. "Why are you doing that to Uncle Garratt's trainers?"

Addy looked at me perplexed as though I was talking in a foreign language. She'd better not try the old 'my invisible friend did it' trick. As a nursery school teacher, I'd had to deal with that one a lot; it was old news.

"Addy," I pressed. "I asked you a question."

"But I didn't understand," Addy replied.

"Okay. Why are you putting soil into Uncle Garratt's trainers?"

She screwed up her tiny little nose and shook her head. "What are trainers?"

"Trainers? You don't know what trainers are?" I picked one up, emptying the dirt back into the flower border. "This is a trainer."

"You mean a sneaker?"

I couldn't help but smile at the way her brow wrinkled and her tone insinuated that I was pretty much the dumbest person she'd ever spoken to.

"Yes, Addy," I replied biting back a laugh. "I'm sorry, I mean a sneaker."

"Oh, why didn't you say that?" She stood up and dusted her hands down against each other. "He put a toy spider in my bed and made me squeal. He knows I don't like spiders. I'm the same as Daddy, he hates spiders." Her little face looked grave as she shook her head in evident disgust of Garratt.

So big, bad, Jesse Connor hates spiders, was my first thought, then I remembered that Addy was in trouble.

"Well that isn't very nice, I admit, but it's also not very nice to put dirt in his trai...sneakers. You don't have to do something bad back if someone upsets you. You just tell them that they made you sad."

"Grandpa always says 'an eye for an eye'."

I gasped that she even understood what that meant. Then her next sentence explained where she'd gained that knowledge.

"Uncle Garratt says that means if someone hits you then you kick them back in the shins. Harder." She grinned at me and stretched out her hand. "I don't want to kick Uncle Garratt, so can I have his sneaker back please?"

Part of me wanted to give Garratt's shoe back to her, payback

29

for teaching her things he shouldn't, but I'd been employed to care for her and teach her things, and not just those of an academic nature.

"No, Addy, you shouldn't be doing that, so empty the dirt out and we will take them back inside and let Uncle Garratt know what you did, and why you did it. Okay?"

She looked at me as though she was going to argue, but then she sighed and emptied out the soil. Addy handed me the shoe and stalked off to the house.

"You're no fun," she muttered as she stomped up the back steps to the house and then slammed the door behind her.

"You're good with her," a deep voice said behind me.

I turned around to see a tall, broad man with dark brown hair and eyes that looked like pools of melted chocolate. He was watching me with a smile that showed perfect, white teeth. What the hell did they put in the water around here? This man was like a model. He didn't make my nerve endings jangle as Jesse did, but he was still extremely easy on the eye.

"Brandon Reed," he announced, offering his hand. "Jesse's best buddy and part-time dogs body this time of year."

"Hi, Brandon, I'm Millie. I'm Addy's new nanny."

We shook hands and Brandon held on to mine for a little longer than was necessary. As he pulled away, his fingers trailed slowly along mine.

"Yep, I know who you are. I've wanted to come introduce myself for a couple of days, but we're calving so..." His words petered off as his gaze drifted over my shoulder. "Garratt."

"Brandon."

The two men stared at each other in silence, and I half expected one of them to pull out a pistol and shoot the other at any moment. I looked from one to the other and the iciness of both their stares was positively arctic.

"Well, I'd better go and find Addy," I said. "Nice to meet you, Brandon."

Brandon's face fell into an immediate smile and his eyes turned back to me. "You too, Millie. Maybe you'll let me take you to

30

Rowdy's one night. Show you how we enjoy ourselves in Bridge Vale."

"I can take her," Garratt said, his tone hard.

Brandon laughed. "No offense Garr, but I think everyone around here knows you're under age and that fake ID you use in the city won't cut it here."

"Don't have to drink, and I think you'll find I'll be legal this time next week."

"Oh yeah," Brandon scoffed. "I forgot that you were finally becoming a man soon. How's that growing up thing going for you then, Garr? Oh sorry, it isn't, you've been sent home from college haven't you."

My eyes widened. These two really didn't like each other that was more than obvious.

"Maybe we can all go together," I said gaily, trying to diffuse the situation.

Brandon smiled at me again and shrugged. "Maybe, Millie. Well, it's been great meeting you and hopefully we'll catch up again soon."

"You two don't get on," I said to Garratt as we both watched Brandon disappear around the side of the house.

"Nope," Garratt replied and stalked back inside.

I followed him in and made my way to Addy's room, sure that's where she would be sulking. As I reached the top of the stairs, one of the framed photographs that hung on the wall drew my eye. It was a picture of Jesse, Garratt, and Brandon and looked as though it was around four or five years ago. Brandon was standing between the two brothers, with his arms draped over their shoulders. They all looked happy and Brandon appeared to be laughing down at a grinning Garratt. I had to wonder what on earth had gone on to change them from obvious friends to two men who evidently hated each other.

CHAPTER 7

♥

JESSE

When I reached the yard, I hadn't expected to see Brandon. He was supposed to be mending a fence, not talking to *her*. I should have known. That damn woman was gonna cause trouble, I just knew it!

CHAPTER 8

♥

MILLIE

The day after Brandon and Garratt's stand-off, the sun was high in the sky and there was very little breeze. It was hot and humid and I was sure that I was going to melt. Addy was doing some coloring at the kitchen table while I sat opposite her, holding a wet cloth to the back of my neck.

"Sure is hot today," Bonnie said as she kneaded some dough. "Have to be honest though, it's not usually this hot at this time of year. You not used to the heat, honey?"

"No," I sighed. "But when I am, it's usually sitting next to a pool wearing a bikini with a nice cold drink. I'm not sure I could get away with walking around here in a bikini."

"Oh, I don't know about that." Garratt entered the kitchen, wearing sleep shorts and a t-shirt; evidently he'd just woken up. His hair was in all directions, and he was yawning while scratching at his chest.

I was just about to respond when Jesse appeared behind him. He huffed and pushed at Garratt's back.

"Move, Garratt," he muttered.

Bonnie looked up from her dough and looked between her sons. "Morning boys."

"Morning, Mommy," Garratt joked as he bent to kiss her cheek.

"Mom," Jesse said and moved over to stand behind Addy. "Morning Addy, honey," he said.

All of us stopped what we were doing and turned our heads in unison to see Jesse run a hand down his daughter's long hair. Addy stopped coloring and turned a bright smile on her father.

"Morning, Daddy. Do you like my picture?"

"Yeah, it's pretty."

There was no mistaking the look of regret in Jesse's eyes as his gaze raked over his daughter's face. While he stared at her, it felt as though we were all holding our breath, not wanting to break the spell. Even I, as a newcomer, could see that this interaction was huge for Jesse. Addy, being the open hearted little beauty that she was, didn't hesitate to climb onto her knees and throw her arms around Jesse's waist.

"Thank you, Daddy."

Jesse raised his hand, looking as though he was going to stroke her hair again, but he allowed it to hang for a few seconds before dropping it to his side.

"I need to go," he said and pulled away from Addy.

"Bye, Daddy," Addy sing-songed, totally unaware that her father was struggling with the closeness of her.

"Bye, honey," Bonnie called with a break in her voice.

As he strode to the door, Jesse said nothing but held a hand in the air to indicate goodbye.

"Shit," Garratt said softly as the door slammed. "Do you think he's finally got his head out of his a-hole?"

Bonnie shrugged and Addy went back to her coloring. I reached across the table and gave her forearm a little squeeze.

"That's really good, Addy," I said as she looked up at me.

"I know." She grinned. "Daddy said."

"Excuse me," Bonnie croaked as she wiped her hands and practically ran through to the lounge.

"Is she okay?" I asked Garratt quietly.

"She'll be good. It's just since the accident he's been a total douche to everyone, especially her." Garratt pointed at Addy who was still busy. "That's the first time he's touched her in…well a long damn time."

"Maybe he's realized what he's missing out on," I said, affording Addy another glance.

"I hope so, Millie, I really do, because if he doesn't change soon he may just lose her forever."

***

Later in the day, the heat had intensified and we were all flagging, even the Connors'.

"It's real hot today, hey?" Ted said to me as he appeared from his office. "Haven't known it to get this hot for a long time, 'specially this time of year."

"I know," I replied, fanning myself with a magazine that I'd bought at the airport. "I've been to the Bahamas on holiday and it wasn't this hot."

"You could always put on that itty bitty bikini of yours," Garratt laughed as he stood in front of me in thigh length swimming shorts. "I'm setting the hose up for Addy."

Addy had already stripped down to her swimsuit an hour before and, slathered in sunscreen and wearing a hat, had been helping Bonnie in the garden.

"It's not 'itty bitty' as you call it," I replied. "With the size of my boobs and bum, there is not a chance of me wearing anything remotely 'itty bitty'," I joked.

"It's tits and ass, honey," Garratt said with an exaggerated twang. "But whatever size it is, you need to get your swim suit on and come outside. Even Mom is thinking of stripping down."

"She is?" Ted asked, his attention suddenly elsewhere and his eyes shining with excitement.

"Ugh, Dad, really?"

"What? We might be older than you son, but we ain't old. These days, men in their early fifties are in their prime." Ted actually flexed his muscles and sucked in his stomach a little – not that he was in bad shape, because he wasn't. Years of working on the ranch had done wonders for his muscle tone, and it wasn't difficult to see where his sons got their looks from.

"Seriously, Dad. If you keep talking like that, Millie will be on the next plane home. It's making me feel sick, and I've lived with you for almost twenty-one years."

"Okay," I interjected with a giggle. "I'll come out and play with you, as long as you stop picking on your dad."

"Why thank you, Millie, I appreciate it. It's nice to have someone respect me for a change." Ted's eyes shone with humor and it was great to see. Between his two sons and their troubles, Ted Connor still had a lightness about him.

"I respect you, Dad." Garratt's words were said with sincerity and a huge smile on his face.

"Yeah I know, Garratt." Ted smiled back and then disappeared into the garden, presumably to find Bonnie.

"I disappoint him so much," Garratt sighed.

His hands were hanging off the back of his neck and he was staring in the direction that his father went.

"I'm sure you don't," I replied. "He's maybe a little mad with you at the moment, but I doubt whether you disappoint him. Has he said much to you about the college thing?"

"I got a lecture from him and Mom. He told me that I get a week to decide what I want to do after summer break. Either try to find another college, which will probably mean me having to go to some godforsaken place that no one in their right mind would attend, get myself a job, or, the icing on my cherry pop tart, work on the ranch."

"You don't want to work on the ranch?" I asked, wondering whether it had anything to do with working with Jesse, or even Brandon.

Garratt shrugged. "I love this place, I really do, and I'm not scared of the work, but I just don't see myself staying here my whole life. Now Jesse, he's different. Working the ranch was all he ever wanted to do. That and raise a family with *Melody*."

The way he said 'Melody' caused me to sit up straight. There was a harshness to his tone. It wasn't my place to ask, but I wondered whether he actually liked Melody, because it didn't sound as though he did. Then surprisingly, Garratt gave me the answer.

"Just so you know, Melody and I didn't get along too well. We did when she first started dating Jesse, when they were seventeen. I was twelve and my hormones were bouncing and Melody was hot, she was a cheer leader, you know what I'm saying? So, I thought that she was amazing."

Garratt smiled and shook his head, memories evidently coming back to him.

"So what changed?"

"Melody changed. They got married just after Jesse's twenty-first birthday, because she was pregnant with Addy, and Jesse wanted to do the right thing. Plus he loved her. He adored her so much that he put her on a pedestal so damn high even he couldn't reach her." Garratt sat down on the edge of the reclining chair, leaning forward with his elbows on his knees.

"After Addy was born, Melody changed a whole lot. She started taking off for the day, going shopping in the city with her friends, or spending money on days at a Spa at the hotel in Knightingale, the next town along, or sometimes in the city. Mom wondered if she was suffering from post-partum depression, but when Jesse made her go to the doctor to get it checked out, he told them both she was perfectly fine."

"That doesn't mean she wasn't," I replied. "She may have hidden it well."

"Maybe, but it wasn't just that, she started to get ideas above her station. Her parents were both dead, so she'd pretty much lived with us since she and Jesse got together. She lived with her uncle, officially, but he was always down at Rowdy's getting drunk and didn't care about Melody one bit, so she'd always been grateful to Mom and Dad, but after she had Addy, she thought she deserved better even though she'd never been to college and only every worked helping Mom doing the cooking and cleaning here. She kept going on at Jesse about the house, how it was dated and too small and that the truck needed replacing, or her clothes were too old. Stuff like that, all the time, and Jesse being Jesse wanted to give her everything she wanted, and worked his ass off to do it. As well as working the ranch, he started to take horses, too, breaking them in for people, and they paid a high price for his services because he was good at it, really good. He ended up working fifteen and sixteen hour days, just so Melody got the latest purse or fashion."

"Jesse loved her, though, so if he wanted her to have those things, it was up to him how hard he worked, surely?"

"I know, and that's exactly what he said, but I didn't agree with it."

"And so you didn't like Melody because of it?"

Garratt stared at me for a few seconds and then stood up from the chair. "That was one of the reasons that I didn't like Melody, yeah. I just couldn't stand what she was doing to my brother, what she's still doing to my brother. The man's in love with a fucking ghost and it's killing me to see it."

At that moment, Addy came running into the house, screeching excitedly. "Uncle Garratt, come quick. Grandpa is chasing me with a bucket of water, we need to get the hose and get him back."

Garratt's sombre expression lightened at the sight of his niece with her gleaming smile.

"Okay, beautiful, I'm coming."

"You, too, Millie," she called over her shoulder.

"Yeah," Garratt said on a grin. "Go and get your swim suit on, Millie, otherwise we might have to get your clothes wet."

"Okay," I sighed. "I'll see you out there."

As I made my way to my room, I thought about everything that Garratt had told me and my heart broke just a little bit more for the Connor family because of what Melody's death had done to them.

CHAPTER 9

♥

JESSE

As I rounded the corner to the back of the house, I saw them all. Garratt, Addy, Mom, Dad, and Millie, all of them having water fights and screaming as if they were all Addy's age. I pulled up short, not willing to take another step.

I'm working my fucking nut sack off to keep this ranch running and they're all having fun. Well hoo-fucking-rah for them. And what the hell does she have on? That's not a swim suit, it's damn underwear!

CHAPTER 10

♥

MILLIE

"Millie, honey," Bonnie cried from the porch steps. "I think all your stuff is here."

Addy had gone out for the day with her friend Elizabeth, who lived in town, and Elizabeth's mother was taking them for ice cream and then to the cinema in Knightingale, therefore I'd been helping Bonnie bake some pies for the ranchers. I say help, but she'd actually been teaching me, as I was not known for my culinary skills at the best of times and pies were way out of my comfort zone.

We'd heard a vehicle beeping as it came up the track, so Bonnie had gone to investigate and seemingly it was all my belongings.

The two men in the truck helped me in with the boxes and piled them in the lounge, then after declining a cold drink and a piece of lemon cake, left with another beep of the horn.

"Is this everything you own?" Bonnie asked.

I shook my head. "Not all of it, just things I thought I'd need for a year on a ranch."

I held up the pair of red stiletto shoes that I had pulled from the first box that I had opened. "Although, not sure I'll need these."

We both giggled as I examined the four inch heels before throwing them back into the box.

"Well, if you leave them there I'll get Ted to help you up with them when he gets back."

Garratt and Ted had gone to see a guidance counsellor friend of Ted's, to find out what Garratt's educational options were, although I had a feeling that Garratt had already decided that college was not for him. After that meeting, Ted was dropping Garratt and a couple of his friends into Knightingale. Today was Garratt's 21st birthday and he couldn't wait to buy his first legal beer. Bonnie had wanted to throw a party, but Garratt didn't want one. Most of his friends were away at college, where he had expected to be, so he didn't fancy 'a fucking tea party with Mom, Dad and Addy playing musical fucking chairs'. Knightingale it was then!

"Okay, thanks Bonnie," I replied. "But I'll just check what's in each one first. I left in such a hurry I have no idea what I shipped over."

"No problem, honey. I'll put the last of those pies in the oven then I'll go over to the bunk house, see what supplies they need."

"Do you need me to come and help?" I asked.

"No honey," she replied, waving a dismissive hand at me. "It's just checking the cupboards, that's all. No, you stay and sort through your boxes."

I sighed contentedly as Bonnie disappeared. She was such a lovely woman and she had made it so easy for me to fit in on the ranch. Everyone had, to be honest. Well, everyone except Jesse, he was like a grizzly old bear that hated to be disturbed.

For the next hour or so, I searched through the boxes and made a pile of anything that I realized that I wouldn't need. I was going to put them in another box and ask Ted if he'd store it somewhere for me for the year that I would be here. I had just pulled out a framed photograph of Dean and me, when Jesse stormed into the house. My pulse quickened and if I hadn't already been sitting, I think my legs would have gone to jelly.

"Oh hey," I said, looking up at him from my cross-legged position on the floor. "Your mum is over at the bunk house and your dad is with Garratt in town."

"And Addy?" he asked, scratching the top of his head. "Where's she?"

My heart jumped a little. Had he come to the house to see Addy? Was Garratt right, was Jesse finally extracting his head from his a-hole?

"She's on a play date with a friend. They've gone to the cinema, sorry, the movies. I'm trying to remember to use the correct lingo," I babbled. "But I keep forgetting."

Jesse gave me a hint of a smile.

"Well if you are, for the record it's my Mom, not my Mum."

The way he said Mum made me giggle, he seemed to struggle to get his tongue around the word. Then as soon as I thought of the word tongue, that was it, my mind started to conjure up other visions of Jesse and what he could do with his tongue. To hide my embarrassment, I looked down at the picture in my hands.

"What's that you've got there?" he asked, lowering his six feet plus frame to crouch next to me.

"Oh, just a photograph. My stuff from home arrived."

Without any warning, he took it from me and examined it. His eyes came up to meet mine and then went back to the photograph.

"Boyfriend?"

"No, not anymore."

"He's not waiting for you?" he asked, handing the photograph back.

I shook my head. "Let's just say we didn't end on a positive note."

"That why you answered Mom's ad' for the job-to get away from him?"

I expected Jesse to stand, but he stayed in the crouched position, with one arm resting on his knee while the other hung between his legs. I could feel my skin start to heat up as the smell of him invaded my nostrils. He smelled of leather and musk and hard work and it was absolutely intoxicating. Putting the photograph in the box, I turned to look at him and felt my heart flutter again; I was going to need a pacemaker at this rate. He looked amazing, despite the dirt smeared across his cheek and the greyness under his bright blue eyes.

"So what happened, you fall out of love with him?"

Jesse's gaze on me was as intense as his questioning. I'd been here eight days and this was the most he'd spoken to me. I had been pretty much invisible to him before now.

"He cheated on me," I said without thinking, Jesse's eyes hypnotising me into laying myself bare. "In fact, he more or less dumped me at the altar. Well, he did dump me at the altar, no more or less about it."

Jesse's eyes widened. "Fuck me, who'd he leave you for, a Victoria's Secret model?"

I started to laugh. "How do you know about Victoria's Secret models?"

"I may work long hours Millie, but I ain't dead from the waist down and we do actually have the TV, newspapers, the internet, running water and all that shit out here."

I thought I'd offended him, but the corner of his mouth lifted into a small smile.

"Okay, point taken," I giggled. "And no, *he* was not a Victoria's Secret model."

"Say that again." Jesse's mouth dropped open as he tilted his head closer to me. "Did you say *he*?"

I nodded as the shame hit me in the chest like a lead weight. Jesse's finger came under my chin, and lifted my gaze to his.

"That's not on you, Millie," he said softly. "If a man likes other men, there isn't a lot you can do about that. You really don't have the equipment to change his mind."

I gasped at Jesse making a joke and started to laugh. Jesse didn't laugh but he gave me a smile that crinkled his eyes, then he stood up and started to walk towards the door.

"Fucking dick head, though, if you ask me," he said with his hand on the door handle. "It's like having prime beef at home and going out for McDonald's every night."

With that he was gone, as was my heart. Jesse Connor was going to be my downfall, I just knew it.

CHAPTER 11

♥

JESSE

The idiot liked guys. Well hell, if that's his choice then that's his choice, but to choose a guy over *that* woman – fucking dick!

CHAPTER 12

♥

MILLIE

The days turned into weeks, and before I knew it, I'd been at the ranch for almost a month. Jesse and I hadn't really spoken again since the day we'd discussed Dean, but he had been a little less grumpy and did actually say hello and goodbye without sounding like a condemned man when he did it. Nothing had changed as far as my heart was concerned though. My crush seemed to be intensifying and I knew that my cheeks colored each time I saw him.

Garratt had decided that after the summer he was going to get a job and was spending a lot of his spare time writing to businesses in the city, to see whether they would give him a job without a degree. He did reveal to me that the success of his escort agency had given him an idea to set up a dating website for college students which meant that any job he got would simply be a means to an end. I was sure he hadn't mentioned anything about the dating service to his parents, because they were both extremely chirpy about the fact that he was finally sorting his head out. In the meantime, Garratt was working on the ranch. He seemed okay about it, but I had heard him say to Jesse that in no way was he working with Brandon. Jesse argued with him, wanting to know what his problem was with Brandon, but Garratt declined to answer and simply stormed out to the porch.

Addy was doing well with the lessons that I'd been giving to her. There wasn't anything too taxing; she was still a little girl who needed to have fun after all. She enjoyed learning though, which made my days an absolute joy; lessons in the morning and then playtime and a nap in the afternoon.

Jesse was still distant from her, but he had progressed to coming to see her at breakfast every day and leaving with a pat to her head. Occasionally at night, he joined us for dinner and then listened to Addy reading before she went to bed. He never sat next to her, his position was always on the recliner while Addy sat on the sofa. Then when it was time for her to go to bed, he'd pat her head once more on his way out to go back to the bunk house; that was where he slept, despite having a bedroom in the main house.

As for Ted and Bonnie, they were just fine, no longer worried about Garratt and happy that Jesse seemed to have found some sort of compromise in his relationship with his daughter. Bonnie also seemed to have gained more energy over the last month, constantly having to keep Addy occupied as well as looking after the ranch hands had evidently been taking its toll. She and Ted had even gone to Rowdy's one evening, although Garratt had refused to let them call it 'date night', saying that it made him feel sick.

As for me, well I was happy. As happy as I could be recovering from being dumped on my wedding day and now falling head over heels for a man who was so closed off to people he may as well live alone, on a desert island. My days were full of Addy and my nights were full of dreams of Jesse. The glimpses that I got of him every day just made my desire for him all the more intense. Every morning I found myself excitedly jumping out of bed, just because I knew Jesse would be downstairs drinking his coffee, waiting for us all to rise.

This morning when I bounced into the kitchen, there was no Jesse, in fact there was nobody there, not even Addy. I looked through into the dining room, wondering whether Bonnie had decided that we would eat there this morning, but nothing. I opened the glass doors that led on to the deck and leaned over the railing, looking down into the garden, but everywhere was deserted.

Walking back through to the kitchen, I had no idea whether to start breakfast or sit and wait. At least I could make the coffee; I had watched Bonnie enough to know how the Connor family like it – strong and black, except Bonnie who liked a drop of creamer and two sugars.

As I finished preparing it and turned on the machine, the back door opened and Garratt walked in. A bruise smudged his cheek and there was a cut on his bottom lip.

"Garratt, what's happened?" I asked, taking a step towards him.

"Ask my brother, the fucking dickwad."

Garratt stalked past me and disappeared towards the stairs.

"Garratt!" I called after him.

Garratt held up a hand to quiet me and snapped, "Millie, just ask fucking Jesse."

As I heard his feet stomping on the stairs, the back door swung open and Ted marched in, closely followed by a sniffling Bonnie, carrying a sobbing Addy in her arms.

"What the hell happened?" I asked Ted. "Why is Garratt bloodied and bruised and why are Bonnie and Addy crying?"

"Jesse," was all Ted replied before storming in the same direction as Garratt.

Bonnie placed Addy on the countertop and kissed her forehead.

"I'll get you some cereal sweetie, okay?"

A tearful Addy nodded and then held her arms out to be picked up. Bonnie picked her back up and carried her through to the lounge. I watched as she deposited her on the sofa and then walked back to me.

"Bonnie, what's happened?" I asked quietly, dragging her into a hug.

Bonnie hugged me back for a while and then with a sniff, pulled away. She wiped her nose with a handkerchief and then flopped down onto a chair.

"Well, from what I've managed to get out of her, Addy got up real early and wanted to go and see Jesse, she'd had a bad dream apparently and just wanted her daddy. She let herself out of the house and made her way to the bunk house."

"She did all that on her own?"

"Yes," she sighed. "We were in here. Garratt was supposed to be riding out early this morning, and Ted had a yearning to go, too; he hasn't been out for such a long time. Well, we heard the door shut, but thought it was Jesse coming in. When he didn't, Ted went to see who it was and he saw Addy running faster than a jack rabbit in the direction of the bunk house. He shouted to tell me, so Garratt and I followed."

"How did I sleep through all of this?"

"Your room is at the back, honey, and it wasn't a major drama, well not until we got there."

"Oh God," I gasped seeing the horror on her face.

"Jesse has a little cabin at the back of the bunk house, it's private. Ted's dad built it when he had a married ranch hand working for him for a time, so Jesse uses it." She took a shuddering breath and then continued. "Ted couldn't reach Addy, that girl is fast when she wants to be, so she got to Jesse's rooms first. She let herself in and...well, Jesse had a woman in bed with him. Ted got there just as Jesse lost it with Addy, shouting and screaming at her to get out, then he started on the woman in his bed. Angie, the damn town whore."

My mouth dropped open on a loud gasp. Bonnie laughed humourlessly.

"Not literally, honey, but she may as well be. That's what Jesse called her, too, while he was throwing her clothes at her. Told her she'd no right staying the night after he'd fallen asleep, and all she was, and I quote, was 'a warm body from time to time, a fuck, and a mediocre one at that.' I don't like that girl, Millie, but I raised my boys better than that."

"Then what happened?"

"Then he took hold of Addy and pushed her towards me and told me to 'get that kid out of here', and that's when Garratt punched him. Ted let them have at it for a while, I reckon he thought Jesse deserved it, but when Addy started to cry for Garratt to stop hurting her daddy, Ted stepped in."

"After everything, she was worried about Jesse?"

Bonnie turned and looked over to where Addy had now fallen asleep, her thumb firmly in her mouth.

"She loves her daddy. As he slumped to the floor, she kissed his cheek and then kicked Garratt in the shins. I think that hurt that boy more than any punch that Jesse landed on him."

***

After breakfast, everyone was still feeling subdued about what had happened, particularly Addy. She wouldn't look at Garratt and ate her breakfast curled up on Ted's lap, with Ted spoon feeding her just to ensure that she ate something. She was now sitting cross legged on the floor, watching a Disney film. I'd taken the decision that today would be all about fun-no lessons.

Bonnie had taken the truck into Knightingale to go to the big food market there, as she needed supplies for both the family and the bunk house. Because she needed so much, Ted had gone with her instead of one of the ranch hands. He said it was because he needed some things for the office, but I had a suspicion he didn't want to bump into Jesse.

Garratt had stayed behind and my suspicion about that was that he wanted to try and put things right with Addy. In his own words, he 'didn't give two shits about Jesse', but Addy was a different matter.

"Hey, Garratt," I said quietly as he sat next to me on the sofa. "How are the war wounds?"

He gently poked at his lip and winced. "I'll live. How's she doing?" he whispered, nodding towards Addy.

"She'll be fine. I think it was all just a big shock."

"Yeah, well, seeing Angie's shaved pussy and floppy tits was no picnic for me either."

I couldn't help but smile. "Garratt!"

"I know," he sighed. "But if I don't laugh about it, Millie, I'll fucking cry."

My eyes turned to the TV as the film was coming to an end, and any minute now Addy's attention would leave the screen.

"Why don't you try and talk to her?" I suggested.

"Because," he replied on a long exhale. "I'm scared shitless that she won't forgive me."

"Oh, Garratt." I reached for his hand and squeezed it. He adored his niece and the fact that he'd upset her was tearing him apart. "Just try."

He nodded and then scooted down onto the floor and shuffled next to her.

"Hey, beautiful," he said softly, giving her braid a little tug. "How you doing?"

Addy ignored him at first, continuing to stare at the TV that was now showing the credits to the film. Garratt pulled on her earlobe and then blew at her cheek. Addy flicked a hand, as though swatting a fly, so Garratt did it again. This time she turned sharply to face him.

"Stop it, Uncle Garratt," she grumbled. "I don't like it."

"I know, but I had to get you to speak to me somehow. I don't like it when we're not friends."

"We're always friends and I always love you, I just don't like you today."

I bit on my bottom lip to stop myself from laughing. Her chubby little face was pulled into a frown; brow furrowed, lips pursed, and nose wrinkled.

"I'm sorry for hurting your dad, Addy, but he upset me because he upset you."

"But he's my daddy," she replied. "I don't want *anyone* to hurt my daddy."

"I know you don't, but I was mad at him because he made you

cry." Garratt edged a little closer and took Addy's tiny hand in his and rubbed it gently.

"Will you say sorry to Daddy, too?" she asked, full of consternation.

Garratt took a breath, considered it, and then nodded on the exhale. "If you want me to."

"Do you want to?"

This child amazed me with her grown up attitude; she could probably teach her father a thing or two.

"I want to, because you want me to." Garratt used a finger to move Addy's hair from her eyes and then smiled at her. "I love your daddy, but I love you, too, so even though I think he's wrong I will say sorry."

Addy thought about it for a moment and then nodded.

"Okay, but not yet."

Garratt tilted his head back and looked at her quizzically. "Not yet, why?"

"Because I want to come with you and I don't want to see him yet. I'm mad at him, too."

Garratt pulled Addy into his arms and gave her a hug and a big sloppy kiss on her cheek.

"Adeline Marie Connor, you are amazing, you know that?"

"What's a maze thing?" she asked, and suddenly she was a tiny little four-year-old again.

I watched uncle and niece as they argued over which film to watch next and hoped that Garratt and Jesse could get over their differences just as easily; but somehow, I doubted it.

CHAPTER 13

♥

JESSE

I fucking hate myself more than I ever thought possible. How could I do that to my baby, push her like that, and *then* fight with Garratt in front of her? The hurt in her face broke my heart, but there was nothing I could do to stop myself. It didn't feel like it was me, it felt as though I was outside my body watching on as the shit storm took place.

I have no damn idea how to do this alone; Melody was supposed to be here with me. No wonder I keep fucking up.

My poor Addy. Damn Angie, I told her she had to leave. Shouldn't have drunk so much and I wouldn't have fallen asleep. I would've made sure she left my bed; but I never expected Addy to come over. She's never come over before. Well, Angie won't be coming here again, I shouldn't have brought her last night. There's only one woman I want in my bed and I can't have her.

CHAPTER 14

♥

MILLIE

The day after the incident with Jesse, Addy had perked up considerably and had even asked Garratt if he would take her into town to get ice cream. I think the clever little minx was playing on Garratt's guilt, but he had been more than willing and had strapped her into her car seat with a huge smile on his face and a promise of not only ice cream, but toy shopping, too. He was definitely overjoyed to be back in Addy's good books.

With Addy and Garratt out, Ted in the office, and Bonnie cleaning and changing the beds in the bunk house, I decided to sort out my things in my room; a beautiful, light and airy room at the back of the house that overlooked the garden and a pasture beyond. On the gorgeous white, wooden posted bed, were crisp white sheets with blue polka dots and a bright duvet cover, or comforter as Bonnie called it, with red and blue flowers on one side, and blue and white stripes on the other. The walls were painted a beautiful sky blue and the woodwork a bright, glossy white. Also on the bed were matching flowered, scatter cushions mixed in with some red fluffy ones. At the two windows were sheer white drapes over blue and white striped blinds and on the wall opposite my bed were a dresser and a wardrobe, both in the same white wood as the bed. I loved it and wondered whether it had been decorated specifically for me, or if this had been part of Jesse and Melody's vision for the house. Whichever, it was perfect.

Ted had told me that I could store some boxes in the barn adjacent to the house. He told me it was water tight and everything would be perfectly safe in there, so I organised what I didn't need into three boxes.

After hanging up my clothes and putting out some of the photographs that I'd brought with me, I sat back on the bed, looked around the room, and sighed; now it was not only beautiful but it looked like home.

I let out a shuddering sigh at that thought. I had spoken to my mum and Javi a couple of times since I'd been here and had felt totally at peace with my decision to up sticks to America. Now though, with familiar things around me, a pang of yearning knocked on my chest bone. I needed to call my mum and just hear her voice. I took my phone from the top of my dresser and dialled her number. Dinner would be finished and she would be settling down to watch TV, so I was hopeful that she would answer. After a few rings, she did.

"My baby," my mother crooned. "How are you?"

"I'm fine, Mum. I just wanted to speak to you. How are you, how's Javi?"

"Oh, he's okay. He's finally dumped that damn girl."

"No way!" I exclaimed, gasping with shock.

Even though he was my brother, I knew he was quite a hottie. His skin was a rich golden brown, his hair was so black it looked almost navy blue in some lights, and his eyes were a gorgeous whisky color. Girls threw themselves at him constantly, but he'd only ever had eyes for Gabby Stevens. Gabby on the other hand seemed to have eyes not only for Javi, but for every other Tom, Dick, and Harry as well. Javi wouldn't believe it, but evidently, he'd finally seen the light.

"Yes, he told me that he'd had enough of her taking him for granted."

I laughed out loud. "Blimey, I can't believe it. I bet you're happy, aren't you?"

"Oh Armalita, I can't tell you. He's also talking of coming out to see you after Christmas."

My heart started pounding with excitement. "Really? Oh my God, that would be amazing. Why don't you come, too?" I babbled.

My mum giggled on the other end of the line. "We'll see. Now, you'd better go, this call will be costing you a fortune."

"I love you."

"I love you, too, sweetheart. I'll call you next time, okay?"

"Mum, it's fine. I have nothing else to spend my money on, so a couple of calls a week aren't going to bankrupt me."

"You youngsters, you have no idea about money."

With laughter and blown kisses, we said our goodbyes and I ended the call, holding the phone against my chest. It had been very short, but very sweet, and very much needed. My mum and brother were everything to me, even more so since my dad had died six years ago. He'd had a massive heart attack while playing golf; Javi had only been sixteen at the time, so it hit him hard. But, we had each other to lean on; our little gang of three. Tears pricked my eyelashes as I thought about Dad and how I'd been a daddy's girl. I adored him and I was his princess, which was why the situation between Addy and Jesse was all the more heart wrenching to me.

With a little sniff and a swipe at my tears, I picked up one of the boxes that I was going to store in the barn, and made my way downstairs.

When I reached the barn, I could see that the bolt was pushed across on the access door. With the box getting heavier with every second, I wedged it between my hip and the door, twisting my body to reach the bolt.

"Let me help you," a voice said behind me – Jesse.

Goosebumps instantly burst out over my skin, a brief shiver rippling through me.

I turned my head to look at him and noticed the deep blue bruise on his chin and a slight redness around his eye. Jesse stared at me unblinkingly.

"I see Garratt got a good punch in," I said, trying to hide the quiver in my voice.

Jesse didn't say anything but reached around me, sliding the bolt back and pushing the small wooden door that had been inlaid into the huge barn door. As his scent reached me, my senses whirled and the air around me thickened. Trying to back away, I stumbled and almost dropped the box.

"Give it to me," he commanded, taking the box from me and stepping into the barn. "Where'd you want it?" he asked from the dim light.

"I don't know," I replied following him in. "Your dad just said to store them in here."

"There's more?"

"A couple, yes."

Jesse turned from me and walked a couple of feet to a tall rack of metal shelves that stood against the wall. He placed the box on and straightened it.

"They'll be better up here than on the floor, it'll make life difficult for the mice."

I shuddered at the thought of opening up my boxes back in England to find an overseas visitor burrowing in my belongings. I dropped my gaze to my feet, my eyes searching for anything scurrying around.

"The cat comes in here daily, I doubt there's any in here."

My head snapped up. "I didn't know you had a cat, I love cats."

"Not this one you won't. It's practically feral and would scratch your eyes out soon as look at you." Jesse moved some other things around on the shelving, presumably to make way for my other two boxes.

"What's it called?" I asked.

57

He stared at me for a few seconds and then shook his head in disbelief. *"Cat."*

***

Ten minutes later and Jesse had deposited my boxes in their new home and bolted the door again. He had hardly spoken since he'd told me about the cat, but the tension that he held in his neck and shoulders said plenty.

"Thank you," I said as he walked towards the house.

"Not a problem."

He reached the steps up to the porch and then stopped and turned back to me with a tilt of the head and a frown.

"Where's Addy?"

"She's out with Garratt. They went to town for ice cream and toy shopping."

"Shitting little fucker," he muttered under his breath.

"Sorry?" I took a step closer to him, not sure that I'd heard correctly.

"Nothing. I'll come back later."

Steam started blowing between my ears as I watched him approach me. It had taken him more than a day to try and put things right with Addy, and just because Garratt had already done so he was a 'shitting little fucker'.

"He's actually not," I said as Jesse got level with me. "He's actually a very kind and sweet uncle to your daughter."

Jesse stopped and stared at me, his blue eyes no longer bright, but icy cold.

"Meaning?"

"Meaning that he's said he's sorry to Addy and to make amends, has taken her for a treat. Something which you should have done yesterday, straight after it happened."

"Millie, you don't know anything about what happened. What my life has been like, trying to hold things together for the last two years."

"I know you've shut your daughter out. Why, I have no idea, but as badly as you feel the hurt, she feels it just as much. You lost your wife; she lost her mummy *and* her daddy."

58

Jesse's jaw clenched as his hands fisted at his sides. "I think it's best if you don't say anymore," he spat at me. "You being here a few weeks does not give you the right to tell me how to be with my child."

"Maybe not," I retorted, my voice getting louder. "But me looking after your daughter and seeing how lost she is without you, does give me that right."

"I'll repeat, stay out of it, Millie. It's no business of yours."

"Every time you reject her, Jesse, either me or your mum, dad, or Garratt have to try and make her smile again. It's going to take its toll on her eventually."

"You know what, I'm not sure this is working out, you looking after my daughter."

I let out a harsh laugh and turned to go. "Whatever, Jesse," I snarled. "But your mum hired me, so she can be the one to fire me."

Before I had moved one step, Jesse's hand caught hold of my arm and pulled me back to his side. One of his arms snaked around my waist while his other hand laced through my hair. He pushed the back of my head so that the tips of our noses were inches apart.

"You want me to fuck you quiet, is that it?" he growled.

"You arrogant pig," I hissed, desperately trying to pull away, yet at the same time loving the feel of his hands on me.

"Don't pretend you don't want this, Millie, because I know you fucking do. So you'd better say no, *now*, if it's not what you want."

His eyes bore into mine as he waited, and when I gave a nod of my head, his lips were on mine and his tongue was pushing into my mouth. His grip on my hair tightened as did that around my waist, as he pulled me closer. I felt the hardness in his jeans and I couldn't help but whimper. Jesse walked us backwards, his mouth never leaving mine, and slammed me against the wall of the barn, pinning my arms above my head with one of his hands at my wrists.

"That mouth of yours is fucking delicious, Armalita," he said and then took it in another knicker wetting kiss.

Desire buzzed through me and I could feel a pulsing between my thighs as his kiss lived up to its description. As I hitched my leg up, and pushed my pelvis forward, Jesse reached between us and popped the button on my denim shorts. He pulled down the zip and then hooked his fingertip into the lacy edge of my knickers. I gasped as he ran his finger along the edge of my pubic hair and then pushed his hand inside.

"So damn ready for me," he groaned as two fingers slipped inside me.

"Jesse!"

I gasped as he thrust them in an out, and then pressed his thumb against my clit.

"I want you shoutin' my name when you cum," he whispered against my ear, his thrusting action never stopping.

I felt the swell start in the pit of my stomach as my orgasm started to take hold. While Jesse used his fingers and thumb, the pressure built, my skin heated, until every nerve ending exploded and the feeling of euphoria burst through on a cry; just as he wanted, it was a cry of his name.

As my thighs continued to tremble, I tried to steady my breathing and leaned my head back, looking up at the sky.

"Oh my God," I gasped.

My chest was still heaving as Jesse pulled his hand from my shorts. He stood back, his hands hanging loosely at his sides, and stared at me. I watched his face and could see a gamut of emotions shadow over it. Pleasure, desire, and finally, guilt.

"Jesse." My eyes never left his as I flattened my hands against the barn wall.

"Leave it, Millie. That should never have happened."

"But it did happen. We can't just ignore it." I couldn't ignore one of the most intense orgasms that I'd ever had.

"I said fucking leave it." With that, he turned and stalked away, never once looking back.

As I zipped my shorts back up, the one thought in my head wasn't regret or shame, but strangely how on earth he'd known that my full name was Armalita.

CHAPTER 15

♥

JESSE

Shit, I should not have done that, but that damn smart mouth of hers was just asking to be kissed. I couldn't stop myself; I needed to have her as much as I needed to breathe to stay alive. I'm still rock hard thinking about her and the way she came apart just from my fingers. Imagine what she'd be like if I got her in my bed – but that is never gonna happen.

CHAPTER 16

♥

MILLIE

"Addy, sweetie," I cried, time for lunch.

Bonnie smiled at me as she placed a plate of sandwiches down on the table. "You okay, honey?" she asked. "You seem a little preoccupied these last few days."

Preoccupied wasn't what I would call it. I'd say I was embarrassed, mortified, guilt ridden, and extremely horny. I was feeling all of those things, after only five minutes against the wall of the barn with Jesse. The orgasm had been spectacular but once that and the aftershocks had worn off, I realized that I'd made a huge mistake. Anyone could have seen us, we weren't exactly hidden from view. My stomach lurched at the thought of Addy and Garratt coming back and catching us, or even Bonnie. The consequences would have been enormous, especially for Addy who had already seen her father in a compromising position, and that hadn't ended prettily.

"Oh, I'm fine," I sighed. "Just a little homesick, I think."

"You can call your momma anytime from the house phone you

know. You don't have to keep using your cell."

I placed a hand on Bonnie's arm and gave it a gently squeeze. "Thank you, but honestly it's not a problem."

"Well so long as you know, honey."

Addy came careering into the kitchen, her breath heavy with excitement. "Granma, Daddy's coming, Daddy's coming."

"He is?" Bonnie asked with a deep frown.

She leaned to look around the shelving that separated the lounge from the kitchen just as we heard the door slam shut.

"Hey, Jesse," she said cautiously. "You okay?"

"Hey, Mom."

As Jesse passed behind me, my skin tingled and every hair on my body seemed to stand to attention, as images of what he'd done to me flitted through my brain. Trying to regulate my breathing, I pulled out a chair at the table. Once I was seated, I took a sandwich and put it on my plate and turned my eyes in the direction of Bonnie and Jesse.

"I'm sorry, okay," he said quietly leaning forward and kissing Bonnie on the cheek.

Bonnie nodded and moved to sit next to me and my gaze followed her son. Jesse looked down at Addy who was staring up at him adoringly; he noticed me staring and held my gaze for a beat, his face giving nothing away.

"Hey, Addy," he said, looking back at her.

"Hey, Daddy," she squeaked in a quiet voice.

"Just wanted to say sorry to you too. I shouldn't have shouted at you like that; you did nothing wrong. It was all me."

"That's okay, Daddy," she replied gleefully. "We can be friends again."

Jesse's eyes brightened and he laid a hand on top of her head. "You sit down at the table now and eat some lunch with Granma."

I inhaled sharply, noting that my name had been omitted.

"Excuse me," I said on a cough. "Went down the wrong way." I reached for the jug of water and filled my glass, taking a long drink.

"You could stay, too, couldn't he Granma?" Addy suggested, tugging on Jesse's hand.

As I banged my glass down on the table, Jesse's eyes darted to mine, and then just as quickly went back to Addy.

"I'm sorry, Addy, I have lots of work to do. We're ear tagging the calves today, I just wanted to come over and say sorry before I ride out again."

Addy let out a sigh and flopped down onto a chair. "Okay, Daddy."

Jesse rubbed the back of his neck and looked up at the ceiling. "I have an idea," he said on a heavy breath. "How about I come over for dinner tonight?"

Addy sat up straight and beamed a huge smile. "You will?"

"Yeah, I will."

"Millie," Addy squealed. "Daddy's coming for dinner."

"I know sweetie, I heard. That's great, maybe you can read him some of your new book that Uncle Garratt bought for you when you went into town for ice cream."

I couldn't help the dig, I felt like being mean. Garratt had spoiled her rotten the day before and Jesse thought one dinner would put everything right; the sad part about that was for Addy, that's all it *would* take as far as Jesse was concerned. Plus, he was treating me as though I was invisible – well I hadn't been when he wanted his damn hands on me.

"Yeah, well, great for Uncle Garratt," Jesse muttered under his breath.

"Jesse!" Bonnie scolded. "No more."

Jesse's eyes darted to Addy and then back to his mother. "I'll see you later. What time's dinner?"

"The usual, six-thirty," Bonnie replied, but the words not vocalised were, 'you'd know if you came more often'.

"Catch you later," Jesse replied and then quickly left.

***

By six-fifty, Jesse still hadn't arrived for dinner and Addy was refusing to eat hers until he got there. Ted had tried calling Jesse on his phone, but he hadn't answered.

65

"Addy," Ted said in a commanding tone. "Eat your mac and cheese, now. It's going cold."

"But Grandpa, Daddy's coming and if we all eat up he'll have no one to eat with when he gets here."

"If he gets here," Garratt muttered.

"Addy, sweetie," I said, ignoring Garratt's remark. "Your grandpa is right, your dinner is going cold. You can always eat your dessert when Daddy gets here."

"Can I, Grandpa?" she asked, narrowing her eyes.

"Yes, sweetie pie, you can. Now eat up that nice meal that Granma made."

With that she started to scoop up her mac and cheese with her spoon.

We had all finished and there was still no Jesse, but Addy was refusing to move from the table. She sat, with her dessert in front of her, elbows on the table and face in hands, waiting.

"She needs to have a bath and go to bed soon," Bonnie whispered as we watched Addy from the lounge. "He's not going to come."

"I'll go and find him," Ted hissed, slamming his newspaper and reading glasses down on to the arm of the recliner.

"I'll go!" Garratt said.

The worry was etched on Bonnie's face; she knew that if either of them went there was likely to be another argument, or worse, another punch up.

"No, I'll go." I stood up on shaky legs and smoothed my cotton sun dress down. I wasn't really sure that I felt brave enough to speak to Jesse alone, but I would for Addy and Bonnie. "He can't be far away, and if he's not in his cabin, I'll ask one of the hands where he is."

"No way," Garratt stormed. "You're not going over there."

"Garratt's right, honey," Bonnie added. "Those boys are good men, but I don't want you over there alone."

"I promise I won't go to the bunk house then, but let me go and see if I can find Jesse." I had no idea why I was offering to do this. The thought of facing him, alone, after what had happened spiked my nerves, but the need to look after Addy's heart was greater than the need to protect my own.

As I rounded the corner to the bunk house, I could hear raucous laughter and shouting. Light was coming through the windows, but the blinds were pulled down, so the shafts of light were all I could see from inside. As a resounding 'fuck you' bellowed out, I quickly walked past and decided that everyone was right and I wouldn't go looking for Jesse in there. I had almost reached the door to his cabin, that was attached to the back of the bunk house, when it was swung open and Jesse came rushing out.

"Millie," he gasped. "What are you doing here? Something happened?"

"Apart from you daughter refusing to leave the table until you come and eat your dinner, no."

"I had a cow caught in some fencing," he replied, continuing towards me. "I couldn't leave it there just so Addy had someone to eat dinner with."

As he stormed past me I let out a growl. "You're unbelievable," I cried and actually stamped my foot.

Jesse stopped and turned back to face me. "Like I said, I couldn't just leave it there."

"I know that, but this was about more than Addy having someone to eat dinner with and you know it. It was eating dinner with *you* that mattered, after what happened the other day, she needed this, Jesse."

"I have fucking work to do, I can't help that."

"You could have called her."

"My damn battery was dead and I forgot to take a radio. Besides, I was a bit busy cutting a fucking valuable cow free of barbed wire. And what the fuck are you doin', wandering around here at night on your own?"

"This isn't about me, it's about you and Addy," I practically screamed, my frustration with him hitting world record levels.

"Fucking point taken then, now if you don't mind I *was* on my way to the house."

It was only then that I took the time to look at him properly. He hadn't even showered and was still dirty with the grime of the day.

"Go then," I replied petulantly.

"You first. I ain't lettin' you wander around here any longer. There's four men in there and a couple of them haven't had a woman in weeks, so as much as I trust them with my cattle and my life, can't say as I'd trust them with you too much. Now move it."

"You're one bossy cowboy, you know that?" I huffed as I walked past him; with a little added hip swing I should add.

"I ain't a cowboy, I'm a rancher," he snapped as he started to follow me.

"What's the difference?"

"Nothing, I just prefer to be called a rancher. I don't just run cows, I work with horses too, when I have time. Now, are you finished talking?"

I looked over my shoulder and frowned. "So sorry your Royal Rancher, I'll shut up shall I?"

"Yep," he growled. "That'd be good."

And so I did as we walked back to the house in complete silence. I say complete, but I huffed and tutted a lot.

As we walked through the door, I could hear Addy in the kitchen, practically screaming at her grandmother.

"No! I want to see Daddy, he promised me."

"Well he's isn't coming, and you need to have a bath. Please Addy, I do not have the energy to argue with you tonight."

"No!"

Addy's high pitched squeal almost shattered my eardrums, so goodness knew how Bonnie felt.

"Adeline!" Jesse barked as he stalked towards the kitchen. "What the hell is going on?"

There was complete silence apart from the ticking of the white, wooden Grandmother clock next to the front door.

"I asked you a question, Addy," Jesse said in a commanding voice not unlike his father's.

"I wanted to wait for you, Daddy. I didn't eat my dessert so we could eat together."

I stood behind Bonnie and watched as Jesse took a step towards his daughter. His face was impassive but strangely, his body was more relaxed than I'd ever seen it during my month on the ranch.

"Okay, you will eat your dessert while I eat my dinner, but first you apologize to your Granma. Then when we've eaten, you go straight to bed, okay?"

Addy nodded and then turned to Bonnie with a huge smile on her face. "I'm sorry, Granma, but I told you he'd come."

I could see Bonnie was torn between calling Jesse out for being late and overriding her decision to send Addy to bed, or getting down on her knees to thank him for calming Addy down. She didn't choose either and nodded at Addy.

"Thank you for apologizing, Addy, but tomorrow Grandpa will not be taking you on a horse ride as he promised."

Jesse turned to look at his mother and opened his mouth to speak. Bonnie straightened her shoulders, daring him to object to his daughter possibly going on a horse. Jesse evidently thought better of it and turned back to Addy.

"But he promised," Addy objected.

"No, Addy," Bonnie said sternly. "I understand why you were upset, but I will not tolerate screaming and shouting like that from you, so your punishment is no horse ride. Do I make myself clear?"

Addy looked at Jesse who shook his head.

"Yes, Granma."

"Okay. Jesse, your dinner is in the refrigerator, you'll need to warm it up."

"Sure, Momma," Jesse replied. "Addy, sit properly in your seat and tell me what you did today."

Bonnie and I moved out of the kitchen and came face to face with Garratt and Ted.

"He came," Garratt whispered.

I nodded. "He had a cow caught in some fencing, he's not

even showered yet."

Ted let out a long exhale and smiled. "I think we should leave them to it," he said. "I've lit the fire pit on the deck. Let's go out there for a while."

Silently we all followed Ted and left Addy and Jesse to eat and talk about their day.

CHAPTER 17

♥

JESSE

As I listened to Addy chatter away about her day, I noticed how much like Garratt and me she was. She had the same blue eyes and face shape; she even wrinkled her brow like we did when we were thinking. She was definitely a Connor and the only part of Melody that I could see was her blonde, almost white, hair.

"And Millie has so many pretty clothes, Daddy," Addy chattered as she spooned pie into her mouth.

"That's great, Addy, but don't speak with your mouth full."

She nodded and had so much to tell me that she chewed quickly and swallowed down what I guess was a big piece of pie, if the way she screwed up her face was any way to tell.

"Yep, she says when I get bigger I can wear her dresses."

I felt myself stiffen. Millie wouldn't be here when Addy was big enough to wear her clothes and I didn't want Addy getting any high expectations.

"Millie may not be here then, Addy," I said.

"Oh she will, Daddy," Addy replied earnestly, nodding her

head. "Millie loves it here. She loves me and I bet she loves you, too, when you're not grumpy."

She looked at me from under her lashes and then burst into fits of laughter, holding her sides and rolling around in her chair.

I smiled widely and noticed that my food had gone cold on my plate. It had been forgotten with my interest taken by the chatter of my little girl.

CHAPTER 18

♥

MILLIE

The day after Jesse had stopped by and had dinner with Addy, the hot weather broke and a thunderstorm hit. The skies turned black and thunder rumbled deep and angry and Addy was petrified.

"Hey, come on, sweetie," I soothed as I rocked her in my arms. "It's just God moving the furniture, that's all. It's nothing to be scared of."

"I want my daddy," she sobbed, clutching tightly to my t-shirt. "Please, Millie, I want Daddy."

I gave Bonnie a withering glance as she came in to the room with the house phone. She shook her head. "I can't get through, it's going straight to voicemail."

"What about the radio?" I asked.

"Tried every frequency and can't get neither him, Ted, nor Garratt. Can't get anyone in fact. This storm is real bad, honey."

I sighed and pulled Addy closer to me. She was slowly getting hysterical, giving great hiccupping breaths.

"Is she always like this?"

"Never seen her this bad. But we haven't had a storm like this for a long time." Bonnie came and sat next to us and held her arms out. "Let me try for a while."

I passed Addy over to her grandmother, but knew it was pointless. We'd both tried to calm her down for the last hour, but it seemed Jesse was the only person she wanted.

"Come on sugar," Bonnie whispered. "Try to stop crying for Granma."

"D-d-d-daddy."

I went to the window and pulled back the curtains, staring into the blackness outside.

"Don't even think about it," Bonnie said from behind me.

I turned and shrugged. "What else can we do? She's going to make herself ill."

At that moment, another huge clap of thunder sounded over our heads and Addy screamed.

"I'll have to go," I said, rushing towards the kitchen. There was a mud room at the end of it where a selection of boots and wax coats were kept.

"No, Millie, it's too dangerous, and you have no idea where to go or even how to ride a horse to get there. Please, honey, she'll be fine soon."

"I had riding lessons when I was a kid," I protested.

"No, honey." Bonnie stroked Addy's head as she pleaded with me. "Why don't you try his cell again?"

With a sigh, I picked the phone up from the chair where Bonnie had thrown it. "What's his number?"

"Oh, just press the redial, he was the last number I called."

I pushed at the button and held the phone to my ear, not expecting it to be answered, but after a few rings, Jesse's voice boomed down the line.

"Mom," he shouted over the background noise of the storm. "Everything okay?"

I moved out of the lounge area towards the dining room, not wanting Addy to hear that I'd got through to Jesse. I didn't want her to be disappointed when he couldn't or wouldn't come back to the house.

"Jesse, it's Millie."

"Millie, what's wrong...hang on a second...Derek," I heard him shout. "Brandon just radioed through, he's got four pairs but said there's another three pairs heading west towards the dry creek bed...sorry Millie, what's going on?"

"It's Addy..." I began.

"What's happened? Is she okay?"

I paused for a second as I heard more horse's hooves and someone shout Jesse's name; it sounded like Ted.

"One minute, Dad," Jesse called. "Millie tell me what the fuck's wrong. I've got cattle running everywhere, spooked by this damn storm."

He didn't need this, the cattle and the men needed him out there and Addy wasn't in any real danger.

"She's fine, she just wanted to be sure that you were okay, and wants to know if you'll stop by later." I closed my eyes and hoped that Addy would forgive me for not getting Jesse to her.

Jesse gave what I think was a sigh of relief down the line. "Yeah, Millie, tell her I'm fine and I'll come over later. She's okay, though?"

"Yeah," I said shakily. "She's fine. I'll let you go."

"Okay, tell Addy that..."

The line went dead.

I went back in to the lounge area to see that Addy now had her hands over her ears and was crying louder than before. Bonnie looked at me expectantly, but I shook my head. Thank goodness, Addy's crying had masked the noise of my voice on the phone.

"I got through, but he couldn't hear me," I lied.

"Oh well, we'll just sit it out and hope she tires herself out."

"I'll make use some coffee," I said, turning away before Bonnie could see the guilt on my face as another rumble of thunder and a crack of lightning caused Addy to scream.

*** *** ***

After almost an hour and twenty minutes, Addy finally fell asleep. The storm had subsided about thirty minutes into our nightmare, but Addy had worked herself up so much that she couldn't settle or regulate her breathing properly. We didn't dare give her any medicine in case she choked, because she was taking in great gulps of air and her breathing was so irregular, so I got her to breath into a paper bag. After a while, Bonnie made her some warm milk with a couple of child's *ibuprofen* dissolved into it. After putting the milk into one of Addy's old Sippy cups, we finally got her to drink it and within ten minutes, she was starting to calm down.

As she slept in Bonnie's arms, I felt I ought to come clean about my call to Jesse.

"Bonnie, I need to tell you something," I said tentatively.

"What's that, honey?" she asked as she stroked Addy's hair from her face.

"I was actually able to talk with Jesse." I winced as Bonnie's head shot up; light grey eyes staring at me intensely.

"Please don't tell me he refused to come."

I shook my head. "God no, nothing like that. I didn't tell him."

"What? What do you mean you didn't tell him?" Thankfully she didn't look angry, just confused.

"It sounded like hell out there, Bonnie. He said that there was cattle running everywhere and he sounded so stressed. I just thought we would be able to handle it, eventually."

Bonnie looked down at Addy and dropped a kiss to her forehead that was covered in a sheen of perspiration.

"Good call, honey. It's dangerous enough out there when the cattle are spooked, he didn't need to be worrying about Addy, too."

I breathed a sigh of relief. "You're not angry?"

"No, honey, you did right."

I was just about to the get up and make us some more coffee when the front door burst open, and a soaking wet Jesse barged in. Water dripped from his hat onto his wax rancher coat, and then travelled down the length of it to puddle on the wooden floor.

"How is she?" he gasped, pulling his hat off and throwing it on the floor.

"Jesse, honey." Bonnie's eyes lit up at the sight of her son.

Jesse grabbed at the poppers on the full-length coat and shrugged it off before rushing over to Bonnie. He looked down at Addy and bent at the waist, put his arms under her body and pulled her to his chest. Cradling her in his arms, Jesse sat down on the recliner, placed one hand behind her head and dropped tender kisses on to her forehead.

Bonnie gasped and slapped a hand to her mouth, her eyes shining brightly with tears of happiness. I swallowed back a huge ball of emotion as I watched Jesse gently rub his cheek against his daughter's tiny button nose.

"I knew," he whispered. "I knew that there was something wrong; my instinct told me that my baby needed me. I came straight away, straight after the line went dead, but I came across a calf stuck in the mud and the mother was getting distressed watching her baby sinking. I had to pull it out. I couldn't let it die, Mom."

"Honey, it's fine. You were on your way here, that's the main thing."

"She's real hot, Momma. Is she okay?"

Bonnie got up to feel Addy's brow. "She's been upset, got herself into a state, I think it's just that. I'll put her in bed with me and she can sleep in her underwear. Your dad can sleep in Addy's bed."

Jesse shook his head. "No, I'll sleep with her."

Bonnie and I both stared at him wide eyed. He'd definitely been making progress with Addy over the last few weeks, but this was a major step forward.

"You'll be cramped in Addy's bed," Bonnie said. "Your bed is made up."

Jesse's face blanched and I saw his grip on Addy relax, the hand on her back dropping to his knee. Then Addy stirred in his arms. He looked down and put his hands back on her, pulling Addy closer to him.

"Thanks, Mom. I'll take her up."

In one swift move, Jesse was on his feet and carrying Addy towards the stairs. As his foot landed on the first tread, he stopped and turned to me.

"Thanks for what you did tonight, Millie, but you could have told me."

"Millie did the right thing, honey. She realized that you had enough to deal with out there."

"Maybe, or maybe she thought I wouldn't come, but I guess that's not surprising since I've been a total idiot for the longest time."

"Jesse..." I was about to say it was purely his stress that stopped me, but Jesse shook his head.

"It's fine, Millie. I'll see you in the morning. Dad and Garratt won't be too long. Dad radioed me just as I got back, they're on their way back in."

Bonnie nodded. "Okay, I'll get some supper ready. Do you want some?"

"No thanks, I'm beat. Goodnight."

Bonnie and I watched him carry his precious cargo up the stairs and we both swiped away a tear.

"That boy," Bonnie whispered.

I flopped back into the cushions on the sofa and thought about 'that boy'. He was strong, brave, handsome, and grumpy as hell. He'd been nothing but rude to me, apart from when he was making me feel as though I was flying just from the use of his fingers, and he had more issues than Prime Minister's Question Time, but when he took his daughter in his arms, that boy took my heart, too. I knew then that I was falling in love with Jesse Connor.

CHAPTER 19

♥

JESSE

As I sat in the chair next to the bed, I watched Addy sleep, willing my own to come, but even the rhythmic rise and fall of Addy's chest wasn't helping. I felt exhausted, but my eyes wouldn't close, and I knew it was because the last time I'd slept in that bed it had been with my wife. Just four hours later she was dead, her gorgeous face ripped to shreds when she went through the windshield of her car on her way to a few days away with her old High School cheerleader friends.

Why the fuck she wasn't wearing a seat belt I have no idea. There is also no clue why she crashed. No other cars were involved, it was a clear stretch of road, she hadn't had a blow out, but she had veered off the road and gone into a ditch, hit a tree, and gone through the windshield. The Sheriff told me that they were putting it down to driver error, and though I hated myself for it, I had to agree with him.

Addy stirred slightly and flopped an arm out of the covers, her tiny little fingers curling inwards. I pulled the chair closer to the bed, took her hand in mine, and rested my head next to hers and waited for the peace.

CHAPTER 20

MILLIE

By the time I went down for breakfast, the morning after the storm, Bonnie was already clearing away dishes.

"Morning," I said on a yawn. "Have the guys gone out already?"

"Yeah," she sighed. "They needed to check the fences. Ted said he thinks all the cattle are okay; the boys managed to locate them all and get them to the run in shed that's out there on slightly higher ground."

"Well, that's something," I replied, pouring myself some cereal. "How was Jesse this morning?"

Bonnie shrugged. "No idea, he'd already gone by the time we got up this morning, and Ted and Garratt were gone by five."

"But they didn't get in until midnight last night."

"The life of a rancher, honey. Anyway, it won't hurt Garratt to be busy from morning 'til night; will keep him out of trouble," she said with a chuckle.

"And Addy?"

"Still sleeping. She looks so tiny in that big bed of Jesse's." Bonnie's brow furrowed and she suddenly looked lost in thought.

"What's wrong, what's worrying you?"

She startled and then sat down in the chair opposite to me. "It struck me the bed only looked slept in on one side, but there was a blanket thrown over the chair in there."

"You think Jesse slept in the chair?"

"Yes, honey, I do. Which means that he's still hurting." Bonnie leaned her elbows on the table. "He hasn't slept in that bed since Melody passed."

My heart lurched. Somewhere in the back of my stupid mind I thought that maybe he had feelings for me; after what we'd done. Evidently, I was nothing more to him than Angie. If he still couldn't face sleeping in his marital bed then I wasn't the one to help him forget. But why *should* he have feelings for me? Aside from giving me an orgasm, basically to shut me up, he'd barely had a pleasant word to say to me. There was no doubt that he thought that I was attractive, his hard on had been evidence of that, and the fact that he thought Dean was an idiot for dumping me, but there was nothing more to it. I had to accept that and get over this stupid infatuation.

"They were high school sweethearts weren't they?" I asked.

"Yes they were. Although, I always thought that Melody would move away; never saw her as a rancher's wife, what she'd do I had no idea seeing as she didn't go to college. But, she worked here with me and then she got pregnant. Jesse was adamant that they get married. Ted and I didn't care whether they were married or not, times have changed from when we were youngsters, but it was what they wanted. Well in hindsight, I think it was what Jesse wanted. Not so sure about Melody."

Bonnie was the second person to talk about Melody in less than glowing terms. Maybe she wasn't as perfect as Jesse evidently thought she was. A burning sensation needled in my chest and I almost gasped with shock; I was jealous of a dead woman.

"She changed after she had Addy," Bonnie continued, bringing me back to the conversation.

"Garratt said."

Bonnie laughed. "That's not surprising. She and Garratt didn't get along, that was another thing that changed after she had Addy. Before that they'd been thick as thieves, but as soon as she started spending time away from the ranch, from Jesse and Addy, Garratt took a disliking to her."

"Do you think he had a crush on her?" I asked, it suddenly occurring to me.

"Garratt? No, honey. He loved his brother, that's what Garratt's problem was. Don't get me wrong, when Garratt was a lot younger and Melody first started dating Jesse I think Garratt thought she was cute, but nothing more."

"Was she a good mother?" I asked, looking down at the table and tracing the chequered pattern of the cloth with my finger.

Questions were running around in my head and I just couldn't help but vocalise them. I needed to know about the woman that still had Jesse's heart.

"I don't like to speak ill of the dead, but she wasn't the best, honey, no. Jesse was the one who did everything when he was home. Melody would say it was so he got to bond with the baby, too, but that didn't explain why I was the one caring for her when Jesse *wasn't* around. Let's just say Melody wasn't the most hardworking of girls, when she worked with me she was more of a hindrance at times."

I let out a long, slow breath, a sense of relief settling on me because Melody *definitely* wasn't as perfect as Jesse thought.

"Yet Jesse worshipped her," I said aloud.

"Yes, Jesse worshipped her." Bonnie looked sad, almost heart-broken, and something flashed across her eyes – a memory maybe.

"Do you think he'll ever move on?" I asked, not daring to look at Bonnie's face. "I mean, I know you found him with the woman from town, but he may decide he wants something more stable one day."

"I don't know," she sighed. "All I know is my boy is still hung up on that girl and, while he's finally let Addy in, I think it will be

83

a long time coming before he lets a woman into his heart. I know he has other women, but I'm not sure he's ready for anything more serious."

I nodded my understanding at her unintentional words of warning and felt my hopes sink. It was exactly what I thought and so having any faith in him having feelings for me was hopeless. I'd been stupid to let myself fall for him in the first place, especially so soon after Dean, and so the sooner I got over my crush the better.

***

In the afternoon, Addy and I were outside feeding apples to a horse that had suddenly appeared in the paddock opposite the house. Bonnie informed me that Wyatt McKenzie, a neighbour – if you can call six miles away a neighbour – had dropped it off earlier while Addy and I had been in the office doing some children's quizzes on the internet. It was a beautiful, lithe, chestnut mare and, according to Bonnie, it had the temper of the devil when anyone sat on its back. Jesse was going to take a few days off from the cattle to break it in for the owner. I couldn't understand what the problem was, she was perfectly gentle as she took the half an apple from Addy's outstretched palm.

"Hey, ladies." Brandon came over and leaned against the fence with us. "You havin' fun?"

"Hey, Uncle Brandon," Addy cried excitedly. "Daddy is going to make her better so that she lets people ride her."

"So I believe. Maybe he'll let you ride her when she's ready."

Addy's eyes widened. "You think so?"

"Well that's up to your daddy, honey," he laughed.

Addy sighed and turned back to the horse, resigned to the fact that she wouldn't be riding her.

"I should have kept my mouth shut. She'll be haranguing him until his ears bleed to let her ride it." Brandon smiled at Addy and patted her head.

"She's certainly insistent. So, what are you doing here, I thought you'd all be busy after last night?" I reached over to Addy and pulled gently on her waist. "Don't lean too far over, sweetie. We don't want you falling."

"Okay," she replied and pulled back slightly.

"I was out until four this mornin' with one of the other guys, just scoutin' around checking that there wasn't major damage, or that we hadn't missed any of the herd. You know it can be hard to count properly when they're all shiftin' around because they're spooked."

"It sounds like it was one hell of a night," I sighed.

"Yep, sure was. But to be honest, Millie, talking about last night ain't what I'm here for." Brandon looked down at his foot that was propped on the bottom rail of the fence. "I was wonderin' whether you fancied coming to Rowdy's with me tonight."

I took a step back in surprise. "Oh, erm, well I don't know," I blustered. "I…"

Brandon started to laugh. "Millie, it's few drinks in a bar, I ain't asking you to marry me, sweetheart."

I looked up at his handsome face and straight white teeth that had definitely had work done on them, and thought, 'why not?' Jesse wasn't interested and I couldn't spend every single minute of my year here, solely on the ranch

"Okay, Brandon, that would be lovely, thank you."

"That's great," he replied with a grin. "I'll pick you up at seven-thirty, is that okay?"

I nodded. "Sounds good. See you then."

Addy suddenly started to giggle.

"What's tickled your fancy pants, little miss?" Brandon asked, giving Addy a playful poke in her side.

"Do you love Millie, Uncle Brandon?"

"Addy!" I exclaimed.

"But you're going on a date. That means you're going to be kissing and that means that you love one another."

God, if only love was that simple. Based on the orgasm he gave me, I'd be engaged to Jesse if that was the case.

"A gentleman never kisses a girl on the first date," Brandon replied to Addy as he slipped his Stetson on. "Remember that when a stinky boy takes you on a date, Addy."

"I will," she sighed.

"See you later, Millie." Brandon winked at me and then walked away.

As Addy and I stayed with the horse for a little while longer, I couldn't help but wish it was Jesse who had said those words.

CHAPTER 21

♥

JESSE

I'd been feeling like shit all mornin'; shiverin' with cold but with sweat pourin' off me. Dad had taken one look at me and sent me back to the bunk house to get some *Tylenol*. It was as I was swallowin' it back with some water that Brandon swaggered in lookin' as though he'd shit a rainbow from his ass and it had a pot of gold at the end of it.

"God," he groaned. "You look rougher than a racoon's nut sack."

"When have you seen a racoon's nut sack?" I asked, tryin' to muster a smile.

"It's a guess."

He laughed loudly and gulped back some OJ, straight from the carton that one of the guys had left out of the refrigerator.

"What's got you so happy anyway?" I asked, taking the carton from him and putting it away.

"Got me a date."

"Yeah who with, and please don't say Belinda Withers. She's

one nasty skank."

Brandon had a thing for Belinda, well it was for her huge double E tits, but the fact that she spent a great deal of time at the doctor's office gettin' antibiotics for her pussy, meant that I gave him shit every time he thought about going there.

"No!" he cried. "It's not Belinda. She may have the best tits in town, but I do not want my dick droppin' off because I've caught something from her."

"Good to hear. So, who is it?"

Brandon grinned wide and rested his hands on his hips and I swear he pushed his dick forwards, like a fucking strutting Silver Back Gorilla or something.

"Millie," he announced. "I've got a date with Millie."

My mouth went dry and a lump the size of Texas formed in my throat.

"Millie, Addy's nanny?"

"Well how many other Millie's do you know? Yeah, that Millie."

"You ask her, or did she ask you?" I shoved my hands into the pockets of my Levi's and leaned against the rough wooden table.

"I asked her, dickwad. As if I'd let a woman ask me out."

"She seem into it?"

"What do you think?" he asked, smoothing his hair back before putting his hat back on. "What women isn't into being seen on my arm?"

As Brandon looked at himself in the old mirror on the bunk house wall, I felt an urge to punch him straight on the nose. He was my best friend and in twenty years I had never felt an ounce of animosity to him; but in that moment I kind of hated him.

CHAPTER 22

♥

MILLIE

I ought to have been spending time on picking an outfit for my date with Brandon, most girls would spend hours brooding over it, but not me. I'd taken out the first thing that I'd laid my eyes on – a pair of skinny jeans and a black vest top with designer rips in it and a white underlay. I teamed it with a pair of black, stiletto heeled ankle boots, big hoop earrings, and an armful of silver bangles.

I hadn't washed my hair, just fluffed it up after my shower, and had put on minimal make-up. I wanted this date to be with Jesse, because while my brain told me that I had to move on, my heart hadn't quite caught up with it just yet. That was the trouble with love; it was selfish and didn't give a shit about your heart.

As I looked at myself in the mirror, I knew that I looked good, but good in a 'popping down to the local bar for a few beers' good, not first date with a handsome cowboy good. But, that was because it wasn't the right handsome cowboy. Taking some cash out of my purse and stuffing it into one of the jeans pockets, and my scarlet colored lipstick into another, I left my room and went down stairs.

"Wow." Garratt grinned at me and wolf-whistled. "Who are you looking so sexy for?"

"I am not," I scoffed, waving a dismissive hand at him. "I'm just off to Rowdy's with Brandon."

"Brandon?" Garratt asked, his eyes as icy as his tone was hard. "What the fuck, Millie?"

"Garratt, language!" Bonnie snapped, pointing at Addy who was curled on Ted's lap, reading.

"You cannot go out with Brandon." Garratt got up from his seat and stalked towards me. "Please, Millie."

"Garratt, honey, please just drop it. If Millie wants to go out with Brandon then leave her be."

Garratt's jaw was clenched tight as he scrubbed a hand through his hair. I really had no idea what his problem was with Brandon, but Bonnie was staring at him wide-eyed, warning him to stop making a fuss.

"Well, I'm coming with you," Garratt said, grabbing his wallet from the shelving behind him.

"Garratt!" Ted barked, looking up from Addy's book. "Sit back down on the couch, now."

"But, Dad…"

"Garratt, sit!"

Garratt looked from Ted to me and then flopped down on to the sofa.

"Ignore him, Millie." Ted smiled at me. "You go and have a good time. You need a ride?"

I shook my head. "No, it's fine, Brandon is going to pick me up."

I heard Garratt growl but chose to ignore him. I checked my watch and it was almost seven-thirty. "I'll go and wait on the porch," I said.

"Enjoy yourself." Bonnie gave me a tight smile that by no means met her eyes.

I smiled back and let myself out.

We walked into Rowdy's with Brandon's hand on the small of my back, and I had to be honest, it wasn't totally unwelcome. We'd chatted animatedly on the fifteen minute trip into town, and Brandon had made me laugh talking about how nervous he'd been to ask me out tonight. He seemed so confident that I doubted it, but it made me feel a little easier and thought that tonight may actually be fun.

Rowdy's had a long mahogany bar down one side, in front of which were round, tall tables with high stools, and to the right of that was a small open area that I assumed was for dancing, with a raised platform at one side with a microphone in the middle of it. Behind the bar were bottles of spirits on a long shelf and above that were dozens of pictures of football and basketball games.

"You'll find me and Jesse up there somewhere," Brandon said as he spotted me looking up at the photographs. "We played on our High School basketball team; Jesse was captain."

"Really?" I said, genuinely interested. "Were you any good?"

Brandon waved his hand in a see-saw motion. "Ah so, so. We were good enough for High School, but we weren't gettin' any colleges bangin' on our doors. That's how Jesse hooked up with Melody; she was a cheerleader."

I swallowed and forced a smile. "Oh okay," I replied.

"Yeah, they really were the golden couple; captain of the basketball team and captain of the cheerleadin' squad. It was kinda written in the stars." Brandon looked down at the bar and sighed.

"Melody was a good friend of yours, too?" I asked, seeing sadness in his eyes.

"Not really, no."

"Sorry, you just looked kind of sad."

Brandon gave me a small smile. "Jesse is my best buddy and has been for twenty years, since our first day at school, and losin' her has pretty much fucked him up. So, if I'm sad it's for Jess. She was the love of his life, and I think always will be."

Despite the vile taste of jealousy in my mouth, I found

91

Brandon's hand and gave it a squeeze. What he'd just said was another reason why I should forget Jesse, and concentrate on Brandon. He didn't seem such a bad guy and I had no idea what Garratt's problem was. Maybe I'd ask Brandon one day; perhaps if we had another date.

"Okay," I said brightly, to change the atmosphere *and* to push Jesse from my mind. "What would you like to drink?"

Brandon looked at me totally horrified. "No way! You are not buyin' me a drink."

"Why?" I giggled. "I'm a modern woman, I can buy a man a drink if I want to."

"Not a chance, sweetness," he laughed, pulling his wallet from his back pocket. "Janelle, two beers over here when you're ready," he called to a tall blonde woman with the perkiest boobs I'd ever seen. "You do like beer?"

I nodded. "Yes, beer would be great."

"Good. Do you wanna grab us a table and I'll bring them over?"

I found us a table, smiling at the few locals that were already in there, and hitched myself up onto a stool.

"Karl, Wyatt, how you doin'?" Brandon asked, doing a chin dip to the two men at the next table. They both lifted their beers and smiled, murmuring that they were okay.

"It was Wyatt's horse that you and Addy were feedin' earlier," Brandon explained.

"Oh yes, I remember Bonnie saying. Jesse's breaking him in, is that right?"

Brandon grinned. "Breakin' *her* in, but yeah, he is. Jesse is amazin' at gettin' a horse to do exactly what he wants."

I nodded and gave him a tight smile. Brandon wasn't helping me to forget Jesse when he kept bringing him into the conversation. But, they were best friends who worked together, I suppose it was natural that a lot of Brandon's stories included the beautiful, dirty blond haired, blue eyed rancher that I couldn't stop yearning for.

"I keep telling him he should make more of a business out of it, but he loves his cattle." Brandon took a swig of his beer and looked at me over the rim of the bottle. "So, what about you, what brings you to the Connor ranch?"

I breathed a small sigh of relief that neither Jesse nor Garratt had told Brandon about my humiliation. It was bad enough that they knew without my date knowing, too.

"Oh, just wanted a change," I replied, which was not totally a lie. "I wanted to get away from the town I lived in for a while. The job taking care of Addy came up, so I thought, why not?"

"Bridge Vale doesn't strike me as the place to escape to, most people wanna escape *from* it."

"That's what Garratt said," I replied before taking a drink from my own beer.

Brandon's smile faded momentarily at the mention of Garratt's name. "You were a teacher, back home?" he asked.

"Kind of. I have a teaching degree but taught the older kids at Nursery – your Pre-school. I did reading and basic arithmetic with the kids Addy's age."

Brandon nodded in understanding. "Addy should be in pre-school, really, but I guess you heard all about that?"

"Yes, I did. Honestly, I think Jesse had a point. She will learn more on the ranch if what I heard about the teacher is true."

"Oh, it's true alright," Brandon laughed. "Muriel Prewitt is mean and too harsh to be a teacher, but when your husband is Principle, maybe it don't matter whether you can actually do the job."

"Maybe."

"Hey, you know you would do a great job there, if we could just get rid of old Muriel." Brandon gently pushed at my shoulder with his beer bottle.

"I'm only here for a year," I said with a shake of the head. "Once Addy goes to school my contract is over."

His gaze roamed lazily over my face and I felt a shiver run across my skin. Want enveloped me, but I knew it was only a natural instinct to a good looking man looking at me as though I was his last supper. It wasn't necessarily want for Brandon the man.

"Maybe you'll change your mind," he whispered. "At the end of the year I might have persuaded you to stay."

Unable to meet his stare any longer, I lowered my head and allowed my hair to fall forward, shielding my face. Brandon reached a hand out and, with a long finger, lifted my chin.

"Don't hide that pretty face," he said softly.

I smiled and was about to say something when the bar door swung open and in walked Jesse and Garratt, looking like one half of a boy band. The two brothers had the same long limbed, confident walk and the same swimmer's physique; broad shoulders and narrow waists, Jesse's a little more muscular.

When they spotted us, Garratt stopped in his tracks and stiffened while Jesse gave us a chin dip and carried on to the bar.

All of a sudden, the optimism that I'd felt about tonight dwindled and I knew that while I was here and still had to see and interact with Jesse, Brandon would never have a chance of persuading me to stay.

CHAPTER 23

♥

JESSE

I'd gone over to the house to put Addy to bed and Garratt's sour mood practically hit me in the chest as soon as I walked through the door. He was sitting on the couch looking at the TV with a look meaner than a steer who'd realized what his balls had been for.

"Daddy," Addy had cried excitedly, scramblin' from Dad's knee. "I missed you."

As she ran into my arms, I felt my heart ache. How could I have ignored her for so long? Okay, I wasn't ready to be full on Daddy just yet; this, being close to her, still hurt because of the family we should have been, but it was getting easier. Shit, the fact that I actually wanted to put her to bed was a miracle, but Millie was right; Addy had been dealt just as hard a heart break as I had, if not harder. Fucking Millie!

When I came down the stairs after tucking Addy in, Garratt was still looking mad. I knew it wasn't me he was mad at, we'd both apologized for our fight and shook hands on a truce, and I knew me making an effort with Addy was all he'd ever wanted.

"What's wrong with him?" I asked my mom.

"He's not happy Millie went out with Brandon," Mom said, casting a weary glance at Garratt.

My poor mom. Between us, Garratt and I made her life shit with our problems. Then what she said filtered from my ears to my brain. Millie was out on a date with fucking Brandon. I'd spent all day pushing that nugget from my head, mostly because I was mad at myself for giving a shit. Millie was nothing to me, just Addy's care giver. Okay, so we'd had some hot action against the barn, but that had been a mistake. I knew it as soon as she'd stopped shaking in my arms from her orgasm. She wasn't a quick fuck like Angie, and she was not…well she was not Melody.

"Actin' like a child if you ask me," Dad grumbled, his eyes never leaving the TV. "She's too old for you and she ain't gonna be here forever."

For some reason my stomach flipped, but I hadn't eaten since lunch, so no wonder.

"I know that," he griped. "And I don't like her like that, but I really dislike Brandon and don't think she should go out with him."

"You can't hate Brandon forever, just because he beat you at cards," my dad said. "Most stupid damn vendetta I ever heard, and I grew up on this ranch when fifteen men worked it."

I had to admit, Dad was right. Brandon and Garratt had barely spoken for almost three years because Brandon had taken Garratt for almost three thousand dollars in a game of poker over at Brandon's one night. I wasn't there, it was a last minute thing and I was home with Addy because Melody was at a Spa. According to Brandon's dad, Henry, when he came downstairs to find out what was going on, Wade, Brandon's brother, was dragging them apart.

"Well, it was all the money he'd made when he sold his Star Wars dolls to that collector," Mom said, trying to make the peace, yet again.

"They weren't dolls, Mom." Garratt rolled his eyes. "He's a

cheat, that's what I couldn't take."

Dad sighed, Mom gave Garratt a twitch of a smile, and Garratt rubbed his temple; a sure sign that he was stressed.

"Wanna go into town, grab a burger?" I asked my brother on impulse, kicking at the sole of his sneaker.

Garratt looked up at me and grinned. "Yeah. I can always eat a burger even after Mom's chicken pie."

"Jesse, honey, I've got your dinner warming in the oven," Mom protested.

"I'll have it tomorrow. I think wonder boy needs to get out of here."

Mom looked from me to Garratt. "Don't cause trouble, Garratt. You leave Millie and Brandon alone."

"We're going for a burger Mom," I sighed. "We're not even going to Rowdy's."

Half an hour later we were walkin' into Rowdy's, under the pretence that tonight was Janelle's chilli night and I preferred that to a burger from the diner. I warned Garratt before we went in not to be a dick, but as soon as I saw her looking so damn sexy and gorgeous, with Brandon's hands on her, it wasn't Garratt's behaviour that I was worried about.

CHAPTER 24

♥

MILLIE

As Jesse walked to the bar, I placed my bottle on the table and sat on my hands. If I hadn't, Brandon would have seen them shaking.

"You ready for another?" he asked, nodding at my almost empty bottle.

I nodded back, not trusting myself to speak, because I knew that my quaking voice would also give away my reaction to Jesse. Brandon grinned wide and walked over to the bar, slapping a hand on Jesse's shoulder as he stood behind him. We were just a little too far away for me to hear what was being said over the rock music that was being played, but Brandon had evidently said something about me, because both he and Jesse turned to look at me, Garratt however kept his eyes firmly on the bar top. Jesse turned to Janelle who was placing a bottle of beer in front of him and Garratt. He said something to her, she nodded and then walked through a door at the back of the bar.

While Brandon waited for another couple of people to be

served before him, I took the opportunity to look at Jesse. My heart sighed. He looked handsome and sexy as hell, wearing jeans and a white t-shirt that stretched over his chest and biceps. He leaned across the bar to grab some cutlery from a metal container, and as he did, his t-shirt rode up, revealing a peak of tanned back and the waistband of his white boxer briefs – unlike his work jeans, those he was wearing tonight were hung enticingly low on his hips. He sat back on his stool and lifted his beer; his bicep bulged and I almost groaned as his lips covered the beer bottle. I sucked in a breath and watched as Jesse dropped his head back and took a long drink. Flashes of what he did to me against the barn flitted through my mind and I felt the throb between my legs start. I shifted uncomfortably, getting a little relief from the seam of my jeans, but it was nowhere near enough. I needed Jesse's hand down there, coaxing my release from me.

"Another beer, miss. Sorry it took so long, Janelle's on her own tonight. Maddie, the girl who was rostered on with her tonight, called in sick."

Brandon startled me, I hadn't even seen him approach and his path back from the bar would have been in my eye line.

"Oh thanks," I said, giving what I hoped was a sincere smile.

I glanced over at the bar, to see that Janelle was placing plates of food in front of Garratt and Jesse which surprised me as Bonnie had made chicken pie for dinner. Garratt had finished off two pieces.

"I can't believe Garratt is having food," I commented, nodding towards the bar. "Bonnie made a huge dinner this evening."

Brandon didn't bother turning around. "Yeah?"

"You two don't get on do you?" I picked at the label on my bottle as I watched Brandon's face turn to stone.

"Nope. We used to be close, but we had an argument over a game of cards."

"Seriously? That's it?"

"Yeah," Brandon answered with a dull smile. "Anyway, why don't you tell me about yourself? Tell me what life is like in England, I've always wanted to go to Europe."

We spent the next half hour or so chatting and I purposefully kept my gaze away from the bar. It took all my strength; I was like a smoker in the first days of giving up cigarettes, or a chocaholic who'd decided to diet. It took everything in me not to give in to my addiction to look at Jesse.

After a while, Brandon went to the bathroom and I decided it was an ideal opportunity for me to buy us some drinks. He couldn't stop me if he wasn't around to say no. Plus, I just needed to be near Jesse, I couldn't abstain any longer. The two bottles of beer I'd drunk had given me a buzz and a state of daring. I took note that Brandon was drinking a light beer and moved across to the bar; my heart thudding in time with my heels on the wooden floor. I headed straight for a spot next to Garratt.

"Hey, Garratt," I said as I leaned against the dark mahogany. "Your mum's pie not enough for you?"

Garratt grinned as he put the last forkful of food into his mouth. "Janelle's chilli is the best, but don't tell Mom I said that."

I felt eyes on me, and as I looked away from Garratt, I saw Jesse quickly avert his gaze.

"Hi, Jesse."

Jesse lifted his head and smiled. "Millie." He then went back to studying his food, taking extra care over the small amount of chilli still left on his plate.

His ignoring me was like a slap in the face. I'd thought that the night of the storm that we'd turned a corner and maybe we could at least be friends, but evidently not. I gave my order and received it from Janelle and was just about to go back to our table when Garratt put a hand on my arm.

"I hope this is your first and last date with Brandon," he said quietly.

"Garratt," I sighed.

"Garr, what did I say?" Jesse hissed. "Who Millie chooses to date is up to her, and there isn't anything wrong with Brandon, he's a good man."

My heart sank. Was this Jesse telling me to get over whatever thoughts I had about him and I? Was he giving me and Brandon his blessing?

Garratt snorted in derision. "Yeah, right."

It was at that moment that Brandon appeared.

"Hey, what did I say?" he asked nodding at the bottles in my hand.

"I wanted to pay my way. So here, take it and drink it."

He laughed, leaned forward and kissed my cheek. I pulled back a little and heard a bottle bang on the bar; Garratt obviously wasn't happy at Brandon's small PDA.

"Sorry," Jesse grunted. "You got something I can clear this up with Janelle?"

I turned and saw a broken glass and beer on the bar in front of him.

"Oh hey, honey," a sickly sweet voice said behind me. "You be careful, I don't want you hurtin' those magic fingers of yours."

Brandon and I both turned to see a woman with long blonde hair, an over made up face, and far too tight clothes standing with her hands on her hips.

"Hey there," Brandon said brightly. "How you doin', honey?"

"I'm good, Brandon, although I'm thinkin' I'll be a whole lot better later." She licked her bottom lip and pointedly looked at Jesse.

"No fucking way," Garratt growled pushing off his stool. "You need to just walk out of here Angie. After what happened at the ranch, do you not understand that my brother is not interested in you?"

This was Angie of the shaven vajayjay and less than perky boobs, according to Garratt's description.

"Garratt, leave it," Jesse commanded as Janelle started to clear away the broken bottle.

Janelle stopped what she was doing and looked at Angie. "I don't want no trouble, Angie. The boys are just enjoying a quiet evening, so if Jesse ain't interested then leave it, honey."

Angie looked at Jesse, her chin jutting out with determination.

"I think we'll leave you to it," Brandon said on a laugh and, grabbing my hand, pulled me back to our table.

As we settled at the table, Garratt stormed out and Angie pulled a stool up close to Jesse, draping her arms around his neck. As for me, I felt as though I was going to be sick. Distractedly I smiled at Brandon and tried to listen to what he was saying, but my mind was over by the bar. I dared to glance over and immediately wished I hadn't; Angie was sucking on Jesse's face.

"Hey," I said during a lull in Brandon's chatter. "I hate to be a kill joy, but do you mind if we go? It's just I have to be up really early with Addy."

Brandon glanced at his watch. "Oh, okay. I was hopin' I could persuade you to dance with me later." He nodded towards the open space to the right of where we were sitting. "Janelle has a singer come in at ten on Friday nights."

"Oh really, that's a shame." It honestly wasn't though, because I couldn't stand the thought of spending another minute with a front row view of Angie and Jesse.

"Sure I can't persuade you?" he coaxed.

I shook my head. "I'm sorry, Brandon, but she's up at six," I lied. "And I really need my sleep to keep up with her."

Brandon sighed good-naturedly and swigged back the last of his beer. "Okay then, miss, your chariot awaits."

He held his hand out for me and led me towards the bar. My breath caught in my throat as I realized that we were going over to Jesse and Angie. Angie, was still hanging around his neck, and Jesse had his head dipped, listening intently to whatever she was whispering to him.

"We're off, Jess," Brandon said, banging a large hand on Jesse's back.

Jesse lifted his head and looked straight past me to Brandon. "Early night?"

I didn't look at Brandon, so didn't see what he did, but Angie giggled and dropped her forehead to Jesse's shoulder. Jesse's face however was impassive.

"See you tomorrow. Don't keep him up too late, Angie," Brandon laughed and then pulled me away.

If Brandon knew that I'd made an excuse to escape our date early, he didn't show it, continuing to laugh and joke on the ride home. The only blip was when we were about two miles from the ranch and we caught sight of Garratt, jogging along the side of the road.

"Hey, that was Garratt," I cried, pointing back through the rear window. "We should stop and give him a lift."

"He ain't got far to go now," Brandon said and stared straight ahead.

"Brandon! You can't just leave him."

"Can't I?" He turned to me, a frown marring his handsome features. "Do you think he'd stop for me?"

"I have no idea, but I won't be happy leaving him on the road, in the dark."

"Millie, he's grown up around here, and probably done that run back from town more times than I've castrated a bull calf, and that's a damn lot. We've all done it, taxis aren't real handy around here."

"Please, Brandon, I don't like to think of him out here."

With a heavy sigh, Brandon slammed on the brakes and shifted the truck into reverse. With his arm over the back of my seat, Brandon turned to look through the rear window.

"You do know that once you go home, Garratt will have to take care of himself?" While his tone was light, I could see in the half light of the car that Brandon actually had a pouty smile.

"I know," I giggled. "But while I'm here I can make sure he's safe when his mum isn't around to take care of him. I'm like his big sister."

"Sheesh, women," he grumbled and shook his head, before pulling up a few feet from Garratt.

In the reverse lights I could see Garratt stop; he put his hands on his hips and was breathing deeply. I opened the window of the truck and stuck my head out.

"Get in Garratt, we'll give you a lift back to the ranch."

"Nope," he said breathlessly. "I'm fine running."

"No you're not, now get in."

"I told you," Brandon moaned beside me. "Just leave the bull headed little dick."

I shot Brandon a look and then stuck my head back out to speak to Garratt.

"Please, Garratt, I won't settle if I know you're running along here. And why are you anyway?"

My question was born out of some sort of masochism, because I knew exactly why he wasn't getting a lift home with Jesse. It was because Jesse had hooked up with Angie in the bar. Thankfully, Garratt didn't put it into words, ignoring my question.

"I'll get in for you, but I've been running this road out of town since I was thirteen, Millie," he muttered as he made his way to the truck.

He flung open the back door and slid into the seat. Before he'd even reached for the door handle, Brandon had the truck in drive and was speeding away.

"Dickhead," Garratt muttered behind me as I heard a text alert sound on his phone.

Once we pulled up outside the house, I expected Garratt to jump out of the truck and make a quick escape, but he stood at the porch steps waiting for me.

"Looks like I don't get to kiss you tonight," Brandon said nodding towards Garratt.

Relief flooded me. "Well, you told Addy that gentlemen don't kiss on a first date."

Brandon grinned in the semi-darkness and lifted a finger to twirl around a strand of my hair.

"I can't wait for our next date then," he said softly.

I knew that I should have been all kinds of turned on by him; he was handsome, funny, and interesting, but there was nothing there. No flutter in my stomach, no throbbing between my legs. That earlier promise of some feelings for Brandon were gone the minute Jesse turned up at Rowdy's.

"Well, we'll have to see won't we," I replied.

I wasn't sure whether I was being a coward by not telling him there would be no second date, or just a bitch by keeping him dangling. Probably the latter, because in the back of my mind, I wanted Jesse to be jealous.

"Goodnight then." Brandon leaned forward and kissed my cheek. "I'll see you tomorrow, maybe."

I didn't reply, but smiled back and let myself out of the truck.

Once he'd disappeared back up the track, Garratt spoke for the first time since we'd picked him up.

"Couldn't even open the door for you," he muttered.

"Garratt, is this really all over a game of cards?" I asked, starting up the steps.

"It's because he's a cheat and a liar," Garratt replied following me. "I hate that he's sucked you in."

"We're just friends, that's all," I said truthfully.

"Yeah until he turns on the charm full throttle; don't believe a word he says, Millie. He's dirt."

With that, Garratt ran past me up the steps and opened the door.

"After you, ma'am," he said with a grin, and good natured Garratt was back.

CHAPTER 25

♥

JESSE

As soon as Brandon and Millie left the bar, I pushed Angie away from me. The sickly smell of her scent made my stomach roil, and I was in danger of barfing up Janelle's chilli. Angie had complained and cussed at me as I'd slapped some dollar bills on the bar and made to leave, but I was not going there again. I should never have let her sit down, but seeing Brandon with Millie had made me feel lonely. I wanted a warm body to curl up to, a woman to lose myself in; trouble was, I soon realized Angie wasn't that woman.

As I made my way out to my truck, I shot Garratt a text telling him that I ditched Angie and would pick him up, guessing he'd be either walking or jogging back home. When his reply came in I chuckled to myself; my fucking brother was a legend.

Garratt: No need - dick head and Millie picked me up. Not letting him fucking kiss her good night even if I have to sit in the middle of them

I needed to at least act like the grown up brother, so shot him back a reply.

Jesse: He's OK don't be a douche. Sorry about Angie. See you tomorrow

When I neared the turning for the ranch, I could see Brandon's truck pulling out, so slowed down. Normally, I would flash him and stop and talk for a few, but tonight I did not wanna hear about his *perfect* date with Millie. Her sweet body filled my dreams as it was, and I didn't want Brandon taking my place in those dreams, because they were all I would ever have.

CHAPTER 26

♥

MILLIE

When I entered the kitchen the next morning, I found Jesse sitting at the table drinking coffee.

"Oh hey," I said as I rubbed Addy's head. "Haven't seen you here for breakfast for a while."

"One of the ranch hands had to go home for a while, so it wasn't so easy to break off and come over. He's back now," he explained. "So, I'm gonna be workin' on Wyatt's horse today."

"Morning, Millie. I'm making pancakes," Bonnie said brightly. "You want some?"

"No, Granola is fine for me, thank you though." I sat next to Addy and grabbed the cereal.

"How was your date?" Bonnie asked, while she emptied the pancake mix into the sizzling pan. "You have a good time with Brandon?"

"Yes, it was good thanks." I added milk to my bowl and started to eat.

"That all," Jesse said, his deep voice rumbling through the

kitchen. "Just good?"

"Yep. What about you, how was yours with Angie?" I asked with a sickly sweet smile.

"Weren't no date, but Angie is Angie."

My insides knotted and I wanted to reach across the table and punch him.

"Jesse!" Bonnie chastised. "I thought that was over and done with."

Addy suddenly stopped eating her cereal and looked to her grandma. Bonnie reached over and cupped Addy's cheek.

"Eat your breakfast, sugar."

Addy's gaze moved to Jesse who gave her a short nod and Addy continued eating, but her movements were slow, and her head was down with her long blonde hair shielding her face. I watched her carefully and saw her shoulders shaking and then heard a little sniffle.

"Hey, Addy, what's wrong?" I asked, putting an arm around her tiny body. "What's upset you?"

"Nothing," she sniffled. "I'm okay."

"Something has, you can tell us."

Her head came up and her bright blue eyes, so like Jesse's, looked at her father. Jesse looked at her impassively, ignoring the pleading in her gaze.

"Jesse," I urged.

Jesse let out a long breath through his nose and leaned forward, placing a hand on Addy's head.

"Stop crying, Addy, and eat your breakfast." He pushed his chair away from the table and stood up. "Sorry, Mom, I don't have time for pancakes."

As the door banged shut behind him, Addy started to sob.

"I made Daddy cross," she cried, scrunching her hands into tiny little fists and rubbing her eyes with them. "Daddy will stop coming to see me again, won't he?"

Bonnie turned off the stove and put the cooking pancakes to one side. "Oh sugar, you didn't make him cross. You shouldn't think that."

"I did, Granma, I did and now he hates me."

Her sobbing was heart breaking as Bonnie drew Addy into her arms. "Oh, Addy baby, tell me what's wrong, tell Granma."

"Daddy loves that lady more than he loves me. He shouted at me when she was there and now he's friends with her again, he'll stop coming to see me again."

My heart totally shattered for the poor child. She truly believed that now that Angie was back in Jesse's life, he wouldn't want her anymore. What also hurt was that I had taken part in shattering her by bringing Angie up, just to be spiteful.

"I'm so sorry," I whispered to Bonnie. "I shouldn't have mentioned her."

Bonnie shook her head and continued rocking Addy. "He shouldn't have taken up with her again and he damn well should be here dealing with this."

I shoved my chair back. "I'll go and get him."

"He'll likely be at the corral, it's around the back of the bunk house," Bonnie offered.

***

I ran all the way but by the time I'd made it to the corral, Jesse was already in the middle, talking softly to the horse while he held a blanket over one arm. I didn't want to shout and startle the horse, but he needed to get to Addy as soon as possible. I skirted the fence until I was in his eye line and waved. It took a couple of minutes but he eventually saw me, spoke something else in the horse's ear, and then strode over to me with his hands on his hips.

"What?" he asked as he took his hat off and wiped his brow.

"You need to come back to the house. Addy needs you."

"I'm busy. She has you or is that not what you are employed for?" He crossed his arms and inclined his head, waiting for an answer.

"It's you she wants, Jesse. She's sobbing in your mum's arms, crying for you." My chest tightened as Jesse sighed and looked down at the floor. "Please, Jesse, if there was any time to show Addy you love her, it's now."

Jesse looked up at the sky and I could see the muscles clench along his jaw line.

"I can't come runnin' to the house every time Addy has a cryin' fit," he seethed.

"This is not just a crying fit, Jesse!" I practically screeched. "She needs to know that you love her."

"Keep your damn voice down." He looked over his shoulder at the horse that was stomping around and kicking up dirt.

"Does your stupid job mean more to you than your daughter?" I asked, my voice lower. "She needs you. You came during the storm, when she needed you, so what's so different now?"

"Because there is no reason for her being upset now." He focused his eyes on mine and thrust his hands to his hips. "Now can I get on with my work?"

"You're a bastard, you know that," I whispered, wrapping my arms around my middle. "That little girl is so special and you have no damn idea what you're losing."

With purpose, Jesse turned and walked quickly back to the middle of the corral and continued to work with the horse.

CHAPTER 27

♥

JESSE

As soon as Millie had disappeared from view, I walked away from Mystery, Wyatt's horse, let myself out of the corral, and punched the wall of the stable.

What the fuck was I doing? Why could I not show emotion to my own daughter? She was four years of age and needed me, yet I ignored and neglected her, leaving everyone else to provide the love that she deserved.

I slumped to the floor and held my head in my hands, allowing the tears to come. Tears that I hadn't let go since that day when the Sheriff came to tell us the news. The pain started in my gut, screwed itself into a huge ball, and got bigger and bigger until it was pushing on my chest, suffocating me. Every part of me wanted to scream at the injustice of it all; I had no wife, Addy had no momma, and there was no real reason why. I hadn't been an evil man; I was a good man, a good husband, and a good father; until that day. That day changed me, it changed my life, and I had no idea how to get it back. The man that I had been. The father that I should still be to Addy. Until that day, she had been my life, my reason to breath; my baby, my Addy. She was special, I'd made her and she would always be mine, yet now I treated her like she was nothing to me. I treated my cattle better at times.

I reached inside my shirt and pulled out the leather cord that Melody's ring hung from, and looked at it through my tears. I had no idea why I'd even kept it; Melody had stopped wearing it a few weeks before the accident. She said that it made her finger itch, but I had an inkling she was angling for a new, more expensive one. I had carried it around my neck for two years and yet my wife didn't even want it in the end.

As Mystery whinnied I looked up and saw a feather was floating around her, spooking her. Stupid damn horse, scared by a feather. A feather was soft, and gentle, nothing to be afraid of.

I quickly got to me feet, swiped a hand across my wet face and ran to the house.

CHAPTER 28

♥

MILLIE

When Jesse came barrelling through the front door, I'd just finished telling Bonnie that he was busy and would try and get over in a little while. Even after him breaking his daughter's heart – again – I still didn't want Bonnie to think badly of her son. Why? Because I knew that deep down he was hurting and the way he was treating Addy was simply a product of his own heartache. Garratt was right when he said that Jesse was in love with a ghost, but who was I or anyone else to say that was wrong? They'd obviously had a deep love and bond that not even death could weaken. He was grieving, and unfortunately, he couldn't see past that grief enough to embrace the fact that he still had Addy. I just hoped he didn't lose Addy, too, because of it.

"Jesse," I gasped as he slammed the door.

His eyes were red and dirt was streaked across his face. He looked shattered and wrung out like a wet rag; his bullish stance in the corral replaced with stooped shoulders and a hand rubbing against his chest.

Jesse took a deep breath and walked slowly over to Bonnie who was now on the recliner, cuddling Addy to her chest.

"Hey, baby," he crooned as he knelt beside the chair. "You wanna tell Daddy what the problem is?"

I chewed on my thumb nail and waited nervously, hoping with everything I had inside me that Addy responded to him reaching out to her.

Slowly Addy lifted her eyes and looked at him, her head still against Bonnie's chest. Jesse stretched out a hand and gently pulled Addy's thumb from her mouth.

"Can't speak to me with that in your mouth now, can you?"

Addy shook her head.

"Okay, so what's the problem? There isn't anything we can't sort out, baby."

Addy took in a shuddering breath and sat up. "Are you going to stop coming to see me now your friends with the lady again?"

Jesse swallowed and looked down at the floor before turning his gaze back to Addy. "No, I'm not gonna stop coming to see you. You're my little girl, why would I stop?"

Addy sucked on her bottom lip and looked at Bonnie.

"Tell Daddy, sugar," Bonnie encouraged.

Addy's lashes fluttered as she took a deep breath. "Because when she was your friend before, you didn't come and see me. But when Uncle Garratt hit you and you told the lady to go away, you started to come and see me. We had breakfast together and you listened to me read at night. And I miss you when you're not here."

As tears rolled down my cheeks, Jesse let out a pained sob and reached for Addy, taking her from his mother's embrace.

"Addy, my sweet baby, I am so sorry," he cried, holding her tightly and gently rocking her. "I love you, baby, and I am so sorry."

"I love you, too, Daddy," she said in her tiny, sweet little voice.

"I'm sorry, I'm sorry," Jesse repeated like a mantra, all the time holding on to Addy for dear life.

I blew out a breath and looked over at Bonnie who was also

crying, her arms clutching at her waist as she watched her son love his daughter. I marvelled at the sight and realized that it wasn't like the night of the storm, when instinct had brought Jesse to Addy's side. We'd thought that Jesse had changed that night, but that had merely been the foundation for what was happening now. This time he'd come because something had broken through the wall he'd put up around his heart the day his wife died.

As I watched the love break through, I couldn't breathe and felt trapped in a place I shouldn't be. This was a private, family moment, so, as Bonnie moved and wrapped her arms around both Jesse and Addy, I silently got up and went to my room.

Once there, I lay on the bed and cried quiet tears of happiness for both Addy and Jesse because I knew that finally they were on the path to getting each other back.

CHAPTER 29

♥

JESSE

"Daddy," Addy said softly.

"Yes, baby."

I reached around her and pulled tighter on the reins, steering the horse that Addy and I were riding on down another track in the woods.

"If you really like that lady, I don't mind."

"I don't like that lady, Addy. She won't be coming around again."

I leaned forward and kissed the back of her head, breathing in the sweet scent of her baby shampoo. Shampoo that Mom, or Millie, or anybody except me, washed her hair in. Well, that was going to change. Breakfast, bath time, and bedtime were mine from now on, and if I had to employ a foreman to run the ranch so I could do that, then so be it. Eventually I would move back into the house. Maybe I'd get Mom and Dad to swap bedrooms first, or maybe I was just being a pussy about the whole thing.

"I don't want you to be lonely though, Daddy." Addy turned

her head to look up at me, and gave me the gentlest smile.

"I'm not lonely, I have you."

"But every daddy needs a mommy," she said, giving her little shoulders a shrug.

"Well honey, this daddy has an Addy and that's enough for me." I tweaked her nose and then kissed her forehead. "Now, eyes front, I don't want you getting hit in the head by a branch."

"Okay, Daddy," she sighed, turning her head back to face the track. "But Daddy?"

"Yes, Addy?" I asked with a huge ass grin.

"I love you."

I wrapped my arm around her chest and hugged her tightly. "And I love you, too."

CHAPTER 30

♥

MILLIE

It had been a couple of days since Jesse's reconciliation with Addy, and she was absolutely blossoming under the warmth of her father's love. A huge grin constantly lit up her face, and her infectious giggle became the theme music for the Connor house.

Jesse was also changed, but not totally, it had to be said. When he was with Addy, he was lighter and more relaxed, playing and cuddling with her at any opportunity. It was as if he was trying to take back the lost two years and cram them into the few hours that he spent with her every day. As for his attitude towards me, well that hadn't changed. He barely spoke to me and when he did, I was lucky to get more than half a dozen words out of him. His family fared a little better with the amount of effort that he put in with them, but he was still a little distant, spending all his time and energy on Addy when he did come to the house.

Unfortunately, my feelings for Jesse hadn't changed either. I still craved for a glimpse of him every day, and my heart still stumbled through any appearance he made. Allowing himself to care about his daughter again had smoothed out the worry lines on his forehead and cleared a little of the sadness from his eyes and he looked rugged and beautiful, all at the same time.

As I contemplated how I'd get through the next eleven months looking at Jesse but not touching, Addy came running in with an old shoe box.

"Hey, what have you got there?" I asked, watching as she placed it carefully on the kitchen table before climbing up onto a seat.

"It's my box of hearts," she exclaimed.

"A box of hearts? What's that?"

Addy smiled at me and shook her head. "Didn't your granma make you a box of hearts?" she asked.

"No, she didn't. She made me a jumper once and the arms were too short."

Addy looked at me a little perplexed.

"A sweater, she made me a sweater," I explained.

"Oh, okay."

She turned back to her box and slowly lifted the lid and placed it on the table. Her mouth dropped open, and with the level of awe on her face as she looked inside the box, you would have expected to see a pot of gold glowing in there.

"Aren't they pretty?" she gasped.

I leaned closer and looked inside to see lots of hearts of varying sizes. There were paper hearts, fabric hearts, one made from thick twine wrapped around some wire and there was even an eraser made in the shape of a heart. On each one was writing, and as I looked closer, I could see that they were names, written in what I recognized was Bonnie's writing.

"They have names on them," I said.

Addy nodded. "Of course, because they are people's hearts. Look."

She reached her tiny hand inside and pulled out the twine heart. It was then I noticed that it had a small tag hanging from it. Addy passed it to me and I read the name *Miss Cynthia*.

"That's the one I wanted," she said as a matter of fact. "Granma

120

is going to take me later to give it to her."

"Okay," I said slowly, not really understanding. "So, did you make it as a present for her?"

Addy frowned. "Your granma really didn't make you a box of hearts, did she?"

"No," I giggled. "She really did only make me an awful sweater."

"I'm giving Miss Cynthia her heart because of Tommy Kincaid." Addy crossed her arms over her chest and inclined her head.

"No, sorry sweetie, I still don't understand."

"Tommy Kincaid is sweet on Miss Cynthia. I know because he goes to the diner every day and sits in her section so that she has to serve him. Elizabeth's mommy told Granma that every time she goes in for coffee, Tommy is making googoo eyes at Miss Cynthia. And Elizabeth's mommy buys a lot of coffee for the sheriff and the deputies. She answers the telephone at the sheriff's office," she explained with an earnest nod.

"So because Tommy Kincaid likes Miss Cynthia, you're going to give her this heart that you made for her."

Maybe it was a local tradition, not that I really understood what Addy meant, but she handled the hearts so carefully that they were obviously very precious to her.

"I'm giving it to Miss Cynthia because it's time for her to give it to Tommy." She carefully placed the twine heart on the table. "He loves her, so now she needs to give him her heart so that they can live happily ever after."

As I watched Addy's little fingers trace the outline of the heart, I felt my nose twitch and tears spring to my eyes. This gorgeous little girl truly had a romanticised view about love; exactly as it should be when you are four years of age. Addy's ideas that if you kissed you were in love and that to be happy forever you simply gave someone a paper or twine heart, were magical and beautiful. She amazed me more each day and I hoped that Jesse knew what an honour it was to be her father.

"Who else's heart is in there, sweetie?" I asked, resting a hand on Addy's head.

"Lots of people." She grinned up at me before turning back to the box and pointing to a heart. "That's Mr Duncan from the library; poor Mrs Duncan died and Mr Duncan is lonely. Uncle Brandon." Addy giggled. "He might give it to you."

I shook my head and tried not to look too horrified. "I don't think so, Uncle Brandon and I are just friends."

Addy shrugged and turned back to the hearts. "Uncle Garratt's is the eraser. I thought he might give it to a girl at his school called Jemma, but he didn't," she gave a sad sigh. "That pretty one, that's yours; look."

Addy held out a piece of white fabric; it had lemon flowers on it and had been cut with pinking shears. On closer inspection I could see that my name had been written on it in black ink. As I stared down at the heart, I gulped back the swell of emotion that threatened to burst out.

"For me?"

"Yes, Granma cut it out for me the day after you got here." Addy put the heart back in the box and pulled out the final one. It looked to be blue foil covering cardboard, and in the middle was the name 'Daddy'.

"This is Daddy's," she said softly. "I made it for him at Christmas. I heard him crying for Mommy on Christmas Day."

Addy gently laid the heart back in the box, on top of mine, and the put the lid back on it. Leaving Miss Cynthia's heart on the table, Addy climbed down from her chair, reached up for the box and then scampered away with it.

As I sat at the table waiting for her, the door opened and Bonnie came in carrying a basket of rolled up sheets and pillow cases – today was linen change day in the bunk house.

"Hey, honey," she sighed and dropped the basket onto the floor. "The damn machine is broken in the bunk house. I'll have to do these over here."

I chewed on my bottom lip and gave her a slight head nod. Addy's little box had certainly done something to my heart.

"You okay?" Bonnie asked. "Jesse hasn't done something has

he?"

"No," I whispered. "Addy showed me her box of hearts."

Bonnie smiled softly and cupped my face with her hand. "Oh honey, she hasn't upset you by making you a heart, has she? She was insistent because she said you looked sad."

"I thought I'd hidden it well."

"Not from Addy." Bonnie gave my shoulder a squeeze and then sat down. "You don't have to tell me, but I'm here if you ever need to talk."

I took a deep breath and told Bonnie all about Dean and Ambrose. Her mouth gaped open and she held a hand to her chest as she listened.

"A man?"

"Yes, a man. But, it wasn't meant to be and to be honest, I don't feel as sad about it as I did."

Bonnie didn't say anything but gave me a knowing smile. Maybe she knew what I'd known for weeks; I evidently hadn't loved Dean but simply the idea of being a couple, being married.

"Is it a tradition?" I asked, feeling distinctly uncomfortable thinking about Dean. "The box of hearts?"

Bonnie shook her head. "No, just an idea Addy had. Just last summer I read her a book about a little boy who kept his wishes in a box under his bed, and Addy loved it. The little boy was magical and he would give his wishes to people who he thought needed or deserved them, and when he did, they would always come true. So," she sighed with a tinkling laugh. "Addy had the idea that if she gave people their heart to give to someone they loved, or who loved them, they would live happily ever after."

"Oh my God," I whispered. "She is the sweetest child I have ever met."

Bonnie's eyes glistened with pride. "I know, and thanks be that her daddy realizes that now, too."

"He's really turned a corner with her, hasn't he?" I said, avoiding Bonnie's gaze, sure that she'd see the truth of my feelings for Jesse in my eyes.

"Yes honey, he has, and I can't tell you how relieved I am. Ted and I were talking about it last night, and we agree we can cope with him shutting off from us, as long as he never does again with Addy."

"He'll get there one day," I replied.

"Let's hope that doesn't take too long either, hey honey?"

Bonnie smiled and got up from her seat and moved across the kitchen to the discarded laundry basket, giving me a wink as she did so.

CHAPTER 31

♥

JESSE

After taking a shower, I rushed over to the house knowing that I had about twenty minutes before Addy went to bed and I was a pissed as all hell that I'd missed bath time. I'd had shit day that had consisted of one dead cow, a ranch hand with a sprained wrist from falling from his horse, and a row with Brandon; over what I couldn't even remember. I knew why, but not what. The why had been because I was sick of listening to him talking about Millie.

Damn Armalita Braithwaite, with her Spanish sassiness. A few days after she'd arrived, I'd sneaked a peak at the resume that Mom had been sent. I don't know why, but I needed to know more about her. I told myself it was because she was caring for my daughter, but I think that fantastic ass of hers had something to do with it, too. I should've known my attraction to her ass would become a pain in *my* ass after what happened by the barn. She took up all my fucking energy, energy that I needed to work the ranch. If strength was measured on what it took for me not to push her up against the wall and have my hand in her panties again, then I was the strongest man in the universe. I was pretty sure that if I let myself weaken, then Millie would be more than willing. She'd loved every minute of what I did to her; Christ the way she'd moaned my name when she came was sexy as hell and the thought of hearing it again was enough to make me hard.

The problem was, Millie had been hurt, and not so long ago. I wasn't the man to heal her heart, fuck my own was barely ticking over and had been grinding to a slow halt for the last two years. Millie was the sort of girl who wanted forever, and even though her heart was hurting, she didn't strike me to be one of those girls that hardened herself to love. She was too damn sassy and sexy to swear off of men forever. She was the opposite of me. I couldn't imagine being anything but hard hearted, except with Addy of course. Now I'd let her back in, I wasn't going to push her away again, not ever.

From now on it would just be Addy and me. As for a woman to keep me warm at night, well a visit to town or Knightingale every now and again would scratch that itch. I had true love once and I'd lost her, and I didn't think my heart could take another beating, so best to keep it hard.

CHAPTER 32

♥

MILLIE

I had been at the ranch for almost two months, and while the days were still warm, they were a little cooler and more bearable for my delicate English disposition. Being half Spanish, my skin could take the sun, but my body just wanted to melt into a puddle, daily. Thankfully, the rising winds meant that I did at least look a little less sweaty whenever Jesse came to the house.

Today was a Saturday, and the town was having a Founder's Day Fair. This meant that instead of working, Jesse and a couple of the hands, Brandon included, were taking the day off to go into town. Bonnie and Ted were going to go into town later, but Garratt had gone on a boys' weekend with some old High School buddies home from college and would be back on Monday evening. Addy was beyond excited about the fair, but when Jesse told her that he was going, too, she almost peed her pants.

"Daddy is going to win me a teddy bear," she told me for about the twentieth time that morning. "He said that I can have cotton candy, too."

"I know, you said," I replied, trying not to punctuate my statement with a sigh. "Although, you won't be going anywhere if you don't get your sneakers on."

Addy scrambled under her bed for her tiny pair of pink converse and after a few grunts, pulled them out and put them on.

"Maybe if you put them in your closet you wouldn't have to go searching for them." Jesse's voice surprised me, causing me to spin around towards the doorway. I felt like my vagina was going to combust when I saw him reaching up to hang his hands from the doorjamb. A pair of Aviator sunglasses were tucked into the open neck of the white, slim fitting, short-sleeved, button down shirt that he was wearing with dark jeans, and he looked like he had just showered as his hair was still damp. My eyes raked further down his body to the edge of his shirt that had the bottom two buttons open. As I spotted the thin line of hair that disappeared inside the waistband of his jeans, my lips parted and I let out a quiet gasp and flicked my tongue along my bottom lip. All I could think about was whether his cock would feel smooth and silky under my lips and tongue.

"You okay, Millie?" he asked, leaning forward with his arms still stretched above his head.

"Yeah, fine thanks. You startled me," I managed to mutter, dragging my eyes up to his face.

"Is that so?"

A smile twinkled in his blue eyes and his mouth turned up into a sexy grin. My nipples tingled with a delicious pain as his mere existence caused them to go hard. I glanced down at my chest and was horrified to see that they were poking against the thin white cotton of my sundress. No wonder he was grinning, he knew exactly what he was doing to me. I quickly turned away from him to Addy.

"Are you ready, sweetie?"

"Laces," she barked, lifting her leg in the air.

As bright as Addy was, she still hadn't mastered tying her laces, no matter how many times I talked about bunny ears. Feeling Jesse's eyes on me, I took Addy's foot and leaned it against my leg and tied the laces on one sneaker and then repeated the same with the other. Normally, I'd try to get Addy to do it, but I needed to be away from Jesse before I jumped him and tore down his jeans and sank to my knees in front of him.

"Okay, off you go," I said, dropping Addy's foot to the floor.

She pushed up from the bed and skipped past me to Jesse, grabbing hold of his hand.

"How you getting to town?" he asked, his body twisted towards me as Addy started to drag him away.

"I'm..." my throat caught, so I coughed to clear it. "I'm going with Brandon."

Jesse nodded and allowed himself to be pulled away down the hall by a chattering Addy.

"Shit," I grumbled.

***

I hadn't wanted to go with Brandon, but he'd been asking me for a second date for three weeks now. Each time I'd come up with an excuse, instead of simply getting up the nerve to tell him I wasn't interested. Yesterday, when he'd asked me, I'd been angry with Jesse, so like an idiot had said yes.

Jesse had been in the corral with a horse which belonged to a friend of Wyatt McKenzie, the owner of Mystery, the horse that Jesse had broken in a few weeks before. Addy and I were watching him from the fence when Brandon came over.

"How's your daddy doing?" he asked Addy.

"He's so clever, Uncle Brandon. The horse is letting him put a blanket on his back now." He'd already managed to get a halter on it the day before, and now the reins were attached, so slowly but surely progress was being made.

"He's damn skilful alright," Brandon replied. He then nudged me with his elbow. "How you doing, Millie?"

"I'm fine thanks, Brandon. This little one has me run ragged," I said, rubbing Addy's head. "But it's great."

We all stood in silent awe as Jesse did his thing with the horse, each of us transfixed as the horse allowed Jesse to put the blanket down. Suddenly the quiet was broken when a bee started buzzing around me and landed on my head and felt like it was burrowing into my hair.

"Oh my God," I screeched. "Get it out."

My feet stamped as I flapped my arms at my side, my skin crawling as I felt the bee going deeper into my messy bun.

"Stand still," Brandon said with a chuckle. "He's probably more scared of you screaming than you are of him."

"Brandon, please, ugh it's horrible."

"He won't sting you, Millie," Addy added. "Not if you stand still anyway."

"I don't like it, Addy," I squealed.

Brandon, still laughing, put one hand on my shoulder, and used the other to take my hair tie out. As my hair cascaded over my shoulders and down my back, he flicked at the bee, encouraging it away from my head. As I saw it fly into the distance, I relaxed against Brandon's side.

"Thank you," I sighed. "I hate creepy crawlies."

Brandon lifted an arm and hugged me against him. "My pleasure, but still think you were being a big baby. What do you think, Addy?"

Addy started to giggle and laughed so much she almost fell off her perch on the fence. Brandon caught her with his other arm and pulled her into our hug. We were all still laughing when Jesse stalked over to us, his face dark and stormy.

"I'm trying to work here, so if you two could take your flirting somewhere else it'd be much appreciated."

"We weren't..." I started to say, pulling from under Brandon's arm.

"Not interested, Millie. And what I *don't* appreciate is you having Addy hanging around while you're swapping spit with Brandon."

Brandon started to laugh quietly and bent to put Addy down on the ground. "I think it's about lunchtime, honey," he said. "Why don't you run back to the house?"

Addy smiled up at him, seemingly not affected by grumpy Jesse. "Okay, Uncle Brandon. See you later."

"Who does he think he is?" I scowled in Jesse's direction.

"Jesse Connor," Brandon replied wryly. "No one interrupts his work, and if you do, then be prepared for him to let you know he ain't happy."

"Egotistical idiot. Ugh, he's so annoying and so..." I turned to look at him again and wanted to scream. Not only was he annoying but he was magnificent. He whispered something into the horse's ear and then in one quick movement was up on its back. There was no saddle, so no stirrup to give himself a leg up, he'd just bounced on his feet and jumped up there and started to walk the horse slowly towards us.

"Shit," I groaned.

"Yep. He's good." Brandon sighed next to me and then followed me to lean back against the fence. "So, I guess this isn't a good time to ask you to the fair tomorrow, seeing as you're pretty angry right now."

I turned to look at Brandon, ready to turn him down again, when I heard Jesse.

"I thought I asked you to go somewhere else and do your dating."

I looked up at him, shading my eyes from the sun with my hand. His jaw was clenched as tight as his hand on the reins.

"We're only talking about the fair," I grumbled.

"Well take it elsewhere, I need it to be quiet." With that, he steered the horse away, and continued to walk it around the corral.

"Sorry I was interrupted, Brandon. Yes, I'd love to come with you tomorrow," I said, pushing my shoulders back defiantly.

"Really? That's great."

His face broke into a grin and as soon as it did, I felt like the biggest bitch. I didn't want to go to the fair with him. He was a nice guy, but my going with Brandon was all about Jesse. When had I become that woman, the one that played one man off against the other? God, Jesse didn't even have any interest in me, so it was a damn pointless exercise anyway.

"I'll pick you at two," Brandon said, pushing away from the

fence. "But I'd better go and get some more work done before he fires my ass."

Brandon laughed as he pointed his hat to Jesse who was still on the horses back, but was now bending forward and talking to it and scratching its nose.

"I thought you only helped out during calving? He can't fire you."

"He still pays me, so yeah he can and don't let us being friends fool you into thinking he wouldn't."

"Hah," I huffed. "Told you he was egotistical."

Brandon kissed my cheek and left me alone wishing I could replay the last ten minutes.

So, there I was waiting for Brandon to pick me and take me to the fair, all because Jesse Connor was an arrogant, bull headed, dick.

CHAPTER 33

♥

JESSE

As Addy talked *at* me from her seat in the back of the truck, I couldn't help but think about Millie's reaction to me when I'd entered Addy's room. I knew what was going through her mind, it was hard not to when her tongue came out and licked along that plump bottom lip of hers. My dick knew what was going through her mind, too. Thank God she looked away because she'd have seen how fucking excited he was by her – shit, I was still hard now.

I had no damn clue what to do about her. I just wanted to taste her mouth again and the need to be inside her, and not just with my fingers, was getting stronger every day.

There was a burning itch deep within me making my skin blaze hot every time I saw her. That soft skin at the bottom of her neck, between her collar bones, was asking for me to lick it, her amazing ass was demanding that I cup it with my hands, and her beautiful face needed to be studied like a piece of art.

For fuck's sake, what the hell was happening to me? When did

I turn into such a pussy? Hah, I suppose that would've been when I first set eyes on Melody. She'd looked like an angel in a cheerleader uniform, with her blonde hair billowing around her like a halo. Now she was gone.

I seriously needed to get laid, and *not* by Millie. I needed a quick fuck with someone who didn't give a shit about feelings. Tomorrow night, when Addy was in bed, I was going to Knightingale to fuck Millie Braithwaite out of my head.

"Daddy!" Addy growled from the back seat. "You're not listening to me."

"What, baby?" I asked, unable to stop the grin that was caused by her bossiness.

"Should I give Uncle Brandon his heart so he can give it to Millie?"

Those words sent my foot to the brake on reflex, sending Addy's sweater and water bottle flying from the seat next to me.

"Sorry, baby. A rabbit ran across the road."

"Oh no, Daddy. You didn't hit it did you?" she wailed.

"No baby, no. I missed it."

She craned her neck up to try and see out of the front windshield and by some fucking good luck, a rabbit skipped out of the grass at the side of the road, saw my truck, and then disappeared again.

"Yay," she squealed. "He's okay, Daddy. You saved him."

"Yeah, Addy I did."

I groaned and rubbed a hand down my face, putting the truck back into drive and continuing into town. Addy was quiet for the rest of the journey, giving my ears a rest, but the sick feeling that I had about Brandon giving his heart to Millie just wouldn't go away.

CHAPTER 34

♥

MILLIE

As we pulled into town, I started to bounce in my seat with delight at the joyous, colorful scene that was unfolding in front of me.

The whole of Central Avenue, the main street that ran through town, was full of stalls and sideshows while balloon sellers walked around clutching dozens of brightly colored strings as the balloons hovered up above them. There were hotdog and burger stalls and a lady wearing a huge floppy hat with flowers on it was making candy floss – sorry cotton candy – while a long line of children snaked along the sidewalk, waiting to buy some. Red, white, and blue bunting was streamed across the width of the street and a huge 'Bridge Vale Welcomes You' banner, above the Civic Offices building, fluttered in the breeze.

"Where have all these people come from?" I asked Brandon as I stared through the window. "I didn't think Bridge Vale was this populated."

Brandon chuckled besides me as he manoeuvred onto the

playing fields at the end of Central Avenue that had become the site of the fair and designated car park for the event.

"We have a population of about nine thousand people," he stated.

"Really?" I gasped. "Where do they all live? I know that there's the small housing development just before you get into town, but I can't imagine there's more than a thousand people living there."

"You're classed as a resident of Bridge Vale if you live in a twenty-five mile radius. You become a Knightingale resident when you hit the bridge."

"The bridge with that huge oak tree next to it?" I asked.

Brandon grinned at me and nodded. "Step over that bridge and you become the enemy."

"Seriously?"

"No, I'm joking about us being enemies, unless its High School basketball, then it's war," he said with a chuckle. "But the bridge *is* the unofficial border."

We drove slowly over the grass, directed by a tall, gangly teenager wearing a high visibility vest, towards a row of cars and trucks that were already parked up.

"Hey," Brandon said. "There's Jesse and Addy." Brandon gave his horn a short burst and stuck his hand out of his open window to wave.

Jesse lifted a hand in greeting, while Addy, too excited to notice us, continued doing a jumping trot next to Jesse while she clutched his hand.

"That child is so excited," Brandon laughed.

I stared at Jesse and Addy as they continued to walk across the field ahead of us. "Maybe we should catch up to them?" I said hesitantly.

Brandon looked at me and arched his eyebrows. "Well I kinda wanted to spend some time alone with you, but yeah we can do that."

"I just thought it might be nice for Addy to have her dad and her Uncle Brandon spend some time with her." And I would get to spend time with Jesse.

Brandon didn't say anything else, but jumped out of the truck, cupped his hands around his mouth and shouted.

"Hey Jess, wait up."

Jesse swung around, and gave Brandon a chin lift.

"We're going to hang with you for a while," Brandon called as I closed the truck door.

Addy looked up at Jesse and beamed at him. She pulled her hand from his and came running back across the field towards us.

"Millie, Daddy is going to win a teddy bear for me."

I couldn't help but laugh. Okay, so now it was twenty-one times I'd been informed of this.

She ran to me and instinctively I held my arms out and scooped her up so that her legs hooked on my hips.

"You're a little excited about this aren't you?" I asked.

Addy nodded vigorously. "Daddy didn't come last time. I came with Uncle Garratt, which was real fun, but I wanted Daddy to come, too."

Her eyes shone like perfectly cut topaz jewels and the happiness she was feeling radiated from her every pore. She adored Jesse and now she had him back I don't think anything could dampen her spirits. I could probably tell her that Santa didn't exist and she wouldn't care.

As we reached Jesse, Addy leaned over for him to take her from me. He held out his arms and Addy practically jumped into them. Jesse's eyes met mine over Addy's shoulder and he gave me a quick smile.

"Millie."

"Hey, Jesse. You don't mind us joining you do you?"

Jesse shrugged. "I don't mind, but does Brandon?"

I turned to Brandon who was walking alongside of me. He reached down and took my hand in his. "No problem, I get to spend time with two beautiful ladies."

Addy giggled joyfully, while I gave a tight smile and glanced down at our conjoined hands, and then up to Brandon.

"You want a hot dog?" he asked.

"Yay," Addy cried. "Hot dogs."

"Hot dogs it is then," Brandon replied and high-fived Addy.

We had eaten hot dogs, cotton candy, jelly beans, and a toffee apple and I felt as though one prick of a pin and I would burst. Jesse had rationed Addy's cotton candy and jelly beans, but I would still put money on her getting a stomach ache.

"She may just vomit later," I said to him as we watched Brandon spin around in a dodgem car with her.

"Yeah, Mom did warn me not to let her eat too much. Good job I'm staying with her tonight, in case she barfs." He laughed quietly.

"How come you're staying with her?" I asked.

"Mom called me before, when you and Addy were on the Ferris wheel. Sorry, I was supposed to tell you, but Addy running off to the coconut game kinda took over."

"Yes, it would do," I sighed.

From the Ferris wheel, Addy had seen that there were teddy bear prizes for knocking the coconuts down, so as soon as we were on the ground, she'd bolted for the stall. Jesse had sprinted after her, trying not to lose sight of her blonde head bobbing in the crowd, but she was determined and fast, only stopping once she'd reached the stall. Jesse didn't win the pink and yellow bear that she wanted, but as we'd moved a sulky Addy away, I turned and noticed Jesse hand over a twenty dollar bill to the stall owner. When Jesse gave the bear to Addy, she was beyond happy, almost toppling a kneeling Jesse over as she jumped into his arms to kiss him.

"Well, she and Dad have had to go out of town. My great aunt Ruby has had a fall. They got the call not long after we left the ranch."

"Oh no, is she okay?"

Jesse nodded. "Yeah, she'll be fine, there isn't anything broken, but she's almost eighty-five and only has Mom. She has no kids of her own."

"How long will they be gone?" I asked casually.

A little shiver ran over my body. It could have been excitement or simply fear at being alone in the house with Jesse; which one I wasn't sure. As Jesse's beautiful blue eyes found mine, I knew it was excitement that I was feeling. I could put money on him being one of those men who wore low slung pyjama pants for bed, and I might just get a glimpse of them.

Jesse shrugged. "Not sure, Mom did say they may have to bring her back with them for a while."

"Okay." I looked down at my feet, and kicked at a tuft of grass. "You don't have to stay at the house, I'll be fine with Addy."

Why those words came out of my mouth, I had no idea, because I wanted to have him close. Close enough that I could try and persuade him that taking me to bed would be a great idea; the best idea that he'd ever had. I knew that if it happened it would be a one night thing, and life would be difficult for the rest of my time on the ranch, but I didn't care. At that moment, all I wanted was to have sex with Jesse Connor. God, I'd go for it now if it wasn't for Addy being with us. As for Brandon, he wasn't even a consideration, and I knew that I needed to tell him that nothing was going to happen between us. I would do it as soon as we got back to the ranch.

"I'd prefer to be in the house," Jesse said flatly. "I don't like the idea of there being only you and Addy there and no men."

"Okay," I replied, trying desperately not to grin, yet at the same time spit out that I was perfectly capable of looking after myself. "Whatever you think is best."

We continued to watch Addy and Brandon for a few more minutes, until their turn was over and Brandon carried her back to us.

"That was fun, Uncle Brandon," she chimed as he put her down. "What are we going to do now?"

I glanced at my watch to see it was almost four, and we'd already been there for two hours.

"I think," Brandon said, putting an arm around my shoulder, "I'm gonna try and win Millie something to remember today by."

"There's no need," I said breathily and feigned a stumble so that I could move away from Brandon's arm. "I've taken lots of pictures on my cell to remind me."

"No," Jesse grunted. "If Brandon wants to win you something then he should try."

I shot Jesse a glance but he was looking down at Addy who was trying to pull her bear from his arms.

"Come on then," Brandon said, moving towards the shooting range. "Let's go and win you a memory, honey."

"You too, Daddy," Addy cried, running up beside me and grabbing my hand. "You see if you can win something, too."

"Now, Addy," Jesse laughed. "We all know that I'm a better shot than Uncle Brandon. We don't want him losing face now do we?"

Jesse gave Brandon a playful punch in the arm, and while Brandon smiled back at him, I got the distinct impression that he didn't find it amusing.

"We'll see," he muttered and strode over to the stall and slapped some money down. "Ten dollars of shots."

"Okay," Jesse laughed. "You asked for it."

He took his wallet from his back pocket and took out a ten dollar bill, putting it on top of Brandon's.

"Same here," he said to the man handing out the air rifles. "Let the best man win."

"What do you want, Millie?" Brandon asked, nodding at the array of stuffed toys.

I looked up at them and shrugged. "Anything, I don't really care."

"You must have a favorite," Brandon insisted.

I scanned the toys again and my eyes landed on a gorgeous, fluffy, white rabbit, clutching a red, velvet heart. It was bigger than the rest but it looked soft and comforting and it was just like one my dad had bought for me on Valentine's Day when I was seven years old. When I was nine, Javi fed it to Buster, our neighbour's Great Dane. He was pooping white fluff for a week and I cried for almost the same length of time.

"That one," I said, pointing at the rabbit with tears in my eyes as I thought of my dad.

"Lady has good taste," the stall owner chuckled. "That's the main prize."

"The rabbit it is," Jesse said. "So let's see what we can do."

In front of Jesse and Brandon were moving targets, and each segment of the target was numbered, the bull's eye being worth 100 points. The more points you scored, the bigger the prize; the ultimate evidently the huge five feet tall rabbit that I had set my heart on.

"You go first, buddy," Jesse said, stepping to one side and waving Brandon forward.

"Okay, oh and don't tell us who got the highest score until we've both had our shots." Brandon addressed the stall owner who grinned and nodded.

As the targets came whizzing past, Brandon's face was one of grim determination, firing off shot after shot, until finally the last target disappeared. He placed the gun down and stepped back, standing a little away from me.

While the man unclipped the targets and replaced them with new ones, I glanced over at Brandon. There was a thin sheen of sweat on his brow and his arms were crossed firmly over his chest, and when Jesse finally picked up the rifle, Brandon's nostrils flared like a bull ready to rampage.

As the noise of the fair buzzed around us, the three of us watched silently as Jesse prepared himself. His stance was a little more relaxed, and he didn't rest his arm on the countertop as Brandon had done, but the clench of his jaw revealed his desire to win.

"Go Daddy," Addy called just as Jesse nodded for the targets to be started.

His shooting was leisurely, despite the speed of the targets, and I couldn't see how he could possibly have hit as many as Brandon. When the last target came past, he waited until the very last second to let off a shot before handing back the rifle.

"Who do you think won?" Addy whispered, although rather

loudly it had to be said. "I think Daddy."

I placed a hand on her shoulder and gave it a gentle squeeze. "I don't know, but we'll soon find out."

The man at the stall flipped through both lots of targets and then took a pencil from behind his ear and wrote a number down on two different targets; one from each pile.

"Here you go guys," he called, holding up the targets that he'd folded so we couldn't see the number. "That's twenty targets each with a possible total of two-thousand points."

Jesse and Brandon stepped forward and took their target from him and each unfolded them.

"Well?" Jesse asked, crossing his arms, with the hand holding the target tucked under one of his armpits.

"One thousand and nine hundred points." Brandon beamed as he slapped the target against the palm of his hand. "What about you, you anywhere near beating that?"

Jesse dropped his hand and placed his hands on his hips. Disappointment flooded over me; Brandon had only missed two bull's eyes.

"I knew it," Brandon cried. "I damn well beat you. Come on then, let's see what you got."

"Sorry Brandon, but I think you're getting a little carried away there." Jesse grinned as he passed the target to his friend. "I'm damn mad that I missed a bull there. Knew I'd left that last one too long, but I still got one thousand nine hundred and fifty."

Addy screamed with delight, and jumped up and down on the spot, alerting passers-by, who slowed down to find out what was happening. The smile on my face was huge and I took a step towards Jesse to hug him, until I realized that Brandon was looking at me. My smile quickly dropped and I shrugged.

"Oh well, that's still a really good score," I said.

"Yeah, I guess so." He turned and slammed Jesse's target onto the counter. "Jess you'd better give the lady her prize."

The stall owner unhooked a black bear from the mass of bears hanging up and held it out to Jesse.

"I thought I got the rabbit?" he asked, refusing to take the bear.

"It's fine, Jesse," I protested. "It's only a bit of fun."

"No way, I want you to have the rabbit."

"Need a perfect score for that son," the man's deep voice rumbled.

"Jess, just take the god damn bear and then we can get to the diner." Brandon impatiently kicked at the ground.

"Honestly, Jesse, the bear is fine."

Jesse looked at me and then at the bear, shrugged, and took it from the stall owner and passed it to me.

"Thank you," I said and clutched the bear against my chest. "I'll call him Lucky."

"Whatever." Jesse held a hand out for Addy. "Come on, baby, let's go and get some dinner."

There was no chatter from any of us as we walked across the field, towards the exit and Central Avenue. Even Addy was quiet, content to have her bear hugged to her chest with one hand, while the other remained securely in Jesse's. Brandon walked slightly ahead of us with his hands in his pockets and his chin dipped low. We passed lots of people that said hello, but all they got from Brandon was a simple chin lift in greeting. Jesse at least did say 'hi'.

As we reached the door of The Vale Diner, Jesse pulled up short and patted his back pocket.

"Damn it," he cursed. "I think I've left my wallet on the counter of the shooting stall."

"You'd better go and get it," I urged. "Hopefully no one else picked it up."

"No one around here would do that," Brandon said. "It'll be there. You want me to order for you Jess?"

Jesse handed Addy off to me and nodded. "Yeah, Joe's special burger, fries, and a coffee. Addy honey, stay with Millie, I won't be long."

"Okay, Daddy," Addy said on a yawn.

"Get her a small bowl of Joe's stew, would you Millie?" Jesse asked. "I think she's eaten enough junk today."

I nodded but had a feeling she wouldn't stay awake long

143

enough to eat anything. And I was right, as she was fast asleep by the time Jesse returned with his wallet.

The three of us ate our meals, interspersed with a smattering of conversation and then Jesse took Addy home, while Brandon insisted on taking me to Rowdy's for one drink. One drink became two, but after that I was yawning myself so Brandon agreed it was time to go home. By the time we pulled up outside the house I was almost asleep, despite it only being just after eight. I was so weary that I couldn't muster up the energy to have 'that chat' with Brandon, so allowed him to kiss my cheek and then I thanked him and got out of the truck with Lucky, my bear.

When I let myself into the house, it was silent, except for the distant giggles and splashing of water that I could hear upstairs. The sound lifted my energy and made me smile as I walked up the stairs to shower and change. As I passed the family bathroom, I heard Addy squealing with delight and Jesse grumbling good naturedly that he was soaking wet. The door was slightly ajar, but because of the layout of the bathroom, all I could see was the basin with a bath towel folded up on the counter. The noises were enough to tell me though that there was one happy little girl in there, so I tiptoed past, not wanting to disturb their fun.

As I reached my bedroom door, I opened it and stepped inside. I let out a loud gasp and my heart thudded. There on my bed, smiling at me, was one huge, fluffy, white rabbit clutching a red, velvet heart.

CHAPTER 35

♥

JESSE

Fuck knows what that woman was doing to me, but I could see it in her face that the damn rabbit brought back some sort of memory for her. Her smile got all dreamy and her eyes were bright with tears, so I knew I had to go back and win it for her.

And what was that pissing contest with Brandon all about? I had never felt the need to do that before. Not even with Melody, when half the jocks in school were desperate to get into her panties. There was one time when the school star Quarterback asked her out, knowing she was my girl, but I wasn't worried. Yeah, I told him that she wasn't interested, but I didn't throw any punches or slam him against his locker, or any shit like that. I caught up with him at lunch one day and asked him not to ask Melody on a date again because we were going steady. Then I just walked away, bouncing my basketball all the way to the gym for practice.

Today though, when Brandon said he wanted to get Millie some sort of memory, I just knew it had to be me that got it for her. I'd tasted her first, and while that wasn't happening again, something about her made me want to tell Brandon to fuck off, she's mine; even though she never will be. Yeah, my head is totally fucked up.

When Addy got into the truck to come home and saw the rabbit on the front seat of the truck, her squeal was so high pitched I swear the local dogs all came running.

"Daddy, you went back and won it for Millie!" she cried.

"Yeah baby, I did. She looked like she thought it was real cute, so I didn't want her to be disappointed."

"She'll be so excited." Addy kicked her little legs as I strapped her into her seat. "I'm so excited, too."

"You are honey, why?" I asked, testing the straps were tight enough.

"Because it has a heart. You're giving her a heart."

If I said my own heart dropped to my boots it wouldn't be an exaggeration. I just hoped to fuck Millie didn't see it that way, because nothing could be further from the truth.

CHAPTER 36

♥

MILLIE

Tears sprang to my eyes as I hugged the rabbit to me. I couldn't believe he'd done it, gone back and won it for me. He made my head spin. He'd made it quite clear that I was nothing to him and that what happened outside the barn was a mistake, and then he'd gone and done something sweet like going to win a toy rabbit for me.

Putting the rabbit, who I'd decided to call Jessica - okay so maybe I wouldn't tell Jesse that - on the bed next to Lucky the bear, I took off my dress, had a quick shower, and put on some shorts and a vest top. Knowing exactly what I was doing, I left off my bra; maybe my nipples would entice him. I dragged my hair up into a messy bun, and left my room to go downstairs.

Addy's bedroom door was cracked open and a pale shaft of light, from her fairy castle night light, shone through the gap. I pushed the door gently and peeked around to see her little chest lifting rhythmically in sleep; her arm wrapped tightly around her pink and yellow bear. My eyes fell on a camp bed, set up on the opposite wall to Addy's bed. Laid out on the end of it were a pair of cotton, plaid pyjama bottoms – I knew it!

With thoughts of Jesse in his PJ's, I left Addy sleeping and tiptoed away and down the stairs. As I reached the bottom stair, I blew out a breath. I could hear Jesse in the kitchen and suddenly felt nervous about being alone with him. The nerves weren't because I didn't know what to say to him, or how to be around him, it was because I knew that as soon as I saw him it would take everything I had not to throw myself at him and, at the very least, beg him to kiss me.

With a nervous cough, I descended the last stair and moved across the lounge area to find Jesse. As I got to the kitchen, he turned from stirring something at the stove and gave me a smile. I almost panted in response; he was dressed in grey sweat pants and a tight white vest, which I'd heard Garratt call a wife beater, and his feet were bare.

"Hi." I leaned against the counter closest to him, my hips pushing against the cabinet.

"Hey, I thought I heard you. Expected you to still be at Rowdy's with Brandon."

I shook my head and scratched at an invisible mark on the countertop. "It's been a long day," I explained. "We only stayed for a couple."

"Things going well with you two?" he asked without looking at me.

"We're not a thing, Jesse," I sighed. "Just friends, that's all."

Jesse continued to look at the pan, but I watched as a muscle in his cheek twitched.

"You want some chicken soup?" He nodded down at the pan that he was stirring.

"More food? Jesse you can't still be hungry?" My hand went to my stomach and rubbed over it. "I'm still full from the diner."

"Well, I'm a growing man," he chuckled.

I looked him up and down, studying his strong arms and broad shoulders and laughed at the thought of him growing any more.

"You'll be growing outwards, that's for sure," I said, pointing at his stomach.

"Hey I'll have you know this is all hard muscle." He lifted up his top and flashed his hard and tanned six pack. "Riding a horse all day and wrestling cattle is a real good workout you know."

I sagged against the counter as desire slinked over my body and heated my veins.

"You okay?" Jesse asked, rousing me from my delicious day dream.

My eyes widened as I realized that he'd caught me staring. "I see you got changed. Did you go to your cabin and grab some clothes?"

I wanted to slap myself across the face; what a stupid thing to say. I couldn't have been less embarrassed if I'd said 'sorry, I was just thinking about putting your cock in my mouth'.

Jesse grinned, knowing exactly what I'd been thinking, but spared my blushes.

"Yeah, Addy came and packed for me, so the fact that I have stuff that matches is a minor miracle."

"Have you heard from your mum and dad?" I asked, directing the conversation to something a whole lot safer than Jesse's clothes.

"Yeah, they'll be gone for a couple of days and then Auntie Ruby is going to come back with them for a little while. She's going to have my old room."

Two things struck me about that statement. We would be alone in this house for the next two nights, and referring to his bedroom as his 'old room' meant he didn't see this as his house any more. A sad indication that he wasn't over his wife and probably never would be. The camp bed in Addy's room wasn't just him being protective of his daughter; he couldn't face sleeping in his marital bed.

"So, what's your great Auntie Ruby like? Is she going to scare me?" I leaned forward and took a grape from the fruit bowl and popped it into my mouth.

"Auntie Ruby, scary? God no, she's a real pussycat." Jesse

149

turned off the stove and poured the soup into a bowl. "You sure I can't tempt you?"

He could definitely tempt me, but not with any chicken soup.

"I'm fine, thanks. I'm going to have a beer though, do you want one?"

Jesse hesitated as his eyes lifted up towards the ceiling.

"She'll be okay, Jesse," I said. "One beer isn't going to hurt or stop you from being able to care for her."

His face broke into a beautiful smile that crinkled his eyes. "Okay, just one."

As Jesse moved towards the table with his soup, I started in the direction of the refrigerator to get the beer. Jesse's arm reached out to put his soup down, and brushed the side of my breast. Our eyes met and instantly my body ached for him.

"Sorry," he said softly, flicking his tongue out to lick his bottom lip.

"No problem." My voice cracked as his nearness threatened to overwhelm me.

Jesse stepped aside and let me pass, but I could feel his eyes on me, assessing my every move. My heart danced with excitement as every inch of my body cried out for him to touch me. He would only need to click his fingers and I would gladly lie down and open my legs for him.

"Did you find your gift?" Jesse's voice broke into my subconscious and I felt the breath rush from my lungs.

"What?" I turned to face him, the two bottles of beer clutched to my chest.

"Your gift, did you find it?" Jesse's eyes drifted to my chest and I knew that my nipples were out and proud. That's what Jesse did to me, so damn easily.

"I did, sorry, I meant to say. Thank you, so much."

"I figured you really wanted it," he replied. "I saw the look on your face."

My heart stuttered and emotion pricked at my eyes. "You did?"

Jesse shrugged. "Yeah."

"It reminded me of a rabbit that my dad bought for me, when I was seven. My brother killed it when I was nine and I cried like you wouldn't believe."

Jesse's eyebrows shot into his hairline. "Your brother killed it?"

"Oh God, no," I laughed. "It wasn't real, it was a soft toy, but Javi fed it to the next door neighbor's dog."

Jesse visibly relaxed. "Oh, I see."

"So, thank you."

Feeling bold, I took a step forward, rolled up onto my tiptoes, and kissed his cheek. Jesse's breath hitched and I felt his arm stiffen at his side. Dropping back down to my feet, I took a step back and went to move away, but his hand reached out and grabbed my elbow.

"I'm probably going to regret this," he said, his voice thick and rough. "But I really need to be inside you."

The wetness that had started between my legs the moment I'd walked into the kitchen suddenly increased and my clit began to throb. I took a deep breath and stared at Jesse's lips and felt the urge to suck on them.

"This won't be anything more than one night, Millie," he said with an air of control.

"Do you think that will make me push you away?" I asked, trying to steady the quiver in my voice. "Because it won't."

He raked a hand across his head and then let it drop to cup my face. "You're like no other woman I've ever met before," he whispered almost reverently.

"And you're like no man *I've* ever met before."

"What if you want more...shit, you deserve more, but I can't give you that."

"At this moment in time, Jesse, all I want is for you to fuck me." I had no idea where this Armalita was coming from. I'd never spoken like this to a man before, obviously not Dean, but neither of my previous three lovers either. At twenty-six I was by no means a virgin, but sweet vanilla sex was all I'd ever known.

"How do you want me to fuck you?" he asked, his fingers

trailing across my collar bone. "Hard or sweet, Millie?"

Jesse took the bottles of beer from me and put them on the table behind him. When he turned back to me his finger slipped the thin strap of my vest top off my shoulder; his eyes never left mine and I swallowed hard. His head dipped and his tongue licked along my collar bone and down to the swell of my breast. With teeth nibbling at the soft skin of my cleavage, a hand came up into my hair and pulled at my hair tie.

"This hair needs to be down when I fuck you," he groaned, throwing the tie to one side. The hand that had been in my hair went to the small of my back and pushed me against him. Jesse was hard against my stomach and a groan whispered from his lips as I pushed my hand between us to feel him.

"Shit," he whispered against my cheek. "You drive me fucking crazy."

Jesse's mouth came down on mine and greedily claimed me. His lips were demanding as his hands explored my skin. I pushed up his wife beater and dug my fingers into the hard, defined muscles of his back, my grip on his cock tightening as I started to pump him.

Jesse took the hem of my top and dragged it up and off my body, throwing it in the same direction as my hair tie. His mouth immediately went to my nipple and he sucked enthusiastically.

"Your tits are perfect," he said as he moved to my other nipple. "So fucking perky."

"Jesse," I moaned as he sucked harder.

The pain was harsh, but it sent a message straight to my pussy. My legs parted and I curled onto my tiptoes, urging him to touch me. Jesse unbuttoned my shorts and pushed them down my legs, along with my underwear. As I stepped out of them, Jesse pulled his own top off, while I pushed down his sweat pants. He *wasn't* wearing underwear and as soon as his hard, beautiful cock was free, my mouth watered and I got even wetter.

Without warning, he turned away from me and swept his arm across the wooden table sending his bowl of soup, two bottles of beer, and a pepper grinder flying across the room. Grabbing my arm, he swung me around and pushed my backside against the edge of the table.

"Remember that this can only be one night, Armalita. So, if you want me to stop, tell me now," he said firmly.

Disappointment flashed quickly through me, but my need and desire pushed it back, and I shook my head slowly.

"No, don't stop," I whispered. "Just fuck me, Jesse."

The next thing I knew I was lying back on the table, with Jesse pushing my legs apart. His head dropped and he sent me into orbit with one long lick of my pussy.

"Jesse," I cried, the pleasure washing over me as I lifted my head to watch him.

He looked up at me through hooded eyes and I felt him grin against my throbbing clit.

"So damn wet," he groaned. "So damn perfect."

A steady, confident hand trailed up my torso and grabbed my hand, linking his fingers with mine. All the time he kept sucking and licking, sending me to the edge of euphoria.

"Oh God," I cried. "I'm going to cum."

"Not yet," he growled. "You covered with birth control?"

"Yes, just get inside me for God's sake," I urged breathlessly.

Jesse chuckled and kissed his way up my body, until his lips were on mine.

"I'm clean, get checked regularly and got the last results three days ago," he said against my neck. "You?"

"Jesse, I've never had sex without a condom, I'm on the contraceptive pill and I haven't had sex in almost two years, so just do it."

Jesse looked at me and frowned. "Two years?"

"He was gay, remember?"

"Fucking dick."

Suddenly, he pushed inside me with such strength that I was forced further up the table. The pleasure was unbelievable as he filled me, pushing my legs wider apart with each thrust. Our hands linked together and held on tighter the further we fell in to ecstasy. As Jesse's pace quickened, my hips matched his rhythm and my limbs began to tremble as my orgasm started to build. The ball of fire started in the pit of my stomach and worked its way around my body, pushing out through my nipples, my pussy, and my clit until I was screaming Jesse's name. My heels dug into his hard backside and my fingertips into his shoulders as the pleasure that was so good, yet too much all at the same time, swaddled me.

"Millie, oh my God," Jesse groaned, his pace quickening. "Fuuuck!"

His body started to shudder as he did one more thrust and push. His grip on my fingers got tighter, his biceps flexed, and every muscle in his body tensed as he emptied himself inside me.

Sweat sheened our bodies as we lay on Bonnie's kitchen table panting as hard as if we'd just run a marathon. Jesse opened his eyes and looked down at me, his gaze searched my face, for what I wasn't sure. Maybe he was checking that there were no signs of any emotion deeper than lust, or satisfaction. Whatever it was, he showed no indication of finding it as he dropped a gentle kiss to my lips.

"You're an amazing woman," he whispered. He gave me another sweet kiss and then pulled out of me.

I propped myself up on my elbows and watched as he bent to retrieve his clothes and pull them on.

"I'm going to clean up and check on Addy," he said, looking me straight in the eye.

"Okay," I whispered, thankful at least that he didn't appear to regret what we'd done.

Then he was gone, leaving me to survey the mess around the kitchen and to feel the loss of his body on mine. I pushed myself up and looked down at my own clothes, strewn in a crumpled pile, a metaphoric picture of how my heart felt at that moment.

"Shit," I muttered into the silence.

I thought that I could do this. A one night thing he'd said, and I'd agreed. I'd lied and I knew I was lying when I said it. One night wasn't going to be enough, not when my heart had belonged to Jesse Connor from the minute I'd seen him.

CHAPTER 37

JESSE

I scrubbed a hand down my face and groaned quietly. What the hell was I thinking, fucking her on Momma's table? What was I thinking, fucking her like *that*? I looked down at my dick that was starting to stir again as I recalled how it'd felt when her muscles tightened around me. The shower I'd just taken may have scrubbed away the sweet vanilla of her perfume, but it couldn't erase that feeling. When she came, screaming my name, no drug in the world could have made me feel as high or as invincible.

I finished drying off and put my clothes back on, taking my time because I was the biggest pussy in the world. Normally I wasn't a man to shy away from my mistakes; I didn't skulk away like a criminal the morning after. Always tell the girl that it was great but it wasn't happening again, be up front about things, that was my take on one night stands. This thing with Millie though, shit, it was different. I couldn't face her; I couldn't go down there and help her clean up the mess in the kitchen. I couldn't do it, not because I was ashamed, but because I was scared. Scared that she would see in my eyes how much I wanted to do it again.

Looking at my reflection in the mirror, my eyes went to my neck, where I usually wore Melody's ring. After that day at the corral, the day that I'd realized my daughter needed me, I'd taken it off and put it in a box in my cabin. A box that had pictures and memories of Melody inside. Addy had her box of hearts, I had my box of memories. That's all she was now, a memory, a memory that hurt like fuck. A memory that at times made me ache with loneliness and grief. My hand instinctively went to my chest, over my heart where the pain was; only it wasn't as bad. Letting Addy in had eased it.

"Fuck it," I muttered as I opened the bathroom door and made my way downstairs.

When I got to the kitchen, Millie was dressed and was washing down the floor. A black trash bag sat next to the table, with what I guessed was the broken glass and Momma's broken dish.

"Hey, I'll do that," I said, taking the mop from Millie's hand

"Jesse, it's fine."

She gave me a small smile and she looked so beautiful that I wanted to kiss her, but I didn't. I just took the mop from her and cleaned up my mess.

CHAPTER 38

♥

MILLIE

As Jesse finished cleaning up the floor and taking the rubbish outside, I sat on the couch, chewing at my thumbnail, and waited. There was no way I was going to sneak upstairs and pretend I hadn't just had the best sex of my life; I was going to stay downstairs and face him. Prove to Jesse that I could do the 'no strings' sex.

Finally, I heard the door close followed by the soft padding of bare feet on the floor. Jesse appeared from the kitchen and sat down on the recliner.

"You okay?" he asked, sitting forwards and leaning his forearms on his legs.

"Yes, are you?" I lifted my legs, hugging my knees to my chest.

He took a deep breath and clasped his hands together. "We on the same page about what happened?"

Frustration pushed inside my chest. What we did was amazing and I know he thought so too. The way he clung to me when he came, the way he shuddered and strained above me. His orgasm was just as spectacular as mine, yet he was still insisting that it was a one-time thing.

"Yes of course, I said, didn't I?"

I hated myself for not being brave enough to tell him 'no, I'm not on the same page, in fact I'm not even in the same book'. What harm would it do to be truthful about how I felt? But, looking at Jesse's firmly set jaw, I knew what harm it would do. He would go back to ignoring me; at least this way maybe we could be friends.

"That's good, Millie, it really is. As damn spectacular as it was, I can't give you anything more than that. I've just got room for Addy in here," he said, patting at his chest. "I can't fit anything else in, so I'm sorry."

Jesse fisted one of his hands and clenched the other one around it, as his eyes narrowed waiting for me to speak; watching me expectantly.

"It's fine, Jesse," I finally said, as I pushed my feet to the floor. "You told me it would be one time, and I agreed. You don't need to explain yourself to me."

"You gotta know, Millie, I think you're amazing and if..." his voice trailed off.

"Seriously, don't worry about it. I don't usually throw myself at men, but you know I've kind of had a dry spell." I stood up and playfully poked him in the shoulder. I needed to lighten the thick atmosphere of sadness in the room.

Jesse smiled up at me, and my resolve almost disappeared in a puff of air. He looked so beautifully sad; his bright blue eyes had lost some of their lustre and the pain and grief he was feeling was palpable.

"Yeah, well I've said before, guy's a dick if you ask me," he replied with a short laugh.

"Maybe." I shrugged. "So, would you like some hot chocolate?"

Jesse nodded and relaxed back into the chair. "Thanks, that would be great."

I gave him my best big girl smile, hoping that I could do this, because I had a feeling Jesse was going to keep pushing his way into my heart, whether he or I wanted him to or not.

The morning after we'd had sex, Jesse and Addy were already eating breakfast when I came downstairs. As I saw them at the table, I couldn't help but let out a small gasp. I'd disinfected it when I'd cleaned up the night before, but seeing Addy leaning against the table as she ate her Cap'n Crunch made me feel a little guilty.

"Morning," I said brightly, brushing away the images of me sprawled where Jesse's hand now rested.

"Hey, Millie," Addy said around a mouthful of cereal. "Daddy is taking the day off today and is going to paint my room for me. I'm too old for bunnies now."

I looked at Jesse and raised an eyebrow.

"You're actually taking a day off?" I asked incredulously as I sat down opposite Addy.

Jesse shrugged. "No biggy."

I begged to differ, but reached for the Granola instead and filled my bowl. I had one hell of an appetite after the previous night's sex with Jesse.

"So, Addy, what color are you going to have?" I asked.

Addy put her head on one side and placed a finger on her lip as she considered my question.

"I think I'll have...let me think...I know," she squealed. "Pink. I'm going to have pink."

Jesse and I both burst out laughing. It wasn't really such a difficult decision when most of her clothes were pink, her Converse sneakers were pink, and her favorite crayon to use when coloring was pink.

"What's funny?" she asked, frowning.

"Nothing, baby," Jesse replied, still laughing softly. "Now eat up your cereal and then we can go into town."

"Okay, Daddy." She grinned at him and then picked her spoon up and continued eating.

"Can I come with you?" I asked on a whim. "I'd like to make dinner for you both, and so need to go to the supermarket."

"Well, if it's a decent grocery store you need, we'll have to go to Knightingale," Jesse replied.

"Oh, okay. No problem, I'll just use whatever your mum has already got."

"No, it's not a problem," Jesse protested. "There's probably more choice of paint at the hardware store there anyway."

"More choice of pink?"

Jesse grinned. "Well, maybe I'll get her to change her mind."

"No you won't," Addy said firmly with her spoon hovering by her mouth. "I'm having pink."

"Okay, baby. If you insist." Jesse shook his head and then ruffled Addy's hair.

"I do."

We finished our breakfast in relative silence and then all went off to Knightingale.

***

"So, you and Brandon," Jesse said as we watched Addy try to decide between six different shades of pink paint. "You said you weren't a thing."

"We're not," I sighed. "Although he might think we are."

"You need to be straight with him then, Millie. You shouldn't mess with his head." Jesse crossed his arms over his chest and played with a piece of cotton hanging from the sleeve of his t-shirt. "Unless of course you think you might become a *thing*."

Jesse turned to look at me, his eyes staring at my face, never once deviating.

"No, I don't think of him like that."

God that was only the half of it. I didn't think of Brandon like that because I *did* think of Jesse like that; every minute of every day.

"You sure? Because I'm kind of feeling a little guilty here if I'm honest. I didn't take much time to think about him when we...well, did what we did." He exhaled and rubbed a hand down his face. "Was too damn caught up in what I wanted to think about what my best friend might feel about it."

"Well you shouldn't," I protested. "We've not even kissed and I'm my own woman, so if I want to do what we did, well then, I will. Anyway, why ask me this now?"

"I don't know, just kind of feel bad for Brandon." Jesse groaned. "Won't be the first time I've taken a girl from him."

"Oh dear, were you high school rivals for the same girl?" I giggled despite the look of pure panic on Jesse's face.

"Kind of, he liked Melody."

"Oh," I gasped.

That was not what Brandon had said. He'd told me that they weren't really friends.

"Yeah, I didn't know, not until Melody told me after we got married. She said Brandon had asked her out in our last year at Junior High, but she was dating Tommy Kincaid at the time."

"Miss Cynthia's Tommy Kincaid?" My eyes widened and I glanced at Addy.

Jesse laughed. "Yeah, that Tommy Kincaid. I guess Addy showed you her box of hearts then, hey?"

"Yes, she did. Wow, this place is small."

"Yeah, not as small as it was a few years back, before the housing development was built. They figured building new affordable houses might get the younger folks to stick around, instead of moving off to Knightingale, or further."

"Did Brandon never tell you that he'd asked her out?" I asked, not really interested in the infrastructure of Bridge Vale at that moment.

Jesse shook his head. "Nope, he's *never* mentioned it. So, you can kind of see why I'm feeling a little guilty over here."

I sighed and nodded. "Kind of, but I swear there is nothing going on between Brandon and me. Has he ever been married?"

"He got engaged about three years back, Alesha Monroe, sweet little brunette who worked at the department store."

"What happened?" I asked, quickly checking that Addy was still being enthralled by pink paint.

Jesse shrugged. "No idea, he won't talk about it. Two years

161

ago, she just up and left one day and went to live in San Francisco. They'd been in Rowdy's the night before, and they seemed happy, according to everyone that was in there, but the next day he was madder than I've ever seen him. Said that Alesha had gone and wasn't coming back. Her mom told my mom that she's married now with a baby boy."

"What? She just left her family and has never been back since?"

"That's about the sum of it. There was only her and her momma, and a step-dad that she hated, so maybe it wasn't such a big thing for her. Her mom visits her a couple of times a year, but Alesha never comes back here. Brandon's brother, Wade, told me that Brandon found out that she'd applied for a job there and when he asked her about it she said she'd already made plans to move, whether Brandon went or not."

"Brandon didn't want to go?"

"Seems that way. Although, if he'd asked me, I'd have told him to get on the first plane out."

"But you love it here."

Jesse gave me a sweet smile. "Yeah I do, this place is everything to me and our land is everything to me. Brandon though, he has nothing to stay for. He helps his mom and dad run their guest ranch, which he hates, and he helps me out when I need him, which I'm also sure he hates."

I looked puzzled, wondering why Brandon would hate working for Jesse. "Why, you seem a fair boss to me?"

"Would you want your best buddy telling you what to do day in and day out? I wouldn't."

"Yes, well, maybe you're just a control freak," I laughed.

"Ooh, looks like we have a winner."

We both turned to watch Addy as she tried to drag a tin of paint over to Jesse.

"I picked one, Daddy."

"You did? And what color might it be?" Jesse asked, rescuing the tin from her. "Ah okay, yep, it's Passion Pink. Not sure what Passion Pink is supposed to be baby, but if that's what you want."

"It is," she sighed. "But I'm so tired, it was a real difficult decision."

I bent down and picked Addy up, hitching her on my hip. "Let me help you out there miss," I said as I tickled under her chin. "When we get back, after lunch you can have a little nap while Daddy starts your room and I prepare everything for dinner. Then this afternoon we can go on a nature walk. How does that sound?"

Addy nodded her head and smiled. "Good," she replied.

As I turned towards Jesse, I noticed that he was watching us. His eyes were sad again and the thought that he was probably wishing that I was Melody made me sad, too.

CHAPTER 39

♥

JESSE

As I picked up the scraps of the bunny frieze that had been on Addy's wall, memories flooded back of the day that I'd put it up. Melody had been too occupied with her pregnancy to think about decorating the baby's room before she was born, so when she went shopping in Knightingale one day, I took Addy into town, pushed her stroller around the hardware store, and showed her every damn frieze they had. Obviously at just six weeks old she had no idea, but when I showed her the bunnies her little legs kicked a little faster – so bunnies it was.

God, what a happy time that had been. We had our whole lives to look forward to, a new baby, and the ranch was doing well. The only problem on the horizon was Mom complaining about Melody all the time. 'Melody wasn't taking any interest in Addy, Melody spent too much money, Melody spent too much time away from the ranch, and Melody barely spoke to anyone anymore'. It had been real hard being caught between the two of them, and while Mom was right, she also needed to see that

Melody was only twenty-one-years-old; she should have been at college not stuck home being a wife and mother. Mom didn't give her any leeway for that and she should've.

While I worked on Addy's bedroom, she and Millie spent their afternoon on a nature trail. They came back with flowers for Addy to press and frame and then put up on her new pink wall. There was also a tub full of blackberries in her hand, although by the color of Addy's shirt and mouth I guess she'd already eaten more than had gone into the tub. According to Addy, Millie was going to teach her how to make something called Eaton Mess – what the hell that was I had no idea, but Addy seemed excited about it.

It was good that she had Millie around to do things with her. Mom was so busy cooking and cleaning for the bunk house and I'd been so far up my own ass I could use my tonsils as a punch bag, that Addy had been entertaining herself for a lot of the time. No four year old should be lonely, but I could see now that Addy had been. If Melody hadn't passed, we would probably have given her a brother or sister by now, although after Addy, Melody wasn't so keen on adding to our family. Now I guess we'll never know what we would've done.

"Daddy!"

I shake my head and laugh quietly to myself as I hear Addy shouting up the stairs. That child just does not have a volume control when she wants something. Fuck, how the hell did I let myself disconnect with her for the last two years?

"What, Addy?" I called from the bedroom doorway.

"Millie made dinner, she said you have to come now before you starve to death. She said that the painting will still be there after dinner." Finally, she took a breath. "And she said wash your hands."

"Okay, I'll be down in two minutes."

"Okay, Daddy."

I looked around the room and was pleased with the result. Two walls were 'Passion Pink' and two walls were white, at the window was a new pink and white chequered blind, and on the bed a matching comforter that Millie had insisted on buying, along with some pink and white feather throw cushions. It was a lot more grown up than the bunnies that was for sure, and would now last her until she became a teenager at least. But that, I didn't want to think about, I'd missed enough time with her as it was.

After washing up I went down the stairs and watched as Addy and Millie giggled together as they set the dishes on the table. I don't know what Millie had said, but it had obviously amused my daughter. I'd never seen her so happy, well not for a long time anyway, and I guess that was on me.

With a heavy heart full of regret, I moved towards them, plastered on a smile, and enjoyed watching the happiness shine from Addy's face.

CHAPTER 40

MILLIE

"But, Millie, these aren't chips," Addy proclaimed, holding what she called a 'French Fry' up in the air on the end of her fork. She was staring at it perplexed.

I'd made an English meal of sausage and chips. I'd managed to get some English Sausage from a deli in Knightingale, along with some potatoes that I was able to make into thick cut, English style chips. All this was to be followed by Eaton Mess, a mixture of meringue, fruit, cream, and raspberry sauce, as made by Addy.

"That's what we call chips," I said with a laugh. "What you call chips we call crisps."

Addy looked at Jesse and shook her head. "The English are silly," she grumbled.

"You think?" Jesse asked with a smirk as he tucked into his food.

"Yep. Millie, tell Daddy what your biscuits are like."

Jesse and I laughed at Addy's pouty little face while she tackled the sausage that she had refused to let me cut up.

"So, go on," Jesse urged. "Tell me about your biscuits."

"Well, they're not dumplings that's for sure."

"What's a dumperling?" Addy asked, still concentrating on her food.

"A dumpling," I corrected, "are what you call biscuits. Our biscuits are sweet and you call them cookies."

Addy dropped her knife and fork and lifted her hands palms up, frowned, and shrugged. "See, Daddy, real silly."

Jesse and I burst out laughing which only made Addy frown even harder.

"Oh, Addy," I sighed. "You are funny."

"I'm not funny, you're funny." She shook her head and started to giggle. "Your biscuits are like cookies, that's just weird."

Jesse reached out a hand and stroked it down Addy's long blonde hair as she went back to her food, still giggling.

"You okay?" I asked him.

Jesse's eyes were bright and shining as he looked at me and nodded.

"Yeah, just wish I'd seen her be this happy more often."

"You were dealing with your own grief," I said. "The main thing is you're here for her now."

"It's not just that," he said, glancing at Addy again. "It's you. You've made her happy. When she was smaller, we just thought she was going to be a quiet kid, you know. When we realized how bright she was, I told Melody that maybe she needed to interact with her more, but it was hard trying not to talk baby talk to a toddler."

"She never laughed or smiled?" I found it hard to believe, Addy had been nothing but a happy child since I'd arrived here.

"Yeah, but usually at bath time. Bath time was always a lot of fun," he said, the memories making him grin widely.

I smiled, thinking back to the night before when I'd heard them in the bathroom, laughing and having fun.

Jesse sighed. "Melody just couldn't get her to do much more than watch TV or draw. Although," he said in a whisper, leaning closer to me, "her drawings were more a scribble, she may be bright but she ain't no artist."

We both laughed quietly as our gazes simultaneously turned to Addy.

"Did you do bath time?" I asked, knowing what the answer would be.

"Yeah, that was my time with her. Bath time and bed time story."

I nodded. Happy times were with Daddy because she'd always adored him.

"Well, she's happy enough now. As for me making her happy, I think it's a lot of things," I said as I started to clear away the dishes. "You're spending time with her, Bonnie isn't so stressed, Garratt is home, and I'm getting her to use her brain, which means play time is all the more enjoyable. I'd say that's a pretty epic group effort, wouldn't you?"

Jesse's eyes closed momentarily as he exhaled slowly.

"Yeah," he said. "Pretty epic."

We both stared at each other, and unspoken gratitude was passed between us. Addy wasn't my child, but I couldn't thank Jesse enough for finally letting her back into his heart.

"Daddy," Addy cried, interrupting our moment of silence. "It's time for the dessert. I made it. But," she whispered. "Millie calls it pudding and pudding is Jell-O, but there's no Jell-O in it. How silly is that?"

"Oh, baby," Jesse laughed, pulling her onto his lap. "I love you."

Addy flung her arms around his neck and hugged him tightly. "I love you, too, Daddy, but Millie is still silly."

After dinner, Addy wanted to play cards and when she said her game of choice was 'Concentration', I was pretty sure that I heard Jesse let out a pained groan. To his credit, he didn't say anything, but got the cards and dealt them with some dexterity it had to be said.

The longer we played, the more I learned that Jesse and Addy were both extremely competitive; there was no letting the child win as far as Jesse was concerned. Unfortunately for him, I was not of the same viewpoint, and on a couple of occasions gave her a little nod towards a matching pair. Jesse's face was a picture when Addy won the deciding 5th game – they had won two each - I on the other hand, won none; probably because I was concentrating on Jesse's laughing blue eyes far more than I was the cards on the table.

"I still think you helped her on that last game," he grumbled as I cleared away the mugs that we'd had hot chocolate in.

"Seriously?" I waved a hand at him and bit my lip to stifle the laughter. "You need to chill out, Jesse."

"I don't," he cried. "You need to stop teaching my daughter how to cheat."

"You have no proof. She's a bright girl and won fair and square."

"Well, she couldn't stop giggling about something when I put her to bed."

"She's probably just happy to have beaten you, that's all," I replied.

"Whatever, Millie," he laughed and flicked the newspaper at my backside.

"Ow." I turned to him with a grin and rubbed at my bum.

His own smile was a mile wide, and it warmed my heart to see him happy and relaxed.

"Well, just remember how that feels next time you want to cheat."

I let out a sigh of contentment and watched as he sat in the recliner, shook out the newspaper, and began to read. The worry lines that were usually in permanent residence on his brow had smoothed out, and his mouth was curled into a small smile. My chest constricted as I watched him and when he reached a hand up to run it through his hair, I had to press my thighs together to relieve the aching throb that was starting between my legs.

Jesse Connor had become my addiction. I'd had a taste, twice, and it was never going to be enough. I needed to taste him every day in whatever way possible; him inside me, his mouth on mine, or my mouth on his cock, I didn't care.

My breath shuddered as I shook my head and moved into the kitchen. This wasn't me; I wasn't the sort of girl who had dirty thoughts. I wasn't a prude, but sex wasn't something discussed in our house; my mother was a practising Catholic who had once made my brother give three 'Hail Mary' for asking her what pre-menstrual meant. Where Jesse was concerned though, I had no filter. My brain just wouldn't stop imagining all of the beautifully dirty things that we could do together.

"Millie!" Jesse was suddenly behind me.

"Oh sorry, yeah?"

"I was just asking if you'd like a beer."

Jesse moved towards the refrigerator and an image of the previous night flashed before my eyes. We'd been going to have beer then, too.

The refrigerator door slammed and Jesse opened a drawer to pull out a bottle opener. He popped the caps and passed a bottle to me.

"Are you okay?" he asked before taking a swig of his beer.

I nodded and held the cold bottle against my heated neck. The warmth from between my legs had rapidly travelled up my body and I was desperate for some relief.

"Okay then." Jesse smiled and glanced quickly at the table.

He was having exactly the same thoughts as I was. His eyes were suddenly hooded and his chest was rising and falling rapidly. I ran my tongue along my bottom lip and drew in a breath as Jesse's hand reached up to push my hair behind my ear.

"Millie," he whispered.

"Jesse?"

He said nothing but let his hand slip to my cheek, where his fingertips whispered against my skin before dropping to his side. I swallowed, taking a step forward, my eyes never leaving his.

"I'm in so much trouble," he whispered.

My free hand reached for Jesse's, and took a loose hold of his fingertips. He looked down at our touch and then back up to me. His eyes were no longer a bright azure blue, but were now a deep sapphire color and were full of promise.

He put his bottle of beer down onto the table and then reached for mine. As he pulled it from my hand, the front door slammed.

"Hey kids, I'm home!"

Garratt was back. Jesse dropped my hand, took a step back, and still holding my beer, walked into the living area to greet his brother, leaving me a hot, wet mess of frustration.

CHAPTER 41

♥

JESSE

I wasn't sure whether I wanted to strangle my brother slowly, or slap him on the back with thanks. If he hadn't come home when he did, I have no doubt that I would have been inside Millie and taking us both towards another mind blowing orgasm. Something that I'd told her would not be happening again; but fuck if the idea of it didn't fill me with excitement.

"What you doing back?" I asked Garratt as he threw his duffle bag down.

"Let's just say Mikey needs to stay away from the drink for a while."

I frowned and thrust my hands to my hips, the beer bottle dangling from my fingers. "What fucking trouble did you get into this time?"

Garratt grinned and held his hands up in surrender. "Nothing, there was no trouble. Unless you call Mikey having alcohol poisoning and spending last night at the City hospital on an IV trouble."

"You bunch of dicks," I stormed. "Don't you know how dangerous it is to spike someone's drink?"

Garratt and his buddies were celebrating Mikey's 21st birthday in the city, so I was guessing that the poor guy had no idea what he'd been drinking.

"Hey, it wasn't me," Garratt protested. "It was some guy, Donny, that John brought along. He kept slipping tequila into Mikey's beer."

"And you're telling me that Mikey couldn't taste it and none of you saw him doing it?"

"Yep, that's about it."

"Bullshit, Garratt," I barked, shaking my head. "You are a stupid bunch of idiots."

"I swear Jess, we had no idea until Mikey passed out. I called an Uber and me and Benjie took him to the emergency room."

I let out a long, slow exhale as I watched my brother and I knew that he was telling the truth. As Garratt flopped down onto the couch, Millie came in wiping her hands on a kitchen towel.

"Hi, Garratt, I was just taking the rubbish out."

Garratt grinned as soon as he saw Millie walking towards us; it was a grin of happiness. A twinge of something dug in my gut as I thought about my brother and his feelings for Millie. But then I felt stupid. You could see in his eyes it was purely the love of a friend that he had for her; maybe even brotherly.

"Do you mean the *trash*?" he asked on a laugh.

"So sorry," she said sarcastically. "I must make sure I do my homework in the future."

"Ah, I'm only messing with you, Millie. So," he said turning to me. "What are you doing here, and where are Mom and Dad?"

I explained about Auntie Ruby and grinned when Garratt's face fell at the news that she was coming home with them. I was Auntie Ruby's favorite and she gave Garratt shit whenever she could.

"Ugh," he groaned. "I think I might go back to the city for a while."

"Now I'm worried," Millie said, her face crumpling into a

grimace.

"Oh, you'll be fine," Garratt replied. "It's just me she hates."

"She doesn't hate you," I scoffed. "She just loves me more."

Garratt shook his head and pushed up from the couch. "I'm going to grab a beer to help soften the blow. You want one, Millie? I see my brother just looked after himself."

I glanced down at the bottle still in my hand and then looked at Millie. A blush touched her cheeks and she shook her head.

"He did pull one out of the refrigerator for me, but I'm going to go to bed, so you have it. It's on the table."

"Stay up with us," Garratt said as he walked past Millie and ruffled her hair.

"No, I've got a new book on my Kindle that I want to read." Her eyes reached mine and I wondered whether she wanted *me* to say something; maybe she wanted *me* to ask her to stay. Like a pussy, I said nothing, because hadn't I made it clear that it would be one night?

"Okay, night Millie. See you in the morning."

"Night, Garratt." She looked at me and paused. "Night, Jesse."

"G'night, and thanks for dinner."

She gave me a small smile and disappeared up the stairs, leaving me wishing that Garratt didn't have such douchebag friends.

CHAPTER 42

💜

MILLIE

"Good morning, honey," Bonnie greeted me with a tired smile.

It was Tuesday morning, after the Founder's fair, and she and Ted hadn't got home until late the previous evening, with a grumpy Auntie Ruby in tow. By the time they'd gotten her settled into bed, caught up with ranch news, and had a hot drink, it was way past midnight.

"You should have stayed in bed. Jesse said one of the guys is cooking for the bunk house again today," I said, noticing that it wasn't even six-thirty.

"I know, but my body just likes the early mornings. Ted went off early with Jesse, anyhow, and while he tried to be quiet, that man is like a herd of buffalo thudding around. Why are you up, honey? I could hear Addy snoring away when I came down."

"I just couldn't sleep," I replied, feeling a heat on my cheeks.

I'd tossed and turned all night thinking about Jesse lying on his camp bed just a few doors down. If he hadn't been in the same room as Addy, I'm sure I'd have gone and tried to seduce him.

"Addy, Ted, and Ruby snoring together *is* enough to wake the damn dead I suppose," Bonnie groaned. "Thank the lord I have ear plugs."

I laughed and poured her a coffee from the jug bubbling away. She took it from me added her creamer and sugar and then took a long drink with a sigh.

"Ooh, I've missed that," she said, putting her mug down on the table. "Auntie Ruby does not spend money on decent coffee, that's for sure."

"How is she feeling, after her fall?"

I hadn't really gotten a chance to meet her at any great length. The poor old lady had been so tired that Ted had practically carried her up to bed as she'd grumbled about the number of stairs.

Bonnie swatted her hand in dismissal. "Oh she's fine, nothing was broken. She's just got a little bruising on her legs and her ego. She didn't really want to come, but Ted insisted."

"Whose aunt is she?"

"Mine, she's my mom's sister. There were six of them, but there's only Auntie Ruby left now." Bonnie looked wistful as she stared out of the window through to the garden. "When I was a child, we'd have some huge family parties. Christmas was magical, usually at our house because we had more room. My uncle Elias always dressed up as Santa Claus for us kids, and his wife, Aunt Jeannie, would tell us ghost stories on Christmas Night. Yeah, we'd always have a house full."

"Six siblings and all their families is definitely a house full," I exclaimed.

"There was usually at least thirty of us. But my momma loved playing hostess for them all. I was brought up on a farm, about eighty miles from here, and we lived in huge house that my daddy built my momma as a wedding present."

"Really? So how did you meet Ted?" I pulled my chair closer to the table. "I know eighty miles isn't much distance around here, but Ted said he didn't go to college, so you didn't meet there."

Bonnie grinned and I noticed that her cheeks were a little red.

"He came with his father to buy a couple of horses from my daddy. I'd just finished college and was at home. I was bored, so while our dads thrashed out a deal, I showed Ted around the farm."

She stopped speaking, rested her chin in her hand and looked dreamily into the distance.

"And?" I giggled.

Bonnie looked coy. "*And* I took him down to the creek and he kissed me. Just one hour and ten minutes after meeting me."

"Oh, Bonnie," I gasped. "That's so romantic."

"Not really," she laughed. "I pushed him in the creek and called him a creeper."

We both burst out laughing.

"You didn't?"

Bonnie nodded. "I did. Didn't stop Ted though. As soon as he got back onto the bank he pulled me into his arms and kissed me again."

"Did you push him in again?" I asked, wide eyed.

"No, honey," she whispered. "I kissed him back and we were married three months later."

My hand went to my chest and my eyes watered with emotion. From the look of love on Bonnie's face, she adored Ted as much now as she did then.

"My boys surely do take after Ted," she said with a shake of her head. "Both romantics, both impetuous, and, even though I'm biased, both as swoon worthy as hell."

Oh God, I couldn't disagree there. Both were handsome, definitely, but Jesse was as delicious a man as I'd ever seen. Unfortunately, the baggage that he carried on his back daily meant that he would never be my 'Ted'.

As that thought ran through my head, I mentally chastised myself. What the hell was I doing, thinking that Jesse and I could be some current version of his parents? I knew my feelings for him were stronger than they should have been, but the heart wasn't the most sensible of organs. My Grandma Armalita used to say that every time your heart fell in love, a brain cell died, and I think she was right. It seemed a whole cluster of mine had bitten the dust since meeting Jesse.

"Wow," I said softly. "That's so lovely. Just three months and you're still together."

"Twenty-nine years this year," Bonnie announced proudly. "Don't misunderstand me, we've had times when things were tough, with Jesse when Melody passed and don't get me started on Garratt. That boy has been a constant worry from the minute the doctor slapped his ass, but no matter what, we've always had love. I'm grateful that my daddy thought his two horses were worth more than Ted's dad was willing to pay. Otherwise, I'd never have taken him down to the creek and he'd have never kissed me."

"That's like one of the romances that I read," I sighed.

Bonnie reached her hand out and taking my fingers in hers, gave them a gentle squeeze.

"Oh honey, it'll work itself out."

As I looked at her, Bonnie's eyes softened and her full mouth, exactly like Jesse's, turned up at the corners. I drew in a breath and curled my lips inwards. The emotion of homesickness overpowered me and suddenly I wanted my mum. I needed to talk through how Dean's betrayal had made me feel so worthless that I'd practically thrown myself at Jesse. And then of course there were my feelings for Jesse; I *really* needed to talk to someone about them.

"You want to talk to me sweetheart?" Bonnie asked softly.

Swiping at the tear that crawled down my cheek, I nodded.

"He made me feel like I was nothing, Bonnie." I held my breath, desperately trying to stem more tears that were threatening.

"Who we talking about here, hmm?" Her hand reached up and pushed my hair away from my face. "That ex of yours or my son?"

My eyes went as wide as saucers and my mouth dropped open. I watched Bonnie warily as she pulled her chair closer to mine.

"Oh God," I whispered, averting my embarrassed gaze.

"Honey," she cooed, lifting my chin with her finger. "You're grown adults but you kind of need to be careful where and when you make out."

She smiled but my heart was thudding like a jack hammer in my chest. Visions of what Jesse did to me up against the barn wall flashed before my eyes.

"W-what did you see?" I stammered.

"Exactly that, you two making out. I was coming back from the bunk house and saw you. It looked kind of hot and heavy, so I found a little more cleaning to do."

Making out was putting it mildly. His fingers were inside me, taking me to another level of pleasure.

"So, what happened, and I don't want the details," Bonnie chuckled. "He's still my son."

"Please, believe me when I say, Addy has never been around, I wouldn't risk her seeing us." A sick feeling rolled around in my stomach, wondering whether Bonnie's smile was a mask and any minute now she would scream at me to pack my bags. It also occurred to me that Addy could quite easily have seen us the night we had sex. She might have woken and come looking for Jesse. I was the worst kind of person. I deserved to be sent packing.

"I know, but are you saying it's happened more than once?"

I nodded slowly.

"The broken soup bowl and bottles in the trash wouldn't have something to do with that, would it?"

I nodded slowly – again.

"I really want Jesse to be ready for you, Millie, but I'm not sure he is." She sighed heavily and folded both her hands around mine. "And to be honest, I'm not real sure that you're ready for him. You were about to get married and only didn't because your man decided he wanted...let's say, he wanted something different. You can't possibly be over that, honey. Not only did you lose him, but you lost your future. And how and why you lost those things must have been heart breaking."

I knew that Bonnie was right in everything she thought I should be feeling, but she was wrong. Since I'd been here, since I'd set eyes on Jesse, the pain at losing Dean and what we'd planned, felt like a tiny scratch on my heart, not the searing pain that I would expect to feel.

"It doesn't hurt like it should," I explained. "I think I was in love with being in love. Dean was my best friend, and I miss that about him, but we weren't even intimate, Bonnie. I never had that physical connection with him."

"And you think you do with Jesse?"

There was definitely a physical attraction, but a connection? Yes, we were compatible in the sense that the sex had been amazing, but I wasn't sure Jesse could connect with anyone who wasn't Melody on an emotional level.

"I don't know. I'm attracted to him, have been since I saw his grumpy self at the airport." I smiled as Bonnie's laugh tinkled in the quiet kitchen. "But I know he can't give me anything else. He told me that."

"You hoping he'll change his mind?"

I shrugged. Shit, who was I kidding? Of course I was.

"You're a beautiful girl, Millie, and if Jesse could wake up to the fact that his life needs to go on, and stop mourning a woman who wasn't all that, I'd say 'you go get my boy', but," she said with shake of her head, "I don't see when that's ever going to happen."

She was being totally honest with me. She wasn't warning me off her son because she was a lioness protecting her cub. She was warning me that her son was broken and nowhere near ready to heal.

"I could be wrong, and you may just be the woman who shows him that his blood still pumps through his body and that his heart still beats hard. I sure hope so, honey, but I don't want to see you hurt any more than you already are, I truly don't."

A lump formed in my throat as I considered Bonnie's words, and I knew that I had to let the idea of Jesse and I go. The next ten and half months were going to be hard, but I'd had crushes before and they'd soon disappeared once someone else had caught my eye. Maybe this with Jesse would be the same. My heart sank at that thought, because I knew it wouldn't. There was no one else around here who would catch my eye, and honestly, I knew that my feelings for Jesse had gone way beyond the crush stage.

"Thanks, Bonnie," I said, standing up from my seat. "It was good to talk."

"Don't bottle things up," she replied. "You talk to me any time, okay?"

I nodded. "Yes, I will. I'd better go and get dressed before Addy wakes up."

Bonnie gave me a nod and as I passed, she took my hand again. "Never lose hope though, honey."

Hope was all I had, because I certainly had no pride left.

CHAPTER 43

♥

JESSE

"Hey, Jess," Brandon called to me as I wrestled the calf to the ground.

"What?" I snapped.

"That one's already been done."

Brandon nodded towards the rear end of the calf and I saw that he was right; there was the Connor Ranch brand in pride of place.

"Fuck," I groaned and let the calf struggle to its feet and run back to its mother, happy not to have the hot brand near its ass again.

"What the hell is wrong with you today?" Brandon asked, punching me lightly in the shoulder. "You nearly took your fucking head off with that over hanging branch you didn't see, you've hardly said a word all morning, and now this. You need to get laid or something?"

"Yeah," I replied. "Something like that."

He was right, I did need to get laid-the real problem was by who. I'd had little sleep the last two nights. My boner had kept me awake on the night that Garratt had come home unexpectedly. I'd been so damn ready to repeat the previous night with Millie; fuck my warning to her. Then my little brother had gone and spoiled it by turning up. Last night hadn't been much better; it's not comfortable trying to sleep with a dick as hard and straight as a lightening pole.

I'd managed to keep busy all day, breaking in Turner Carlisle's horse, but then we'd all had dinner together. As soon as I'd come down stairs from my shower I saw her dancing around the living room with Addy, while Garratt clapped along to the music coming from the radio. Her long black hair was down, her smooth, silky shoulders were bare and were a gorgeous golden brown from the sun. She was wearing a pale blue sun dress that, when she stood in a certain spot, the light through the window made it see-through and I could make out the outline of her gorgeous long, toned legs. Instant fucking boner once again.

As soon as Addy saw me, she ran up to me and begged me to dance with them. Millie said she was tired and flopped down on the couch, but not before I'd brushed past her and breathed in the smell of her perfume and the hint of mint in her shampoo. If there is anything harder than steel, then that was how hard my dick went. Thank Christ I was wearing loose jeans and a shirt long enough to cover any sign of a bulge in my pants.

The only time it had even felt as though it had softened a tiny bit, was when Mom, Dad, and Auntie Ruby got home. They'd called earlier to say they were on the way back, so we'd waited up for them. Truthfully, I should have been in bed trying to get some sleep before my five a.m. start, but I knew it was pointless if the previous night had been anything to go by. Plus, I hadn't wanted to leave her downstairs with Garratt. Not that I thought anything was going to happen between them, but I hated the thought that he was getting closer to her, while I, like a dick, was adamant about keeping a distance. Who was I kidding; I could no more keep my distance than Garratt could go a month without getting into some stupid ass trouble of some sort or another.

Then bed time had arrived and I lay there listening to the damn orchestra of snores around the house; Addy's soft one, Dad's deep throaty one, and Auntie Ruby's that sounded like a hissing cat. All the time thinking about a certain woman just a few feet away.

So, I think you'll find that's what the fuck is up with me today.

CHAPTER 44

♥

MILLIE

"So you're telling me that you were gonna marry a man who preferred wiener to cooch?" Auntie Ruby asked as she reclined the armchair.

"Erm, well, yes I suppose so," I replied hesitantly as I took a stab in the dark at what she meant by 'cooch'. I groaned quietly, not even sure how she'd managed to get the information from me in the first place.

"Sheesh, that's a bummer sugar. Oh my goodness, *'that's a bummer'*." She looked at me expectantly and then burst out into a cackling laughter, showing me the few teeth that she had left.

"Auntie Ruby!" Bonnie stared at her wide eyed. "Behave yourself."

"Oh, shove it, Bonnie. I'm damn well ninety years of age, I'll say what I like.

"Not while Addy is around, and you're not ninety. You know full well that you're only eighty-four."

"That's practically ninety. Anyway, who gives a shit?" She

waved her hand dismissively and turned back to me. "How did you not know, sugar, that your guy preferred a game of hunt the sausage to stuff the taco?"

I gasped and my head shot around to Bonnie, needing clarification that I'd heard correctly.

"Did she...?" I asked.

Bonnie nodded and sighed. "I'm sorry, Millie. You should excuse my aunt, she has a mouth fowler than a backed-up sewer pipe."

"Ah, you're just a damn prude, Bonnie. I'm betting you'd never seen a johnson until your wedding night."

"And what's wrong with that?" Bonnie protested, pulling Auntie Ruby's skirt down where it had ridden up to show her spindly legs.

"Nothing, I s'ppose. But betcha wouldn't buy a hat without trying it on."

"Well I never said I hadn't," Bonnie protested, with a hint of pink to her cheeks. "Now, less of your dirty mouth. Addy will be back in with Garratt in a minute."

Garratt had taken Addy to feed the horse that Jesse was breaking in, and then clean out the stables of the ranch horses. I had a feeling that he'd volunteered simply to get away from Auntie Ruby for a little while. Her opening words to him as he'd come down for breakfast were, 'so have you popped your cherry yet, or you still playing with it yourself?'

"The child lives on a ranch, she'll hear worse than what comes from my mouth," Auntie Ruby grumbled.

"Doesn't mean you have to speak that way in front of her. Now," Bonnie sighed. "Are you sure you'll be okay here while I go over to the bunk house?"

Auntie Ruby looked at me and shrugged her shoulders, accompanied by an eye roll.

"Yes, I've told you once. Go and do some damn work woman. Millie here will keep me company."

I groaned inwardly, because the thought of keeping her company didn't exactly fill me with joy. I'd have to find something to distract her with while I did some reading with Addy. Either that or get Garratt to entertain her; but then that would be cruel, because he seemed petrified of her.

As Bonnie called goodbye, Ruby gave another cackling laugh.

"Right, now Bonnie's gone with her twisted panties, you can tell me all about the gay guy and whether he always wanted to do you in trap number two."

***

Garratt shuddered as we shut the door behind us and made our way down the porch steps. We had both offered to go and tell Jesse that dinner would be a half hour away; both of us anxious to get away from Auntie Ruby.

"How does one little old lady make me feel like such a damn fool?" Garratt moaned. "And don't say it's because I am one."

"I wasn't going to," I protested. "She makes me feel the same way. I just don't know how to answer her without giving her more ammunition to take the mickey out of."

Garratt stopped walking and tilted his head. "Take the *what*? What's Mickey Mouse got to do with it?"

"Not Mickey Mouse," I laughed, pushing at his shoulder. "Taking the mickey. It's an English phrase for mocking someone with sarcasm."

"Ah, so she's screwing with you?"

"Yes." I nodded. "She screws with me whenever she can."

"I'm with you on that one," Garratt sighed. "She asked me why I'd be thrown out of school and when I told her, she asked me if it was the only way I could get girls. Then she said if I was a pimp did it mean I could get her some drugs as well. I never know when she's being serious."

As we walked around the edge of the pasture, Garratt hooked an arm over my shoulder. It was nice and brotherly and it made me miss Javi just a little less. Garratt had been good for me in that sense, just as Bonnie had been an amazing stand in for my mum when I'd needed to talk about Jesse.

"So, what's going on with you and the dick head?" Garratt asked as we passed the barn.

"W-who?" I stammered, glancing at the barn guiltily.

"There's only one dick head on this ranch," he growled.

I let out a little gasp – he meant Brandon. For one horrible moment, I thought Garratt knew about Jesse and me, too.

"Nothing," I stated firmly. "He took me to the fair at the weekend, but there's nothing there…not for me anyway."

"You could do worse than my brother you know, if you're on the lookout for a man that is."

The air rushed from my lungs and spluttered out of my mouth in a huge choke.

"Hey, you okay?" Garratt asked, slapping me on the back. "Is the thought of my brother that awful?"

I shook my head and waved my hand to indicate no. No couldn't be further from the truth.

"Sorry, think I swallowed a bug, or something," I was finally able to croak out.

"Yeah, well," Garratt sighed. "I doubt he'd get his head out of his ass long enough to realize how beautiful you are anyway."

"Garratt!"

"Not that you're my type, Senorita, but you are beautiful in a…well Spanish sort of way."

My laughter was loud as I linked arms with Garratt. "A Spanish sort of way? I'm guessing English wasn't your major."

"No," he chuckled. "I'm a math genius, I told you."

We were both laughing hard when we reached the corral, and found Jesse leaning against the fence.

"Hey, you two," he called as we approached him.

I waved a hand and Garratt saluted him.

"You come to see someone doing some real work?" he asked with a twinkle in his eyes.

Garratt nudged my side with his elbow and said in a loud stage whisper. "He got out of bed on the good side this morning."

Biting on my lip to stem the laughter, I kept my eyes on Jesse and watched to see his reaction. He shook his head and gifted us the most beautiful, crinkle eyed smile.

"You're a fucking douche, you know that, right?" he aimed

189

towards Garratt.

"Yeah I know, but you love me."

Jesse didn't respond, but the growing width of his smile showed that he did indeed love his brother. Those who received the gift of Jesse Connor's love were extremely lucky. I'd seen how the strength and depth of it had helped Addy to blossom over the last couple of weeks, and when I looked at Garratt, he was basking in the light of it, too. His eyes were glowing and his back had straightened, his height appearing to have grown a few inches. That was what Jesse Connor's love did, and he had no idea that his family yearned for it; they needed it because him giving it meant that he was living.

Taking in a deep breath, I moved over to the fence where Jesse was standing. I tried to kid myself it was to pet the horse that he had tethered there, but it wasn't, I just wanted to be next to Jesse and maybe grab a little bit of that light he was giving.

"He's gorgeous," I said, reaching a hand out to the horse's nose and giving it a rub.

"Yeah, he's a beauty alright."

Jesse reached for the stallion's ears, but his fingers whispered over mine, making my heart and stomach do a synchronised dive. As I glanced at Jesse, I saw his mouth twitch up on the side of his profile that I could see. Holding my breath, I dared to hope that he'd done it purposefully, because he'd needed a connection with me as much as I needed one with him.

"What's his name?" Garratt asked, moving to the other side of his brother.

"Corazón," Jesse replied.

"Heart," I whispered and looked at Jesse, who was bending his head to nuzzle the stallion's nose with his own.

"Yeah, apparently Turner's wife, Rosaria, named him. He was an anniversary gift from him to her, but she's never been able to ride him."

"And now?" Garratt asked.

"A couple more days and he'll be ready."

The beautiful, sleek, black stallion whinnied happily as Jesse gave him one last scratch of the ears before feeding him a mint Lifesaver from his pocket.

"So, what do you two want, anyway?" he asked, his eyes never leaving Corazón.

"Mom said dinner will be ready soon. She doesn't want you to be late, you're the only one who can keep Auntie Ruby on the straight and narrow."

Jesse dropped his head back and laughed loudly.

"You bunch of cowards," he cried. "She's a little old lady."

"Well Mom's had to put up with her for the last four days, Dad says he's sick of her asking whether he needs to take 'the little blue pills yet', and as for me and Millie, well she just keeps taking the mickey out of us!"

"The what?" Jesse asked, incredulously.

Garratt sighed, put an arm around Jesse's shoulder and started to lead him back to the house.

"Oh, you have a lot to learn, big brother. Let me explain."

We'd finished dinner and Jesse and I were clearing the dishes. Garratt actually offered to help me, but as he was still watching an episode of The Big Bang Theory when Jesse came down from putting Addy to bed, he said he'd help instead.

"She go down okay?" I asked, loading the last dish into the dishwasher.

Jesse sighed happily and smiled. "Yeah, don't know what you did with her today, but she was pooped. Or do you think she's coming down with something?" he asked, worriedly.

"She's fine. She helped Garratt with the horses this morning before we did some reading. Then this afternoon we planted a vegetable patch."

"You did?" Jesse looked surprised and then a frown wrinkled his brow. "She never told me. Why do you think she didn't? Do you think she's pulling away from me because I've been so distant?"

He pulled at his hair as he looked up at the ceiling, to where Addy's room was above us. I put a hand on his bicep and

191

squeezed it gently.

"She wants it to be a surprise, I wasn't supposed to tell you, but I didn't want you worrying that she's not well."

I smiled gently at him, amazed at the change in his attitude towards Addy. He'd obviously always loved her, but now he cared about her, too. He cared about how she was feeling, what she needed, and how he could make her happy.

Jesse let out a sigh of relief. "You sure that's all it is?"

"Yes, Jesse, I'm sure."

On instinct, I reached up and brushed his hair from his eyes. He hadn't been wearing his Stetson while he'd been in the corral, and the sun had added some lighter golden highlights to his usual dirty blond, and it made him look younger; or maybe that was because he didn't seem to frown quite so much these days.

As my fingertips lingered on his hair, Jesse swallowed, his eyes darkened and his hand came to my hip. His fingertips rested on the curve of my backside, while his thumb found its way under the hem of my t-shirt and rubbed against my stomach.

Neither of us spoke, and the only sound was that of the TV that Garratt was watching from the recliner, with his back to us. My breath hitched as Jesse's thumb pushed down to the waistband of my jeans and when he took a step closer to me, I felt the satin of my bra tighten against my breasts with the hardening of my nipples. Jesse inhaled deeply through his nose and inclined his head slightly as we heard a tread on the stairs.

"Say you need to get something from your things in the barn," he whispered. "Leave the flashlight here and don't go in, but wait for me outside."

"Why?" I questioned, breathily.

"I think you know why," he murmured quietly and then pulled away from me.

I gave Jesse a short nod and watched as he joined his dad and brother in the living room. My heart was thudding fast and hard and the expectancy of what we were going to do meant that I was already wet.

CHAPTER 45

♥

JESSE

Millie had been gone about two or three minutes, when I 'spotted' the flashlight still sitting on the side table next to the door. It was next to the basket where we kept the keys, exactly the place where you would leave it by accident. I smiled at her smart thinking.

"She's left the damn flashlight," I groaned, pushing up from the couch.

Dad looked over at it and sighed. "You want me to take it? You said you were going up."

"Nah, I probably should check on Turner's horse anyway. He was a little restless when I stabled him earlier."

I turned away so that they couldn't see the grin on my face. There was nothing restless about that horse anymore; he'd been one of the easier ones to break.

"Okay," Dad yawned. "I'm gonna go up myself. Garratt, don't stay up too late, son. We're helping out with the branding and vaccinating tomorrow."

"Yeah, I'm coming, too. I need my beauty sleep seeing as boss man over there is having another easy day with his horsey."

I turned to see Garratt grin at me and I gave him one back. We were getting back on track and it was good to be friends with my brother again.

"Night guys," I called and snatched up my keys and the flashlight. Locking the door behind me, I ran down the porch steps towards the barn. My pulse was racing and my dick was already hard.

I knew that I shouldn't be doing this, but she was so damn well addictive. This was nothing like Angie. Fucking Angie once had been a mistake, doing it three times was a disastrous decision of monumental standards, but this with Millie didn't feel like that. It was still just fucking, no emotions involved, but she wasn't just another lay. I liked her as a friend, and as long as we could keep it on that level then there was no reason why this wouldn't work. I decided that I was going to suggest it to her; maybe not use the phrase fuck buddies, but that's what we'd be if she agreed.

As I approached the barn, I could see Millie, her back to me, pacing up and down, her arms wrapped around herself against the chill that the breeze had brought with it.

"Why didn't you put a jacket on?" I said as I reached her.

"Oh shit, you scared me," she gasped.

Taking hold of her hand, I dragged her to my side and continued walking.

"Where are we going?" she asked, jogging to keep up with me.

"The cabin. You didn't think I'd fuck you in the barn did you?"

Who the hell was I kidding? I'd had every intention of fucking her in the barn, then I'd seen her beautiful features, the curve of that spectacular ass, and her amazing rack and I knew I couldn't explore that body how I wanted to. Not on a dirty sheet of tarpaulin surrounded by boxes of shit that no one had a use for. Besides which, she was too classy for that. Okay, so I'd had her against the barn and on Mom's kitchen table, but now she deserved more, so my bed was about to become the altar where I'd worship Armalita Braithwaite.

CHAPTER 46

♥

MILLIE

I didn't have time to survey the cabin, because as soon as we were inside, Jesse had me pushed up against a wall and was kissing the breath from my body.

As he pushed his tongue inside my mouth, my hands went into his hair, pulling at it. My hips bucked forwards, desperate for some friction to ease the throbbing between my legs. Jesse's hand pushed under my t-shirt and gently kneaded my breast, eliciting a moan of pleasure from me.

"Millie," he groaned and pulled his mouth from mine.

"What's wrong?" I gasped, the anxiety that he'd changed his mind overwhelming me.

"You drive me crazy, Armalita. I'm so damn addicted to you and your pussy that I can't think straight."

"So," I breathed out, taking his mouth in a kiss. "Don't think, just do."

Jesse pulled back again. "I know I said one night, but I can't help myself and I don't want to give you any idea that this is going to be more than it is."

His soft eyes gazed at me as his hands gently framed my face, pushing back my hair. Then he let out a long exhale before kissing the end of my nose. My heart stopped as he opened his mouth to say something. I just knew he was going to tell me to go back to the house.

"No Jesse, I'm not leaving," I cried, wrapping my arms tightly around his waist.

His mouth lifted into a smile. "I wasn't going to say that. I couldn't let you leave now even if my life depended on it."

"What were you going to say then?" I asked.

"I was going to ask you how you'd handle us being friends, but adding sex into the equation. No strings, just friendship and sex."

My pride should have told me to tell him no, it wasn't what I wanted, but after being stood up at the altar I had very little of that left. More importantly my body was screaming at me to agree. My skin was on fire, my clit was throbbing, as usual my nipples ached they were so hard, and boy, I was wet. I could do this. I was a twenty-six year old woman who had barely got to first base in almost two years.

"The sex has to be mutual, not just on your terms," I replied, trying to sound controlled, when all I really wanted to do was be fucked by Jesse whenever and wherever he liked.

"I'm never going to force you, if that's what you mean," he growled.

"That's not what I meant. I mean I have needs, too, and if you're one of these old-fashioned men that doesn't like a woman taking control and asking for sex, well then we may have a problem."

I bit on my lip to stop it from trembling. I had never taken control where sex was concerned, *ever*. But this man, he made me want to push the boundaries and I knew that I needed to hide my insecurities where he was concerned. He could never see that I was hanging on his every word, his every movement, just to be able to have snatched moments with him. Jesse needed to think that I was as in control of the situation, and my emotions, as he was.

"Well?" I pushed. "Is this all going to be about your wants and needs, or do I get a say in things, too?"

I held onto his arms, gripping the cliff edge, hoping not to fall off if he told me 'no'.

"You need me any time at all, then just fucking say," he groaned before taking my mouth in a feverish kiss.

With a tangle of arms and hands, we practically ripped each other's clothes off, panting in unison as our need for each other sky rocketed with each piece of clothing that fell to the floor.

"Fuck," Jesse groaned, as he ran his hands down the sides of my naked body. "You're damn near perfect."

With one hand in my hair, he cupped one of my breasts with the other, pushing it up to meet his mouth. He sucked hard on my nipple, increasing the ache between my legs. As his tongue continued to lick and torment me, I arched my back, urging him to suck harder. Jesse's mouth latched on and as he gave me what I needed, I whimpered and moaned, grabbing his hair and pushing his head closer. I rolled onto my tip toes and started to slowly thrust against his thigh, trying to gain some relief.

Suddenly I was being lifted, and my legs were around Jesse's waist. I continued to move my hips, and with every thrust, my clit hit his hard cock, causing an electric pulse to throb throughout my body, ending its journey between my legs. Jesse started walking across the room, and then climbed onto his bed. My legs were still wrapped around his waist, his mouth was still on mine, and my arms were still coiled around his neck. Slowly, he laid me down and only then did he stop kissing me.

His head dipped back to my breasts and this time he took the other one into his mouth, grazing his teeth against it. I drew in a breath as he pulled the nipple into his mouth and sucked on it, hard and long.

Jesse's hand feathered down my body and dipped between my legs. His calloused fingers brushed against my swollen nub and when I moaned, Jesse drew in a ragged breath.

"Perfect," he whispered against the swell of my breast. "So

fucking wet for me."

His words, so deep and dirty, sent another thrill of desire straight to where his fingers were playing with me, and already the pressure was building. Jesse pushed two fingers inside and I started to pulse around them. As I clutched at the bed covers beneath me, Jesse kissed down my body, dropping sweet, and feather lights kisses on my sensitive skin.

"Your skin is so damn soft."

"Oh God, Jesse." I pushed my hips up, desperate for more.

Jesse kissed a trail along my hip bone, down my leg, and then on the inside of my thigh, all while his fingers gently stroked my inner wall. With a groan, he pulled out of me and pushed my legs apart, his hands on my inner thighs.

I lifted my head to look at him, to savour the view of his hard and toned body kneeling in front of me. As I devoured the sight of his deep V, slim waist, and broad shoulders, Jesse watched me, his breathing uneven and his eyes dark. Taking hold of his hard length, Jesse pumped it, while his other hand rested on my bent knee, keeping my legs apart. He lowered himself down, so that his mouth was inches from mine, and kissed me tenderly at the corner of my mouth and then down to my neck, before coming back to my mouth. One more kiss, a gentle nip of my chin, and he pushed into me.

As his hips started their rhythm, Jesse reached for my hands and pushed my arms above my head, entwining his fingers with mine. His eyes never left mine as his long, languorous thrusts pushed me to the brink. Neither of us spoke as we continued to move in unison, instinctively building up the speed of our thrusts, chasing our orgasms.

"Fuck, Millie," Jesse groaned, and gripping my hips, flipped us over so that I was straddling him.

My head dropped back so that my hair skimmed against my calves. Jesse's hips thrust upwards while his hand moved to my clit. His thumb circled it and I could feel myself starting to fall into ultimate pleasure.

"I need more, Jesse," I cried.

Jesse pulled himself into a sitting position and gripped my hips. His mouth found mine and his tongue darted in and out of my mouth in time with his cock moving in and out of my pussy. His movement was hard and quick and when he started to shake beneath me, I knew that he was almost there. Jesse's hand pushed between us and his fingers moved against my swollen clit once more. I came with one single stroke.

"Oh shit," I screamed. "Jesse, fuck!"

As I grasped his shoulders, Jesse gasped, his hips jerked, and then he shuddered.

"Millie!"

Still inside me, Jesse fell back onto the bed, pulling me on top of his chest. We were both breathing heavily and were covered in a light sheen of sweat. I lay on top of Jesse, my hands gripping the pillow on either side of his head. Jesse moved my hair from shoulder, and dropped a kiss on it.

"That was unbelievable," he whispered against my damp skin.

"Hmm," I mumbled, against his ear. "I think I've lost the use of my legs."

"Yeah?" he chuckled and started to trace circles on the small of my back.

"Yep. Do you think paralysis by cock is a real medical condition?"

"Maybe, honey, maybe."

We lay like that for a few more minutes and as Jesse continued to stroke my skin, I almost believed that I'd broken through. We were so sated and peaceful, just like any normal couple who had just had mind blowing sex. Deep down, though, I knew nothing had changed. We would get dressed, go back to the house, and I would continue to fall while Jesse continued to cling on; breaking my heart in the process. But even that wouldn't stop me from doing this again and again, because a little bit of Jesse was better than none at all.

CHAPTER 47

♥

JESSE

I was seriously fucked. The gorgeous woman lying on top of me was working her way into my fucking heart, and I really should stop it; it was not an option. I had Addy to think about, and Millie wasn't staying. Besides, all we were was comfort for each other to get through our own heartache. The guy who ditched her may have been a dick, but just two months ago she was in love with him. She must be devastated. Then there was me and my fucking problems. I still had feelings for my dead wife, and in what world was that even sane? I knew that I needed to move on, but the thought of falling in love again and possibly losing those feelings and memories wasn't something that I was willing to do. Especially not with Millie. Addy already loved her and it was going to hit her hard when Millie left; I would need to be there for my baby girl, not wallowing in my own fucking grief like I had over Melody.

No, I should stop it before we went any further. Then she made a little circular motion with her hips, causing my dick to go hard again.

Yep, I was seriously fucked.

CHAPTER 48

♥

MILLIE

After another quick round of sex, Jesse and I made our way back to the house. We walked back in silence, but it was comfortable. Jesse wasn't ignoring me because he was regretting what we'd done. At least I didn't think he was. He'd winked at me as we'd got dressed and then as we sneaked past the bunk house he held my hand, dragging me along. He hadn't let go straight away, only as we approached the barn near to the house.

"Oh bugger," I hissed. "I need to get something from my boxes to take in."

"Ah fuck, I forgot about that." Jesse looked to the house and then the barn. "Hey, don't worry about it, they were going up when I left."

"How long have we been gone?"

He fished his phone out of his pocket and looked at it. "Shit, almost an hour and a half."

"Oh God, your mum is going to know exactly what we've been up to," I groaned.

I could see from the light of his phone that Jesse was a little perplexed.

"Firstly, she's sleeping and secondly, why would she even think that something was going on between us?"

"Oh shit," I muttered, looking down at the ground.

"Millie?" Jesse ducked his head to look up at me.

"She knows about us." I grimaced and chewed on my bottom lip. "She saw us against the barn that day."

"You have got to be joking," he hissed.

I shook my head. "And she knows something happened while they were away. She found the broken dish and bottles in the rubbish."

"How the fuck does some trash prove that I fucked you?" he asked incredulously.

"I don't know." I shrugged. "She's a very astute woman, obviously."

"Did you tell her?" he demanded.

"No! I didn't tell her, why would I do that?"

There was no way I would have risked my job by telling Bonnie that I'd shagged her son in her kitchen. Thankfully, she'd taken it well, but that was probably because she had no idea about what had gone down on the family breakfast table.

"I don't know, maybe you thought you'd get her on your side and she'd persuade me that we should be something more than fuck buddies."

My mouth dropped open as I stared up at him. "What did you just say?"

"You heard me," he replied, widening his stance and putting fisted hands to his hips.

"I think I heard you say that I told her because I'm desperate to be more than your fuck on the side."

"Those were not my words, Millie." Jesse shook his head and sighed.

"They may as well have been, you egotistical prick."

"Seeing us against the barn, yeah, I can understand that, but how the hell does she know what happened while they were getting Auntie Ruby? Come on Millie, you tell me."

He inclined his head, putting a cupped hand behind his ear waiting to hear what I had to say.

"I did not tell her, she put two and two together by the words that I used, and she asked if the rubbish had anything to do with it," I hissed in a controlled tone, despite the fact that I was actually boiling inside.

"So you *did* tell her. Fucking great." Jesse waved his arms in the air and made to go to the house.

"I didn't actually say the words," I snarled. "I said we'd never done anything when Addy was around. She had already said she'd seen us by the barn, but assumed that you were just kissing me."

Jesse turned and stalked back to me. "Well to me that's as good as telling her. Great, Millie, just great. Now I'm going to be getting a damn lecture every day on why I should just move on from my wife and give you and me a chance. Well let me tell you this, sweetheart." Jesse moved closer and pointed a finger close to my face. "It ain't happening. You will never take her place, no matter how much you suck up to my Mom or ingratiate yourself with my daughter. You may be a great fuck, Armalita, but that's it."

With that, he stormed off and ran up the porch steps, letting himself into the house, with a slam of the door. I stood frozen to the spot, not able to move or process what had just happened. The horrible words that had spewed from his mouth had left me feeling sick to my stomach. The tears fell slowly, and the crushing pain of my heart took my breath away. Standing alone in the silence of the night, I swiped at the wetness on my cheeks and decided that Jesse Connor didn't deserve to be happy, and I hoped he never found peace.

The next day, I woke up surprisingly refreshed. Despite how upset I'd been, I'd slept really well, better than I had done in days. Evidently, Jesse's snide comments were no match for his sexual prowess when it came to my sleeping habits.

That being said, I was still in a rage with him and I was thankful he hadn't shown his face at breakfast. According to Bonnie, he'd gone out early with the boys before coming back to the corral mid-morning. Thankfully, I had no reason to go around there, so steered clear, because I wasn't sure I'd be able to hold my temper.

Then, at lunch time, I was given the opportunity to find out. I had just set out Addy's lunch on the table, when the door burst open and Jesse stomped in.

"Mom!" he shouted, ignoring Auntie Ruby who was dozing in the recliner. "Mom!"

"She's not here," I ground out through clenched teeth.

"Hey, Daddy," Addy said, offering him her lips.

Jesse bent down and kissed her. "Hey, baby. Where's your granma?"

Addy shrugged. "Don't know."

Jesse gave an exasperated sigh and stalked over to the refrigerator and took out a jug of lemonade and filled a glass.

"I know where Bonnie is," I said.

Jesse continued to look out of the window. "Where?"

I moved up beside him, took the jug of lemonade from where he'd left it and put it back where he'd got it from.

"Well, if you had the manners to look at me, I might tell you," I replied quietly so that Addy couldn't hear.

"Just tell me. I'm not in the mood for your games, Millie."

"Oh go fuck yourself, Jesse," I hissed. "Hey, Addy sweetie, make sure you eat all your sandwich."

"Okay, Millie," Addy sing-songed as she took a huge bite of her sandwich.

I started to run some water into the sink to wash Auntie Ruby's lunch plate, and some other dishes. Squeezing in some detergent, my back stiffened as Jesse stood behind me.

"I think you'll find it was you I fucked, *Millie*."

He took hold of my elbow and slowly turned me to face him. He then reached around me and turned off the water, allowing his fingers to touch my forearm as he pulled his hand back. My traitorous body let me down as my skin goose bumped and my breathing hitched. Jesse lifted a hand and picked something off my shoulder. I tried to take a step backwards, but my back was already against the sink.

"Okay, Millie," he said quietly. "Where is my mom?"

My eyes narrowed on him and I really wanted to slap his stupidly handsome face. There was dust on his cheek bones, his hair was mussed up and his shirt sleeves were rolled up to display his tanned forearms. How dare he stand here with his damn arm-porn?

I took a deep breath and pushed my shoulders back. "She's gone to Knightingale with Garratt. He's heard that the bank are recruiting for their management program that starts in October."

Jesse looked at me quizzically. "And Garratt went willingly?"

"It was his idea." I knew that Garratt only wanted a job to help get the capital for his dating website idea, but I wasn't sure Jesse did.

"Thought he wanted to start up some damn website?"

There was my answer.

"He does but needs money to do it."

I moved to turn back to the dishes in the sink, but Jesse put a hand on my shoulder.

"Does Mom know what he's up to?" he asked.

"Contrary to what you believe, Jesse, I don't tell your mother everything. Now if you don't mind, I have things to do."

He leaned around me and looked in the sink. "Yep, I can see you've got important business to attend to."

I didn't say anything, but curled my lip and turned away from him, giving a little huff.

"Did you just sigh at me?" he whispered in my ear.

My heart stuttered as I turned my head to look at him.

"Go away," I whispered. "Your presence offends me."

Jesse opened his mouth to say something, closed it again, shook his head, and burst out laughing.

"Fuck me," he muttered and walked away, giving Addy another kiss as he passed her.

Well, at least when I left here at the end of my year I could say I'd actually made Jesse Connor laugh – miracles would never cease.

CHAPTER 49

♥

JESSE

As I started to walk out of the house, after my little spat with Millie, a hand came up and grabbed my arm; Auntie Ruby.

"You been upsetting that girl, Jesse?" she whispered, her dark brown eyes surveying me carefully.

"Now what gives you that idea, Auntie Ruby?" I gave her my sweetest smile, not wanting to get into the shit that Millie and I had going on.

"I'm old Jesse, but I ain't blind. Now I know your momma and daddy did not raise you to lie to old ladies, so spill it cowboy."

"I'm not lying, there's nothing to tell," I said in a low voice, glancing towards the kitchen where Millie was chatting to Addy.

Her lips thinned and she gave me the stink eye. "That little incident at the sink wasn't nothing."

My mouth gaped open as I stared at my wizened, old, great aunt. "Were you spying on us? I thought you were asleep."

She cackled out a laugh. "When you sleep in the wilderness, always do it with one eye open, my daddy used to say."

"But you're not in the wilderness." I shook my head and laughed.

"So you say, now tell me what's going on between you and the Spanish beauty. Have you had your way with her and now want something new?"

I sighed and rubbed at my tired eyes. "It's not like that, Auntie Ruby. It's complicated."

"Let me guess, you still hankering after that flighty piece you were married to?"

"Auntie Ruby." I growled a warning at her. "Don't speak about Melody that way."

"Why? She *was* flighty. I liked her well enough, but she's gone Jesse and she ain't coming back, and if you were honest with yourself, you know she wasn't the best wife in the world."

I lifted my hand to stop her. I didn't need to hear this.

"Nope," she growled quietly. "You listen to me. When my Samuel died, I spent years grieving for him, and where did it get me?"

"You..."

"It got me nowhere," she interrupted me. "Nowhere, except lonely and childless. I was twenty-seven years of age and was young enough and pretty enough to marry again. I could have had a family around me now; children and grandchildren. As it is, your poor momma has to drop everything and come and take care of me."

"She loves you, Auntie Ruby, she wouldn't want it any other way."

"Not the point. I hankered after a dead man, when I could have been having a good time with a living one. Now, I know you ain't stopped putting yourself about, your momma told me about the women, but those women aren't the sort to look after you when you're old and decrepit. Yes, you'll have Addy, but who'll keep you warm at night when those damn good looks of yours start going?"

"Hey, who says I'll lose them?" I asked with a smile.

"Maybe you won't, but those memories of Melody will fade

and one day you'll wake up and wish that you'd taken off those rose colored spectacles when you had a chance."

I closed my eyes and took a deep breath. She was old and she should be respected for that, but I wouldn't have her muddying Melody's memory.

"Listen, Auntie Ruby, I hear what you're saying about me being alone, but please don't speak about Melody as though she was nothing."

"Not what I said. She was something, she was your wife and Addy's momma, but she weren't the be all and end all that you seem to think." She pushed the button on the recliner, so that she was fully sitting up. "Could be wrong, Jesse, but something tells me that young woman in there actually could be your be all and end all. You've just gotta get your head from up your ass and stop thinking with your dick."

I had no idea what to say to her, so shook my head and made to leave.

"Hey," she hissed."

"What, Auntie Ruby?" I asked on a sigh.

"You hear what I'm saying, cowboy?"

She started to laugh and I couldn't help but join in. You could never be mad at her for long.

"Yeah, Ruby. I hear you."

"Good, cos those babies you'd have would be damn beautiful."

I looked over at Millie again and realized that Ruby was right, she'd make some beautiful babies. Trouble was, whether I wanted to be the father of those babies or not, I was pretty sure I'd burned my bridges where Millie was concerned.

CHAPTER 50

♥

MILLIE

It had been a couple of days since Jesse and I had argued outside the barn, and now that my anger has subsided, I felt deeply hurt by his words. I still couldn't fathom how he could be so lovely and tender one minute, and then an absolute prick the next. I'd never once intimated that I wanted to take Melody's place. Okay, maybe I'd been obvious about my feelings for him, and who wouldn't love Addy? But I'd never tried to take the place of the wife or mother that they both loved; I'd never do that.

"You fancy coming into town with me?" Bonnie asked me. "I need to go and get a few supplies and Addy needs some new clothes. She's shot up so much in the last couple of months."

I looked out to the garden where Addy was helping Ted make a bug house, something that we'd read about in a book from the library. Needless to say, between Addy's high expectations and Ted's desire to give his granddaughter anything she wanted, the bug house was fast becoming an apartment block.

"Come on, honey," Bonnie urged. "Those two will be occupied

until sun down with that little project, and Ruby is having a nap and it would take an earthquake to wake her."

I laughed and nodded. "Okay, I'll just go and grab my bag."

***

When I got outside, Bonnie was already waiting in Ted's truck for me. The engine was running and the windows were up, so I guessed she had the AC running at full blast. It was a warm and muggy day, but I was getting more used to it. I was skipping down the porch steps to her when Jesse appeared at the bottom.

My heart jumped a beat and took my breath with it. His face was impassive as he lifted his hat off and wiped his forehead with his forearm.

"Hey," he said, putting one foot on the bottom step. "You headed out?"

"Yes. Town with your mum."

Swallowing back the tears that were threatening, I continued down the steps, determined that I would not look at him and let my face betray the fact that he was affecting me. I didn't even feel this used when Dean dumped me, probably because we'd never had a physical relationship. God, I was so stupid. How did I not realize that something was wrong with Dean? And, more importantly, how did I let myself fall for Jesse, when all along I knew that he would never feel the same way about me?

"Millie," he said in a low tone as I was about to pass him. "I'm sorry."

My eyes lifted to reach Jesse's and saw that his were soft and pleading. He rubbed the back of his neck and sighed.

"I didn't mean anything that I said, I was just mad is all."

"You said it Jesse, so it must have been in your mind somewhere."

I dropped my gaze; I just couldn't look at him any longer. His perfect face and shining blue eyes hurt my heart.

"Please, Millie."

His hand dropped from his neck and reached out to mine that was hanging limply at my side. His fingertips brushed mine before I jerked my hand away; I couldn't let him touch me, this was hard enough as it was.

"It's fine," I sighed. "I accept your apology. I have to go, your mum is waiting."

"Can we talk later?" he asked. "We're getting the calves in that need castrating, but we'll be finished around five. Maybe we can go for a ride before dinner, say five -thirty?"

My head shot up and I stared at him wide eyed. I had never met anyone whose mood changed so quickly.

"I don't understand," I replied. "You made it clear that I was just a 'great fuck' and now you want to talk and go for a ride? I don't think so, Jesse."

Taking a deep breath, I made to move past him, but his hand came out and snagged my elbow.

"Please, Millie. I feel like a big enough douche as it is. Just give me a chance to explain."

Staring at him, I watched as his jaw tightened and his breathing got heavier.

"Please."

I nodded and then walked away to the truck.

***

"Everything okay?" Bonnie asked as I clipped my seat belt into place.

Not daring myself to speak, I just nodded.

"You know, honey, it's been hard for him, getting used to being without Melody."

"He seems to do okay," I snapped.

My head turned to Bonnie, who was looking out of the windshield towards Jesse who was sitting on the bottom step, his head in his hands.

"I'm sorry, Bonnie," I whispered, my eyes now on Jesse. "He said some things that hurt me and I..."

I trailed off, not sure how to tell her that I was in love with her son and he was breaking my heart because he couldn't feel the same way. Yes, I was in love with him. His gentleness, his black moods, his heartache, his everything. I couldn't help it.

"Looks to me like he's sorry for those words," Bonnie said,

laying a comforting hand on my knee. "Was that he was doing then; apologizing?"

"Yes," I sighed. "He wants to go for a ride and talk, after he's brought the calves in, whatever that means."

Bonnie tinkled a laugh as she put the truck into drive. "We like to manage their pain and discomfort as much as possible when we castrate them, so we bring them and their momma's in for a couple of days beforehand, and after. It helps to keep them calm. Jesse made that change," she said proudly.

She didn't have to try and prove to me that her boy wasn't all bad. I knew he wasn't. He couldn't help the fact that he didn't have feelings for me beyond those of sexual attraction

"So," Bonnie continued. "You going for that ride?"

I chewed on my bottom lip and thought about it.

"If I do, I'll just make things worse for myself."

"How so, honey?"

I took in a deep breath, and watched her profile as she concentrated on maneuvering down the dirt track to the road. When I didn't answer, Bonnie glanced at me and gave me an encouraging smile.

"Because, if he apologizes and we become friends again, I'll be forever waiting and hoping that it moves on to the next level."

I blew out a breath and pinched the bridge of my nose. Why on earth did he have to be so damn desirable?

"Maybe I should just go home," I cried out. "I'll soon get over him if I don't see him."

My nose tickled, warning me that tears were on the way, so I held my breath, willing them not to come.

"Don't you dare go home!" Bonnie barked. "How do you propose to ever snap him out of his damn Melody funk if you're on the other side of the world?"

My head shot around to face her. Bonnie's impish features were determinedly tight as she looked at me, before putting her eyes back on the road.

"But you said you couldn't see him ever getting over her," I gasped.

"Yes well, maybe I changed my mind. I've seen how he looks at you. Saw that same look in his eye when he first started dating Melody."

My heart clattered against my breast bone like a bell hammer. Bonnie must be mistaken. Jesse had told me himself that he didn't think of me like that and never would.

"Seriously, Bonnie," I stammered. "He really doesn't. I promise you."

"Fiddle," she said, waving a hand at me. "What that boy says and what he actually means are two totally different things. You forget I know him better than he knows himself. I was the one that brought that stubborn ass into this world. Almost two days it took me, because he couldn't make his damn mind up whether he wanted to come out our not."

"Two days!" I gasped. "Oh my God."

"I know, honey," she sighed. "You don't need to tell me. The point I'm making is, he's stubborn, but he's also a deep thinker. He'll have thought a lot about you and him and the consequences of it, and he'll do what he thinks is right; doesn't mean it is though. He'll think it's right that you just have a relationship based on sex...I'm guessing that your visit to the barn wasn't exactly to get some photographs from a box."

"H-how did you know?" I groaned, my humiliation complete.

Bonnie giggled. "Ted told me where'd you'd gone when he came up to bed. When I went to check on Addy, I looked through the window and there was no light coming from the barn, so I kinda guessed."

"I'm sorry."

"Oh, Millie," she laughed. "You're both young, you're single, and I've told you as long as it doesn't affect Addy then I'm happy about it, but you have to be prepared for the heartache that goes with him."

"Because he's not ready," I said on an exhale.

"No, because he thinks he's not ready. That's different. Like I said, he's doing what he thinks is right, but he'll realize in the end. Just be patient, don't push him, and listen to what he has to say."

215

"So, go for a ride with him then?"

"That's about it, honey, yep."

As we drove down the long, straight road into town, we fell into a comfortable silence, giving me time to think about Jesse. I would do what Bonnie said, I'd listen to him, but I wasn't sure I could risk my heart anymore

CHAPTER 51

♥

JESSE

In all my life, I had never been so frustrated bringing calves inside. I wanted to be finished in time to wash up before I met up with Millie, but the damn cattle had other ideas. Two of the little bastards had gone walkabout with their mothers, and when we finally found them at the perimeter of our land, they decided they wanted a game of *Catch Me If You Can*. Finally, they were all in the stalls, with fresh hay and being fed. Little shits had no idea that in a couple of days they'd be missing their balls.

"I'm going to leave you to it, Garr," I shouted to my brother who was fastening the last pen.

Garratt nodded and raised a hand. "Enjoy your *ride*," he called with a smirk on his face.

I'd told him that I was taking Millie for a ride to talk. He'd wanted to know what we'd needed to *talk* about, so I'd told him everything while we sat and ate our lunch over by the old lightning tree. We'd called it that since we were kids because one of the branches had broken off at an angle. Our grandpa told us it was because it had been hit by lightning years before, but Dad said it was just rotten. The rotten tree just didn't have the same ring to it.

"Who you off riding with?" Brandon asked as I passed him on the way out.

I ducked my head, not wanting him to see the guilt in my eyes. I knew he liked Millie, and maybe I should just give it up, tell her to date him. He'd treat her good, and he wouldn't mess with her head like I had. Problem with that was, I wasn't willing to give her up. I may have said some dumb things to her, but the truth was she'd breathed life into me. She'd got my blood pumping again. That damn ache in my chest that had been there every day for the last two years, had all but gone; at least it disappeared when I was around her. Yeah, it came back when I was alone, but the hurt was nowhere near as painful.

"Just got a few errands to run," I said vaguely.

"So what's he grinning like a fool for?" Brandon nodded towards Garratt, who was watching our exchange.

"Ah, he's just being a dick as usual. Anyways, I'd better get going."

"Okay, but you fancy a beer later?"

I stopped in my tracks and looked up at the ceiling of the barn. What the fuck did I say to him? 'No because I'm hoping to be wrapped around Millie, making it up to her for being a dick'?

"Yeah, maybe." I chickened out. "Let me see how it goes. I'll shoot you a text."

Brandon raised his hat in acknowledgment and then turned back to emptying feed into the trough attached to one of the pens.

Shit, I hated lying to him. He was my best buddy, and had been since we were six years old, but I couldn't tell him this. I didn't think he was in love with Millie or anything like that, but I hadn't seen him this interested in a girl since Alesha. He'd been pretty devastated after she left; he was always angry and saying he missed her, drunkenly crying on anyone's shoulder who'd listen about losing the love of his life. He'd been pretty lost by all accounts; he even went by her mom's house demanding she tell him where Alesha was. I hated to admit though, I'd heard all this second hand. I had no damn idea what was going on with him, I'd just lost Melody so had pretty much checked out on everyone.

Checking the time on my phone, I saw that I had just over fifteen minutes to get ready. I ran to my cabin, knowing that if I went to the house, Addy would distract me, and as much as I loved her, I needed to talk to Millie while I still had the nerve to say what I wanted to say.

CHAPTER 52

♥

MILLIE

While Bonnie and I were in town, she'd persuaded me to buy a pair of gorgeous cowgirl boots. They were dark brown with hot pink butterflies and flowers trailing up the side and fit me as though they'd been hand measured for every part of my feet. I'd argued at first that I didn't need them but, as Bonnie pointed out, what else was I spending my money on? When we got home, I'd pulled my hair into a high ponytail and changed into jeans and a hot pink tank top for my ride with Jesse. Bonnie insisted I should wear the boots. I wasn't sure where we were going and thought I may be too hot in boots, but they did look cute. So, when five-thirty came around, despite the rollercoaster going on in my stomach, I felt confident in my appearance; understated yet kick ass.

"You should go wait outside, honey," Bonnie whispered, nodding towards Addy. "If she sees Jesse, she'll want to come and I don't think that would be quite what he had in mind."

I nodded and snuck out, trying not to clomp too much on the

wooden floor in my beautiful new boots.

When I got to the bottom of the porch steps, Jesse came around from the side of the barn leading two horses.

"Wow," he said. "You look real pretty."

I blushed and looked down at myself. The boots really were magical. Then suddenly my head shot up as I realized what he'd meant by a ride.

"Erm, are we going riding on them?" I asked, pointing at the horses.

"Yeah," Jesse chuckled. "What did you think I meant?"

"Your truck?" I questioned.

"Hah, sorry, sweetheart, but a ride around here means on the back of a horse. Well some rides are anyways," he said with a wicked grin.

Damn it, I was not ready for naughty Jesse. I'd wanted him to grovel before I was willing to give him even a hint of a smile. I couldn't help it though, his was infectious, and so I returned it.

"Jesse!" I warned.

"Sorry," he replied, bowing his head. "I know, you're still mad at me."

"Yes I am, and not just because of what you said. I'm now mad that you didn't tell me that it was a horse ride that we'd be going on."

"Millie, you live on a ranch. Come on, *really*?"

"But I haven't ridden since I was about eight years of age," I groaned. "And that was a little, fat pony that went the same speed as a turtle."

"You'll be fine, you never forget how to ride a horse," Jesse urged, moving towards me with the huge horse. "We'll take it slow, I promise."

"You'll bloody well have to," I hissed quietly, so as not to startle the horse. "Because I'll probably end up falling off otherwise."

Jesse's hand came up and a finger touched my cheek. "I won't ever let you fall," he said softly.

I suddenly couldn't breathe properly as the air left my lungs in a rush. Adrenalin coursed through my veins, sending my heart into a whirling dervish. Heat pooled between my legs. Jesse's lashes swept against his cheek as he blinked slowly, waiting for me to trust him. Whatever he had done and said to me previously didn't matter in that moment.

"Okay," I croaked out. "Let's do it before I lose my nerve."

Jesse smiled, and nodded on an exhale. He led the horses over to the fence surrounding the paddock and tied them up.

"Come on then," he called, beckoning me over with a lift of his chin.

"This won't be pretty, I promise you."

Jesse chuckled and held a hand out to me. "You'll be fine. Miss Daisy here is real gentle."

I stared at the extremely tall, chestnut mare who stared right back and blew down her nostrils at me.

"She doesn't look gentle," I grumbled.

"Come on, you'll see."

Jesse led me around to the side of the horse, giving her a gentle rub as he did.

"Okay, so put your right foot in there." He held out the stirrup with one hand, and patted my right thigh with the other.

"I know which my right leg is, and what the stirrup is," I giggled. "I'm not totally useless."

He shrugged. "You're a city girl, I just figured you would need help."

"Rickeby is hardly the city, and I told you, I used to ride ponies when I was little."

I put my foot in the stirrup, took hold of the horn on the saddle and pulled myself up, swinging my left leg over, and...landed in a heap at Jesse's feet.

"Fuck, Millie," Jesse cried. "You okay?"

He knelt down next to me and cautiously ran a hand down my arm.

"Don't move until I can see if you've broken anything."

I shrugged him off and sat up on a groan. "I'm fine, I haven't broken anything."

"You sure?" His eyes widened as he dared me to lie to him.

"Honestly. Just a dented ego, but nothing is broken."

Jesse stood up and held his hand out. I took hold of it and allowed him to pull me to my feet.

"You said you wouldn't let me fall," I chastised, poking him in the chest with my finger.

"I wasn't expecting it," he replied. "You told me you knew what you were doing."

"Evidently not." I let out a huff, rubbed my bum and pushed Jesse's hands away. "Okay, let me at it."

"I'll help you," he offered.

"No. I can do this. My backside is evidently a lot heavier than it was when I was eight. It's just going to take a little more effort to heave it up there."

Jesse started to laugh as he stood back and crossed his arms over his chest.

"Go on then, let's see what you got."

Throwing him a glare, I took a deep breath and stepped back towards the horse.

"Okay, Miss Daisy. We'll try again shall we?"

This time I made it, albeit landing a little skew on the saddle. Jesse stepped forward and with a chuckle, placed a hand against the right cheek of my bum, and pushed me further onto the horse.

"Did you do that just so I'd touch your ass?" he asked, walking around to his own horse.

"Yeah," I replied sarcastically. "Of course I did."

I watched in amazement as Jesse did his little trick of bouncing on the spot and jumping straight up into the saddle. No mean feat for anyone, but especially someone of around six feet two inches tall.

"Show off," I muttered under my breath.

"You either have it or you don't," he replied with a cheeky grin.

"Yep and you have it."

"I do, hey?" He sat up straighter in his saddle and winked at me.

"Yeah, you do. An ego the size of North America."

He shook his head. "Not just my ego, honey, as well you know."

I swallowed hard and fanned myself, knowing that riding a horse while in the company of this gorgeous cowboy was going to leave me feeling extremely horny.

***

Jesse had led us to the perimeter of the Connor land, through dense woods that eventually led to the edge of the mountains and hills. We rode halfway through the woods until we came to a clearing where a brook ran through it. It looked as though it came down from the mountains; it was so clear, you could see the pebbles at the bottom.

Jesse dismounted, as elegantly as he'd mounted, loosely tied his horse to a low tree branch, hooked his hat on the saddle horn, and then walked over to me and held up a hand.

"You need help?" he asked with a smirk.

I didn't answer, but swung my leg over the horse and dismounted all by myself. Once I had both feet on the ground, Jesse tied up my horse and then put his hand in the small of my back, guiding me towards a large flat rock.

"Let's sit here, while I talk," he said on a sigh.

My stomach clenched as I glanced at him. His mouth was downturned and his brow was pinched. This was the 'I like you but we can only ever be friends – without the sex' speech.

"Jesse, you don't have to say anything. I get that you're sorry, it's fine. We can go back to being friends." I flopped down onto the stone and looked out to the brook, watching the water bubble along on its journey.

"I'm glad about that," he replied, sitting next to me. "But I need to explain."

"No you don't."

I turned to see Jesse was leaning forwards, resting his forearms on his knees, looking straight ahead.

"Yeah I do, Millie. What I said to you was wrong, it was cruel, and I didn't mean it."

I doubted that statement. Of course he didn't think I would ever replace Melody; I would never expect to.

"I've never tried to take her place," I sighed. "I like you Jesse and I adore Addy, but at no point did I ever think that you or I would ever be any more than friends, admittedly friends with benefits, but friends nonetheless."

"You have to understand how hard it's been for me," he groaned and rubbed a hand down his face. "When Melody died, I couldn't see any future for myself without her. You know that included my relationship with Addy, too. I just couldn't be near her without feeling the intense pain of Melody's loss. We were a family, it was the three of us, and suddenly a real important part of that family was missing."

"It must have been an awful time for you, I do understand that. I know we've argued about you and Addy, but you've turned a corner now with her." I laid a hand on his forearm and gave it a gentle squeeze.

"Yeah well," he groaned. "I was a total douche to my own daughter, and I have to live with that."

Jesse stood up and paced towards the brook. He stood on the edge, looking down into the water for a few seconds and then turned back to me.

"Melody was my first love. As soon as we started dating, I knew that she was the one who I'd spend the rest of my life with, the one who'd be the mother of my children." He paused momentarily and took in a deep breath. "We were seventeen, but I knew, even then. We had a lot of firsts together, you know?"

I nodded, understanding his heartache. The loss of your first love always cut deep, but to lose them when you've started to have a future together, and to lose them through death, must be the deepest cut of all.

"Melody was with me the first time I got drunk, when I got my driver's permit, when I broke my first horse. And I was the one lucky enough to be hers when she went from a pretty girl into a beautiful woman. I was the one lucky enough to be holding her hand when she brought life into this world for the first time. I was just damn lucky that she was mine."

Jesse's voice broke on the last word, and I desperately wanted to rush over and hug him to me; to tell him in time that the pain would ease, but I wasn't sure it ever would for Jesse.

"Jesse, please don't upset yourself. I really do understand and I know that you're sorry, so let's just forget it. Thinking about losing her is upsetting you."

Jesse's head shot up and he stared at me with shining eyes.

"No, Millie. You don't understand. I loved her with all my heart, still love her, but that's the reason why I struggle with us, what we've been doing," he cried, taking a step forward.

"You love her," I stated. "You'll never stop loving her, and no one will take her place."

My heart practically folded in on itself. I knew that he wasn't ready for anything more with me, but I recalled Bonnie's words about him never being ready, and I had to agree. That was the saddest part of all of this, because even if it wasn't me, Jesse Connor would, I was sure, love long, hard, and deeply. The sort of love that any woman would cherish.

"But that's what I'm trying to say. I loved her, she was the love of my life, but you," he said, pointing a finger at me. "You have sent me fucking crazy and I'm feeling as guilty as shit because of you."

"Why me?" I snapped, standing up and positioning myself a couple of steps away from him. "Angie didn't make you feel guilty, so don't put all this on to me, Jesse. We had sex, the same thing you did with Angie, but you didn't seem guilty about that when you brought her back to your cabin or let her suck your face in Rowdy's."

"No, I didn't," he said, moving another step closer. "And I'll tell you why. Because it's not the damn sex that I feel guilty about, it's the damn feelings that I have for you. I like you, Millie, it's not just about you being a great fuck, no matter what I said."

"So what the hell is it?"

"It's because I'm falling for you. It's because you've made me question every thought I ever had about Melody being my soul mate. It's because I fucking see you in here." He stabbed a finger at his head. "I fucking see *you* now in here as my future, *you're* the one I now see holding my babies and *you're* the one that I damn well dream about every fucking night. The pain in my chest because Melody isn't here has gone, and it's been replaced with excitement and light and you're responsible for that. That's why I feel fucking guilty, Millie."

With one stride, Jesse was inches from me, his hands framing my face as he pulled me into a hard kiss. His tongue duelled with mine, our breaths synchronised in perfect harmony, and we moaned each other's names.

CHAPTER 53

♥

JESSE

Christ, she tasted so sweet and delicious, and I never wanted to stop tasting her. But, I knew I had to; what sort of man would I be if I let my feelings for her erase all those I had for Melody?

"Millie," I groaned and pulled away from her. "We have to stop this."

"Oh God, yes you're right," she gasped. "We should get back."

I shook my head. "No, Millie. We can't do this again. We can't be friends with fucking benefits. I can't kiss you anymore, we can't keep having sex."

Millie pushed away and stared at me with tears pooling in her eyes. Fuck, I'd hurt her once again. This was getting to be a damn habit.

"I'm so sorry, but the more we do this, the more my memories of Melody fade, and I can't do that to Addy. She needs to know all about her momma."

Millie's eyes almost bulged out as she thrust her hands to her hips. "You've got to be fucking kidding me," she bawled. "How dare you put all of this onto Addy? I get that you're grieving and you may never get over that grief, but do not try and tell me that we can't be together because of Addy!"

"I've told you I feel guilty about my feelings for you," I protested. "Everything about you is taking over my head space, so what happens if I forget everything about her? I can't do that to Addy; I can't forget those memories that I need to give to her because she was too young to remember."

"Whatever, Jesse, but you can't keep pushing and pulling me like this. You're messing with my brain, too."

I shook my head and groaned. "I'm sorry, but this is so damn difficult to deal with, I have no idea where I'm at half the time."

"Well you know what, come and find me when you do," she slammed and stormed off towards her horse.

"Millie, where the fuck are you going?" I yelled.

"Away from you, giving you the space to sort your damn head out." She stopped and turned to face me. "If you think you want me, Jesse, then at least have the guts to go through with it. If you truly don't think you can do this, then leave me alone, and stop kissing me, stop flirting with me, and keep your bloody dick in your pants when you're around me."

She untied Miss Daisy and pulled herself up into the saddle, and with surprising ease, steered her away from me.

"Millie, you have no idea how to get back," I snapped, rushing towards Dillinger, my horse.

"Fuck off," she shouted over her shoulder and galloped off.

"Shit!"

I untied Dillinger, jumped into the saddle and kicked at his flank to chase after her.

I was five minutes into the forty minute ride back to the ranch, and I still hadn't come across Millie. There was no way she could have gotten so far ahead; there were too many low hanging branches to make it easy or safe for an inexperienced rider like her to go at any speed other than a trot.

"Fuck it, Millie. Where the hell are you?" I muttered.

229

I looked up through the canopy of trees and could see that the sky was darkening. I had about an hour before it went dark. Pulling Dillinger up, I stood up in my stirrups and looked around. I couldn't see anything except the dark green and brown of the trees. I knew then what she'd done. The path that we followed forked about half a mile back and I was betting that she'd taken the wrong route. The route that would take her deeper into the woods and would eventually incline up into the hills and then up to the mountains.

As I thought about her lost and alone, my gut clenched with fear. Thank God I'd brought a radio with me, because my cell would be useless out here. I reached behind me and pulled it from the saddle bag. Forgoing our usual radio protocol, I selected our main channel and pressed the call button.

"Someone fucking answer me, now," I snapped.

Within seconds I heard the buzz of someone on the other end. "Hey boss, what's wrong? Over."

It was one of my men. "Zak, I'm out in the woods with Millie, but she fucking rode off without me and I can't find her. Over."

"Ah shit," he groaned. "How long? Over."

"She was ahead of me three minutes at most, but I'm five minutes or so in and haven't seen her. I think she might have taken the wrong route where the path forks. I'm going to go back that way, but I need a couple of you out here with flashlights. We've got a little less than an hour of daylight left. Over."

"Okay, boss. I've just come back in with Marty. We'll be with you as soon as we can. Over."

"Make it quicker than that, Zak!"

I quickly steered Dillinger around and sped off back down the path.

CHAPTER 54

♥

MILLIE

I wasn't sure how long I'd been riding, but I did know that the woods were getting denser, to a point that I almost couldn't go any further. I didn't recall it being like this on my way in, but then I'd been concentrating on Jesse's rear end for most of the way.

"Oh God, Miss Daisy," I groaned, leaning forward to rub her ears. "I'm really sorry, I think I've got us lost."

As I looked around me, there was nothing familiar for my memory to grab onto, plus there was now a chill in the air. The light had definitely dimmed and I wondered how much daylight there was left. I'd been stupid and not brought my mobile phone or even a jacket with me. But, I hadn't expected Jesse to be such a dick head that I would want to run away from him. Admittedly, that hadn't been the best decision I'd ever made. I should have just followed him back to the ranch and *then* unloaded my crazy onto him.

I tried to think back to any survival programs that I'd ever watched, wondering what the best plan of action was, but the only thing I could remember was to pee on a Jelly fish sting; not helpful in this situation. What should I do; double back, or stay where I was and hope that someone found me? The problem was, I'd been so red with rage that I hadn't taken any notice of my route back out and so didn't have a clue which way to go even if I decided to. I was pretty sure that I had veered off the path quite drastically. No, the best plan would be to stay put. Then it occurred to me that Jesse may not even be aware that I was missing. Knowing him, he'd have gone back to the ranch and gone straight to his cabin to sulk, or even worse, gone into town to meet Angie at Rowdy's.

That thought made me feel sick, and messed with my head as much as his words had earlier. He'd said that he had feelings for me and that I was making him question those he had for Melody. Words, that in any other circumstance, would have me giddy with happiness, but then he'd burst my bubble good and proper. Plus, what use were those words when I'd probably die out here, eaten by some weird forest creature.

Not sure what to do, I looked aimlessly around, searching for shelter of some sort. There was nothing, except for a fallen tree, but that looked decidedly uncomfortable and was probably home to all sorts of creepy crawlies.

"Looks like you might be my bed for the night," I whispered to Miss Daisy, giving her head a rub.

The problem with that was I was already feeling saddle sore, despite the adequate padding on my behind. It was also cruel to expect her to stand all night with me on her back. Chewing down on my bottom lip, panic started to set in, and tears brimmed at my eyelashes. I'd been totally stupid and irresponsible by leaving Jesse, so this was my own fault.

I started to shiver through the tension in my body, and desperately wanted to cry, but I knew that if I did I wouldn't stop and getting hysterical wouldn't help me to think straight. Taking a deep breath, I thought about the consequences of going back, and decided to stay put. Even if Jesse didn't realize I was missing, someone at the ranch would. I didn't know how big the woods were, but he'd told me that they skirted most of the Connor land and that was pretty vast. This was going to be a long night.

With some trepidation, I dismounted from Miss Daisy and led her over to the fallen tree and tied her up. I would sit there for a while, and then, when it got darker and scarier, I'd maybe get back up on Miss Daisy to avoid any creatures scurrying around my feet. I swallowed, thinking of what might live out here, and shivered.

***

Darkness had fallen and every noise had me jumping out of my skin. Miss Daisy seemed pretty calm about it all; totally cool and collected. I on the other hand had now started to cry; silently so as not to alert any animals or creatures that may fancy me for dinner. I hadn't even shouted for help as I wasn't sure if it was the right thing to do. I made a mental note to research survival methods in woods before storming off on my own again.

It had also occurred to me that there may be snakes in here, so I had my knees up with my arms wrapped around them, trying to stave off the cold. With the darkness had come a drop in temperature, and while it wasn't freezing, my tank top really wasn't adequate. I was just grateful that I had jeans and boots on. I thought about getting back on Miss Daisy and maybe using her to keep warm, but she was so quiet and still I wondered if she was actually sleeping. With what little bravery I had dying with each passing minute, my mind wandered back to my earlier conversation with Jesse.

The fact that he'd been honest about his feelings for me had given my heart some relief, but he was pretty adamant that he wouldn't be doing anything about it. I tried to see it from his point of view. There were times when I forgot what my dad sounded like, or what he smelled like, and it petrified me. I'd get all panicky and anxiously put on the DVD I had of him doing a speech at his and mum's Silver Wedding party. Just hearing his voice and seeing him living and breathing, albeit on the TV, calmed me, allowing me to carry on for a few more months without the grief suffocating me. That must be exactly how Jesse felt, but maybe worse. Melody had been his wife, she had been young and vibrant and that in itself would be difficult to come to terms with. Plus, he was right, he needed to keep the memories for Addy's sake. She needed to grow up remembering things about her mum. Things that only Jesse could tell her.

With a deep sigh, I realized that Jesse and I were never going to happen. If he couldn't let go now, two years on, and after admitting those things about me, then he never would. I had to accept that, work out the rest of my contract, and then move on. I had no doubt that I would always think of him, he would always be special to me, but my time with him would just be a memory; something to smile fondly about when I was old and grey.

With that miserable thought in my head, I laid my head on my knees, closed my eyes, and even though it wasn't late, tried to block out my fear and get some sleep.

CHAPTER 55

♥

JESSE

"How long has it been now?" I asked into the receiver.

"An hour and ten. Over," Marty replied, almost on a groan.

I'd been asking him the same question every five minutes for the last hour and ten, since he and Zak had got to me with flashlights. That meant it was just under two hours since I'd seen Millie.

I'd gone back to the fork in the path, and scouted around there while I waited for Zak and Marty, not going far off the track, though, because I didn't want to miss them. Once they'd gotten there, we'd split up; each of us with a radio, a flashlight, and luminous chalk to mark our routes. Zak and I had grown up playing in these woods, but over the years it had grown a lot denser, and with the dimming light, even we weren't confident about not getting lost.

"You see anything? Over." I knew I sounded desperate, but I was and I didn't care who knew it.

"Nope, sorry Jesse. I've shouted until I'm hoarse but either she's deaf or she ain't anywhere near where I am. Over."

"Zak? Over."

"Nope. Same as Marty, been shouting but nothing. I reckon we should maybe think about coming back in the morning. It's gonna get dangerous out here, last thing we need is to have to shoot a damn horse because it's broken a leg. Over."

Zak sounded beyond pissed. His folks lived on a farm a couple of miles down the road, and he still lived there with his wife and twin boys. This time of year was real busy and we worked all hours, so when the guys got an opportunity to finish early, they grabbed it with both hands, which was what Zak had done. Today was his wife's birthday, so he was at this minute supposed to be sitting down to dinner and birthday cake. Guilt pricked at my conscience.

"Zak, buddy, you go home. Get Garratt to come out here instead. I know it's Sarah's birthday. Over."

He sighed on the other end of the receiver. "I already called home before I came out to you. Sarah's cool, although its cost me a damn new, expensive as all shit, designer purse. Over."

I couldn't help but smile. That was what it was like working on a ranch; you knew that you could rely on your men, your buddies, even if it got them into shit with their women.

"Well you let me know what that expensive as all shit purse costs and it's on me. Over."

Zak chuckled. "Fuck, Jess, you might just regret that. You know Sarah and how she likes the good stuff."

I did know Sarah, and she did like the good stuff, but unlike Melody, she didn't go out and just buy what she wanted. I knew from Zak that if she saw something she liked, she either saved the money for it or asked her family to get together and all of them buy it for her as a gift at Christmas, or on her birthday. So for her to *ask* for the purse, meant that, although Zak had said she was cool, she was probably real mad that her birthday dinner had been ruined. She was a great girl though and I knew she wouldn't be angry at Zak for too long.

"Okay guys," I said, opening both channels. "Let's give it

another half hour and then we'll rethink what we do. Over."

They both agreed and I was left with silence once again.

"Millie!" I shouted, moving Dillinger forward. Nothing except the scurrying of some animal that I'd startled. "Millie!"

Again, no response. Now I was real scared. The three of us were searching a wide span of the woods and she should have been able to hear at least one of us. If she couldn't, then maybe she was hurt. Bile threatened my gut as my fear spiked. We were about three miles from the edge of the mountains, but that distance was nothing to a hungry Mountain Lion on the prowl for food.

I had to find her. I couldn't leave her out here, alone, all night. Zak and Marty could go back if they wanted to, but I wasn't giving up. I wouldn't give up until she was in my arms, safe and secure.

I carried on along my route, numbering trees as I went and shouting out her name. Not having a watch on, and my cell having died a while back, I guessed it was almost time to meet up with the guys. I was just steering Dillinger back around when the receiver buzzed at the waistband of my jeans where I'd clipped it.

"Jesse? You there buddy? Over."

"Hey Zak, what's up? Over."

"I've found her. We're about two miles in. How the hell she wandered off the path this far I don't know. Over."

I heaved out a huge sigh of relief. "Fuck," I groaned. "Is she okay? Over."

"Yeah, a little scared and cold, but she's fine. Over."

Zak had a smile in his voice, so I knew he was telling the truth, but my stomach was still knotted.

"Let me speak to her, Zak. Over."

There was a few moments of silence and then I heard that sweet, sexy, British accent.

"Jesse, it's me. Do I need to say over?"

I heard Zak's laughter and then some muttered words.

"Over."

"Are you okay?" I breathed out. "You hurt? Over."

"No, I'm fine. I just feel stupid. I'm sorry, Jesse, I shouldn't have left you like that. Over."

I shook my head and smiled. "No baby, you shouldn't. I'll see you soon and do not, I repeat, do not lose sight of Zak on the way back. Over."

There was silence and I wondered whether I'd lost transmission.

"Millie, you there?"

"Sorry, Jesse," she said quietly and then sniffed.

"Hey, don't cry," I soothed, not waiting to hear whether she'd finished speaking. "You're going to be okay, Zak will take care of you, I promise." Silence again. "Millie?"

"I was waiting for you to say 'over'."

I started to laugh and the relief that she was okay brought a lump to my throat and I couldn't speak.

"I'm so over this over thing." I heard her hiss at Zak.

"Jesse? Over."

"I'm here," I sighed. "I'll see you soon. Over."

"Okay, bye...*oh alright, Zak.* Over."

"Tell Zak, to meet me at the fork. Over."

"I heard ya. Over." Zak replied.

I let Marty know that Millie had been found and then headed back to the fork, desperate to see her, and I knew then that whatever was happening between us was far from over, no matter what I'd damn well said.

CHAPTER 56

♥

MILLIE

As Miss Daisy trotted behind Zak's horse, I could see a beam of light through the trees.

"Looks like Jesse's waiting for you," Zak called over his shoulder.

"I am sorry, Zak," I replied, trying to quell the feeling of nausea rolling around my stomach. "Tell your wife I'm sorry, too."

"Stop stressing about it, maybe you could go to Rowdy's with her one night. She don't get out much, so it'd be good for her and you could buy her a few of those damn sugary sweet cocktails that she likes."

"It's a date," I agreed. "And all on me."

"Jesse." Zak gave him a chin dip. "One English lady for you buddy."

"Thanks, Zak. Really appreciate your help, and don't forget about that purse for Sarah." Jesse got down from his horse and held a hand up to Zak.

Zak took it in some kind of hand clasp/hand shake and nodded. "Well I've told Millie here that maybe she can take Sarah to Rowdy's one night. She'd like a girlie night out, I reckon."

Jesse nodded and then said something that almost had me falling out of my saddle.

"Yeah, maybe the four of us could go. Kinda like a double date." He growled out the words, his eyes never leaving me as he said them.

"Sounds good to me," Zak replied without any surprise. "Guess I'll be off. Maybe Sarah will still let me have some birthday cake."

"Thank you again, Zak," I said, feeling terribly guilty.

"No problem, but please, Millie, next time you're mad at Jess, just slap his face like any other woman." With a chuckle he rode off, urging his horse to go a little faster.

Jesse watched him go and then turned to me. He lifted a hand and with one finger, beckoned for me to get off Miss Daisy and go to him. If I didn't think I was already in trouble for causing so much worry, I would tell him to get lost. I would not be bossed around by him and certainly not by using a damn accusatory finger. Aside from which, it was really hot the way his jaw was clenched and he had one hand at his hips.

Slowly, I slid out of the saddle and landed on the ground. I didn't move, but stood and watched Jesse cautiously.

"Here," he growled, pointing at a spot in front of him. "Now."

God, he was so sexy when he was being bossy, and my whole body went on high alert.

I walked towards him and stopped exactly where his finger pointed.

"What the fuck was that all about?" he ground out.

"You know what it was about," I replied defensively. "I was giving you the space that you wanted."

"Bullshit, Armalita." Jesse removed his hat and pointed it at me. "Do you have any fucking idea what could've happened to you out here?"

I shrugged and looked down at the floor. This was worse than

240

being hauled into the headmaster's office at school. The anger was positively seeping from every single pore of his body; you could almost smell it.

"Damn well look at me when I'm talking to you," he hissed.

That made my head shoot up. "Who do you think you are, speaking to me like that?"

"I'm the fucking man that's been searching these woods for nearly two hours, looking to save your damn ass from a freezing cold night out here. That's who I think I am."

"I know, and I'm sorry, but you can't speak to me as though I'm a child."

"I damn well can, especially when you behave like one. I should fucking smack that ass for what you did."

My hand went instinctively to my bottom, but at the same time, my breath hitched.

"You like the sound of that, don't you?" he asked, his voice still laced with anger. "Well I can certainly oblige if that's what you want."

"No, I do not!" I protested, my eyes wide.

"Well don't ever do that again. Marty and Zak should not have to be out here looking for you, just because you've had a little hissy fit."

"I did not have a hissy fit," I mumbled, like a sulky child.

"Yeah, well I think you'll find you did."

"Oh, whatever, Jesse. Let's just get back to the ranch and then you never have to worry about me again."

"Is that what you think, Millie?" he asked, taking hold of my chin with his thumb and forefinger. "That I'd never worry about you, that it'd be that easy?"

I shrugged again.

"What the fuck is it with this damn shrugging?" he cried. "Since when did you have nothing to say?"

"What do you want me to say? I've told you I'm sorry, I admit I was stupid. I'm sorry I wasted your evening."

"Wasting my evening, you think that's what I'm mad about?"

"Well that and putting your horses in danger, maybe?" I

241

watched as he stormed back to Dillinger and hooked his hat on the saddle.

"You think it's that simple?"

"God Jesse," I cried to his back. "Just drop it please. I'm grateful you looked for me, I'm sorry I was an idiot and stormed off, I'm sorry I reacted badly, in fact, I apologize for absolutely everything from getting lost, to the American Civil War. There, does that cover everything?"

I covered my face with my hands and groaned into them. I had no idea what else he wanted me to say. I knew I'd been stupid and reacted badly to his honesty. At least he hadn't let me think we could be something, only for him to wave me a happy goodbye in ten months' time. While I was contemplating what to say next, I felt his hands on mine. He pulled them from my face.

"I don't give a shit about any of that," he said softly. "Yeah okay, you shouldn't have gone off on your own, but I'm past being mad."

"What, you're furious now?" I huffed. "Deep joy."

Jesse sighed and shook his head. "You fucking drive me crazy, you know that?"

"Yep, I'm kind of getting that," I grumbled. "Just say what you have to say."

I was resigned for the full force of Jesse's anger or ferocity, whatever he was feeling at the moment.

"You think that this is me being mad?"

It was obviously a rhetorical question, because he simply ploughed on.

"Well this isn't me being mad, baby, this is me being as scared as fucking shit that something had happened to you."

I looked at him, my mouth gaping with bewilderment. He called me baby again. The first time I'd thought it had been a slip of the tongue, or I'd misheard over the radio, but there was no way I'd misheard that. Not only had he called me baby, but he'd said it with such tenderness that it had made my heart sigh. With a smile and a stroke of my cheek, Jesse continued.

"I couldn't breathe while you were out there on your own. My heart was yelling at me to find you, because if I didn't, I was damn sure it was going to give me pain like I've never felt before."

"Jesse," I whispered, emotion gripping at my throat.

"No listen to me, Millie. What I said to you, I really did think that was what I wanted. To carry on living in the past, being married to a ghost, but she's gone and she isn't coming back. I loved her with everything I had, but the way I feel about you is so damn intense, I feel as though everything that went before was just practice for this, *for us*." Jesse reached up and wiped away the tears that were slowly running down my cheeks, tears I wasn't even aware that I was shedding. "Baby, the guilt that comes with the feelings that I have for you is suffocating and the only time I feel any peace is when I'm with you."

"Which then makes you feel guiltier," I said, with a sniffle.

Jesse nodded. "Yeah, it does, but you know what? I have to work out how I live with that, because I'm not sure I can live without you."

The sob that escaped from me was one of relief, happiness, and fear all mixed together. To hear those words gave me a feeling of euphoria, but I was scared at what the 'but' was going to be, or that once I fully gave my heart to Jesse he would suddenly change his mind.

"You need to be sure about this," I said, gripping onto his shirt and leaning my forehead against his chest, not daring to look at him. "If you're not sure, Jesse, tell me now."

Jesse lifted my chin with the palm of his hand and then stroked my cheek.

"I can't promise that this is going to be easy. I've had two years of hardening my heart to everything and everyone, but if anyone can help me through this, you can. You've helped me so fucking much already." His hands framed my face as his thumbs wiped away more tears. "I haven't felt happy for so long that I'd forgotten how to even smile, but then you came here and I started to remember. But, you have to know there's still so much more I need to get through."

I nodded. "I know, and I know it won't be easy for you. But I promise I'll be patient and I'll help you as much as I can."

"I know you will. You're the one who got me to open up to Addy, you're the one who made me realize that what I'd been doing was empty and meaningless."

I took in a deep breath as I realized he was talking about Angie and all the other women he'd been having sex with since Melody died. Thankfully, Jesse had enough sensibility not to be specific.

"Being with you, Millie," he continued. "It meant something to me. I felt the difference in here." He patted a flat palm against his chest, swallowing hard as he did so. "You've brought light to my life again, when I thought I would always be in the dark; when all I wanted was to be in the dark. Now, I want this, I want us, and I may struggle from time to time, but I want to try and be the man that you deserve, that Addy deserves and that I deserve to be."

There were no words that I could say that would even come close to those Jesse had just said, so I simply threw myself into his arms and kissed him until we were both breathless.

***

Jesse decided that we were both riding home on Dillinger, so I sat in front of him, while Miss Daisy trailed behind us. As we made a slow journey back, Jesse's arms kept tightening around me and then he'd gently pull my face around to kiss him. He'd given me his shirt, leaving him in a white t-shirt, but he didn't seem to care about the cold, and as his arms wrapped around me to hold the reins, I rubbed my cheek against his bicep, loving the feel and smell of his bare skin.

"You warm enough?" he asked, dropping a kiss on my neck, just below my ear.

"Yeah," I sighed dreamily. "What about you? I feel bad that I have your shirt."

"I'm fine, I've never felt better." He chuckled. "In fact, I have the most amazing boner at this moment."

"Jesse," I scolded and playfully slapped at his thigh. "This is supposed to be a romantic ride home, and you're talking about your cock."

Jesse laughed loudly and squeezed his arms around me. "Now who's turning this into something dirty?"

"Not me," I protested.

"You used the word cock, not me. Although, you did miss a word out of that description."

"And what would that be?" I asked, as if I didn't know.

"Huge, of course."

Jesse laughed some more and my ears fully appreciated the sound of it. He rarely laughed, but when he did, it was deep and joyous, and I loved it.

We carried on in silence for a few more minutes and I felt Jesse tense behind me. Surely he hadn't changed his mind already.

"What's wrong?" I asked with a quaver in my voice.

"Shit, you know me too well already," he sighed. "Nothing bad, I'm just wondering what we tell everyone is all."

"Do you want to keep it quiet?" I looked at him over my shoulder, and could see, even in the dim light, that his eyes were soft. There was no fear or anxiety, just tenderness.

Jesse shook his head. "No, I want us to be open about this. We're not a dirty little secret Millie, and I'm sorry I made it sound like that the other night when I was a dick."

"Are you sure?"

"Yes, baby, I'm sure. We're us and I want everyone to know that."

"Oh my God, I think my womb just did a back flip. Jesse Connor, you're one smooth cowboy."

"You idiot," Jesse laughed and kissed the back of my head. "Seriously though, what do we say to Brandon? Addy will be high as a kite when I tell her. Mom, Dad, and Garratt won't be surprised, but Brandon, shit I have no idea."

Waves of nervousness washed through my stomach. I'd never promised him anything, but I never got around to telling him that I didn't feel that way about him either.

"I should tell him," I stated with a sigh.

"Nuh uh," Jesse replied with another kiss to my neck. "We do it together. We're us now, remember?"

With that, I leaned back into his chest and sighed, feeling happier than I had in years.

CHAPTER 57

♥

JESSE

I was fucking petrified at what I had committed to with Millie; not because it wasn't what I wanted, but because I just hoped to God that I didn't let her down. For so long I'd been a miserable bastard, I wasn't sure I knew how to be a good man any more. But, if anyone could help me make that change it would be her. She made me want to be better.

She'd been real quiet for about ten minutes, and she was leaning heavily against me, so I was pretty sure that she'd fallen asleep. Dillinger was a good, steady, and calm horse, and his gentle gait made sure she didn't wake. I tightened my arms around her and breathed in her smell, thankful that she was safe.

When I'd told her that I couldn't be with her, I'd meant it. I had feelings for her, real ones that were growing deeper every damn day, but the guilt and fear that I was being disloyal to Melody was greater. Until I thought she might be in danger, and then I realized that there was nothing that could keep me from being with her. I, above everyone, knew that life was too short, and if I went from this life not trying to be with Millie, then it would be a life half lived. My only worry now was Brandon. I wasn't sure how he was going to take me and Millie being together.

As I thought about how to tell my best friend that I'd stolen the woman he wanted, the very object of his affection stirred in my arms.

"Hey, beautiful," I whispered against her ear. "You enjoy your little nap?"

"Hmm," she moaned sexily and stretched out her arms.

I peeked over her shoulder, knowing that with the arch of her back, those gorgeous tits of hers would be pushed forward. Yep, even with my shirt on, I could see the luscious swell of them.

"We nearly home yet?" she asked.

"Ten more minutes. I just hope Mom saved us some dinner, I'm starved. It's almost ten and I haven't eaten since midday."

"Yeah, me too." She shifted in the saddle, pushing her backside into my dick that was already uncomfortably hard.

"Quit moving, baby," I said. "I do not want to go into the house with a steel rod dick tenting my jeans."

Millie's head shot around and she gave me a narrow eyed glare, but her mouth was curled into a smile and I knew she was feeling frisky.

"You fancy spending the night in the cabin with me?" I asked.

I needed to sleep with her in my arms, but wasn't sure how Mom and Dad would feel about me doing it in the house. I wasn't sure how I felt about it until I told Addy.

"I don't know," she replied. "What about Addy? What if she needs you? She's got used to having you there."

Suddenly, I felt like the biggest shit ever where my daughter was concerned. The fact that Millie had thought about her, though, warmed my fucking heart to Millie even more. I gave her a quick kiss on the cheek and then rested my chin on her shoulder.

"Yeah, you're right. How about I come visit you in your room, and set an alarm in case we fall asleep?"

Millie's room was at the back of the house, away from Mom

and Dad's and my old room, where Ruby was sleeping. Yes it was closer to Addy, but she always slept soundly, and if she did wake I'd hear her.

"In fact, I think there's an old baby monitor in her closet, how about I bring that in, too?"

Millie thought about it for few seconds and then nodded. "Okay, but you need to check with your parents first. Make sure it's okay with them."

"Millie, honey, I'm twenty-six years old, and it's officially my house, so I don't really want to be asking my mom and dad if it's okay if me and my girl have a sleepover."

Millie started to giggle.

"What?" I asked.

"You called me your girl."

"And you are, or did I imagine that deep and meaningful conversation in the woods, followed by a sexy as fuck make out session?"

"No, but it's just so...country," she laughed again and buried her face in her hands. "Sorry, but I feel like a teenager."

"God, you're crazy," I groaned and nipped at her ear. "But, if you really want me to I'll ask my mom and dad if it's okay to fuck you in your bed tonight."

"Jesse!" she cried. "You can't do that!"

"Just watch me," I growled. "You unleashed the beast, so now you have to take the consequences."

As we both sighed happily, the house came into view and a feeling of contentment swept over me. It was a nice surprise because I hadn't felt that way about this house for a long time. It hadn't felt like home for two years, but seeing it now, I knew it was the only place I wanted to be.

CHAPTER 58

♥

MILLIE

"You ready?" Jesse asked, pulling at my hand.

I blew out a breath and nodded. "I think so, but if anyone hates the idea, what do we do?"

"Nothing. We carry on doing what *we* want to do. The only person's opinion I care about is Addy's, and there's no way she's going to hate the idea. Anyone else can suck my pecker."

I started to giggle and melted into his side. I opened my mouth to say something then quickly shut it. I shuddered at my near miss at what had almost slipped from my mouth. Jesse had only just come to terms with wanting me to be 'his girl', so I was pretty sure if I mentioned that I loved him at this stage, Dillinger would be ridden out of here as though the devil himself were after him.

"Come on," he said with a grin. "Let's go and tell them the news."

I tried to pull my hand from Jesse's, but he wouldn't let it go. He looked down at our hands and then inclined his head, waiting for an explanation.

"I just thought you'd want to do this slowly."

"Nope," he said resiliently. "I've finally grown some balls and admitted how I feel about you, so we do this with pride, because I'm proud as fuck that you're mine, Millie. Okay?"

Shit, there went by nipples again. "Yes."

"Good."

He pulled me to him, gave me a closed mouth kiss, and then led me up the porch steps.

"Oh my goodness," Bonnie cried as we walked through the door. "You found her. Honey, are you okay?"

"I'm fine thanks, Bonnie. I just feel stupid and selfish that the guys had to stay out there looking for me."

"What did you do to make her run off?" Bonnie wagged a finger at Jesse and then scuffed him on the shoulder.

"Hey," he laughed. "That hurt."

"Good, it was supposed to. Anything could have happened to her. Sit down, honey," she said, plumping up a throw cushion on the couch. "Garratt, move up so Millie has more space to sit down."

Before either I or Garratt had chance to move, Jesse flopped into the space that Garratt had made, and pulled me onto his knee, wrapping an arm around my waist, causing me to let out a startled cry.

Would the real Jesse Connor please stand up! Who the hell was this man who was sending my head and heart into a spin? One minute he could barely speak to me in public, limiting any conversation to dirty words while he's having sex with me, and then, before I've had time to catch my breath, he's staking his claim and showing everyone that I'm his.

"Shit, Jess," Garratt said. "Why don't you just piss on her and be done with it?"

"Garratt!" Ted barked.

"Oh my," Bonnie gasped, her eyes firmly fixed on Jesse's arm around me.

Ted stood up and moved behind Bonnie, placing a large hand on her shoulder. "Take a breath, sweetheart," he said into her ear.

"About damn time," Ruby cackled from the recliner. "Glad you've finally seen sense, cowboy."

"Thanks, Auntie Ruby," Jesse replied, and then gave my waist a squeeze. "You okay?"

"Yeah, I think so," I answered tentatively.

"Okay," Jesse announced. "You can all see that we're together. We've kinda been seeing each other for a few weeks…"

"Kinda is the word," Garratt quipped.

Jesse turned to face him, and I have no idea what sort of glare he threw at his brother sitting next to us, but Garratt looked scared and threw his hands up in surrender, and shied back.

"So, as I was saying," Jesse continued. "We've kinda been seeing each other, but tonight I finally got myself some guts and admitted how I feel about her. How she makes me feel."

"How's that son?" Ted asked quietly, a tender smile on his face.

"Like I'm alive." Jesse lowered his forehead to my shoulder and took a deep breath in, before continuing. "I don't feel that pain when she's around."

Bonnie leaned forward and kissed my cheek and then the top of Jesse's head.

"We don't know how this is going to go," Jesse said looking up at his mother with the smile of a young boy. "But I'm going to try and do this right, Mom."

"So," Ruby said. "You staying longer than the year then, sweet cheeks?"

I shifted slightly, not sure what to say. "Well, I don't know, Ruby. I guess…well."

"Auntie Ruby," Bonnie scolded. "They've only just got together, do not be putting pressure on them."

"I ain't," she protested. "I'm just asking."

"Mom's right, Auntie Ruby," Jesse said, rubbing a hand rhythmically up and down my arm. "We're only just figuring things out. Let's see what the next ten months bring before anything is decided."

"Ah bilge," she retorted with a wave of her hand. "I'm

guessing you have great sex, you've just said she's made the pain go away. Don't see what the damn problem is. Dillydallying never won anyone nothing."

"Auntie Ruby," Ted said in his rich, deep voice. "Leave them be and listen to Bonnie when she says no pressure."

"Ah whatever," she scoffed. "I'll be home soon anyways, so I won't have to listen to all your shedaddle nonsense."

"What the fuck does shedaddle mean?" Garratt whispered to me and Jesse.

"Damned if I know," Jesse answered.

"Okay," Ted said, clearing his throat. "I'm pleased for you both, I am, but what about Addy?"

I stiffened on Jesse's lap and held my breath. Addy was who I worried about the most. She'd already lost her mother at such a young age, and I didn't want her to think I was going to join the family only for things not to work out between Jesse and me and Addy lose me, too.

"That's what I need to talk to you all about," Jesse said. "I want to tell her, I don't want any secrets between us, but I'm worried it might confuse her."

I turned to look at him, and could see the concern etched in his features.

"It's not that I don't think she'll be happy, because I do," he continued. "But this is new to me, shit being in a relationship with someone other than..." he checked himself, coughed and then carried on. "Being in a relationship is all new to me, and I may just mess this up, no matter how hard I try not to, and if that happens I'm worried it will hurt Addy as much as when Melody died. She was so young then, she had no idea what was going on. Now, she's older and she's bright and she loves Millie, so you can see how I'm struggling with what's right."

I put my hand on Jesse's at my waist and held it tightly, wanting him to know that I supported him and whatever decision he made. Jesse leaned forward and dropped a gentle kiss to my shoulder, making me sigh inwardly.

"Well," Ted said, putting an arm around Bonnie. "I for one

think, while it's a risk, it would also give that little girl some joy. I have a good feeling about you two, but if it doesn't work out, we'll all be here for Addy. Plus, you can't sneak around for the next ten months hoping she doesn't find out. Shit, you've been downright bad at it for a few weeks, and that child is sharp, she'll figure it out herself."

I stared up at Ted in astonishment, and then looked at Bonnie.

"No, honey, I didn't tell him. He figured it out for himself."

"The fact that I saw you both sneaking to Jesse's cabin kinda gave it away," Ted laughed. "Shoulda just said you wanted some alone time."

"Maybe they won't mind me fucking you in your bed after all," Jesse drawled quietly into my ear, setting off a daisy chain of goose bumps over my skin.

"Well," Bonnie sighed. "I'm real pleased for you both. But if he doesn't treat you right, honey, then you come and tell me."

Bonnie's twinkling smile lit up her face and the honesty in it calmed me.

"You're really okay about this?" I asked, earning me a squeeze at the waist from Jesse.

"Hey," he growled. "This is our decision."

"I know," I said, turning to him. "But I care what your family thinks. I'm an employee, after all, and if this is going to be awkward, me working with Addy and being with Jesse, then I'd rather someone say. That way we can try and work something out."

"Well?" Jesse demanded. "Does anyone have a problem? Not like *I* care whether you do, but Millie does, so tell me now."

"Ah chill, Jess," Garratt grumbled, knocking Jesse's knee with his own. "The only problem I have is that my friend is probably going to be too wrapped up with you to want to spend time with me now."

Garratt pouted sulkily and sighed.

"Garratt, you know you'll always be my favorite Connor boy," I joked.

Garratt grinned and winked. "Yeah I knew that, just wanted to hear you tell Jesse. Keep him in his place, you know."

"I dated brothers once," Ruby chipped in. "Damn beautiful they were. When girls saw me on both their arms they was green with envy."

"Both at the same time?" Bonnie cried, holding a hand to her chest.

"Yep, what's wrong with that?" Ruby asked, perplexed.

"But you were only seventeen when you met Uncle Samuel. So, you're saying you dated two brothers, at the same time when you were what...sixteen?"

Bonnie's mouth gaped as she stared at her aunt. Ted looked decidedly uncomfortable and Garratt was looking at Ruby with a new found respect.

"Fifteen actually," she replied, nonchalantly. "Way I see it, you gotta try the bath water before you step in Bonnie; you need to know how hot you want it." Ruby cackled and wheezed, waving her hands in the air at the look of horror on Bonnie's face. "Shit, sometimes your ass is so tight I think I hear it squeaking, girl."

"Oh my God," Jesse groaned. "I do not want to think about Auntie Ruby dipping her toe in the waters of sex."

"Hey, cowboy," she cried, pointing a finger at him. "You youngsters didn't invent sex you know. Them fancy positions of yours have been going for years, long before you got your pecker wet for the first time. Not much I ain't tried."

"Please, no," Garratt spluttered. "I think my dick just shrivelled up and died."

Jesse and I burst out laughing while Bonnie scuffed her youngest son across the back of the head.

"Ruby!" Ted warned with a small smile twitching at his lips. "Let's not, hey."

"Ah, whatever, I'm going to bed."

She flicked the button on the side of the recliner, lowering her feet to the floor. Holding her gnarled old hands out to Ted, she huffed as he pulled her to her feet.

"Now," she said, nodding at Jesse and me. "You keep the noise to a minimum. I don't want to have to listen to you two going at it. Bad enough hearing your mom and dad early this morning."

"Ruby!" Ted growled.

"Oh damn it, Auntie Ruby," Garratt whined. "Now my balls have gone, too."

"I'm with you there, brother," Jesse moaned, burying his face in my neck.

"Go to bed, now!" Bonnie barked at Ruby, pointing towards the stairs. "And we'll talk about your behaviour tomorrow."

"Ah, go shove a finger up your tight ass, Bonnie." Ruby waved her away, and with a wink, went to bed.

"Well," Ted sighed. "I think we all need a drink after that."

"I need hypnotherapy to make me forget," Garratt replied, giving himself a little shake.

"Make mine a large brandy, sweetie," Bonnie said with a shake of the head. "That woman will be the death of me."

"Ah, she's okay," Jesse replied. "She's old Mom, let her have her fun."

"Shit!" Garratt said, flopping his head back on the couch. "You really have done a number on my big brother, Millie. He's being nice to everyone. Oof," he moaned, as Jesse nudged him in the ribs with an elbow. "Well, maybe not everyone."

"You want a drink, Millie?" Ted asked, ignoring his sons.

"Nope," Jesse replied, before I could open my mouth. "We're going up."

He pushed up from the couch, gently lowering me to the floor, stooped to kiss Bonnie, who was now in the recliner, and pulled me towards the stairs.

"Shit. Mom, do we have any earplugs?" I heard Garratt ask as Jesse smacked my behind, urging me up the stairs.

CHAPTER 59

♥

JESSE

This morning when I woke, I felt lighter than I had in two whole years, and it was all down to the beautiful woman sleeping in the next room. Despite what everyone, particularly Garratt, might have thought, when it came down to it, I couldn't disrespect either Millie or my parents by fucking her in her bed until I'd spoken properly to Mom and Dad about it. Plus, I wanted to tell Addy first before she accidently found us together.

Like the decent man my folks had always hoped I'd be, I left Millie at her bedroom door, with a long kiss. A kiss that left me with a boner for a damn long time, but it had been the right thing to do. That didn't mean though that once all those conversations had been done, I wouldn't be spending the night with her, because I would. Now I'd finally admitted how I felt, I wanted to sleep with her wrapped around me.

First off, though, I was about to have a little chat with Addy. We were in the barn checking on the calves that were going to be castrated. I'd asked her to come with me, and while she'd jumped up and down in excitement, I'd seen the look of worry on Millie's face. Personally, well I didn't think she had cause to be concerned, but Millie loved Addy and it would kill her if she hated the idea.

"When do they go back outside to their friends?" Addy asked, stroking the head of one of the calves.

"Couple of days, baby."

I rubbed a hand across her head and looked down at her as she let the calf lick her fingers.

"Do their momma's come, too, so they don't miss them?"

"Their momma's come so that they can feed them, but I guess they'd miss them if they didn't."

I knew that this was my opening, so I took a deep breath, suddenly nervous at how my four year old might respond to my news.

"Do you miss your momma?" I asked, crouching down next to her.

Addy turned and looked at me, her huge blue eyes staring out at me from her beautiful, cherubic face. She bit on her bottom lip and turned back to the calf.

"Hey, I'm sorry. It doesn't matter." I took her little hand in mine and rubbed it gently. The last thing I'd wanted to do was upset her.

"I don't know, though, Daddy," she whispered. "I think I do, but I don't remember her."

"Well, you were only a baby when she went to heaven, so that's okay."

She turned back to me and tears were now brimming against her lashes. "Did she do lots of things with me?" she asked, a tiny break in her voice.

I flicked through my memories, trying to recall those of Melody as a mother.

"She used to make your breakfast and wash your hands and face after because you were such a messy eater," I replied with a huge smile.

"What else? Did she read to me?"

258

No, she didn't, I did.

"Well, I liked reading to you, like I do now. That was my special time with you."

Addy grinned and kissed my nose. "And Millie."

"Yeah," I sighed. "And Millie."

"Did she do my bath?"

No, she didn't, I did.

"You know, that was my special thing, too." I shrugged and laughed.

"You still like to do that now, so does Millie. But," she said coming closer to my ear. "Your bath time is more fun. You let me have more bubbles, but don't tell Millie, it would hurt her feelings."

I swallowed the lump caught in my throat as I watched Addy's earnest little frown.

"I won't, baby."

"So, what did my momma do with me, Daddy?" Addy folded here arms and cocked her head to one side.

Absolutely nothing. Either I did it or Mom did. The thought hit me in the middle of the chest with the force of a rampaging bull. Other than feed Addy and stick her in front of the TV, Melody did nothing for our child.

"She liked to take you shopping," I lied. "Girls like shopping."

"Not me," she replied with a shake of the head. "I get bored when Granma takes me shopping."

"Well, maybe next time she goes you should ask her if you can stay home with Millie," I suggested.

"Oh, that's okay," Addy replied, turning back to the calf that was desperate for her attention. "Millie comes, too, sometimes and she makes it fun."

"She does, hey? How?"

I watched the calf as it licked out its tongue and desperately tried to get to Addy. Once it succeeded, Addy giggled and wiped her hand on her jeans.

"We look for pairs of things, and we do numbers and she lets me read Granma's list and sometimes, if Granma needs a lot of supplies, we go to the library. She's real fun."

Addy gave me a huge smile and my heart melted, not only for her but for Millie, too. She was more of a mother than Melody ever was. Yeah, she was being paid to do a job, but she made sure my baby was happy while she did that job.

"You like, Millie, baby?"

"Yes, of course I do," she replied, pouting at me. "That's a silly question, Daddy."

"I guess it is." I laughed and hugged her to me. "How would you feel if Daddy took Millie on a date?"

Addy spun around and stared at me, her eyes bugging out comically. "Really?"

"Yes, really." I rubbed her head and let out a deep breath. She seemed happy enough by that.

"Are you going to give her your heart?" she asked, excitedly jumping up and down. "Please, Daddy," she squealed. "Give her your heart. I can get it for you. Let's go now."

She grabbed my hand and tried to pull me to my feet, almost dragging me over, she was so forceful.

"Hey, wait," I said, pulling her into my arms. "I think that might a little premature."

"What does that mean?" she asked, the pouty frown back.

"Well…" shit she was so bright that I sometimes forgot that she was just a baby. "It means that I like Millie and she likes me, but we're just good friends. She's not ready to have my heart yet."

"Not like Miss Cynthia and Tommy Kincaid?" she asked dejectedly.

I really wanted to say, 'yeah, just like Miss Cynthia and Tommy Kincaid', but I knew it was too soon. I'd only just come to terms with my feelings, and they still scared me, so there was a damn good chance that I'd fuck this up. Rushing things with Millie would only hurt her and Addy if I made a hash of it.

"Baby, giving your heart to someone is a real important thing to do. You have to be sure that they want it and won't give it back, otherwise you just get upset."

"Millie wouldn't give it back," Addy argued. "She'd keep it, because when that man gave hers back to her it made her cry, and she wouldn't do that you."

Maybe she wouldn't, but what if I couldn't get it back from Melody in the first place? There was no way that I could give Millie half of my heart; she deserved more.

"I know that, Addy. Millie tries not to upset anyone, she's a good person."

"So give her your heart!" she cried, tugging on my shirt.

"Addy, sweetheart, maybe one day, but just now we're going to be real good friends. I just want to be sure you're okay with that. I mean, you may see us kissing, or holding hands. How would you feel about that?"

Addy looked at me as thought I was the dumbest of all dumb animals.

"You said you were just friends but you said I might see you kissing."

"You might, is that a problem?"

Addy shook her head. "No, Daddy. But when you kiss someone that means you love them."

She looked so confused, it was comical. Addy and her idealistic viewpoint on love.

"It can mean you care about them...a lot."

"Do you care about Millie a lot?" she asked.

"Yeah baby, I do." I let out a sigh, the words a balm to my fears. "I really care about Millie."

"But you don't love her?"

"No," I laughed. "Not like that." Not yet, but I was damned close.

Addy shook her head. "You're silly, Daddy."

"How so, baby?"

"Because you said you don't love her," she breathed out exasperated. "You want to kiss her, you always smile when she's around, and you watch her all the time. Just like Tommy Kincaid does with Miss Cynthia and he took her heart when she gave it to him."

I'd heard from Mom that Addy had insisted that they took

Cynthia her heart. The whole town knew about Addy's little tradition and had bought into it. The thing was, most of the time she was right about who people should give their heart to. Who the fuck thought one town would rely on the match-making skills of a four year old?

"Okay," she sighed. "If you're not ready, I'll save it, but don't wait too long, Daddy."

"Why's that, baby?" I asked, standing up with her in my arms.

"Because if you don't give her yours, Uncle Brandon might."

That thought made my guts do some sort of flip with a twist thrown in. Pulling Addy closer, I kissed her head and took a deep breath. Brandon was another conversation that I needed to have, and the sooner the better.

CHAPTER 60

♥

MILLIE

Jesse and I had been 'a thing' for a couple of days, and we still hadn't told Brandon, something that had been playing on my mind greatly. I had wanted to speak to him the day after my 'hissy fit' as Jesse had called it, but Jesse wanted to speak to Addy first. Thankfully, Addy had taken it well; in fact, as soon as she saw me, she squealed and ran into my arms telling me that her daddy was taking me on a date. And so, here we were, going out on our date. Jesse was taking me into town. He'd wanted to go into Knightingale to some fancy restaurant, but I'd put my foot down and told him the diner and Rowdy's was perfectly fine. Brandon was out of town for a couple of weeks, on some business for his parent's guest ranch, so there wasn't any chance we'd bump into him. It did worry me, though, that someone else may tell him before we had the chance, so Jesse promised to do it as soon as Brandon got back.

"I'm not happy taking you there when that's where you went with Brandon," he grumbled, lifting the diner menu to read it.

"Oh, stop being a grump," I giggled. "I told you, you're not driving into Knightingale when you have to be up so early tomorrow. You've got all those calves to castrate, so you'll need to be rested."

"Millie, I've been castrating calves since I was thirteen years old. I could do it with my eyes closed. A late night in Knightingale isn't going to hurt me."

"No, but that horrible nut nicking contraption might if you're tired."

Jesse's dropped his menu and grinned at me. "'Nut nicking contraption'? Shit, Millie, where do you get this stuff?"

"Well I don't know what it is," I grumbled, lifting my own menu. "What is it called, anyway?"

"It's a Burdizzo, but to be honest, I'm liking nut nicker. I dread to think what you call the dehorner *'contraption'*." He laughed softly and continued reading his menu.

"I know that's a hot iron," I said proudly.

"Yeah, and how on earth do you know that, sweetness?"

I looked up at him and sighed. How could one man turn me to a hot, needy mess just by calling me sweetness?

"Well? Or is it a secret?" He smiled over the top of the laminated pictures of burgers, ribs and fries.

"Oh, sorry, Garratt told me," I replied, quickly pulling myself from my Jesse daydream.

"Yeah well, I could work both the Burdizzo and the Hot Iron perfectly well, on two hours sleep if I had to."

I sat back in my seat and watched him decide on what to eat. His brow furrowed with deep concentration while his hair fell boyishly over his forehead. He looked handsome and sexy, as his tanned biceps flexed under the sleeves of his plain white t-shirt.

"Keep looking at me like that, Armalita, and we'll be going home with empty bellies," he said in a low voice without looking at me.

"How do you know I'm looking at you? You're reading the menu."

He looked up at me and there was a twinkle in his eyes.

"Because your breath hitched and I felt you push your thighs together."

God, he was right, and calling me out on it had only increased the throbbing between my legs.

"I can't help it," I sighed, dreamily. "You're too beautiful not to look at."

Jesse let out a laugh and, lifting up from his chair, reached a hand across the table to the back of my neck. He captured it and pulled me to meet him before kissing me softly and nibbling at my bottom lip.

"I think you'll find you're the beautiful one," he whispered before flopping back into his seat. "I think I'll get the Tower burger, what about you?"

"I'm going to get the same." I put the menu down on the table and looked up to see Jesse grinning. "What?"

"A Tower burger? You know how big that thing is, right?"

He reached for my hand across the table and took my fingertips in his, while his other hand played with the sugar dispenser.

"Yes, your mum and I came in for coffee when we went shopping, and there was a guy eating one. It looked really nice, so I asked Cynthia what it was."

"You think you'll eat it?" Jesse asked incredulously.

"Well, you obviously don't think I will."

Jesse sat back in his chair, keeping a hold of my hand. "I know you won't."

My eyes widened and my mouth gaped open. "Jesse Connor, that's practically a bet."

"No way, I'm not taking your money from you."

"You may not win, and anyway, who said I was going to bet money on it?"

I gave him a cheeky wink, kicked off my shoe, and lifted my foot to brush it up the inside of his thigh. Jesse's eye's darkened and his breathing became laboured as I edged my foot further up his leg.

"You sure you know what you're doing?" he asked, his grip

tightening on the sugar.

I nodded. "Yep."

"So," he grunted out on a deep exhale. "What's this wager going to be?"

I licked my lips while I pretended to think about it. I already knew what I was going to offer as my stake.

"Okay," I finally said. "I eat it all, you have to give me a lap dance back at your cabin later. If I don't eat it, then I give you one."

I pushed my bare foot against Jesse's rock hard cock and gave it a rub before pulling back. As I did, Jesse grabbed it and held it against his hardness. His jaw was tight and I could see that he was having difficulty keeping control; I loved it.

"That's a no lose situation," he said, moving my foot up and down his length. "If I dance for you or you dance for me, I still get to fuck you afterwards."

I shrugged. "Not all bets have to be a poor investment."

"You are the most…"

Before he had time to finish, a woman I didn't recognise bounced over. She was probably in her mid-thirties, but the lines creased around her mouth and eyes meant she could have been older. Her waitresses' uniform was unbuttoned a little too low, displaying a neon green bra that pushed her chest almost to her chin.

"Jesse, honey. How ya doin'?" she asked, flicking her tongue along her top lip.

She'd obviously read somewhere that it was a sexy move, but it had no effect on Jesse, whose eyes remained on me. His hand was still clutching mine, but neither that nor Jesse's apparent lack of interest bothered her.

"Not seen you since Founders Day," she giggled, landing a hand on his shoulder and squeezing it.

Jesse looked up at her and flashed a quick smile before gently shrugging away her hand.

"Hey. Janet, been busy," he answered. "So, we'll have two Tower burgers, fries, and salad."

"You going to Rowdy's later? It's open mic night."

No, she was still openly panting for him, despite his brush off.

"Not sure, depends what Millie wants to do."

Jesse nodded towards me, and finally Janet noticed me. Her smile slipped momentarily when she noticed our joined hands, but it was quickly back when she turned her attention to Jesse.

"Thought maybe we could get together some time. It's been a while."

Jesse's nostrils flared and I felt nauseous at what that meant. Surely he hadn't slept with *Janet*? Angie I understood; she was an attractive, if not a little bit brassy, girl. But Janet was definitely older and apart from the huge breasts, wasn't particularly attractive. Her bleached hair was the color and texture of straw, and besides the lines of a well lived life, she had poor skin and uneven teeth. Yep, it was official; I was a nasty, jealous bitch!

Jesse looked up at her. "Janet, I don't want to be rude, but you can see I'm here with my girl, so if you wouldn't mind taking our order and then leaving us alone."

That still didn't do it and Janet giggled, poking Jesse in the arm. "You always was a kidder. So, Rowdy's, you gonna sing, darlin'? And then maybe we can get a beer together."

I could see that any control Jesse was holding on to had now firmly disappeared. He let go of my foot under the table and gently pried his other hand from mine. Turning in his seat so that his knees almost touched Janet's, he took a deep breath.

"Okay, I'm sorry about this, but you obviously aren't getting what I'm saying." He paused, giving her time to respond. When she didn't, he continued. "We had one night over a year ago, a night that you know full well was when I was a mess in my head. I told you then and I'm telling you now, it was a one-time thing and would not and will not be happening again."

I held my breath as I watched the exchange, wishing that Janet would just turn and leave to get our order. The way she was looking at Jesse told me that whatever scrap of hope she had, she was going to hang onto it until the very last. There was a need in her eyes, a look that I was sure was in my own more often than not. She was in love with him. One night had given her that, and she couldn't give it up.

"We had a good time," she protested, still smiling, but it was more forced now.

"Janet," he sighed. "It's not going to happen. I'm with Millie, who to be honest, you're kinda disrespecting by doing this."

Janet glanced at me and her smile finally slipped.

"Now, do you want to go and get our orders, with two beers, so I can enjoy a meal with my girl before I take her over to Rowdy's to drink and dance and maybe sing, then depending how things go with the food, there's going to be some more dancing back at my cabin, and well, then you can guess what happens next. Do I make myself clear?"

Janet looked between us and then nodded. "Two beers and two Tower burgers with fries. Gotcha."

Then she was gone.

"You sing?" I asked.

Jesse stared at me and burst out laughing. "Everything that just went down, and all you took away was me singing?"

"Really, you sing?" I breathed.

"Yep and play guitar, why?" he asked, grinning like a Cheshire cat.

"Oh shit, I may need fresh knickers."

Jesse roared with laughter again, then reached forward and took my mouth in a long, sweet kiss and bang went another brain cell.

CHAPTER 61

♥

JESSE

Sweet fucking Jesus, she ate every damn bit and I have no damn clue where she put it all. The last few mouthfuls were a struggle, I could tell. She practically had to push the last bite in, but props to her, she did it. Shit, that meant I was going to have to give her a lap dance! Never mind, I could do that knowing what I'd get afterwards.

"You sure you want to go to Rowdy's?" I asked as Millie unbuttoned her jeans and groaned.

"Hmm, yep." She breathed heavily and took a huge gulp of water. "Just give me a few minutes."

I started to laugh and waved to Janet for the check. Thankfully, she'd delivered our food without saying much else, other than asking if we needed any relishes. Yeah, she'd been one massive mistake when my head was fucked over Melody, but that was how I used to get through the days; sleeping around, getting drunk, and ignoring my family, especially Addy. At least I'd come through that and things were changing for the better.

"Okay," I announced. "You've had long enough, I'm taking you dancing to work off some of that food. I don't want you falling into a meat coma later."

Millie gave me a small smile quickly followed by a grimace. "I may lose my jeans, I don't think I can fasten them."

"I'll help you when we get outside," I replied in all innocence.

"Yeah, I'll bet you will," she scoffed.

At that moment, Janet appeared and quietly placed the check on the table. I picked it up and fished my wallet from my back pocket, thumbing a couple of twenties and a ten out, placing them on the check; a good tip was the least I could do after what I'd said to her.

"I want to pay," Millie protested, fishing around in her purse.

"Nope, not a chance. Now shift that sweet ass, we've got dancing to do."

***

When we got over to Rowdy's, the place was starting to fill up. It was Saturday night and most people, unlike me, didn't have work the next day. With Millie's hand in mine, I moved through the locals that were gathered and pushed to the bar.

"Hey, Janelle, busy night," I stated.

Janelle smiled and threw a bar cloth over her shoulder. "It's open mic' night, and it's a Saturday, never changes. So, what can I get you, honey?"

"Two beers, but make one light would you?"

Janelle nodded and reached into the refrigerator for two beers; she popped the caps and placed them on the bar.

"You singing tonight?" she asked, taking the money I handed over.

I glanced at Millie, who was still holding my hand but was talking to Cynthia and Tommy.

"Maybe, depends how much I need to impress the lady," I said, nodding my head to the side.

Janelle looked down to see Millie's hand in mine. "Wow," she said with a huge smile. "That's a change. For the better."

"We're just taking it slow," I replied.

"Pleased for you, honey. But, hey, didn't she come in here with Brandon a few weeks back?"

My back stiffened and my grip on Millie tightened.

"Yeah, it was just a date."

"Well whatever. Like I said, pleased for you, Jesse. Okay, Frank what can I get you?"

With that, Janelle moved a little further down the bar to the next customer in her section.

"You okay?" Millie asked, placing a hand on my forearm.

"I'm fine." I forced a smile and passed her a beer. "Let's go find a table."

I hated that she'd been on a date with Brandon, but there wasn't anything I could do about it now. I just dreaded telling my buddy that there would be no more dates, because Millie was mine now.

We were lucky to find a high table free, right next to the small dance and stage area. But, as soon as we sat down, I wished it hadn't been vacant. At the next table was Angie and another girl, Wanda, who had been on the cheerleading squad with Melody. I sat Millie with her back to them; if Angie decided to pull any shit I wanted to be the first to see it coming. I nodded at her and sat down once I knew that Millie was comfy.

"It's really busy in here," Millie said, leaning closer to me. "Is everyone here just to hear you sing?"

"Hah, doubt it," I laughed. "I can throw a tune out, but I'm not some local celebrity, you know."

She had a wicked glint in her eye as she quickly glanced over her shoulder. "Amongst the ladies you are. Any more likely to creep out of the woodwork tonight?"

Thankfully, she was smiling, so she wasn't upset – at least I hoped not.

"No baby, no more."

I dropped a kiss to her shoulder and thanked God that I'd only shit on my own doorstep twice; the other women I'd slept with over the last two years lived out of town.

We talked and laughed for a while, all the time I kept an eye on

Angie, but apart from throwing me the stink eye occasionally, she behaved herself and I was grateful she wasn't spoiling our night. The more time I spent with Millie like this, the deeper I was falling. She was fun to be with, not caring about laughing at herself, or me for that matter. Too many women that I'd been with tried to be something they weren't, but not Millie. We'd laughed hysterically when she'd belched the alphabet for me; some friend of hers had taught her apparently – go figure.

A few people had started dancing when a slow number came on and I knew it was an opportunity to have her in my arms.

"Wanna dance, Miss?" I asked, holding out my hand as I got up from my seat.

Millie gave me the most beautiful smile and nodded.

I led her onto the dancefloor, and all eyes were upon us. Most folk around here would probably be thinking she was another of my one night stands, but some, like Janelle, those who knew me, would know this was something more. They'd know because they'd seen us talking and laughing and being affectionate. I was never like this with Janet or Angie. They were lucky to get three words from me, which were usually 'just one night'. The eyes of Angie, on the other hand, were probably crossed with being so bat shit crazy mad at me.

As I pulled Millie into my arms and we swayed to Ed Sheeran's 'Thinking Out Loud', I listened carefully to the words, and the face in my mind was Millie's. The thought that it wasn't Melody took my breath away, but she would never be the one I grew old with, could never be. Millie could, and the fact that I wanted her to be, scared the shit out of me

CHAPTER 62

♥

MILLIE

Once the Ed Sheeran song had finished, I expected Jesse to lead us back to the table, but he held me tight as Elvis started crooning *'Can't Help Falling in Love'*. I thought my heart had stopped beating when Jesse started singing along, his raspy voice deep and melodic in my ear. I could not think any more of this than him just singing along to a classic song. I *would* not think any more of it. But how could I not let my heart just have a little hope?

He was starting to mean everything to me; he was the man who I could see all my tomorrow's with, the one I wanted to share my future with. My Grandma Armalita always said that I would know when I'd met the man worthy of trusting my life with, and for a time I'd thought that was Dean. As time had gone on, I realized that we didn't have that deep, passionate love that pulls you by the seat of your pants through life. I now know why, but at the time I thought we were comfortable and lacking in spontaneity because we were so attuned to each other.

With Jesse things were immeasurably different right from the first moment I saw him. There was the amazing sex for a start, and the fact that he obviously liked women and not men, but it was more than that. The chemistry and passion were evident, but he took my breath away with every look, every touch, and every word. I was falling more in love with him every day, and while he wasn't at that place, I knew that I couldn't give him up. I was just like Angie and Janet; in love with a man whose heart was with a dead woman, and just like them, I couldn't give up hope. Hope was still all I had.

"Your voice is beautiful," I whispered.

Jesse laughed quietly. "I'm beautiful, my voice is beautiful. Shit, my head will be too big to get out of the door soon."

"Well, you do have some faults," I sighed.

"Oh yeah, and what are they?" he asked, pulling me closer as another slow song kicked in.

"You're grumpy before you have your first cup of coffee," I answered. "Oh and you're bossy, and you hate losing at cards to your four year old daughter."

Jesse's head went back as he let out a deep belly laugh. "Okay, I'll try and work on those areas for you, ma'am."

"Good," I sighed and snuggled back against him.

His body was hard from working on the ranch, but even the softest pillow wasn't as comfortable as laying my head on his chest. I breathed in his scent and linked my arms around his narrow waist. As we danced in one spot, Jesse bent his head to my ear.

"What do you want me to sing to you, baby?" he asked softly, smoothing down my hair.

"Anything." I looked up at him, my chin resting against his chest. "But you don't have to, I just got a personal rendition."

"Ah, but that wasn't a song of your choice, or mine for that matter."

The disappointment left a bitter taste. He really didn't mean those words, I knew he didn't, but that thing called hope had reared its head again.

"You pick," I said, clearing my throat. "So, shall we go back to our drinks?"

"Erm, yeah okay," Jesse replied, evidently confused at my sudden desire to stop dancing halfway through a song.

I couldn't help it, I felt deflated and couldn't summon up a smile.

"Hey, you okay?" he asked, tugging gently on my hair as we walked back to our seats.

"Yes, I'm fine," I lied, flashing him a smile.

Jesse pulled out my stool for me then when I was seated, he pecked me on the cheek and went to the bar for more beers.

Once he came back, I had pulled myself out of my funk and realized that I was being stupid. He couldn't help how he did or didn't feel and he'd been honest in that we should take this slowly, and that I'd need patience. So, while he was at the bar, I'd taken a deep breath and given myself a talking to.

Halfway through our beer, the music stopped and a tall, well-built man with a long ginger beard tapped on the microphone.

"Who's that?" I whispered to Jesse.

"That's Rowdy."

"Oh my God, that's him." I started to clap, excited at seeing the real Rowdy.

"He's not a celebrity either, baby," Jesse laughed.

"I didn't realize that there was a real Rowdy. Oh, this is so exciting." I pulled my phone from my pocket and snapped a quick picture of him while he tested the microphone.

Jesse shook his head, kissed my temple, and then walked over to Rowdy and whispered something in his ear. Rowdy nodded, said something to Jesse, and then gave me a wave. I waved back, highly embarrassed, but Rowdy just continued talking to Jesse without drawing any attention to me.

"What was that about?" I asked Jesse when he came back and stood behind me.

"Wait and see," he said, an arm reaching around me for his beer.

He grinned, wrapped his other arm around my chest and continued to sip from his bottle. A few minutes later, Rowdy stepped up to the mic' again, this time holding an acoustic guitar, and shouted for everyone to be quiet.

"Okay ladies and gentlemen," he bellowed, probably not needing any technical aid to be heard. "First up tonight is Jesse Connor."

"Jesse!" I gasped, and tilted my head up to have his lips land on mine.

"See you in a few," he said, putting his bottle on the table and walking towards Rowdy.

"Okay," Rowdy continued. "He asked me to tell you that this song is for a very special young lady."

He passed Jesse the guitar and stepped down from the small platform that acted as a stage. While Jesse tuned the guitar, Rowdy put a stool behind him, then when he was ready, Jesse looked up at everyone and gave a wave.

"Hey. Hope you enjoy this."

As soon as the first notes of John Mayer's *Daughters* sounded out, the room went silent, except for Jesse's guitar playing. When he started to sing, I held my breath; it was amazing. His voice was bluesy and raspy, but there was a lightness to it as well when he effortlessly moved into a falsetto; everyone was enraptured. Mesmerised by him, tears ran down my face as Jesse sang every word with passion and feeling. I loved the song and knew straight away the message he was giving. It was his way of atoning for his behaviour with Addy; he was admitting that he could have damaged her for any man to come if he hadn't changed. As he sang the last few lines, Jesse's voice broke and he was visibly moved by the song.

Everyone clapped and cheered and Jesse took a little bow, waving away their praise.

"I guess you thought that he might be singing a song for you, did ya?" Angie had sidled up beside me and was watching Jesse intently as she spat out her venom.

"No, I knew he was going to sing for Addy," I lied, wiping my face with the back of my hand.

Okay, at first when Rowdy had introduced him, I had thought

it might be me he was going to sing for. There was no disappointment though, none whatsoever; he couldn't have sung anything more fitting or beautiful.

"Ah, really," Angie scoffed. "Like I believe that."

I was about to bite back when Jesse's voice came over the microphone again.

"Okay, so that song was about my beautiful baby, you've all met Addy, right?"

"Shit, she got some of us together." It was Tommy Kincaid and he was standing on the edge of the dance floor with his arm firmly around Cynthia.

Jesse grinned and shook his head. "Yep, my baby loves her hearts. Well, anyways I'd like to do another song for you and this is for someone who has helped heal *my* heart over the last couple of months. Someone real special to me."

I gasped as Jesse stared at me, blew me a kiss, grinned, and then struck up the chords for Bob Marley's *'Is This Love'*.

As Jesse started to sing, Angie slammed her drink down on the table, and with her friend running behind to catch up, exited the bar. She only took my attention momentarily, because all I could concentrate on was Jesse as my breath caught in my throat and my heart hammered triple time in my chest.

Jesse's gaze never left me as he asked me the question 'is this love?' I could answer him right at this moment; emphatically and unreservedly. The real question was, could I *risk* telling him, knowing that Jesse wasn't even sure whether he could properly move on from Melody?

As he sang the last verse, I no longer had any doubts. I knew that no matter what, I'd have to tell him. I needed him to know that for me, it was love, but that I'd be patient and wait until he was sure, too.

Finishing the song, Jesse passed Rowdy the guitar, strode towards me, and pulled me into his arms.

"Let's go," he commanded, close to my ear.

I nodded and, taking hold of Jesse's hand, followed him out of Rowdy's to his truck.

CHAPTER 63

♥

JESSE

By the time we got to my cabin after leaving Rowdy's, I was about ready to just rip Millie's clothes off, fuck any buttons or fasteners. I drove past the house and parked next to the cabin, ran around to the passenger door, and helped her out. I practically pulled her out in fact, I was so desperate to be inside her.

"The fucking lap dance will have to wait," I groaned as I pushed her against the wall.

"A bet's a bet, Jesse," she moaned breathily as I hitched up her skimpy little top.

"I'll pay, but it'll be after I've come inside you."

Millie lifted her arms in the air, allowing me to pull her top off, and then arched forwards, giving me access to her impressive tits. Hungrily, I took one in my mouth and caressed the nipple with my tongue, pausing for a few seconds while Millie undid my jeans. Her hand went inside my boxer briefs and she gently stroked my iron hard cock.

"Fuck," I said on a long breath as she started to pump me.

The next thing I knew, Millie was pulling away from me, dropping to her knees, and taking my pants and underwear down. I looked down as she looked up, her big brown eyes peeking from under her dark lashes.

"I'm going to give you the best blow job you've ever had," she whispered, before taking me in her mouth.

She was true to her word, sucking and licking me like she was savouring the best lollipop she'd ever tasted. She took me deep, until I touched the back of her throat, and moaned softly around me. Her licks were slow and long. She dropped kisses on the end of my cock, and her hand cupped my balls as she pumped me, and I came, shouting her name.

"Millie," I gasped, pulling her to her feet as she licked her lips. "Oh my God, that was...damn it was amazing."

Pulling her to me, I kissed her hard, dragging my fingers through her hair and squeezing that amazing ass of hers. Shifting slightly, I pulled her legs up around my waist and carried her to the bed where I took off the rest of my clothes and then spent time slowly removing hers, adoring every bit of naked skin as it was revealed to me with soft kisses.

When she was totally bare, and on the edge of screaming at me to take her, I slowly pushed inside. Her back arched and her fingers dug into my shoulders as I moved in and out, rolling my hips with each thrust. I linked my fingers with hers and pushed our arms up above Millie's head, and then kissed along her jaw, her cheeks, her neck and finally took her mouth. We were silent and slow and I knew this wasn't fucking anymore. I'd only ever had this with one woman before, and I wasn't even sure it had even been this good with her. Pushing that thought from my mind, I continued to worship the woman beneath me. Her hair was fanned across my pillow, her cheeks were flushed a light pink, and her eyes were hooded as gasps of pleasure escaped her swollen lips; she looked more beautiful than any sunrise I'd ever seen.

With our bodies covered in a thin sheen of sweat, we both began to breathe heavily, and I knew that she was close, as close

279

as I was.

"I think I'm falling in love with you," I whispered.

"I know I'm already there," she replied softly.

As Millie's hands gripped mine tighter, her legs that were wrapped around me started to tremble. My own orgasm was about to hit as the electric current from the pit of my stomach hit my balls.

"Jesse," she cried, as her inner muscles spasmed around me.

I pumped quicker and kissed her harder, desperate to bring us both to climax. Millie pushed her hips higher, taking me deeper, and we were both gone, crying out as we orgasmed together.

I flopped to my side of the bed, my arms out and breathing heavily.

"Fuck," I said breathlessly.

"Yeah," Millie gasped out.

I reached over and pulled her to me, kissing the top of her head as I wrapped her in my arms.

"I think you can forget the lap dance," she giggled. "For tonight at least."

"Yeah, I don't think I could move again. Let's get some sleep and talk about our wager tomorrow, okay?"

She nodded her head and snuggled into my side. Within minutes, sated from food, beer, and amazing sex, she fell asleep. But, despite having to get up at the bare ass crack of dawn, I lay awake, staring into the darkness.

What had just happened between us had been incredible, and I'd felt things that I hadn't felt in a long time, maybe ever. Millie was getting under my skin, into my soul, my head, and my heart, but instead of feeling excited and happy that I was actually feeling alive again, I felt sick to my stomach.

Melody had been my soul mate, the woman that I'd grieved for, the woman that I'd thought I'd never replace. I'd been a piece of shit to my family, my friends and, worst of all, my baby girl, all because I'd lost her. Then Millie came along and with her beauty and her no nonsense attitude, turned everything upside down.

She'd breathed life back into me, into this ranch, into Addy, and I was falling in love with her. Love that I knew was going to be big, deep, and for a lifetime, but I hated the idea of it. I hated feeling that way about her, because what the fuck did that mean about my feelings for Melody? Why the hell had I put everyone, including myself, through hell for two years, if what I had with my wife was only a fraction of what I could have with Millie? What I already felt for Millie?

She'd made me question everything and I wasn't sure I could get past that, no matter how deep my feelings.

CHAPTER 64

♥

MILLIE

When I woke up the blinds were still pulled down, but I could see that the sun was up. It wasn't too bright in the room, so I guessed that my body clock had woken me at its usual time of six-thirty. I wasn't sure what time Jesse had left his bed, but I had a vague recollection of him kissing my forehead before he'd left.

After stretching lazily, I kicked off the covers and looked around the floor for my bag and clothes. Once I'd found my bag, I fished around inside it for my phone to check the time. I'd been right; it was almost six-thirty. Hopefully, I could get back to the house and change before Addy woke at seven.

I wasn't sure whether Jesse would go to the house for breakfast today, seeing as he was going to be so busy, so I wrote him a quick note and left it on his pillow. I then let myself out and went back to the main house.

When I let myself in through the mud room, Bonnie was there cooking breakfast. With the click of the door, she stopped and looked over her shoulder.

"Morning, honey. You have a good night?" she asked, perusing my wild woman hair and smudged eye makeup; everything about me suggested sex.

"Hi," I replied, shyly. "I'm sorry."

"What are you sorry for?" she asked, taking the frying pan off the stove and turning to me. "Has something happened?"

"Oh God, no. I'm sorry for sneaking in like some naughty schoolgirl. I promise it won't happen again."

She came over and pulled me into a hug. "Oh, hush now, don't be so silly. You deserve to have some fun, and if it means that Jesse had fun, too, then I'm perfectly happy about it. You did have fun, right?" she asked, letting me go.

I nodded. "We had a great time. I didn't know Jesse could sing, though."

Bonnie preened like a mother hen fluffing her feathers. "Doesn't he have a beautiful voice?"

"He does," I agreed, remembering his songs to me and Addy.

"You should hear Garratt, too. They used to sing together when they were young boys, usually at church or the Founder's celebration meal for the town dignitaries, but not for a long time."

"Wow, they could have been famous rock stars if they'd kept it up," I said excitedly.

"Ah, I don't know about that, but they were good and we were real proud of them. So, I guess he sang at Rowdy's last night?"

"He did, starting with a song for Addy."

I went on to tell Bonnie all about our evening, leaving out what had happened at the cabin but making sure to include Angie storming out. Bonnie laughed loud and hard at that, telling me that it was about time Angie got the message. Her laughing stopped though when I told her why she stormed out, and she listened with a dreamy smile on her face.

We were still chatting and had lost track of time, when Addy stumbled into the kitchen rubbing her eyes with one hand and clutching a teddy bear with the other.

"Good morning, sweetie," Bonnie said, stooping to kiss her granddaughter. "You sleep well?"

"Yes, thank you, Granma." She gave a big yawn and pulled out a chair at the table.

"I'd better go and get showered and changed before the boys come back for breakfast," I said.

"But you look pretty," Addy said as she brushed her messy hair from her eyes that were barely open. "Did you have a nice time with Daddy?"

"I did, sweetheart, a really nice time."

Suddenly, the door from the mud room was flung open and Garratt and Ted stepped inside, talking loudly about calf testicles.

"Oh, please," Bonnie groaned. "Do you really have to?"

"Sorry, sweetheart," Ted laughed, kissing her cheek. "But when you've cut off thirty pairs of balls and horns, you get obsessed."

"Believe me, Dad. I am not obsessed with testicles of any kind," Garratt stated, going to sit next to Addy. "Morning, sunshine."

"Morning, Uncle Garratt," she replied, reaching up to kiss him. "Where's Daddy?"

"Oh, he's going to have breakfast with the boys in the bunkhouse," Garratt answered.

"If it's not ruined," Bonnie grumbled. "I left it warming in the stove as usual, but it's been playing up. I really think we need a new one, honey," she said to Ted.

"I'll check it out tomorrow, see what deals I can find. We need a new washing machine for over there, too."

Poor Bonnie, no wonder she'd needed my help with Addy. She got up at five-thirty every morning to cook breakfast for the bunkhouse and then come back here to cook for the family. I'd offered a few times over the last couple of months to cook for the family, but she said it was enough that I was here helping with Addy, I didn't need to cook as well. Honestly, I don't think she thought I *could* cook, but she was adamant, so I didn't push her on it.

"Why is Daddy eating with the boys?" Addy asked.

Yes, I thought, why is he? Jesse hadn't had breakfast with the boys in weeks.

Garratt shrugged, concentrating on something on his phone. "Something about wanting to talk to Marty about the weaning."

"Weaning is weeks away," Bonnie said, busying herself with dishing up breakfast. "Oh well, that's more for you boys."

"Sounds good to me," Ted said. "Garratt, lets wash up, son."

"Yes, Daddy," he said with a wink at me. "Nice outfit, Millie. Just like the one you wore last night."

I gave Garratt a smile, but it was forced. Something felt off about Jesse not coming for breakfast, and I was determined I'd ask him when we met up later.

***

I didn't see Jesse later; he sent a message back with Garratt that he wasn't coming over but was driving over to a place called Booker, three hours away, to talk with a man who was going to buy some of the calves in the fall. Feeling slightly aggrieved, I sent him a text.

Millie: Hi you okay? Not seen you all day x

I finally got a text back about half an hour later.

Jesse: Yeah busy with the calves. Got to see this guy in Booker and make a deal.

Okay, so no kisses and a little dismissive, but I wasn't going to let that be it.

Millie: Will you be back late? I could wait up for you x

His response was immediate, but didn't relieve my anxiety.

Jesse: No. May be gone a couple of days. See you when I get back.

With a sick feeling in my stomach, I responded with shaking

hands.

Millie: Okay. I'll miss you xx

I got no response from that text and Jesse didn't return the next day. I didn't send any more messages, because even I had my limits.

CHAPTER 65

♥

JESSE

I knew that I was being a bastard, but I had no idea what else to do. My head was in the toilet thinking about Melody, and I had to have some distance from Millie. I knew coming to Booker was a coward's way out, but I needed to think. I wasn't meeting Andy Merrill until Wednesday afternoon, so I had almost three full days to come to terms with what I had to do.

CHAPTER 66

♥

MILLIE

It was Wednesday and I hadn't seen Jesse for four days. He'd been in Booker for three of those days, without any contact whatsoever. He'd spoken to Addy on the phone every night, and had a quick chat with whichever member of his family was around, but he'd never once asked to speak to me.

Bonnie had noticed, and each time Addy chatted animatedly about her daddy, Bonnie would give me a sympathetic smile and try to turn the conversation elsewhere. As for me, I was sad, angry, and distracted, with a propensity to bursting into tears when I was alone. I'd hardly eaten for the last three days and once Addy was in bed, I curled up in my room crying into my pillow. Ruby, being the straight up person that she was, had tried to talk to me about him, but I brushed her off and found something else to do that was away from her.

Tonight though, I was in town with Sarah, Zak's wife. My promised apology for the night he'd missed her birthday. Zak was going into Knightingale with his Dad to play in a pool tournament, so they had dropped us off on the way and were picking us up later.

"Okay," Sarah said, leaning up against the bar. "What are we having first?"

She was a gorgeous looking red head with curves to die for and the most beautiful green eyes that I had ever seen. I could also see that she was good fun, and if anyone could rouse me from my despair, it was probably Sarah.

"A beer is good," I replied, handing over a twenty dollar bill.

Sarah pushed it back at me. "Hey, it's my round and I do not want you thinking you have to pay all damn night just because Zak missed my birthday. Jesse already made up for it when he gave me three hundred dollars for a designer purse I wanted."

"He did?"

"Yeah, he did. Said it was his fault you went off and it was the least he could do. I'd told Zak that was his penance for being late, but was only kidding. Jesse insisted though."

I was shocked. I thought he totally blamed me for that night.

The guilt overwhelmed me again. "I am sorry, Sarah. I shouldn't have just gone off like that."

"Ah, sweetie, don't worry about it," she cried, waving a hand at me. "Zak gave me some real good head and crazy monkey sex to make up for it."

Sarah was so matter of fact about it that I burst out laughing and my mood was broken.

"What?" she asked innocently. "He did. Don't tell me you didn't use that little tiff of yours to get Jesse to set you off like a damn rocket."

I shook my head. "No, he gave me a really romantic kiss though."

"Ah shoot, you're further gone than I thought." Sarah leaned over the bar and clicked her fingers at the barman who was chatting to a couple of girls at the other end of the bar. "Hey, Dusty, get your frickin' ass down here and serve us. It's not damn singles night, you know."

Dusty, the barman, shook his head and strolled over to us.

"What do you want?"

"Some manners to start with, now move your damn ass and get me two Slippery Nipples."

"Ugh, you disgust me," Dusty said with a roll of the eyes.

"Shove it and do your job."

My mouth gaped open as I watched Sarah shove some money at Dusty.

"Sarah!" I exclaimed. "You can't speak to him like that."

"I can and I will," she replied with a grin. "He's my baby brother."

Oh my God, she was just what I needed. My worries over Jesse were pushed to the back of my mind as we commenced trying to drink ourselves into oblivion. Garratt, evidently feeling sorry for me, had offered to be on Addy duty the next morning. He'd given me a hug and a peck on the cheek, so his brother's behaviour evidently hadn't gone unnoticed with him, either

***

"Please, tell me that's not true," Sarah screamed, holding her sides. "Oh God, I'm gonna pee my panties."

"It's not funny," I moaned. "Imagine how you'd have felt if Zak had dumped you at the altar for another man."

A part of me was hurt that she thought it was hilarious, but the rest of me had to agree. After the last three days of Jesse rejecting me, Dean ditching me for cock was merely a blip in my life plan, and in hindsight damn funny.

"If Zak had done that to me, firstly I'd have asked for a threesome and then, when we'd finished, I'd cut his balls off," she said, pouring more Sangria into her glass. "Come on, pretty girl, drink up so I can get us another jug."

I shook my head and waved a dismissive hand at the jug. "Nope, no more Sangria. I need something less sweet. I have a coating on my teeth."

Sarah opened her mouth and rubbed her molars with her finger. "Ugh yep, fluffy as all fuck. We'll have Tequila next."

"Hey ladies, can I get you a drink?" a deep, rich voice asked.

We both turned to see two tall, blond haired men dressed in

jeans and polo shirts standing behind us at our spot at the bar.

I opened my mouth to say 'no' but Sarah slapped a hand on my arm and gave the man a pouty smile.

"Why, that'd be kind of you," she purred. "Patron would be lovely. Silver."

The man only winced slightly, knowing how much it cost, but nodded and lifted his chin to Dusty, who was watching in amusement.

"Sarah, we can't," I hissed.

"Sure we can," she whispered. "Tequila makes me randy, and if Zak finds out I drank it but didn't pay for it, that'll make him come like a train." She giggled and turned to the men. "So, I'm Sarah and this is my friend Millie, she's from England."

"Hey, nice to meet you both," the man who was buying the drinks replied. "I'm Trent and this is Corbin."

Corbin gave me a smile, and while he was handsome, he was not Jesse. But, Jesse clearly didn't want me, so I decided that maybe Corbin was just what I needed.

"Pull up a stool boys," Sarah said. "Now you should know, I'm married and have twin boys, so I'm sorry you won't get any fun with me. Hoooweeever," she giggled, elongating the word. "Our English Maiden here is well and truly single."

Trent suddenly looked uncomfortable and I noticed him nod his head towards the door, silently telling Corbin that they should leave. Corbin, however, had other ideas.

"No problem," he said, taking the money from Trent's fingers. "It's just a drink, no harm in that."

Corbin moved down the bar a little, with Trent following.

"Sarah, I don't know whether I'm single or not," I said, my eyes firmly on Corbin and Trent who appeared to be arguing.

"Did you or did you not tell me that Jesse had been MIA for three or four days and never once spoke to you?"

I nodded. "Yes, but…"

"Not buts about it lady, except that mighty fine one in those Levi's that Corbin is wearing. Now, sit back and enjoy some attention, and let Jesse Connor go suck his own dick for a change."

291

I think I loved this woman and she may very well turn out to be the best friend I'd ever had.

Almost an hour later, Trent had relaxed and was happily chatting to Sarah. He'd told us that he'd just split with his girlfriend of four years because he hadn't been ready for the next step, but within ten minutes, Sarah had persuaded him that he was being a 'dickwad' because he was obviously miserable without her. Trent had agreed. He sent his ex a text and she'd called back immediately. They agreed to meet up at the weekend, when he got back from his business trip, to talk things over. He and Corbin ran a stud farm in Florida, and were here to look at some horses that Wyatt McKenzie was selling. They were staying with the McKenzie's but had come into town for the evening.

"I still can't believe you're single," Corbin said, looking at me over the top of his beer bottle. "There must be someone."

I sighed and shook my head. "No, not really."

"No or maybe?" he asked. "Not really sounds like there may be."

What should I say, and what difference would it make anyway? Corbin was nice, he was good looking and had a great sense of humor, but he lived in Florida and besides, that buzz wasn't there.

"I am in love with someone, but he doesn't feel the same," I explained, pushing my tequila to one side. "He's my boss actually."

I'd never thought of it like that before, but he was. It was Jesse's daughter that I was taking care of, it was his name on my pay check.

"Unrequited?"

I shrugged. "I didn't think so, but he's been away on business for a few days now and I've not heard anything from him."

"Maybe he's busy," Corbin offered.

"Not too busy to talk to his daughter or his family; just me."

I couldn't help the tears that slipped down my cheek. All the emotions that I was feeling, plus alcohol, meant that they were inevitable.

"Hey," Corbin soothed, reaching a thumb out to swipe at my cheek. "Don't cry, he really isn't worth it."

I leaned into Corbin's touch and smiled. "Thank you, I really appreciate it."

"What the fuck is going on?" A voice boomed behind me.

I swivelled on my seat and gasped.

"Oh fuck," Sarah cried. "Call Mulder & Scully, and tell them aliens haven't taken Jesse Connor after all."

CHAPTER 67

♥

JESSE

When I'd gotten home and Mom had told me that Millie was at Rowdy's with Sarah, I knew that I had to go and see her. I needed to tell her right away what I'd decided before I lost my mind and talked myself out of it. Then, when I walked in and saw that douche's hand on her, I was in no doubt that I'd made the right decision.

"Jesse," she gasped. "What are you doing here?"

"To get you and take you home. Now get your things."

My eyes remained on the douche, daring him to say a damn word.

"Sarah," I snapped. "You're coming, too."

"Oh, Jesse," she cried. "Stop being a caveman and sit down and have a drink with us. Trent and Corbin are doing no harm, and Zak and Pop will be here soon to pick me up."

My eyes switched between the two preppy boys. I didn't know which was which, but the one who'd had his hands on Millie looked about ready to say something.

"I wouldn't," I growled. "Nothing you can say will be a good enough explanation as to why you have your hand on my woman."

"Oh for God's sake, Jesse," Millie hissed. "Corbin was just being kind."

"Yeah really, well if being kind is his dick getting hard for you, then good for him, but it stops now."

"Hey man," the Corbin guy said. "She was upset, talking about you."

I looked at Millie questioningly.

"I haven't seen you in four days, and had no contact whatsoever in three. What did you think Jesse? That I'd hire a marching band to celebrate?"

She looked hurt and I saw now that she'd been crying, making me feel like the biggest tool on the planet. That being said, it still didn't explain why *Corbin* felt the need to touch her. Fucking Californian frat boy if ever I saw one.

"We'll talk about that when we get home," I replied, picking up her jacket. "Let's go."

"No," she spat back at me. "I'm staying with Sarah and waiting for Zak."

I huffed a sigh and crossed my arms over my chest. I could see by the look on her face that she was not budging.

"Fine," I sighed. "You mind?" I nodded at Corbin, wanting him to move.

He hesitated at first, but when I took a step closer, he got down from the stool and pushed it towards me. That would have made me happy, but he pulled another one over and sat on it.

"Well this is fucking cozy," I muttered.

"Jesse, stop being an idiot." Millie gave me a look that pretty much told me to shut the fuck up.

The next twenty minutes, while we waited for Zak, were more painful than a tooth extraction. Millie and Corbin tried to continue a civilized conversation, but I have to admit, every time preppy spoke I sighed or rolled my eyes, until in the end he gave up and suggested to Trent that they left.

When he hugged Millie and kissed her cheek, I felt like punching him, but when he offered her a place to stay if she ever went to Florida, I actually pushed up off my seat. If it hadn't been for Zak and his pop arriving, I think there may have been a bar fight. Zak came over to me while Pop went to talk to Sarah's brother, Dusty, at the bar.

"Hey, Jess," Zak said, placing a hand on my shoulder. "How did Booker go?"

"Okay, got the deal I wanted. He's going to take all of them."

"Sheesh, well done, buddy." Zak looked over at Sarah and laughed. She was talking *at* the Trent guy and giving him a hug. "She been flirting with guys for drinks again?"

I looked at him and shook my head. "And that doesn't bother you?"

"No way. I'm betting she told them she was married and had kids, but invited them to sit down and buy her some fancy assed drink anyway. It's me she loves, me she's married to, and it's me she gives unbelievable blow jobs to, so no, it doesn't bother me."

I could not imagine being that cool about Millie asking another man to sit and drink with her.

Zak started laughing. "We're all different buddy, you're a fighter and I'm a pacifist. We love our women hard, but just in a different way, doesn't mean that either of us is wrong. Hey, baby," he called to Sarah who was now cupping Trent's cheek while she spoke to him. "What've you been up to?"

Zak went to join his wife, leaving me watching Millie as she took her turn to say goodbye to Trent. Corbin, thankfully, kept his distance, eyeing me warily. Finally, they were gone and Millie came back over to me, but she was not happy.

"What was that all about?" she snapped, snatching her jacket up and putting it on.

"He had his hands on you," I stated. "And I didn't like it."

"Well you have no right to say whether you like it or not."

I narrowed my eyes and took hold of her hand. "*Excuse me?* I have no right?"

"Yes, you have no right."

296

She bit on her lip and I knew she was desperately trying not to cry, and once again I felt like a shit.

"Baby," I whispered. "I have every damn right. You're mine, I thought I made that clear."

The words almost made me want to punch myself in the balls. Running away and not speaking to her for almost four days was not me making it clear that she was mine. It was the total opposite, but that's exactly what I'd been thinking at the time. Push her away and she'll soon forget about loving me. I didn't want what she was offering, because if I took it, what I'd had with Melody would've been a lie.

It had only taken a three hour drive to make me realize that, but I was such a dickhead I'd waited three more days to tell her. Seeing another man's hand on her was even stronger proof that whatever had been going through my head four days ago was, in fact, a crock of shit. What I'd had with Melody had been different. We'd been younger and she'd been my first love, so it was only natural to grieve for her in the way I had. This with Millie was just as good, it was intense and deep, but it didn't take away from what I'd had before.

Millie's bottom lip trembled and she echoed my own thoughts. "Leaving me is your way of telling me that I'm yours. You're joking right?"

"Nope, never been more serious in my life."

"You fucking pig headed idiot," she cried and slapped my face. "I absolutely hate you."

With that, she turned on her heels and stormed out, leaving me with a smarting cheek.

"I did tell her to slap you next time," Zak laughed. "What did you do this time?"

"Shut up, Zak," Sarah chastised, slapping at his arm. "You need to go after her, Jesse."

"Yeah I know, Sarah. I don't need telling."

"Well, maybe you do, you great big lug. Leaving her here while you go and contemplate your asshole is not the way to show her how you feel. If you don't want her, tell her, and if you

297

do want her, then tell her, because she won't wait forever, Jesse."

"I know that too, Sarah."

I rubbed my cheek and moved towards the door, stopping in my tracks and turning back when Sarah started to talk again.

"You know, some people are not always how they appear," she said, taking hold of Zak's arm and wrapping it around her waist. "But Millie, well she is. She's an open book, Jesse, and what you see is what you get. She loves you, and if she didn't, you'd know it because she'd be honest about it."

Thinking on her words, I gave Sarah and Zak a chin lift, pushed open the door, and went to find what was mine.

CHAPTER 68

♥

MILLIE

I stood on the pavement outside Rowdy's, wondering how the hell I was going to get home. There was a distinct lack of taxis in this stupid place. In fact, I was going to suggest to Garratt that he should start one, as his business. Trouble was, there were probably only a handful of people who would use it; everyone, and I mean *everyone*, around here appeared to have a huge penis replacement truck. I sighed and kicked at a stone. I shouldn't really take my anger at Jesse out on every other resident of Bridge Vale. It was just him who had a penis replacement truck - as decrepit as it was - everyone else's was perfectly acceptable. Actually, not even that was true; there was nothing wrong with the size of his penis. It was more than adequately sized.

"You standing on the sidewalk waiting for me?"

I spun around to see Jesse watching me from Rowdy's doorway.

"No!" I snapped. "I'm looking for a taxi."

"Hate to disappoint you, but you won't get one on a

Wednesday night. Not unless you call an Uber, and I believe I've just seen Bobby knocking back a shot of bourbon. He's the only Uber driver around here"

"Well what sort of businessman is he, drinking when he could be making money?" I grumbled, glancing up the street.

"Like I said, not much call for cabs on a Wednesday night. So, you'd better come home with me."

Jesse started to walk towards his truck that was parked a few feet away.

"You can't just waltz back home and expect me to fall at your feet, you know," I called to his back.

"Didn't expect that for one minute," he replied, not even turning around. "Now get in the truck."

God, he was so damn annoying and I hated that he thought it was okay to treat me like shit and get away with it. Well, he could think again. Yes, I was in love with him, but he'd hurt me and I had some level of pride left.

"I'll get a lift home with you, but that's it," I said, flinging open the creaking passenger door. "I can't bear to speak to you right now."

"Don't need you to speak, Armalita, just need you to listen."

Jesse thrust the truck into drive and sped off down Central Avenue towards home.

***

Considering Jesse had told me that I just needed to listen, he hadn't said a word on the ride home and we were now pulling up next to the house.

I unclipped my seatbelt and moved to open the door, but Jesse's arm shot across me, his hand grabbing the handle.

"I need to say something first," he said, watching me intently.

"I don't want to hear it, Jesse," I sighed. "I'm a little bit drunk and I'm tired, and I'm afraid that if I listen to what you've got to say I may just slap you again."

Jesse chuckled and shook his head. "Seriously, baby, if that's what makes you feel better, then go for it."

"No, Jesse," I replied, my voice cracking. "It wouldn't make me feel better. You've hurt me so many times with your inability to make your damn mind up, I'm not sure I'll ever feel better about you. I understood your issues, I really did, but after what you said the other night, what you heard me say to you, well I thought we were almost on the same page. To then run away and ignore me for days is unacceptable."

Jesse hung his head and moved his hand from the door, dropping it to my thigh. I hated that my body tingled at his touch, and it would have been so easy to have crumbled and given myself over to him again.

"I'm so damn sorry," he finally said. "It was a shitty coward's trick, but I was confused."

"So you keep saying," I muttered.

"But I am, or I was. The last few days have given me a chance to think, and I needed distance from you to be able to do that."

"Don't you see how wrong that was?" I cried, pinching the bridge of my nose, trying to stem the pain that was growing between my eyes. "You should have talked to me. Did you not consider how hurt I would be, you disappearing after I'd told you that I loved you?"

I know I hadn't actually said the three words, but there was no mistaking what I meant when I'd said 'I'm already there'.

"Yep," Jesse breathed out. "I did know, but I was a selfish dick who could only think of himself. I was freaked out about my feelings for you. They're like nothing I've ever felt before, even with Melody."

His voice went quieter as he said her name, and I was in turmoil again. I understood that he was still grieving, but I was so over being compared to her and having her damn saintliness pushed in my face.

"The thing is," he said, taking my hand in his. "That scared the shit out of me. What sort of person was I, if I felt like this about a woman I'd only known for a couple of months? What sort of person was I, if I'd treated my daughter and my family like shit for two years because I was grieving for a woman who I could replace so easily?"

"Believe me, Jesse," I sighed. "There is nothing easy about me and you, about being in love with you."

"I did tell you that, Millie. I said it'd be hard and that I'd probably fuck things up."

"Yes, I know," I cried. "But you still shouldn't have ignored me. All you had to do was say 'I'm struggling, Millie, I just need a couple of days'. Instead you disappear, make it obvious it's because of me, and then stroll back in acting like *He Man* and scaring off someone who was just being nice to me."

Jesse's breathing got heavier and his grip on my hand tightened. "I didn't like how he was touching you and looking at you."

"Well tough fucking luck," I yelled, pulling my hand away. "I can't talk to you, Jesse. I'm so hurt, you have no idea."

"Please, baby, I do, but I just want you to know that I've come to terms with everything. I realize that feeling this way about you doesn't mean what I felt about Melody wasn't real. I'm ready to move on."

I was done. My blood was pumping loud in my ears and I could feel the anger emanating from every one of my pores.

"You know what, Jesse," I said in a measured tone. "I'm really pleased for you, and so glad that *you're* ready to move on, but maybe I'm not anymore. I deserve to be treated better than that. I may not be Melody, but that doesn't mean I should be treated like shit, just because I'm first reserve."

I flung open the truck door and jumped down. As I stalked towards the porch steps, I heard Jesse shouting my name, begging me to come back, but the way I felt at that moment, I wasn't sure I would ever turn around and go back to him.

CHAPTER 69

♥

JESSE

"Fuck," I snarled, kicking at the hub cap of my back wheel. I had really messed up this time. Well, she could argue all she liked; she was mine and I was going to prove to her that we should be together.

CHAPTER 70

♥

MILLIE

The next few days, after Jesse came home from Booker, I managed to avoid him. It was really easy to do as he was busy, having taken on a couple more horses to work with. They took up all his time and he didn't sit down for dinner until after he'd put Addy to bed. I would then escape to my room to read, and usually cry.

Brandon came back early from his business trip; apparently, it hadn't gone as well as he'd been hoping. The trip had been to get some big travel company in Chicago to put his parent's guest ranch on their 'preferred list', but the facilities weren't to their standard. Brandon had come back with a long list of improvements that were needed, and the temper of a grizzly bear with a stomach ache, according to Bonnie. I also knew this because he'd snapped my head off when I'd asked how the trip had gone. Ted told me not to take any heed, while Garratt threatened to punch him for being so rude to me.

Obviously, Jesse and I having to talk to Brandon about 'us' was no longer necessary, but I knew that once Brandon cheered up, if he asked me out again, I'd have to be honest and tell him that I wasn't interested. Until I could erase Jesse from my heart, I was staying well and truly away from men. The problem with that was, I wasn't sure I'd ever be able to stop loving him.

Addy seemed unaware of the fact that Jesse and I weren't really conversing, which was good. I would hate to think that she was affected by our fall out; she didn't need any more upheaval. On the couple of occasions where I'd been with her and Jesse had appeared, I'd been civil to him for her sake, and then made myself busy elsewhere. She was a bright child, though, so I wasn't sure how long it would be before she started asking questions about why we hadn't been on another date. But, that was something that we'd have to deal with when it happened, because I really wasn't at a point where I could sit down and discuss it calmly with Jesse.

Life was therefore continuing, as best as it could when you had a broken heart, but I had a job to do. Which was why I was currently calf deep in pond water while Addy sat on the grass giggling.

"It's not funny, Addy," I groaned, pulling my face into a grimace. "It's all slimy."

Addy and I had watched a video on YouTube about the things that live on plants and in pond water, and she'd found it so fascinating that I'd bought her a microscope so that she could look at things more closely. It was only a child's version, but she was really excited when it arrived earlier in the day, and was insistent that we collect some pond water and plants.

"You look funny," she giggled. "Your nose is all screwed up."

"That's because it smells. Oh my goodness, it's horrible."

"Daddy, look at Millie!"

I lifted my head to see Jesse, standing on the grass bank behind Addy, with his hands on his hips and a stupid grin on his face.

"What in the Sam Hill are you doing?" he asked with a deep belly laugh.

"We're getting water bugs to look at," Addy explained, looking up at her father. "Millie got me a micropoke."

Jesse inclined his head to one side and looked at her questioningly. "A what?"

"A microscope," I said.

"A microscope? Wow." Jesse looked at me wide eyed.

"That's what I said," Addy grumbled. "A micropoke."

"You didn't have to do that," Jesse said softly.

"It's just a kid's one. It's good, but it wasn't too expensive."

"Even so." He tapped a finger on Addy's head. "I hope you said thank you, baby."

Addy nodded vehemently. "I did, Daddy, and I gave Millie a big kiss."

"A big kiss, hey? You're one lucky girl." Jesse's eyes shone brightly as he took a step closer to the pond.

"I know, I've never had a micropoke before."

Jesse's lips twitched and we both knew he hadn't been talking about the microscope.

"We'd better get washed up for lunch," I said breathily, pulling my gaze away from Jesse.

I tried to take a step forward, but couldn't move. The mud at the bottom of the pond, pulled on my foot, like a hungry baby sucking on a bottle – it wouldn't let go.

"What's wrong?" Jesse asked as I cursed under my breath.

"I'm stuck," I ground out, as I tried once more to pull my foot out of the mud.

"What do you mean, you're stuck?" Jesse asked with a hint of laughter.

"Exactly that, what do you think it means, you idiot?" I hissed at him with my nostrils flaring.

"You can't be." He was full out laughing now, as he took off his Stetson and plonked it onto Addy's head. "Baby, go and get Grandpa, ask him to bring some rope."

"I'm not being roped out of here like a damn cow!" I protested, stamping my foot that wasn't stuck. Water splashed up at me and then…

"Your other one is stuck now, isn't it?" Jesse bit on his lip and then doubled over, letting out a deep rumbling laugh. "Go, baby, get Grandpa."

"Okay, Daddy." Addy skipped off, pushing Jesse's hat to the back of her head.

"This is not funny, Jesse," I snapped, trying to move again.

"I think you'll find it is." Shaking his head, he sat down on the bank, kicked off his boots and socks and started to roll up his jeans. "Don't move, I'm coming to get you."

His head dropped back and he let out another laugh.

"I hate you!"

"Yeah, I know, sweetness, so you've said," Jesse replied with amusement as he stood up. "So you can either let me help or Dad can wrangle you like a cow. Which one, Armalita?"

Letting out a loud huff, I held my hands out to indicate my decision.

"Good choice," he replied with a shit eating grin.

"What if you get stuck, though?" I asked as Jesse stepped into the water.

"I won't, but if I do, Dad can wrangle us both."

When he reached me, Jesse took hold of my hands in his, rubbing his thumbs over the backs of them. I tried to tug my hands free, but Jesse held firm.

"I guess I have you just where I want you now," he said softly. "You're going to have to listen to me."

"No, I don't." I pouted, averting my eyes from his gorgeous Atlantic blue ones. They were just too mesmerizing and made me do and say things that I didn't want to.

"Look at me," he commanded.

"No, I don't need to look at you for you to pull me out of here."

I knew that I was acting like a child, but being so close to him was making my body fizz with excitement; looking at him would have just pushed me over the edge that I was already so close to.

"Armalita, I said look at me." His tone was deep and controlled, dripping with masculinity.

I looked at him and...I wanted to cry. I was right, just seeing his strong, square jaw and his long, straight nose with the tiny bump in it, made me melt like snow in a spring thaw. He was perfection to me and I knew then that I would never get over him.

"What?" I asked on a swallow.

Jesse reached up and pushed a strand of my hair away from my face. "You are so damn beautiful," he whispered, his fingertips tracing the line of my jaw.

"Jesse, stop." My lie was thick with emotion, because no matter what words came from my mouth, I never wanted him to stop saying those things, or touching me in that way.

No matter how much I tried to forget him, it wasn't going to happen. He had my heart.

"You need to listen to what I have to say."

I held my breath, trying to stop the tears, but seemingly I had no control over them. Jesse wiped at a tear that trickled slowly from the corner of my eye. "Please, listen."

I nodded slowly and this time gave a long exhale; fortifying myself against the words that could break me, or make me whole again.

"I know I've gone about this all the wrong way. Running away to Booker wasn't right…"

I was about to agree, but Jesse shook his head.

"Just let me talk, then you can let loose on my ass, okay?" he asked with a sweet smile.

"Okay."

"Running away to Booker wasn't right," he continued, wiping away more moisture from my cheeks. "But the last time I did this sort of thing I was seventeen and thought I was the best thing to walk this damn earth. I had no fears about anything, all I cared about was what I wanted, and that was Melody."

My breath instinctively hitched at the name of the woman who truly had his heart. Jesse heard it and dropped a sweet kiss to my lips and I hated myself for being jealous of a dead woman. A dead woman who'd loved him a long time before I ever had.

"We were kids, Millie. I wanted her, she wanted me, and life was simple. Then Addy came along and I loved Melody even more, for giving me the best thing I'd ever had in the world. My heart was full of her and Addy. I had a beautiful baby and wife, and I treasured them both. When she died, I never thought I'd get over it, I thought I'd drown in the grief that suffocated me a little bit more each day and I didn't care. I wanted to die."

I let out a shuddering gasp and clasped a hand to my mouth.

"Jesse, no," I sobbed quietly, the tears moving faster now.

"Please, let me say this." He took a deep breath before continuing. "Death was all I wanted, because I couldn't see how I would ever find joy in the day ever again. Not even Addy could make me want to carry on, so what sort of father did that make me? It got to a point I couldn't even touch her, because I felt like I didn't deserve her. If I loved her like a father should, I wouldn't want to leave her alone, without any parents, but that's how I felt and I hate myself for it."

"Grief makes us feel so many different things though, Jesse. You weren't to blame."

"I know, but that's how I felt."

With my body wracked with emotion and the coldness of the water, I started to shiver, and wrapped an arm around my waist. Jesse pulled me to his chest and rubbed my back with his big hands. After a short time, he let me go and tugged his shirt over his head, leaving himself in a thin wife-beater.

"Here, put this on." He dropped it over my head and held tight onto my waist as I pushed my arms through. "Better?"

I nodded. "Thank you."

Jesse looked over his shoulder, and I guessed it was for Ted, but there was no sign. He turned back and carried on talking.

"When I picked you up at the airport, I hated how you made me feel. From the minute I saw you, I wanted you. You were so damn beautiful, like a new born calf with your big brown eyes and skittishness."

I giggled amidst a sob. "A calf? I'm not sure that's much of a compliment. And I was not skittish."

"Firstly, you *were* skittish. I thought you were going to puke when you saw me, and secondly, I love my cattle and there is nothing more beautiful than a calf with big eyes and long lashes."

"Okay, maybe I'll take your compliment, but if I looked like I was going to 'puke' as you so nicely put it, it was because I fancied the pants off you."

Jesse's brow furrowed.

"I thought you were cute."

He laughed and shook his head. "Okay, I'll take *your* compliment too. What I'm trying to say is, right from the off you made me question everything I'd thought and done over the last two years. The more time I spent with you, the less I thought about Melody, and the less it hurt, and so, the guiltier I felt; that's why I pushed you away. Then that night after we'd been to Rowdy's, and I sang to you, well I..." He looked up at the cloudless blue sky and sighed. "Well that night I knew how I felt about you. I lied when I said I was falling, Millie. I'd already fallen from a great fucking height, and it scared the shit out of me; made me question the sort of man I was. In two months, you'd wiped away most of the pain and hurt, and I felt things for you that I'd never felt before, ever."

Knowing that he meant Melody, I understood the sadness that must have brought to him; thinking that he'd betrayed her. But, hearing his words of realisation, made my hopes for a future with him soar.

"I felt all that, yet had spent two years treating my daughter, my parents, my brother, and everyone I knew like shit because I'd lost the love of my life."

I couldn't help but stiffen as the stab of jealousy hit my stomach again, and self-hatred reared its head once more.

"But she wasn't, was she?" he whispered, dropping a soft kiss to my forehead as he gripped my shoulders.

"What?" I held my breath as I looked up at him through my lashes. "Jesse?"

"She wasn't the love of my life, Armalita. If she was, I wouldn't love you as damn much as I do. I couldn't rest without you near me when I was in Booker. Every day it was like being stuck in this damn pond," he gave a quiet laugh and looked down at the water. "I was trying to move and not getting anywhere, because you weren't there. I couldn't eat, I couldn't sleep, all I could do was think about you and how I wasn't complete without you. I realized that what I had with Melody was different than what I had with you, and while I was grieving for her passing, I was also grieving for the life that I thought we were going to have. You know something though?"

"What?" I asked on a sniffle, as his words tugged at my heart again.

"I loved her, I did, but my greatest loss was the idea of what I thought she had been. She wasn't the woman that was up here," he said, tapping at the side of his head. "She wasn't the Melody who I loved at seventeen, who loved me to distraction because I was the basketball captain and Prom King who loved her back. She was a different woman."

"She still loved you, though," I stated. "And you still loved her, despite her being different."

"Yeah, I did. But, you see, all Melody ever wanted was someone who doted on her, someone who worshipped her from sunrise through to sunset. And I did, until Addy came along, which for Melody meant I didn't love her enough. I can see now that my sharing my heart between her and Addy wasn't enough for Melody."

I chewed on my bottom lip and looked at him warily. His words backed up what Garratt and Bonnie had said, but it wasn't for me to agree with him. I didn't even know Melody, but what I knew of her she didn't cherish her family enough.

"I guess being so busy, trying to build a life for us, I never realized until now. Now, I can look back and see what our life, our love, should've been like. Addy should've been her first priority, and she wasn't, and because of Addy, she couldn't love me like I loved her. But you," he said with a sigh. "You love me like that, Armalita. You love me unconditionally, even when I've been an idiot and you're screaming at me, it's because you love me. And I do know you love me, even after I've hurt you so damn much."

Jesse gazed at me, and his lips turned up into a soft smile as he brushed my hair from my face. I smiled back and let my tears track down my cheeks and drop off the end of my chin.

"You know what the best part of all this is, though? It's that you love Addy like that, too. You put her first, always, even though she's not your child. You didn't want me to leave her on the night you got lost, in case she needed me. That was the first time I'd admitted how I felt about you, yet you put her before your wants and needs. You've risked your own feelings where I'm concerned by putting me straight on her, and how she needed me. You didn't care whether I never spoke to you again, as long as I treated Addy right. And, these last few days, I know you've been avoiding me and maybe that was to save your own heart, but I'm *damn* sure it's because you don't want Addy upset. You love her like her mother should've and you love me the same way. That, Armalita Braithwaite," he said on a shaky exhale, "is why I fucking love you with all my heart, and why I'm not letting you go."

Without thinking of anything else except for how much I loved him, I pushed myself into Jesse's embrace, winding my arms around his neck and kissing him. My momentum took me forward and released my feet. Jesse yelled and clung to me as he fell backwards, taking us both into the water.

"Shit," he cried. "That's fucking freezing."

"I'm sorry," I spluttered as I lay on top of him. "At least I'm not stuck anymore."

He wrapped his arms around me and craned his neck up to kiss me. "No, sweetness, you're not stuck anymore." He kissed me hard and one hand went to my bum, giving it a squeeze. "Fuck, I love you."

"I know," I gasped, breathlessly.

"Hey, I'm guessing you don't need the ropes."

I looked up and Jesse tilted his head back, to see Ted standing on the grass, a thick rope wrapped around his shoulder.

"Daddy, you're kissing," Addy cried. "So, do you love Millie yet?"

Jesse looked at me and nodded. "Yeah, baby, I do."

I wouldn't have any brain cells left at this rate.

CHAPTER 71

♥

JESSE

Millie and I were in my cabin, having spent the night there, the third night we had since we'd finally sorted things out and I'd told her I loved her. Okay, it hadn't been the most romantic of settings, in a stinking pond, but the sentiment was there.

Mom and Dad had been great about us getting together, and every couple of nights listened out for Addy while we stayed in the cabin. It wasn't going to be a long term thing, and I'd said no at first, Addy was my priority, but they'd insisted. Mom said she understood me not wanting Addy to find us in bed together just yet, but Millie and I should have some time together, alone. The nights we didn't sleep in the cabin, I stayed in Millie's bed for a couple of hours, setting an alarm to make sure I didn't fall asleep in there all night. We also had Addy's old baby monitor set up, that way if she did wake I could get to her before she found us. It wasn't ideal, because I wanted Millie with me all night, but we agreed we needed to do this carefully to make sure Addy didn't get upset or hurt, any more than I already had. Something that still filled me with guilt.

As Millie shifted next to me in the bed, I tightened my arm around her, not wanting her to move even an inch away from me. I'd taken my time vocalising how I was feeling, but now I had, I was beyond pussy whipped. She made me feel seventeen again, the knot of excitement in my belly every time I saw her, and feeling of anxiousness when she wasn't around. Yep, it had taken me a while to get to the party, but now that I was, I wasn't fucking leaving any time soon; I was going to be the last one on that damn dancefloor.

"Hmm, morning," Millie moaned in a sexy rasp laced with sleep.

She yawned and stretched, her beautiful tits popping out from the comforter. Not one to miss a chance, I leaned over and took her nipple in my mouth.

"Hey," she said on a giggle. "No boob action until you promise me something."

"Really, baby, you sure?" I groaned, giving her nipple one last lick.

I knew what she wanted me to promise, because it was the last thing we'd talked about the night before. Just before I'd fucked her so hard, twice, that she'd fallen asleep, pretty much straight after her last orgasm.

"I promise I'll speak to him today," I groaned, making a grab for her.

Millie rolled away and pushed a pillow between us to create a barrier. "No, you need to say the words; 'I promise to talk to Brandon today about me and Millie being a couple'."

I groaned again and sat up, my back against the headboard. "Okay, for you." I coughed to clear my throat. "I promise to talk to Brandon today about me and Millie being a couple, and me loving her so hard I can't damn breathe when she's not around."

Millie whimpered and the next minute straddled me and rode me like an experienced cowgirl.

CHAPTER 72

♥

MILLIE

I was in Ted's study, replying to emails from Javi and some ex-colleagues while listening to a music streaming service, when the door creaked open. I knew it wasn't Addy as she had gone to the library and then for ice cream with Bonnie and Ruby, while Ted had gone into Knightingale with Garratt for his final interview at the bank for the Management program. I knew, therefore, it had to be Jesse, so the grin I sported was huge.

As the first notes of the piano on Des'ree's *'I'm Kissing You'* started, the door clicked shut and I felt his presence behind me. Without saying anything, he reached around me and turned up the volume on Ted's computer. I turned my head up to look at him, and was greeted with the most intense gaze; one that told me, without words, exactly how he felt. My own emotions bared to Jesse, I gave him a shy smile and swallowed.

As Des'ree started to sing, Jesse dropped his head and started to kiss along my shoulder. They were open mouthed kisses with the tip of his tongue seductively tickling my skin, moving up to

NIKKI ASHTON

my neck and back down to my shoulder. While his lips trailed a hot path, he pushed my t-shirt off my shoulder, and let his hand dip inside it, and into my lace bra to gently caress my breast. His fingertips were at my shoulder, digging into my skin, as his kiss moved to the top of my spine. The intensity of the moment took my breath away, and created a fire in the pit of my belly.

"Jesse," I whispered.

Jesse remained silent as he licked up my neck until he reached my earlobe and nipped it with his teeth. With one hand still playing with my breast and the other squeezing my shoulder, Jesse's mouth moved back to my neck where he dropped butterfly kisses. The hand on my breast moved to grab my ponytail, with Jesse giving it a gentle pull to give him access to the other side of my neck. The kisses became more intense, his lips putting more pressure on my electrified skin as his arm dropped to wrap around me, just under my breast, his thumb skimming over my nipple. Stretching my body up, I moved my head around, desperately searching for his mouth. As I pulled on his lip, my fingertips feathered over his jaw and Jesse's breathe hitched, his grip on my hair, while still tender, tightening. He moved his mouth from mine and kissed along my jaw, turning my head away from him. He pulled the band out of my hair, letting it fall down my back, before lacing his fingers through it, pulling it aside to suck on my neck. The marking of my skin caused a heavenly mix of pleasure and pain, and I couldn't help but gasp out Jesse's name.

I had never felt so desired in all my life, as heat pooled between my legs. Arching my back to try and ease the ache that the fire within me was causing, I licked my lips and moaned. Jesse reached around and, taking my chin in his thumb and forefinger, pulled my mouth back to his and kissed me. He took me captive, his kiss a perfect balance of soft and hard, before sucking on my bottom lip. While the music played on, he went back to kissing me, and his arm moved to wrap around my shoulder and across my chest, his hand over my heart, feeling every beat, before dropping and fondling my breast over my t-shirt. He kissed along

316

my jaw, back to my neck, and the hand that had held my chin gathered up my hair, allowing him access to the back of my neck. My head dropped forward and I bit down on my bottom lip as Jesse accompanied each kiss with a squeeze of my breast. His teeth nipped at my skin and each bite was soothed with a tender kiss as his breathing got heavier. The hand at my chest slipped inside my t-shirt and his thumb rubbed a rhythm across the swell of my breast. Jesse's tongue swirled over my skin, and his fingers worshiped me with their reverent touch, as my body yielded to him. His hand moved from my chin, closing lightly around my neck, maneuvering my face up to his so he could kiss me, hard and deep. Then he was holding my shoulder, his grip strong as he kissed between my shoulder blades, the touch of his lips making me shudder with desire. As the song built to its climax, the music getting louder and the piano faster, Jesse's kisses got more intense and his arm around me got tighter, and he wound my hair around his hand. Then, following the journey of the music, his kisses became feather light and his hand lifted from my breast to cup my face. As Des'ree's voice got softer, nearing the end of the song, Jesse turned my mouth to his again and went to kiss me, before pulling away with a grin. As I reached up, desperate for his mouth, he dropped a sweet kiss on my lips, giving me a beautiful smile. He leaned forward, took my hair band from the desk where he'd placed it, pulled my hair into a pony tail, and secured it.

As the song finished, he reached forward and I felt his breath at my ear and tried to calm myself. It was no use; I was too close to the precipice to regain my balance.

"I love you," he whispered, before leaving the room and closing the door quietly behind him.

CHAPTER 73

♥

JESSE

As we walked into Rowdy's, I felt ten feet tall. Millie looked beautiful and sexy as all hell. She was dressed in skin tight leather pants and a skimpy little blouse that it was impossible to be wearing a bra with; not exactly the usual attire for the women of Bridge Vale, but she wore it damn well. Her blouse was bright red, with tiny straps and the back was real low; so low in fact, that if she wasn't wearing pants I'd probably be able to see the top of that perfect ass of hers, but don't get me started on the ass. Her pants were so tight, I was hard just wondering whether she was wearing any underwear at all.

Then there was that beautiful raven hair that she'd styled in loose curls; it almost touched her ass when it was straight, and I loved it. Loved wrapping it around my hand when she was beneath me. Loved everything about her to be truthful, so no wonder my jeans were uncomfortable; I'd turned into a walking hard on since she'd become mine.

That thought – her being mine – was the best feeling ever, but it kinda worried me, too. It meant that I had to talk to Brandon. He'd only done one day on the ranch since he'd come back from Chicago, as he'd been trying to sort his folk's place out. That meant we'd been able to keep our relationship on the down low, but I'd have to tell him sooner rather than later. He may be my best buddy, and I didn't want to hurt him, but I wouldn't tolerate him asking Millie out on any more damn dates.

"Jess," Garratt called over his shoulder. "What do you want to drink?"

We'd given Garratt a lift into town as he was meeting up with some buddies and going to a house party later. He'd thought he'd been funny and sat in the front seat of the truck, so that Millie had to sit in the back. I'd soon put him straight and practically dragged him out by his ear. He'd been laughing so much I think he nearly wet his pants. It was good to see him laugh; shit it was good to laugh *with* him because we hadn't done much of that for a while. The little fucker got payback though, when I'd subjected him to a show earlier, while waiting at a stop light when coming into town. I'd leaned across to kiss Millie, making sure it was long and hard and had plenty of tongue. Garratt said he was going to barf, but I knew how happy he was for us really.

"Get me a Coors Light," I said, and then turned to Millie. "What about you, sweetness?"

"I'll have a beer, too," she replied with a gorgeous bright smile. "It's kind of growing on me."

"Beer for Millie, Garr. So, what do you drink back home?" I asked, ignoring the sick feeling when I thought of her 'back home'.

"Prosecco."

"We have that here, if you'd prefer it." I moved to tap Garratt's shoulder, but Millie pulled me back.

"No, seriously, beer is good. I really quite like it and it makes me feel like a local."

She grinned at me and gave a little wink, sending my heart in a tailspin.

"You like being a local, then?" I asked, taking one of her curls in my fingers and pulling on it.

"Yeah," she said with a hint of surprise, pulling her shoulders back and tilting her head. "I do."

"Well, that's good, but I have to say, you're too fucking sexy to be a local." My breath stalled as I raked my gaze over her. "Shit, Armalita, you're going to kill me."

"I am. Why?" she pouted.

"Because," I replied, moving my mouth close to her ear. "I'm not sure that it's healthy having every drop of blood rushing to my dick all the time."

"Jesse!" She pushed at my shoulder, a huge grin on her face.

Taking hold of her hand, I pulled her to me and dropped a kiss on her smiling lips.

"You look beautiful," I said, my hand moving down to her ass.

Then, without any warning, she pulled away from me and took two steps back. Her eyes were wide and her gaze was somewhere over my shoulder.

"Baby?" I turned to see where she was looking. "Fuck, Brandon," I cursed under my breath.

"Jesse, what do we do?" Millie hissed. "I told you we should have told him."

"Well, he's going to find out now," I muttered.

Millie shook her head. "No way, he's not finding out like this."

"Well what else do you suggest I do?" I looked towards Brandon, who was talking to Bobby Sloane, the owner of the department store.

Millie looked at Garratt, who was still at the bar, and then back to me. "We don't say anything, except that we've all come out together. I'll go and stand with Garratt."

"Nuh uh," I grunted. "You're not standing six feet away from me all night. Let's just tell him."

"Jesse, no. That's not fair on him. I don't think for one minute he'll be too upset, but even so, he's made it clear he likes me."

I let out a long breath and looked down at the floor, my hands fisted at my hips. She was right, it wasn't fair to tell him like this. Brandon was my oldest friend, and I owed him more respect than to just let it out by kissing her senseless in front of him. Anyone else, I wouldn't give a shit, she was mine and everyone needed to know that, but Brandon deserved to be told in private. Hopefully, Millie was right and he wouldn't be too upset. They'd only been on one date, for fuck's sake – the double date with me and Addy at the fair didn't count – so maybe he'd take it okay. But, looking at the beautiful, sexy woman who was now staring me down, I think I'd be pissed as all hell if I was in his shoes.

"Okay," I breathed out. "But if he so much as touches you in a way I don't like, I'm telling him. Agreed?"

Millie looked over my shoulder and was suddenly panic stricken. "Okay, agreed. He's coming over."

She scooted over to Garratt who was on his way back with our drinks. Garratt stopped in his tracks and stared at her. Millie rolled up on her tiptoes and whispered into Garratt's ear. He looked over and burst out laughing. I still had no idea what that little fucker's problem was with Brandon. Three years of hating each other over a game of damn cards was just stupid.

Brandon appeared at my side at exactly the same time as Garratt and Millie. Brandon slapped me on the shoulder, Garratt practically growled at him, and Millie begged me with her eyes not to say anything. Me, well, I grabbed my beer from Garratt and took a long swig.

321

CHAPTER 74

♥

MILLIE

As Brandon slapped Jesse's shoulder, I stared at Jesse, hoping that he wouldn't say anything; not at that moment anyway. Thankfully, Jesse simply took a drink of his beer and grinned around the lip of the bottle.

"Hey, Jess." Brandon smiled tightly. "You didn't say you were coming here tonight."

"Didn't realize that he had to tell you his every move," Garratt muttered, turning to look around the room.

"Garr!" Jesse warned. "Leave it."

"Ah, fuck this. I'm going to speak to Poppy and Marnie, see if they fancy going to the party," Garratt replied and shoved past Brandon, barging shoulders with him.

"What is the problem with that little fucker?" Brandon complained, watching Garratt cross the room to two girls who were giggling in a corner.

"He just can't forget your game of cards, buddy. You bled him dry and he thinks you cheated doing it." Jesse inclined his head and gave Brandon a wry smile. "So, did you?"

A rush of crimson travelled up Brandon's neck as he shook his head. "You know I wouldn't fucking do that, Jess."

"It's been three years, Brandon, so you must have done something to get up his ass crack."

"He just hates losing," Brandon muttered, turning his head towards the bar. "You need a drink, either of you?"

We both shook our heads and watched as Brandon stalked away.

"They really hate each other don't they?" I gasped.

"Ah, they're just both stubborn," Jesse said with a short laugh. "It's about time they sorted things out. Acting like a pair of kids."

"Somehow that doesn't look like it's going to happen." I looked over at Garratt, who had one of the girls hanging onto him and whispering in his ear. "Not tonight anyway."

Jesse followed my gaze and shook his head. "That's the last we'll see of Garr tonight. I'm guessing he'll be taking both of them to the party with him, unless they decide to enjoy a more intimate party, just for the three of them."

"Garratt wouldn't do that would he?" I asked, astonished.

Jesse grinned and took another swig of his beer. "My brother is not as quiet as you may think, baby. Let's just say that he made more of his high school years than I ever did."

"He had lots of girlfriends?"

"Wouldn't call them girlfriends as such," Jesse laughed. "More like hook ups. He's the only math nerd that I know that had more girls than the school football and basketball captains added together; and that was just senior year."

My mouth opened in shock. Garratt was a good looking boy and I could see why girls would be attracted, but he appeared to be someone who would prefer to have a serious relationship. He'd looked really upset when he'd told me about his college girlfriend, Jemma.

"I just assumed he was a good boy," I said, now watching Garratt being kissed within an inch of his life by the taller of the two girls.

"He is; he's respectful and polite when he tells them goodbye the next morning. And every single one of them stays his friend. They adore him and all send him Christmas and birthday cards; he gets dozens of them in the mail every year."

I opened and closed my mouth like a ventriloquist dummy.

"Oh, come on Armalita, he's twenty-one years old, he should be enjoying himself."

"I know," I replied turning back to Jesse. "I just didn't think he'd be a manwhore, one night stand sort of man."

Jesse started to laugh. "I don't think he'd call himself a manwhore. I think I've heard him call himself a 'generous love giver'."

We both turned towards Garratt, and burst out laughing as we saw him still kissing one girl, while holding hands with the other.

"What are you two laughing at?" Brandon asked, as he arrived back from the bar.

"Oh, nothing," Jesse said on a sigh.

"Must be something." Brandon looked from Jesse to me expectantly. "Or is it a private *little* joke."

Jesse furrowed his brow as he looked over the top of his bottle at his friend. Brandon stared him down, an angry fire in his eyes.

"No," Jesse replied. "It's not private, we were just laughing about Garratt so I didn't think you'd be interested."

"Yeah well, there ain't much about Garratt that amuses me." Brandon took a drink of his beer, his lip curling into a snarl.

Jesse opened his mouth about to say something, but suddenly closed it again, evidently sensing that it was better to keep quiet.

We stood in silence for a few minutes, and it was not a comfortable quiet. Jesse and Brandon were pointedly looking at opposite sides of the room, while I stood in the middle of them, not really sure what to do or say. Finally, Brandon broke the silence when he turned to me.

"How come you're out with Jesse?" he asked, pointing at each of us with his bottle. "Thought you two didn't really care for one another."

I shifted uncomfortably on the spot and quickly glanced at

Jesse, willing him to rescue me.

"We called a truce," Jesse replied, trying to sound nonchalant. "Plus, we couldn't stand Auntie Ruby's farting much longer, so the three of us decided to get out of the house."

Brandon nodded his head in acceptance of Jesse's explanation. "Right." Then we were back to silence.

"You want another beer, swee…Millie?" Jesse asked, correcting himself with a quick grimace.

"Erm, yes please." I passed him my empty bottle and glared at him, warning him to not only be as quick as possible, but also to ensure he didn't slip up with any more pet names.

"I'll check on Garratt," he said. "But he'll probably be going soon."

I gave a nervous giggle and looked over at Garratt and the two girls.

"He's a dark horse," I said to Brandon, desperately making small talk. "I had no idea he was such a ladies man."

Brandon gave a quick look over his shoulder and turned back to me with a sneer. "You know those Connor boys," he said. "Real hit with the girls; both of them."

Jealousy almost had me spitting out that Jesse wasn't like that, not anymore, but I bit back the words and gave Brandon an understanding smile.

"Must say you look damn good tonight, Millie." Brandon's tone didn't match his words. He might have been complimenting me, but his voice was hard and cold. His eyes grazed slowly up and down my body, and it struck me; he knew about me and Jesse.

"Thanks, Brandon." I crossed my arms over my chest, wondering whether I should just ask him outright.

Brandon reached out a hand and took a strand of my hair, holding it between his fingertips.

"Like how you've done your hair, too."

I swallowed hard and glanced towards the bar, thankful that Jesse had his back to us. I took one step back, and Brandon let my curl drop from his hand.

"Anyways," he said, around a drink of beer. "We never did have another proper date. Maybe we should go somewhere tomorrow. I'll take you out for a drive, how about it?"

He definitely knew and was trying to make me squirm; it was working.

"I don't think so, Brandon. I really like you as a friend, but…"

"Hah, fuck, Millie," he interrupted. "You're really going to do the old 'I like you as a friend' shit? Come on now, you ain't really given us much chance have you?"

"I'm sorry, Brandon, but I'm just not looking for that sort of relationship with you."

He gave a hollow laugh. "Ah, come on, just be honest with me."

"I am," I protested, desperately willing Jesse back from the bar.

"But you ain't, are you? Not really. You're kinda being a little bit economical with the truth."

"Brandon," I pleaded, not really sure what to say to him.

Brandon lurched forward and took my face in his hand, his thumb rubbing along my cheek.

"I would be so much better for you than him," he hissed. "He'll make your life a fucking misery, working all hours on that damn ranch and not giving a shit about you. Look at what he's been like with Addy, and she's his flesh and blood. You ain't anything but a convenient fuck for him, Millie."

Any sympathy I felt for him vanished at that moment.

"How dare you?" I gasped. "You have no idea what our relationship is like."

"Yeah, and why's that? Because you sneaky fuckers kept it from me," he snarled, dropping his hand from my face.

"But you and I had one date, it's not as though I'd promised you anything."

Brandon looked me up and down as though I was dirt, and shook his head. "You have no fucking idea about him. You've known him five damn minutes, I've known him nearly all my life."

"Yes and you're supposed to be best friends." I moved to walk past him, but Brandon caught hold of my arm, gripping it tightly. "Let me go."

"Not until you've heard all about your precious Jesse," he hissed.

That was when all hell broke loose. I heard Garratt before I saw him, pushing through the crowd.

"Don't you touch her, you slimy fucker!"

He manhandled people to one side, trying to get to us, but before he did, Brandon was swung around by his shoulder.

"Get your fucking hands off her."

Jesse pulled at Brandon's shirt, dragging him into his space so that their faces were inches apart.

"You touch her like that again and I don't care whether you're my best friend or not, I'll fucking end you!" Jesse's voice was cold and controlled, and there was no doubt that he meant what he said.

"Whatever, Jesse." Brandon pushed away from Jesse and turned to look at me. "You'll always be second best, just a convenient fuck, like I said."

That was when Jesse swung Brandon around and punched him square on the nose. Blood splattered everywhere, dotting my face and arms and spraying a few locals standing close by. People stopped, their drinks hanging midway to their mouths, as they watched Brandon stagger backwards. He dropped his bottle on the floor with a crash, beer washing the wooden boards as Jesse grabbed him, stopping him from falling.

"Jesse!" Garratt cried as Jesse pulled his fist back again. "Leave him. Just get Millie out of here."

Jesse stopped and looked at me, and then at Brandon. He pushed Brandon away, letting him drop onto his backside onto the floor. He stepped over him and pulled me into his arms.

"You okay?" he whispered against my hair.

I nodded and stared over his shoulder at everyone in the bar. Having stopped to watch Brandon and Jesse's argument, they were now drinking and talking again, as though nothing had happened. Scuffles between best friends, evidently, weren't enough to stop beer being drunk around Bridge Vale. Garratt was looking down at Brandon, his jaw clenched and his hands fisted at his sides.

"You're a fucking cock sucker," he snarled and spat at Brandon.

"Garratt," I gasped. "Don't!"

Garratt looked up at me with hatred swimming in his eyes, his chest heaving with emotion. "He fucking deserves it."

Jesse pushed me from his body and looked down at me. "Don't listen to a damn word he says. You know that's not how it is, don't you?" He bit on his bottom lip as he waited for me to answer.

"I know," I said quietly. "Please, just take me home."

"Garr?" He turned to look at Garratt over his shoulder.

Garratt shook his head. "I'm going to stay. Just get her home."

"Please, Garratt, don't do anything silly," I begged, looking down at Brandon who was still on the floor. He was lying on his side, propped on one elbow, his eyes firmly on the ground.

"He's not worth it," Garratt sighed. "I promise, for you, Millie."

"Come on, baby." Jesse leaned in and kissed me gently before leading me on shaky legs out of Rowdy's and to the truck.

When we got into the truck, Jesse turned in his seat and took my hand in his, rubbing it gently.

"Talk to me," he begged. "Please tell me you don't believe a word he said."

"I don't, but it was still humiliating."

"I know, and I'm sorry. It shouldn't have happened."

"No, it shouldn't have," I sighed, running a hand through my hair.

"He's a dickwad."

"He's upset."

"That doesn't excuse him for saying those things and laying his fucking hands on you," Jesse protested.

"Maybe not, but you should have told him about us before," I snapped.

"So it's my fault?" Jesse let go of my hand and stared at me. "Yes it is."

Jesse leaned forward, his brows arched in surprise.

"Seriously?"

"Yes, seriously. I asked you to tell him, you didn't and he found out. That's why I ended up being humiliated in there."

Jesse shook his head and turned to sit forwards in his seat. He turned the ignition and banged on the steering wheel.

"Seriously!" he cried, rubbing at his brow. "You think it's my fault?"

"Yes, I've said." I crossed my arms and turned to stare out of the passenger window. Deep down I was mad at Brandon, his words had been cruel and uncalled for, but it should never have got that far. I'd been asking Jesse to tell him for days, but no, he'd known best. So, yes, at that moment I was blaming him.

"You are joking, right?" he asked, incredulously.

I gave him a look of disdain and then turned away again. "Just drive, Jesse."

"Un-fucking-believable," he moaned and drove away at top speed.

CHAPTER 75

♥

JESSE

As we drove home, Millie's silence screamed loudly around the cab of the truck. I say silence, but she did a lot of tutting and sighing and tapping her nails on the screen of her phone. Only ten minutes into the ride home, I had to turn the radio on just to drown out her damn quiet. By the time we pulled into the ranch, I'd had enough. I did a sharp turn into a clearing, a few feet inside the ranch entrance.

"What are you doing?" Millie asked, turning her head so sharply I was worried she'd cracked her neck.

"We're fucking talking about what went down in Rowdy's."

"Well, I don't want to talk about it," she snapped.

"Yeah, well tough, I do. The days of radio silence between us are over."

"Hah," Millie scoffed. "I think you'll find you're the expert at that, not me."

"Really?" I arched a brow and unclipped my belt, then leaned over and did the same with Millie's, letting my arm skim the side of her rack that was heaving with angry breaths.

I felt her shiver at my touch, and sighed in relief, hoping it meant that her level of angry was pissed rather than nuclear.

"Weren't you the one who rode off into the woods and got lost?" I said, as I sat back in my seat.

"Yes, because you were horrible to me," she pouted as she rubbed at her leather pants with her finger.

"I was just trying, or thought at the time I was, to be honest, but that isn't what we're going to talk about. We're going to talk about tonight and why you're mad at me now."

Millie huffed and shook her head. "I told you why. It's because I asked you to speak to Brandon days ago, you didn't and now I've ended up being made to look like a fool in front of half of Bridge Vale."

"Sweetness, the residents of Bridge Vale that were in Rowdy's were so full of booze they won't have any recollection tomorrow of what went down in there tonight. And you did not look a fool. If anyone did, it was Brandon, ending up on his ass with a bloody nose. No one in there will have a damn clue what he said to you. All they'll know is me and Brandon got down to it. The damn gossips will all be wondering why, but the only people who know are the four of us. Garratt and us aren't going to say, and if Brandon knows what's good for him, he won't tell either. So stop worrying about folks who have no importance."

Millie drew in a shaky breath and turned to look out of the window. "I know, but..."

When she didn't finish, I took hold of her hand and tugged on it.

"Millie, baby. Is it *what* he said to you, is that what's upset you most?"

She turned back to me and nodded. "Partly. But I'm really mad at you for not doing as I asked and telling him. It wasn't fair that he found out from someone else, whoever *that* was," she grumbled.

"Yep, you're right and I am sorry I didn't tell him, but you should not feel sorry for that fucker after what he said to you."

Talking about it got me angry all over again, and I wanted to drive back to town and put Brandon back on his ass. He was my oldest and best friend, but I would not tolerate him speaking to Millie like that. She and Addy were my priority, not Brandon.

"Do you feel like that?" Millie asked quietly, dropping her lashes quickly to hide the hurt.

"Oh, baby," I soothed and reached for her, pulling her across the seat and onto my lap. "I don't think of you like that, and deep down you know that. I love you."

She looked up at me with her huge eyes brimming with tears and her bottom lip quivering. "He said I would always be second best and just a convenient fuck," she said, her voice cracking with emotion. "I know I'm not her, and I'll never try to replace her, but if you're always going to be thinking of Melody, comparing me to her, then I don't think I can do this."

Fear gripped at my throat, at the thought that Millie might end what we had. All because Brandon was a jealous cock who had no idea what went on in my head. Yes, there had been times when I'd compared her to my dead wife, but most of the time it had been a positive comparison; it had been Melody who'd been lacking. That thought in itself filled me with guilt, but I had to push those feelings away if we were going to move on.

"Do not listen to what he said. I don't want you to be like her; you're two totally different people and I don't see you as second best and neither should you." I shifted her so that she was face to face with me and kissed her gently. "I swear to you, I love you. He won't understand that, all he'll see is that we've probably had sex a few times, and with my recent past, that doesn't hold much store for a long term relationship. But, Brandon doesn't know what's going on in my head, or what we've been through, what you've done to help me. He hasn't seen us together and has no idea what I think or feel about you. I usually tell him everything, so maybe he thinks it's just casual between us; but it isn't, baby, I promise you. He's hurt because we didn't tell him, which I know," I sighed, "is on me. And he's hurt because he liked you and now he can't have you."

"I get that, I really do," Millie sniffed. "But he was so nasty, Jesse."

"Yeah, well, I'm going to be making sure he apologizes for that."

Millie shook her head and opened her mouth to protest, but I shot her down.

"No, he's not speaking to you like that. I'll apologize for not being upfront with him, but he needs to apologize for being a dick to you. Okay?"

Millie nodded and ran her fingers through my hair as she gazed into my eyes. "Please tell me now if this isn't what you want."

She looked so vulnerable and scared, so as that Enrique guy quietly started singing about being someone's Hero, I pulled her against my chest and hugged her tight.

"I want this," I whispered against her hair. "I love you so damn much."

My words must have rung true because she pushed back and kissed me. The urgency immediate as she grabbed my hair and tugged at it, while her tongue explored my mouth. Her lips on mine were soft and warm and every touch sent a thrill through my veins.

"Millie," I moaned, against her mouth. "I fucking need you, baby."

She smiled slowly, and lifting her arms, pulled off her blouse. Her beautiful, round breasts were revealed and made my dick throb in my pants. As my eyes drank her in, Millie reached and started to unbutton my shirt. She took her time and with each button that was opened, she landed a soft kiss to my chest, her tits rubbing against my skin. I felt as though I was going to force the zipper on my jeans open, I was so hard. When we were both naked from the waist up, Millie went for the button on my jeans. The whole time she was silent, the sparkle in her eyes telling me exactly what she was thinking. Once my jeans were undone I lifted my hips and allowed Millie to pull them down my legs, earning a cute giggle from Millie when she realized I had no underwear on. When my jeans were around my calves, she lifted up on her knees and undid her leather pants and, along with the tiny piece of lace that was her panties, she pushed them down and then sat back to shimmy them off, throwing them on the seat behind her.

"How do you want to do this, cowboy?" she asked, reaching around to gather her hair over one shoulder.

I could barely speak. Her beautiful pink nipples were rock hard and were inches from my lips, asking to be sucked. I leaned forward and took one of them into my mouth, eliciting a moan from Millie.

"Jesse," she said breathily.

"How do *you* want it?" I asked, looking up at her, and I almost came there and then. Her eyes were closed, her lips were slightly parted, and her hand was at her chest, her fingertips trailing slowly over the swell of her breast. Not waiting to hear how Millie wanted me to fuck her, I put my hands at her waist and lifted her further up my thighs.

"Looks like you're on top, baby," I groaned before dragging my tongue back to her nipple.

Millie's hand went to my granite hard dick and she wrapped her long fingers around it. Mom would call them 'piano player's fingers'; me, I'd call them 'dick playing fingers'. They fit perfectly around me, and pumped me hard, before she lifted her ass and guided us so that we met perfectly.

"Fuck," I gasped, as her beautiful pussy tightened around me. "You're so damn perfect."

"Perfect for you," she whispered as she placed her hands on my shoulders and started to move her hips.

One of my hands went to the back of Millie's neck to pull her in for a kiss, while the other went to her delicious ass. With each of her thrusts, my fingertips dug deeper into the soft plumpness.

Our breaths were hot and heavy, and were the only sound in the truck, as Millie thoroughly fucked me. As the rhythm of her hips sped up, my hands went to her waist and I began thrusting upwards to help her to bring our orgasms home. As we got closer, Millie buried her face in my neck and moaned; her lips warm and soft against my skin. I jacked upwards, hard and fast. Millie held tightly to my shoulders and called out my name as I lifted my hands to push her now wild hair back from her face.

"I need to see your beautiful eyes when you come," I groaned as my fingers tangled in the thick strands of her hair.

"Jesse!" Millie cried, as our bodies moved against each other hot, sweaty and perfectly matched.

My woman felt amazing; she was everything, filling my soul and my heart and pushing me over the edge of pleasure as she screamed her own release into the stillness of the night.

Totally drained, I pulled Millie against my heaving chest and kissed her.

"I love you, Armalita," I whispered breathlessly. "Don't ever forget that." She gave me a satisfied grin, kissed my chest, and then snuggled into my arms, exactly where she was meant to be.

CHAPTER 76

♥

MILLIE

The morning after my confrontation with Brandon, I was surprised to see Garratt at the breakfast table. I assumed that he'd be staying overnight at the party. I'd still been upset when we got into the house, despite the amazing truck sex, so Jesse had stayed with me, in my bed, all night until he'd had to get up at five to get started on work.

"Hey, Garratt," I said, giving his shoulder a squeeze. "Didn't expect to see you this morning."

Garratt shrugged and took a drink of his coffee. "Wasn't really in the party mood so I caught a ride home with Preston Jennings. He lives five miles down the road, going out towards Missington. He's a complete jock who doesn't drink, so cheaper than an Uber."

"You weren't enjoying the company of those two girls then?" I said with a grin.

"Poppy and Marnie?"

"If they are the ones who were at Rowdy's, yes."

Garratt shook his head. "Nope, just wasn't feeling it." A shadow crossed his face and the usual gregarious Garratt was missing.

"Have you tried contacting her again?" I asked, giving him a gentle nudge.

Garratt stared at me with arched brows. "How did you know?"

"Good guess, and I have a younger brother who wore that same expression every time his bitch of a girlfriend let him down. Not that I'm saying Jemma was a bitch, or that she let you down."

He sighed and gave me a thin lipped smile. "I sent an email to her Gmail account, but it bounced back. She's totally disappeared off social media and according to her friend, Hannah, she isn't going back to college. She just sent Hannah a text to say she wouldn't be back and to tell me she'd had a great time and was sorry it had to end."

"But she didn't text you anything?" I sat down next to him and pulled the coffee jug towards me, pouring myself a mug.

"Nope, nothing except for the first message to say about her sister and how she had to go home." Garratt blew out a breath and circled the rim of his mug with his finger. "Anyways, how about you? How are you feeling this morning?"

"Good change of subject, Garratt," I said, before taking a sip of coffee.

"Nothing more to say, and same goes for you. So now tell me, how are you feeling after what that dickwad did?"

"Hurt by what he said, I thought we were friends."

Garratt took my hand and gave it a squeeze. "He's a prick and you shouldn't listen to him. Jesse put you straight, yeah?"

I smiled and felt warm inside as I thought about how Jesse had 'put me straight'.

"Yes, he did. He made it quite clear how he feels about me. I just don't understand how Brandon can be like that. He was awful about Jesse, too."

"What?" Garratt growled through clenched teeth. "What the hell did he say about my brother?"

"Nothing too much, just that I ought to hear all about 'my precious Jesse'. What do you think he meant, Garratt?"

Garratt shook his head, and I could see he was desperately trying to hold onto his control. "Nothing, he was just trying to stir some shit between you. Jesse hasn't done anything you need to know about. You've seen him at his damn worst, the way he was when you first got here is the only time Jesse has fucked up. Before she died, he was the best son, the best brother, the best husband, and the best fucking father ever, so do not listen to what Brandon Reed has to say."

A vein in Garratt's temple throbbed and his jaw was tight as he looked at me and gave my hand a squeeze.

"So why would he say that about him, and what he said to me? I don't for one minute think it's because he liked me that much. We'd only had one date. I hadn't even kissed him properly."

"There's things about Brandon that you don't know, and I'm not going to tell you, but what I will say is he's a lying, cheating, cock sucker who shouldn't be trusted."

"Is this about the card game where he won all your money?" I asked, trying to understand why Brandon had been so nasty. "Is there more to it?"

Garratt swallowed and ran a hand through his already messy hair. "I wish I could tell you, but I can't. Just promise me you won't listen to him. You and Jesse belong together, and if he found out what I know about Brandon, it could ruin things for you, because it would kill Jesse."

My heart was thudding, banging a beat against my breast bone, as I opened my mouth to tell Garratt I wouldn't listen to Brandon. I didn't get chance.

"What would kill me, Garr?" Jesse's voice was low and controlled. "Tell me what the fuck Brandon has done that I shouldn't know about?"

I swung around in my seat to see Jesse standing behind me, hands fisted at his sides and his chest heaving.

"Jess," Garratt said, his voice quavering. "Nothing, it's nothing, just about him cheating at cards, and that he's done it before."

My eyes went back to Garratt who was chewing on his bottom lip. He was physically shaking and there was no way he was telling the truth. The tortured look on his handsome face gave him away.

"I know about his cheating," Jesse replied. "Now tell me what I don't want to hear. Because I'll be honest with you, Garr, I'm freaking out a little here."

He ran a hand through his hair, the exact same way that Garratt had only minutes earlier. Garratt stood up from his chair and leaned forward, his hands on his knees as he exhaled a shuddering breath.

"Please, Jess," he begged, looking up at his brother. "Just leave it. All you need to know is that Brandon can't be trusted."

Seeing how distressed Garratt was, I turned to Jesse. "Baby, let's just leave it. Everything is fine between us, we're good, and Brandon won't change that."

Jesse shook his head. "I need to know, Armalita, and Garratt is going to tell me. It doesn't involve you; this is between me, my brother, and my best friend, so damn well stay out of it!"

"Please Jesse," I whispered, trying to ignore the hurt as I put my hand on one of his shoulders.

Jesse shrugged me off, taking a step towards Garratt and leaning down to face him.

"Tell me, Garr," he snapped. "If this is anything to do with Addy you'd better tell me."

Garratt straightened and shook his head vigorously. "God no, it's not Addy, I swear."

"Well what the fuck is it then?"

As they stared each other off, both with grim determination, the door to the mud room opened and Bonnie strolled in, looking at a list in her hand.

"Morning," she said distractedly before looking up. "Oh, hey honey, I thought you were out this morning."

Jesse shook his head. "Came back to check that Millie was okay."

"You not well, sweetie?" Bonnie asked, her brow wrinkling with concern.

"She had a run in with Brandon," Jesse said, his eyes still pinned to Garratt.

"Oh really, is that why he's shuffling around outside then?"

Before anyone had chance to blink, Jesse turned for the door.

"Jesse, no!" Garratt yelled and lunged for him, managing to grab Jesse's arm.

Jesse's upper body strength, through years of working on the ranch and roping cattle, meant he was able to shrug Garratt off easily, aiming an elbow at his brother's chest as he swung the door open.

"Shit!" Garratt took the blow and staggered after Jesse.

"What's going on?" Bonnie cried.

"Jesse heard Garratt say Brandon wasn't to be trusted and wanted to know why." My words were rushed as I started to follow Garratt and Jesse. "Jesse hit him last night, for things he said about me."

"Oh my God, no," Bonnie yelled and ran after her sons.

"Bonnie, what's going on?"

I chased after her, across the lounge and through the door that was swinging open. When I got to the top of the porch steps, Jesse had a blustering Brandon by his shirt, while Garratt was trying to pull his brother away.

"Jesse, leave him!" Bonnie cried as she reached her sons.

Jesse turned to Bonnie and took a deep breath. "He's done something that Garratt says will kill me, and I need to know what the fuck it is. I want to hear it from his mouth."

"Sweetheart, just leave it be," Bonnie pleaded.

As I gasped, Jesse's eyes darted towards me and then back to his mother.

"You know, too, don't you?" he accused.

"We just thought..."

"Mom," Garratt said, shaking his head. "Please don't."

Bonnie turned to her youngest son and placed a palm on his cheek. "We have to, he won't rest until he knows. He deserves to know the truth. He's strong enough to hear it now."

I could hardly breathe as I watched Jesse's face crumple. I instinctively knew what was going through his mind and I was sure that he was right. It explained why Garratt hated Brandon.

"Someone better tell me, now!"

Brandon shook his head, as if pleading with Bonnie and Garratt.

"You tell him!" Garratt snapped. "You tell him what you did, you be the one to break his fucking heart, because I can't."

Garratt let out a heart wrenching sob as he collapsed back against the side of Brandon's truck. Bonnie lifted a hand to her mouth and started to cry as Jesse looked between her and Garratt and then back to Brandon.

"Why?" Jesse asked in a quiet voice.

While Brandon stood silently, I took the steps and moved to Bonnie's side, taking her hand in mine and giving it a squeeze.

"I asked you a question?" Jesse said, prodding Brandon in the shoulder. "Why?"

Brandon opened his mouth, but didn't speak. He turned to Bonnie. "I can't."

"Yes, you can," she said sharply. "You were man enough to do it, so now be man enough to tell him." Her face hardened as she lifted her chin in disdain.

"Tell me!" Jesse yelled, inches from Brandon's face. "I want to know why you were fucking my wife!"

CHAPTER 77

♥

JESSE

"Tell me," I spat at Brandon. "I want to know why you were fucking my wife."

Mom whimpered behind me, and from the corner of my eye I could see that Millie was upset, wrapping an arm around herself.

"Jess," Garratt mumbled behind me. "Please."

"Shut it Garratt, you've had plenty of time to speak, so don't fucking start tweeting like a damn parrot now."

Brandon was breathing heavily and he looked scared shitless, and so he should, because once he said the words I was going to kill him.

"Tell me, Brandon, were you having an affair with Melody?"

"I swear, Jess, I wasn't."

"Yeah right, now tell me the truth."

"He wasn't, Jess," Garratt croaked out behind me.

I heard Millie gasp as Brandon slumped in my grip, relief washing over his face. I let his shirt go and spun around to my brother.

"You better not be lying to save me jail time for killing him," I growled.

"I'm not, he wasn't having an affair with Melody, I swear."

"Bonnie?" Millie whispered. "What the hell is going on?"

"That's exactly what I'd like to know. Now what the fuck did he do that you felt it necessary to hide from me?" I asked through gritted teeth, pointing at Brandon.

"Tell him, Brandon," my mom snarled.

"Bonnie," he pleaded.

"Just fucking tell me, now."

My pulse was racing as I watched my best friend of twenty years sweating and squirming under my gaze. The sick feeling in the pit of my stomach hadn't lessened any from hearing he wasn't having an affair with Melody, because somehow I knew it was much worse.

Brandon moved to lean against his truck, prompting Garratt to push away from it. He went and stood behind Mom, placing comforting hands on her shoulders.

"She wasn't meant for this life," Brandon started quietly. "Melody, she was a princess who should have been living in some fancy house with a swimming pool and diamonds on every finger."

"And you know that how?" I asked.

"Because I was in love with her. Had been since Junior High, but she was happy with Tommy and then eventually you waltzed in there and did what I didn't have the balls to do, and asked her out."

"You're hardly shy, Brandon," I scoffed.

"With her I was. I could hardly breathe when she was around, never mind ask her out on a date."

Millie stepped forward and wrapped her arm around mine, but I couldn't have her near me so I shrugged her away. When I heard her distressed whimper, I gave her a cursory glance before turning back to Brandon.

"So, that's what this thing with you and Garratt is about?" I said. "Garr knew that you loved Melody and was trying to protect me?"

"If only," Garratt muttered.

"Ssh, honey," Mom said.

Brandon gave Garratt a sneering look and turned back to me. "I tried to keep my feelings on the down low, but it was hard, and when I started to see how unhappy she was, I got to thinking that I could save her. I could be the one to give her the things she deserved."

"You fucking bastard." I pulled my hand into a fist and tried to raise it, but Millie's arm held tightly to mine.

"Jesse, let him finish," she whispered against my bicep.

"I asked her," Brandon said, his voice breaking. "I asked her to come away with me. I was convinced she'd say yes. She'd flirted with me enough times, she'd even let me kiss her, and a little bit more, one New Year's Eve at Rowdy's. We'd both gone to the bathroom at the same time and I caught up with her in the hallway. You were arguing with Jed Aspen about beef over dairy."

"Fuck!" I gasped, dropping my hands to my knees. I remembered when that was, because Jed and I almost came to blows. "She was fucking pregnant with Addy then."

Millie gasped. "Oh my God, you bastard."

"It takes two, Millie," Brandon snapped at her.

"Millie, I've told you, keep out of this," I growled.

Millie didn't say anything, except to try and lay a comforting hand on my back, but I stepped away.

"Is that it?" I asked. "You loved her, you kissed her, and then she fucking died?" My voice broke with the emotion of it all and I couldn't stop the tears from falling.

Brandon looked at my mom and then shook his head.

"Jesse," Millie said soothingly in my ear. "You don't need to hear any more."

I didn't mean to snap at her, but I couldn't help it; I needed to hear every damn word.

"Yes, I do, now if you don't like that just go."

"Jesse!" my mom scolded. "Don't speak to Millie like that."

"It's okay, Bonnie, he's upset."

I heard Millie sniff as she moved back a step, not leaving me totally, but distancing herself.

"Just get it over with, Brandon." I looked down at the ground, not wanting to look at my 'best friend'.

"I asked her to come away with me, and she laughed in my face," he sighed. "She said I had nothing to offer her and when she did leave, it would be for someone a whole lot richer than me. So you see, Jess, she didn't really want either of us. It was 'drop dead Brandon', and it wasn't *if* she left, it was *when* she left."

"You're not making yourself look any better, you know," Garratt said with an angry growl. "So, just tell him what I found out you sick fuck."

"I followed her, okay? I was so much in love with her I couldn't think straight. I just needed to make her see; I was the one that she should be turning to for comfort while you were busy with your damn cows. Trying to convince her became my whole life. Nothing else mattered. Not this place, not my folks place, not you, not Alesha, just her; it was always just her."

"So you weren't helping your folks with the guests when you couldn't work here," I said accusingly. "You were too busy trying to persuade *my* wife to run away with you?"

"I guess I was, so I failed them. They were struggling without me and that's why the place is such a fuck up now. They couldn't cope and let things slide."

"And it gets worse," Garratt said. "Tell him the rest you sick fucker."

"Garratt," I warned. "Let me hear it from him."

Brandon yanked his hat from his head, and wiped his sweaty brow with his forearm. His pits were sweating onto his dark shirt, and I could also see a sheen on his top lip. It wasn't even seven-thirty in the morning, so it wasn't that hot.

"She was cheating on both of us, Jess," he spat out quickly. It was as though saying it fast meant he didn't have to hear the words. He looked destroyed and I saw then how much he'd loved my wife. "It was some trust fund pretty boy who took her to that spa she liked to visit so often. He drove a car that probably cost five times your yearly income on this ranch, and I wanted to kill him. I confronted her about him and she laughed in my face again, told me to mind my own business and that he was going to marry her. She admitted that she'd met him on one of those girly weekends she went on, and she also admitted he knew nothing about you or Addy."

"What the fuck is Garratt talking about, Brandon?" I needed to know now, because I was dangerously close to snapping. "Just tell me."

Brandon took in a long, deep breath and then let it out slowly.

"Her lies were escalating and I hated how she belittled me when I confronted her, so I forced her to sleep with me in exchange for keeping quiet to you and keeping quiet to fucking *Heston*. What sort of damn name is Heston?" he said on a hollow laugh.

"What the fuck?" Garratt groaned and dragged a hand through his hair. "I had no idea about this, Jesse, I swear. That's just sick."

"He *raped* her!" Millie cried. "Oh my God, you need to call the police."

"No, Millie, I didn't fucking rape her. She was more than willing in exchange for me keeping her secret. And she damn well enjoyed it, too, said I was better than you and Heston."

His sneering accusation didn't create any reaction from me, I didn't have it in me to care what lies Melody had or had not spilled to save her own ass.

"So why does Garratt hate you then?" I asked. "If you weren't having an affair with Melody, and he didn't know what you did. What else have you done to make my brother hate you so much?"

Brandon looked down at the ground, shaking his head.

"I'll tell him then shall I, Brandon? Well, I found his stash of Melody memorabilia," Garratt sighed. "The night we played cards, I had a feeling he was cheating and using marked cards, so when I went to the bathroom, I had a quick look in his room for other sets of cards. I didn't find any but I did find a top of

Melody's, and a pair of her panties, not to mention dozens of photographs of her, some with you ripped out of them. And the whole damn lot stunk of that god awful perfume she wore, which would be because *he'd* bought a bottle of it."

Mom gave a guttural groan, and Millie cursed, and from the corner of my eye I saw her shudder.

"You sick bastard," I said in a hushed tone. "No wonder Garr fucking hates you."

"Garratt has no idea what it was like loving her, *you* have no idea. You never cherished her the way I did. I came to see her and tell her that I loved her and wanted to take care of her, but she was leaving. She'd left you a letter she said." Brandon gripped his hat in his hand, and started to pace up and down, looking between me and Garratt. "Fucking Heston would never love her like I did, that's why I had to stop her," he rambled. His gaze was now on the ground and he was muttering to himself as he stalked up and down. "I couldn't let her go, she had to stay with me, I didn't mean for it to happen, but she needed to stay here, not go with him."

"What the hell are you talking about, Brandon?" I asked on a heavy breath.

Brandon glanced at me, pain and suffering clouding his features.

"It was an accident; she was going too fast. You know how she hated driving fast, Jess," he cried, his hands twisting his hat. "I only wanted her to talk to me. To listen to me so that I could tell her that I wanted her, her and Addy. I wanted Addy as much as I wanted her. I would have been good to them, Jess, you know that."

At the mention of Addy, my adrenalin surged and my hands fisted involuntarily.

"Addy is my fucking daughter and I would *never* let you have her."

Brandon shook his head. "But don't you see, Jess, that doesn't matter. What matters is that I loved her, but she wouldn't stop. She kept going, faster and faster, so I tried to catch her and I almost did, Jess, I almost did, but then..." Brandon stopped talking and looked up at the sky, gulping in deep breaths. "She just skidded off the road," he whispered. "Straight into that old tree. I couldn't do anything, she was going too fast. She hated driving fast."

He turned to me and bile rose in my throat as Brandon let out a strangled cry of despair, dropping his hat to the ground.

"Did you go to her?" I asked calmly. "Did you comfort my wife while she died?"

Brandon's face crumpled as he opened his mouth to speak and then quickly turned away.

"I'm sorry," he sobbed.

It was then that the world tipped on its axis, my knees gave way, and I crumpled to the ground.

"Jesse," Millie cried and rushed towards me, closely followed by Mom and Garratt.

"Get off," I snapped. "All of you, just leave me alone. Get away from me."

"Jesse, son," Mom said, reaching out for me.

"Did you know?" I cried. "What he did, that he left her to die?"

She shook her head and clutched at her stomach. "I would have told you, honey," she replied. "I would never have let him get away with that, I swear."

"We only knew about him having Melody's things," Garratt said, moving to Mom's side and placing an arm around her shoulder. "Alesha knew, too. She found his Melody stash the night before she left, and he was so drunk he told her about being in love with Melody and that Melody had been having an affair. Alesha came over to tell Mom and Dad on her way out of town, but they'd taken Addy out for the day, so she told me. I'd only known about the things in his drawer, and that was bad enough, but then I told Mom the rest."

"And why the fuck didn't you tell me?" I bellowed as the pain in my gut increased.

"We thought you'd gone through enough," Mom sobbed. "I

did what I thought best, honey. You knowing that he was in love with her wouldn't have changed anything, neither would you knowing she had an affair. Melody would still be dead."

"Dad, does he know?"

Mom shook her head. "He knows Melody was having an affair, but not what Garratt found, or that Brandon loved her. I feared what he'd do more than you."

She was right, Dad would have just shot Brandon between the eyes. He loved us boys and nothing was more important to him than us; that's why he'd put up with so much shit from us, especially me.

"The letter, where is it?"

Mom drew in a breath. "I have it."

"Get it for me!"

Millie moved forward and knelt next to me. "Jesse, I'm so sorry." Tears crawled down her cheeks and I couldn't stand looking at her sadness. I had enough of my own to work through.

"Mom, get the damn letter."

"Let me help you," Millie whispered.

"No!" I yelled. "Get away from me, I don't want to see your face."

"Talk to me, Jesse," she begged.

"Talk to you and tell you what, Millie? How I can't face my daughter after finding out that her mother didn't give two shits about her? Or do I talk to you about how the woman that I loved, the woman who owned my heart, was cheating on me? Or maybe the fact that I worshipped her, yet I never really knew her at all? Do you really want to sit down and chew the fat over that shit, Armalita?"

She didn't answer, but stared at me with tears in her huge brown eyes.

"No, I didn't think so, so just leave me alone, all of you, and Brandon get the fuck off my land and never come back here again. I will never forgive you. You killed my wife, the woman I loved more than life itself. You fucking snuffed her life away, and watched her die in pain."

The howling cry that came from my throat was that of an injured animal, and at that moment, I wanted to die.

CHAPTER 78

♥

MILLIE

Garratt took mine and Bonnie's hands and walked us quickly towards the house.

"We can't leave him," I sobbed, looking over my shoulder and dragging my feet. "He needs us."

"Millie, just get inside." Garratt tugged at my hand.

"We need to go to him," Bonnie said.

As Jesse let out a painful cry of grief, she gasped and tried to go back to him, but Garratt held her tightly, too.

"Mom, he needs to be alone."

"My baby," she cried. "He's hurting."

"Garratt, please," I begged.

"I said no," he commanded. "Now get inside, both of you."

He dragged us up the last few steps, and as we hit the porch, the door burst open and Ruby pulled Bonnie into her arms and inside the house. Garratt guided me inside and then closed the door behind us.

"Oh, sweetheart," Ruby soothed, holding Bonnie close. "He'll be fine, just let him get it all out."

"Uncle Garratt, what's wrong with Daddy?" a tiny voice asked.

We all stopped and turned, surprised to find Addy standing at the window, the drapes pulled to one side and her hand on the glass. Garratt rushed towards her and scooped Addy up into his arms.

"Hey beautiful, let's get you some cereal. What would you like?"

Addy struggled in his arms and tried to push her tiny body away from his.

"Let me down," she cried. "I want to go to Daddy. He's crying."

"Addy, sweetheart," Bonnie cooed, swiping at her tear stained face. "Daddy's fine, he just had some bad news, that's all."

"But I want my Daddy."

Somehow, she squirmed out of Garratt's grip and dropped on her feet to the floor. She rushed towards the door, and before anyone had chance to stop her, she had it open. Just as she was about to go out of it, Garratt made a dive for her and just managed to grab hold of her pyjama top.

"Daddy!" Her scream was loud and screeching, coming from her throat. "Daddy, please, I want Daddy."

Her cries were piercing and tore at my heart, making my chest ache for her.

"Daddy, daddy!" she screeched.

Garratt pulled her against his chest, burying her face and her sobs against his shirt. I ran towards them and as Garratt shuffled back on his backside, away from the door, I put my hand on the wood to close it. But, I couldn't do it. I stood rooted to the spot watching the man I loved, kneeling in the dirt with his heart breaking. It was hopeless, because I knew I couldn't help him. As I started to close the door, Bonnie pushed past me and took a step onto the porch. I instinctively followed her, and stopped as she pulled up at the edge of the steps.

"Jesse!" she called, her voice breaking. "Please, son."

Jesse was doubled over, his arms wrapped around his waist,

rocking in time to his sobs.

"Bonnie, sweetheart," a voice behind me pleaded. "Come on in. You can't do anything to help him."

I looked over my shoulder to see Ruby leaning against the door frame for support. Her face was ashen and her eyes red, as though she too had been crying.

"But he needs someone, Auntie Ruby," Bonnie said as tears careened down her face. "He's dying out there."

"I know," she said. "But he has to come to terms with what he's found out. Just give him time." She held her hand out for Bonnie, her eyes begging her to go inside.

I turned back to Jesse again to see he'd stop rocking and was now leaning forwards, with his hands on the ground. Bonnie edged forward hesitantly.

"Millie, sweetheart," Ruby pleaded. "Go to him, see if he'll talk to you."

I took a step closer to Bonnie and placed a hand on her shoulder. "Bonnie, go inside," I whispered.

Jesse looked up and saw me watching him.

"Get out of my sight, Millie!" he screamed. "Now!"

With a shocked gasp, I stumbled backwards; a hand came to my elbow and Ruby guided Bonnie and I back inside.

"He'll calm down soon," Ruby said as she closed the door and ushered us further into the room. "Come on, sit down, honey, I'll make you some tea."

As Ruby got Bonnie settled on the couch, I stood at the window and watched as Jesse dragged himself to his feet. His shoulders were heaving as he looked up at the sky and continued to sob for his wife, and I wanted to scream. I wanted to go out there and shake him, to ask him why I hadn't been enough for him. I didn't expect to be his priority above Addy, I wouldn't want to be, but I certainly didn't want to come third after his dead wife. I'd been second choice for Dean, and that had hurt, but nowhere near as gut wrenching as this was; the man I loved choosing a dead woman over me.

Dragging myself away from the window, I turned to the room

and felt more alone than I ever had before. Garratt was talking softly to Addy, cradling her in his arms, while Ruby rubbed rhythmic circles on Bonnie's back. The arms I needed didn't want me, and the loneliness was overpowering.

***

Garratt finally managed to calm Addy down, while Bonnie and Ruby took turns to watch through the window to see if they could see Jesse. After an hour, Garratt decided to go and make sure he was okay. No one asked me if I had wanted to go, but simply gave me a sympathetic smile. They knew that it would kill me when he sent me away again. Within twenty minutes, he was back. He was just sitting down to tell us, when the mud room door swung open and Ted walked in. As soon as he saw all our faces, he knew something was wrong.

"What the hell has been going on?" he asked, cupping Bonnie's face in his large hands. "Why've you been crying, honey?"

"Hey, sweetie pie," Ruby said to Addy. "How about me and you go and get you a nice bubble bath?"

"Bath time is at night," Addy whispered, her little chin trembling. "Daddy does my bath."

"Yeah, well today is a special treat day. You can have a lovely bubble bath and maybe have some of your dollies in there with you. Whaddaya say?"

We all held our breath as Ruby gave Addy a wide-eyed, expectant grin. After what seemed like an eternity, Addy nodded and held her hand out for Ruby.

Once they'd disappeared up the stairs, Ted turned to Bonnie.

"Okay, what's he done now?"

I burst into tears and Bonnie pulled me into her side, kissing the side of my head.

"I think you need to sit down, Dad," Garratt sighed. "You're really not going to like this."

***

"I'll damn well kill him myself," Ted yelled, pushing up from his chair and sending it tumbling backwards.

"Ted, honey, no. That's exactly why I didn't tell you about

what Garratt found in his room." Bonnie looked shamefaced at her husband as he righted his chair.

"Well, I ain't happy about that, Bonnie, but that ain't what's important now. Jesse is. Where'd he go, do you know?"

"He's in the cabin," Garratt said solemnly. "I was just about to tell Mom and Millie when you came in."

"You sure he's there?" Ted asked, rubbing a hand down his face. "He ain't gone after Brandon?"

Garratt shook his head. "Nope. He's in his cabin drinking straight from a bottle of bourbon."

"Good. Hopefully he'll get drunk enough to pass out so he can't do anything stupid."

"Oh my God," Bonnie gasped. "What if he chokes on his own vomit?"

Ted rubbed her back reassuringly. "I'll go over there in a few. Now where's the damn letter?"

Bonnie stood up wearily, pushing down on the table. "I'll get it."

"You read it, honey?" Ted asked.

Bonnie shook her head. "No, do you think we should?"

Ted leaned back in his chair and looked up at the ceiling. He was silent for a few moments and then looked back to Bonnie. "Go get it."

When Bonnie came back, she passed the lilac colored envelope to Ted. My heart skipped a beat as I saw Jesse's name, scribed on the front in looping, feminine writing.

Ted looked at it for a few seconds and then slipped his finger into the flap and pried it open. Two years must have dried out the glue, because it opened easily and without tearing. With a deep breath, he pulled out the two sheets of lilac paper and read. Finally, he folded them and placed them back into the envelope.

"Ted?" Bonnie placed a hand on his forearm.

"I'm going to see my son, and take this to him," Ted sighed and stood up. "This letter won't necessarily make things better, but it may give him some peace."

"What did the bitch say?" Garratt snapped. "That she was

running away with someone with a bigger car and a swimming pool?"

Ted placed a hand on Garratt's shoulder and gave it a squeeze. "Jesse will tell you if he wants you to know, but she did say she loved him, can't say she said the same about that poor baby upstairs, though."

I let out a sob as I thought of poor Addy and wondered how Melody could be willing to just leave her? Then there was Jesse; he'd had his heart broken all over again. I couldn't help but think about our future and how this had probably ruined things. You only had to watch him grieving all over again to know that he wasn't really over Melody. I'd been kidding myself, thinking he was ready to move on. He wasn't, and I couldn't hang around to be rejected once again. My heart would never get over Jesse Connor, and it certainly would never heal, especially if I had to hear him tell me that we had no future. He was broken in so many ways because of Melody, and even in death she'd been able to shatter those broken pieces even more.

CHAPTER 79

♥

JESSE

Dear Jesse

To start with, I need you to know that I did love you, once upon a time. We were seventeen when you asked me to the movies, and I thought that I was the luckiest girl alive. There you were, the captain of the basketball team, all the girls wanted you, but you, you wanted me. God, I thought I'd never love anyone the way that I loved you then. I know now that was just puppy love.

You've always treated me real good, honey, and I am so grateful for that, but it's not enough anymore. This life isn't enough anymore. I can't stand it and feel like I'm suffocating living on this damn ranch. When I first found out I was pregnant, I nearly left then, but I couldn't do that to you. I knew you'd be a great daddy, and Addy loves you, and is better off with you.

Please don't hate me for leaving, I'd only make you miserable in the end, so it's better this way. You probably guessed I met someone, if you haven't, Brandon will tell you anyways. He knows about me and Heston, the guy I met, and he tried to cause trouble. I guess if he were a good friend he'd have told you, but Brandon has his own reasons for keeping quiet. He says he loves me, but I don't think a guy should be pestering his best buddy's wife, do you?

Heston is a good man and says he wants to marry me, so I guess we'll need to get divorced sometime soon. I'll be in touch once I'm settled in Boston. Heston is already there, he doesn't know I'm coming yet, but I can't stand this place any longer. It's time for me to go. He's a good man and will look after me, but I know he won't love me like you do, but, as long as he looks after me I can handle not being worshipped. He's a lawyer at his dad's firm, so I figure I'll be okay.

You take care, honey, and have a good life. When you meet the right person for you, just don't spend all your time on the ranch, it gets real boring for a girl.

Melody x

p.s. kiss Addy for me.

CHAPTER 80

♥

MILLIE

"Why are you hugging me so tight if you're only going shopping?" Addy asked, her little brow furrowed.

"Oh, I'll miss you, that's all. Now remember, be good for Granma while I'm gone and remember that I love you very much."

Addy sighed and flung her tiny arms around my legs. "Okay, I will and I love you, too."

I swallowed back the lump in my throat and bent to kiss the top of her head. "I'd better go. You go and see Granma in the garden, and don't forget it's a surprise."

"I know," she sighed. "I won't tell Granma you're going to get her a present, I'll tell her you've gone to town to get us ice cream for a treat."

I nodded and sucked back the tears. This was so hard, but it would only get harder the longer I stayed.

As Addy skipped outside, I retrieved my carryon case from Ted's office where I'd hidden it, and went out to the truck.

Luckily, no one was around. Jesse still hadn't come out of his cabin and Ted and Garratt were helping with the cattle, while Ruby and Bonnie were in the garden.

With a last look around, I let out a quiet sob and got into the truck. I felt bad that I'd have to text Bonnie and let her know that the truck was at the airport, but I knew if I spoke to her she'd persuade me to stay and I couldn't. My heart couldn't take any more.

CHAPTER 81

♥

JESSE

As I roughly scrubbed a towel over my head, I winced at the pain. I'd really gone to town on the bourbon last night and had a headache to prove my stupidity this morning. Thankfully, the bottle had already been half empty, otherwise things could have been a whole lot worse. I could still taste the vanilla of the Wild Turkey and felt a little queasy every now and again, but I'd manage. The shower had certainly helped.

I looked in the mirror above the sink in my bathroom in the cabin, and sighed. Apart from the grey under my eyes, I didn't look any different. Not that I'd expected to see a sign around my neck saying, 'Stupid Husband Last to Know' or anything like that. But you'd think finding out a whole bunch of shit like I had, might just leave you looking haunted or broken. Yet I didn't, and I didn't feel it either. Finding out my wife was a cheat, surprisingly wasn't the thing that hurt the most, neither was it the fact that she was leaving. It *was* heart breaking that Brandon had left Melody to die at the side of the road. That had torn my insides apart; for her. No one deserved to die alone like that, especially when the man who claims to love you is watching nearby. No, the thing that crucified me the most, the thing that caused me pain and suffering, was Addy. She was leaving Addy, hadn't even acknowledged her existence to the man she was running away to. And I couldn't fathom how, as a mother, Melody could do that? Then I'd pushed Addy away, too. I abandoned her all over again, and as long as I live, I will never forgive myself. For two years, my poor baby had only my parents and my brother to rely on, when she should've had her momma and daddy.

When Dad had brought me the letter, I screwed it up and threw it on the floor, with no intention of reading it, but curiosity killed the cat and all that. Yeah, so she'd said she loved me once, hoo-fucking-rah for Melody. Once isn't how you should love your husband, it should be for life. And as for your child, that love should be beyond life, into death. Melody though, well she'd just about mentioned Addy in her damn letter. Christ, the 'give Addy a kiss for me' had been a fucking p.s. That's all Addy was to her, a p.s.; an afterthought. She didn't even say goodbye for fuck's sake.

As for Brandon, well I didn't know what to do about him. I ought to go to the sheriff and tell them about him leaving Melody, but who would that hurt except his mom and dad? They were getting older and needed him to help with their guest ranch. His brother, Wade, lived in Alaska working at Prudhoe Bay Oilfield, and only came home every six months, so he was no help. I'd see to it that Brandon never worked another ranch again, but I couldn't hurt his parents while doing it. At least that might make him focus on getting his folk's place right. Anyway, I thought with a sigh, life was too fucking short. I at least had Millie, my beautiful girl who had put me back together when I was broken, almost beyond repair.

With a deep breath, to push back another bought of nausea, I grabbed my clothes, suddenly in a rush to get to Millie and Addy.

When I walked into the house, Mom almost dropped the plate of sandwiches that she was holding.

"Daddy," Addy screamed and ran super-fast towards me, her arms outstretched.

"Hey, baby," I said, catching her and pulling her up against my chest and squeezing tight. "You okay?"

"Yes, Daddy. Are you okay? You were crying."

I looked at Mom who was chewing on her thumb. I could see the trepidation in her eyes and while I'd screamed at her the day before, I'd calmed down enough to realize she'd done what she thought was best.

"I'm fine, Addy. I just felt sad about something."

"Granma said you had bad news," she replied sagely. "Did you all have bad news? Because you were all crying."

"Yes, baby, we did, but it's okay now. I'm better now." I smiled at Mom and my heart lurched when her shoulders sagged with relief. I fucking hated that I'd put her and Dad through so much shit over the last two years, but it was over now.

I kissed Addy and put her down on the floor and moved over to Mom, taking her into a hug.

"I'm sorry, Momma."

"Oh, sweetheart," she said on a broken sob. "I should have told you, it's my fault. I made Garratt keep quiet."

"No Mom, there's only two people to blame for what happened yesterday and neither of them are in our lives anymore."

"What are you going to do about him?" she asked hesitantly.

"Nothing." I kissed her cheek and moved over to the coffee jug. "I figure it's enough he has to live with what he did. He'll never work another ranch, I'll make sure of it, so maybe now he'll do what he was supposed to be doing and sort his folk's ranch out."

"He deserves to go to jail, though," she said, her chin wobbling as she spoke. "He blackmailed her and left her."

"Hey," I soothed, rubbing a hand over her hair. "Pay no mind to him, Mom. Just make sure you keep Dad away from him. As for Melody, well she made her own bed, so to speak."

We both laughed quietly and then dropped into silence. Finally, Mom turned to me.

"You want something to eat?" she asked as she moved to the counter where bread and cheese were sitting.

I did feel kind of hungry, and maybe it'd stop the sickly feeling.

"Yeah, that'd be good Mom. I need to speak to Millie first though, where is she?"

"Her room I think, I told her I'd look after Addy this morning." She looked at me from under her lashes. "I don't think she slept too well."

My heart dropped as I remembered how I screamed at her. Yelled at her to get out of my sight. God, I'd been a total shit, but I couldn't think straight. The only thing I had in my head was pain and the need to be alone.

"I'll go get her," I said and made my way to the stairs.

"Daddy," Addy hissed as I passed her.

"What, baby?"

She beckoned me down to her level.

"Millie isn't there," she whispered. "She's gone to buy Granma a present."

I frowned, wondering why she was buying a present for Mom. It wasn't her birthday, and we were four months off Christmas.

"What sort of present?" I asked.

"I don't know," Addy shrugged. "But I think she's getting it from the airoport."

"Do you mean the airport?" I asked, a little concerned, but not sure why.

"That's what I said, the airoport," Addy pouted.

"Okay, baby, but what makes you say that?"

I looked at Mom, and I knew that she was pretending not to listen because she was cutting the cheese real slow, and her head was cocked towards us.

"I heard her on the telephone," Addy said leaning closer to my ear. "She said, I'll pick up at the airoport."

"Mom, when did Millie go out?" I asked anxiously.

"A couple of hours ago, why?" Mom put the knife down and took a step towards me. "Jesse?"

"I need to check something." I rushed up the stairs and to the back of the house, into Millie's bedroom.

I turned in a circle, my eyes trying to spot something, anything, yet hoping I didn't. I flung open the door to her closet and flicked through her clothes. I had no clue what I was looking for because, while I always feasted my eyes on Millie, I couldn't tell you if any of the clothes I'd seen her in were missing; her beautiful face was what I always looked at, not her clothes so much. The slinky red top wasn't there, that she'd worn that night at Rowdy's, but it might well be in the laundry for all I knew.

"Fuck," I cursed, slamming the door shut.

"What's got into you, cowboy?"

Auntie Ruby appeared at the open door, looking tired and a little dishevelled. I guess I'd woken her from her nap.

"I think Millie's left, but I can't be sure."

"Well, call me Uncle Walter with a dress on, but have you tried her cell phone?"

I let out a groan, wondering why I hadn't thought of that. I took out my phone, pressed her number, and waited while the cell rang out in my ear. No answer, with it finally going to voicemail.

"Millie, baby, it's me just checking where you are. Call me back, sweetness."

"Jesse!" Mom's voice was loud as I heard her running up the stairs.

"What is it?" I asked, meeting her outside Addy's bedroom door.

She shoved her cell in my face.

Millie: Hi Bonnie. So sorry I didn't say goodbye but I can't stay and be rejected again. I love Jesse but he isn't ready to move on. I said goodbye to Addy but she thinks I'm shopping. Please tell her I love her very much and I'll call her soon. The truck is at the long stay car park at the departure gate of the

airport. Level 3 Row W. Paid for three days in case you can't get here. Thank you for everything and I'll call you soon – Millie x

"No fucking way!" I yelled, throwing Mom's cell phone down the hall, towards Millie's bedroom door.

"Jesse, what are you going to do?"

"Go and get her," I snapped, moving past her. "She's the damn love of my life, Mom, and I am not losing her, no matter how stubborn and annoying she damn well is."

Auntie Ruby started cackling "Yay, go get her cowboy."

CHAPTER 82

♥

MILLIE

The great, big, fat man who was sitting next to me had the worst body odor I had ever had the displeasure of smelling. It was a mixture of sweat and tobacco, with a hint of garlic, and it was making my stomach churn. That along with the fact that I'd just left behind the man I loved, and I was feeling as though I could quite easily vomit. The heat in the departure lounge didn't help with my pounding head or the man's body smell.

All I wanted to do was curl up in my seat and sleep the hours away until I touched down in England. Although sleep hadn't come last night, so even though I was shattered, I doubted it would come easily now. My mind was full of Jesse; how he kissed me, how he made love to me, replaying every word he'd ever said to me, what he looked like, his smell and the sound of his voice. Everything about him.

Tears pricked at my lashes and my nose started to tingle, and if it didn't mean I'd lose my seat in the packed departure lounge, I'd go to the bathroom to cry in the solitude of a toilet stall. However,

I didn't want to lose my seat, because while it was awful sitting next to stinky, I didn't have the energy or strength to stand up for the next half hour until we boarded; so stinky it was.

"It's hot in here, isn't it?" Stinky said, wiping sweat from his brow with the palm of his hand.

"Yes," I replied, trying not to breathe in. "Really hot."

"Betcha that damn plane is the same," he growled. "I hate flying, I always end up with some sort of bug. It's all that stale air you know."

"Hmm, I suppose so." I flashed him a small smile and started to fish around in my bag, hoping he'd stop talking.

"You're from England then?" He nodded at me. "It's the accent, I spotted it. Where are you from?"

He wouldn't know if I told him, so said the place that most people had heard of. "Manchester."

"Oh, Manchester United!" he said excitedly, grinning.

I shook my head. "God, no. Manchester City, although I don't really watch football." My brother would never forgive me if I'd said anything good about United, he was a real City fan.

"Ah now, we call it soccer. Football is a man's game, not what you English call football."

I just smiled and seriously considered going to the bathroom; who cared if I lost my seat? I just couldn't stand this any longer.

I zipped up my bag and was just about to push up when I heard a commotion from the row of seats near to the entrance.

"Sorry, ma'am," a familiar voice shouted as they pushed past people.

My chest tightened and I felt a hot sweat blanket my skin. Jesse was here and I had no idea what to do. I was stuck to my seat, staring at the top of his head bobbing along, as he ploughed through the people standing around. As he got closer and closer to the row that I was sitting in, my breathing got faster and my legs started shaking uncontrollably.

Then, as he reached the end of the row, he spotted me and his eyes locked with mine. Tears flowed as I watched him walk towards me. His hair was mussed up, he was wearing his casual jeans, the ones that were well worn and hung from his hips, and his black t-shirt was covered in some sort of pink sticky liquid, but he'd never looked more beautiful.

"Armalita," he said in a low voice, stopping a couple of feet in front of me. "Where the hell do you think you're going?"

"Home," I whispered around the lump in my throat.

"Why?" He crossed his arms over his chest and tilted his head to the side, waiting expectantly for my answer. "Well?"

"Because it's what's best," I replied.

"For fucking who?" he asked, leaning forwards from the waist.

"Hey, do you mind?" Stinky asked. "There's no need for cursing in front of the lady."

I held my breath as Jesse turned to him and furrowed his brow.

"I'm sorry, but I'm trying to talk to my girl here. I apologize for my language sir, but this is fucking important." He then turned back to me. "Now, tell me who is it best for that you go home?"

"Me," I said, taking a deep breath. "You too, you're not ready to move on."

"How do you know what I'm ready for? And tell me, how do you feel sitting here waiting to go back home, without me, knowing that once you get on that plane you'll probably never see me again, hmm?"

Jesse's hands moved to his hips, and his legs parted. His muscular chest flexed underneath his t-shirt and I could see a few people were now starting to quiet their chatter to watch and listen.

"Answer me, Armalita," he said. "How the hell do you feel?"

"What's that on your t-shirt?" I asked distractedly.

Jesse glanced down at his chest, and scrubbed a hand over his head. "It's not important, now tell me how you damn well feel about getting on that plane."

"Hey, miss, if you want me to get security, I will," Stinky kindly offered.

I looked at him and shook my head. "No, it's fine, thank you, though."

He sighed. "Whatever, but if that man is harassing you, then I think you should call them."

"He's not," I assured him. I turned back to Jesse, who was still staring at me, waiting for my answer. "I feel as though I have an open wound in my chest, and someone keeps poking it," I replied. "I feel that if I get on that plane I'll just shrivel up and die."

My voice broke on a quiet sob, and I placed a flat palm against my stomach, trying to stem the nausea.

Jesse gave me a slow smile and let out a long breath. He took a step closer to me and dropped to his haunches, taking my shaking hands in his.

"Shall I tell you how I feel?" he asked. "How I feel about the thought of you getting on that plane?"

I chewed on my bottom lip and nodded.

"If you got on that plane, baby, I'd feel as though my soul had been ripped out. The pain I would feel if you left me, would be nothing like I have ever felt before, and I mean *ever*. You are mine, sweetness, you're meant to be with me, and I don't just mean for the next ten months. I mean forever, for always, until I have no breath left in my body."

I heard a gasp behind Jesse, and when I looked around him, I saw a lady dressed in a pink velour tracksuit, and lots of gold jewellery, fanning her eyes.

"That's so beautiful," she cooed in a broad British, Yorkshire accent. "Andy, why've you never said anything like that to me?"

The man, who I guessed was Andy, simply shrugged.

"Well if you don't want him, love, I'll take him off your hands."

I let out a nervous giggle and sniffled. Stinky shoved a tissue into my hand, one that was thankfully clean.

"Do. You. Get. It. Armalita?" Jesse asked, nodding his head on each word, to bring home the point.

"Get what?" I asked, dabbing at my nose.

"How much I love you." He gave me a soft, gentle smile, the sort that warmed my heart, my blood, my soul. "I love you beyond words, beyond actions, but it means nothing if you don't believe it. You need to know, to understand and believe, because if you don't, then you may as well get on that plane."

"No!" Pink velour lady shouted. "Of course she knows, don't ya love?"

Jesse swivelled to look at the lady and I guessed that he'd given her a smile, because her cheeks suddenly matched her tracksuit. He then turned back to me.

"Do you know?" he asked quietly, his blue eyes pleading with me.

"What about what happened, when you found out?" I asked. "You were hurting so much, and I don't expect you to brush it off, not something like that, but it felt like you still loved her."

Jesse ran a hand through his hair as he contemplated his words.

"It was a shock, I admit, but the thought of her with someone else didn't give me the pain I thought it would. What I couldn't handle was the agony it had all caused Addy. She's my baby, Millie, and she's been through so much damn hurt and she's only four years old. I hated that her mother denied her and was just going to leave her without a care. I hate that Melody dying meant that I pushed her away, too, and that was part of the distress I felt that day. And what sort of man would I be if I didn't feel sadness at the way Melody died, alone and in pain? You know the autopsy said she probably survived about five or ten minutes after she went through that windshield. Five or ten minutes when she might have been conscious, knowing she was dying." Jesse dragged in a breath and looked down at the floor. His shoulders sagged and I knew reliving what Brandon had told him must have been hard.

"Jesse," I whispered, reaching out a tentative hand. "I understand all of that, I really do, but I can't live in her shadow. But what sort of woman would I be if I tried to push her from your memories?"

"Oh, baby, you won't live in her shadow, you could never live in anyone's shadow. You shine much too brightly for that." He reached forward and took my hand, rubbing his thumb along the back of it. "I have to keep some memories alive though, for Addy, not because Melody deserves it, but because Addy does. Addy needs to think her momma loved her more than life itself, more than diamonds, fast cars, and swimming pools. The Melody I loved left me a long time before she passed away. I think she left me the day I married her."

He dropped to his knees and moved over to me, cradling my face in his hands.

"I love you, Armalita Braithwaite, and I will do everything in my power to make you happy. You deserve happy, *we* deserve happy, and I know we can get that together. So, are you getting on that plane?"

I didn't even need to think about it. A sob escaped as I shook my head and flung my arms around Jesse's neck. "No," I cried. "I'm not getting on the plane."

"Thank fuck for that," he said, his lips finding mine and kissing me hard.

"Bloody brilliant," Pink velour shouted.

Jesse pulled away from me, so I tried to drag him back. He laughed and shook his head.

"There's something I need to do," he said, giving me another very quick kiss.

He sat back on his calves and put his finger and thumb in his mouth and gave two short whistles. The next thing I knew, a tiny little blonde princess was running towards us, dragging a fluffy, white rabbit holding a red velvet heart behind her.

"Millie!" she yelled, her eyes bright with excitement. "I brought your rabbit."

"Yes, sweetheart, you did," I replied, with tears falling rapidly down my face.

"Well, there's a special reason for that, isn't there, baby?" Jesse pulled Addy to him and sat her on his knee.

"Yep," Addy said with a resounding nod. "Do I give it to her now, Daddy?"

Jesse kissed the back of her head and laughed. "Yes, you can give it to her now."

Addy thrust the rabbit at me, almost pushing it in my face, so I had no choice to take it from her.

"Thank you," I spluttered.

"Look at the rabbit's neck," Addy said, bouncing up and down on Jesse's knee.

I looked down to see a ribbon around the rabbit's neck, and hanging from it was a blue foil heart. On it was the word, 'Daddy'. I gasped, knowing exactly what this meant, and peered at Jesse over the top of the fluffy bunny. Addy was watching me wide eyed, a bundle of nervous energy.

"Did you see it?" she asked.

I nodded, not able to speak.

"It's Daddy's heart," she said. "He wants you to have it."

"He does?" I asked with a sniff.

"Yeah, I do," Jesse answered, his voice deep and full of emotion. "Although we had an incident with a strawberry milkshake on the way here, and it nearly got soaked."

I looked at his chest and giggled.

"I told you not to keep it in that pocket," Addy complained, poking at the breast pocket of his t-shirt. "Daddy's are so silly sometimes."

"So, Armalita," Jesse sighed with a smile and shake of his head. "Do you accept my heart?"

I nodded and clutched the rabbit to my chest. Addy squealed, jumped up, and reached inside the little pocket of her jeans.

"I brought you this," she said, shoving something at me.

I looked down and there was a piece of white fabric with lemon flowers on it in the shape of a heart, and on it was my name. It was *my* heart, made for me by the warmest and most loving little girl I had ever met.

I took it from her tiny fingers and looked at Jesse. "Will you take my heart, Jesse Connor?"

Without hesitation, Jesse took it from me and placed it in his t-shirt pocket. "Too damn right I will." He leaned around Addy and kissed me, but then pulled back again.

"One last thing," he said, holding up a finger. "Okay, you ready, baby?"

Addy nodded and grinned widely. "Yep, sure am."

Jesse cleared his throat and, placing Addy on one knee, he lifted the other and put his foot on the ground. As soon as I recognised his kneeling stance, my hands started shaking and my heart began punching its way out of my chest.

"Armalita Braithwaite, I love you more than I can say in words. You're my beginning and my end, and I don't want to spend a day without you, so if that means moving to England then we'll do it, won't we, Addy?"

Addy nodded. "Granma argued with Daddy about that all the way here, but she was okay in the end."

I glanced over my shoulder in the direction that Addy was nodding and saw Bonnie. She was standing a few feet away, behind us, and her face was tear stained, too. She gave me a beautiful smile and nodded her head.

"That won't be necessary," I said, turning back to Jesse and Addy. "I love it here, and I love the ranch."

Jesse seemed to relax with relief, but I loved that he was willing to come to England with me.

"As long as you're sure," he whispered.

"I'm positive."

"Okay, so the final thing then." He coughed and held Addy's hand. "I don't have a ring yet, but Armalita, will you do us the honour of marrying us?"

Before I'd even finished the word 'yes' I was dragged into their embrace and kissed thoroughly by Jesse, while in the background I heard Stinky crying and Pink velour lady whooping loudly.

Jesse Connor was the love of my life and he had my heart forever.

EPILOGUE

♥

7 YEARS LATER

MILLIE

To say that Jesse was freaking out was an understatement. His baby girl was about to fly the nest and he was hating every single minute of it. Addy had been accepted on a Gifted Child program at a specialist School two hours away, and Addy being Addy, said she wanted to board. She was just eleven, so Jesse being Jesse said, 'hell will freeze over first'. Addy being Addy, had wrapped her daddy around her little finger and he was now packing up the truck to take her.

"I fucking hate this," he muttered to me as he heaved a suitcase into the flatbed of the truck. "I don't know why she can't come home every day."

As he turned to face me, I saw the utter grief etched over his handsome features. I ran my fingers through his hair, brushing it away from his beautiful eyes and kissed him gently.

"Baby, she wants to do this. She's going to be home every

Thursday evening."

"Yeah, until some science club or reading group starts, or she makes friends with some rich kid who wants her to do sleepovers, or some other shit. Then," he cried throwing his hands into the air, "the next thing, there'll be some little dickwad with hormones who thinks he's a fucking stud!"

I couldn't help but laugh at my husband's little temper tantrum. It was evident now where our youngest, Hunter, got his temper from. He was only two, but could throw a fit with the best of them. Clemmie, or Clementine to give her proper name, our six year old, was all me. With her olive skin, big brown eyes, and black hair, her Spanish side was prominent. Thankfully, she hadn't inherited a Spanish or Connor temper and was so relaxed she should have had a mattress strapped to her back. Hunter and Addy, however, were Connor's through and through, both in looks and temperament.

"It ain't funny, Armalita," Jesse growled, and I knew that I was in trouble. I was only ever Armalita when I was in trouble.

"Oh, come on, it is," I giggled. "You know none of that is going to happen."

"How do I?"

Jesse pouted and kicked at a stone that ricocheted off the hub cap of his old truck. Yes, he still had it. He said he couldn't get rid of it because of the happy memories it gave him; memories of us having amazing sex on the front seat, the night we'd argued over Brandon. In fact, we couldn't be sure, but we think Hunter was conceived on that front seat. We'd been to Rowdy's and I'd got drunk, so when Jesse parked up at the side of the house, I pounced on him and rode him until he bellowed my name. In return, Jesse gave me two amazing orgasms and possibly a baby. We'd loved it, and over breakfast neither of us could stop grinning. That was until Ted told Jesse he needed to sort the suspension out on the truck, 'because it made the noise of a creaking gate the whole time you were going at it'.

"She loves you too much to not want to come home," I replied. "Plus, there's Dapple, she will not leave that horse for long."

Jesse grinned, realising that the horse that he'd finally bought and given in to letting Addy break in by herself, was probably going to ensure his baby girl came home every weekend.

"Told you it was a good idea," he muttered.

"You told me?" I gasped. "I think you'll find it was me that kept hearing 'Momma please ask Daddy if I can have a horse to break in by myself...Momma did you ask Daddy... Momma why is Daddy so mean about me having a horse'."

Jesse let out a laugh and dragged me into his embrace.

"Did I tell you today that I love you?"

"Nope," I said with pouty lips. "You didn't."

"I sure did show you this morning though, didn't I?"

Jesse's low, sexy drawl had me wanting to drag him to our room and rip his clothes off. Nothing had changed in that respect over the last seven years; I still fancied the pants of him, and did whenever possible.

"How about you show me again, when you get back. I'll get the kids to bed and then maybe I'll put on that sexy underwear that you bought me for Christmas."

Jesse moaned and pushed himself against me, so I was in no doubt what his answer was. The rock hard dick straining against his jeans said it all.

"Good thing Mom and Dad moved out of the house," he groaned. "Because I'm gonna fuck you so long and so hard you'll be screaming my name."

"Don't I always?"

Jesse took my mouth in his and gave me a long, intoxicating kiss that fired up all my senses.

"Baby, we need to stop, Addy will be back from seeing your mum and dad in a minute."

Bonnie and Ted had moved out of the house once Hunter was born. Not only did we need the room to accommodate three rowdy, growing children, but Hunter was not a good sleeper and he disturbed everyone in the house pretty much every night. Jesse had built them a cabin house just on the other side of the pasture, opposite our house. He'd got a construction company to come in and build them a fantastic home, all done to Jesse's specification. It was beautiful and modern, yet still retaining the rustic feel that Bonnie had missed from the main house after Jesse had developed it. I told Jesse that once he finished ranching, if Hunter didn't want to take over, then he should sell up and go into construction design because he had a great eye for it. He just laughed and said hell would freeze over before this ranch belonged to anyone but a Connor. He really did have a thing about hell freezing over one day.

"Okay," Jesse said, pulling away from me. "You're right, but you'd better be naked and waiting for me when I get home."

"You can count on it."

"So, did Garratt say what time he was getting here this weekend?"

I grinned, knowing that Jesse's change of subject was to try and erase pictures of me naked from his mind and ease his hard on before Addy came back.

"Probably early evening on Thursday. He wants to be here when the bus drops Addy back."

"Ah, she'll love that."

Addy still adored her Uncle Garratt and had no idea that he was coming over next weekend, because we hadn't told her we were going to have a party to celebrate her first week at her new school.

"I'm still not happy about her coming home on a bus, though." Jesse ran a hand down his face and I knew that he was starting to struggle again, but the bus was the best option.

Because it was a school for gifted children, and lessons were much more intense, they only attended school for four days of the week then, on a Thursday afternoon, various buses transported all the kids home. That's why Jesse's truck was full to bursting. We'd had to buy Addy a duplicate of everything that she had at home, just so she wouldn't have to haul things on the bus every weekend.

"We'll see how it goes and if she doesn't like it, or you're not happy, then maybe I can collect her."

"No, honey. That's a four hour round trip that I do not want you doing, especially if you had to take the kids with you. Can you imagine my fucking stress levels? My whole life in one fucking car, without me. Nope, not happening. If necessary, I'll hire a driver, or send one of the boys."

Before I could say anything else, Addy came skipping around the corner from saying goodbye to her grandparents. She was really excited, but when she saw Jesse's face, she slowed to a walk.

"Baby, don't spoil this for her," I whispered.

Jesse looked up at me and nodded.

"Come on then, Adaline Marie Connor, let's get you to school." He plastered on a smile and held his hand out to Addy.

It was at that moment I saw it hit Addy; she was going away from her family and while it was an exciting time, the realisation of not being on the ranch every day and being with all of us was suddenly a little daunting.

I knew how she felt, leaving Mum and Javi behind permanently had been heart wrenching, but I loved Jesse and Addy and couldn't imagine a life without them. Thankfully, Mum and Javi were able to visit at least every eighteen months or so and Jesse had even spoken to them about coming out here to live. Mum missed her grandbabies and Javi wanted a fresh start, so I was forever hopeful.

As I looked down at Addy, I saw her bottom lip tremble, just as it had that first day I met her. Then tears started to roll slowly down her cheeks.

"Hey," Jesse soothed, pulling her into his arms. "It's gonna be fine, you'll love every minute of it."

I watched him brush his hands through her long blonde hair and I couldn't have loved him any more if I'd tried. He could easily have used her fears to persuade her to stay, but he didn't; he was doing what he knew she wanted and what was best for her.

"Momma," Addy sobbed and pulled away from Jesse to wrap her thin little arms around my waist. "I'm going to miss you, so much."

"I'll miss you too, sweetie, but you'll be home before you know it. It's just four days, that's all. Think of it this way. It's four days without Clemmie wanting you to play tea parties, or Hunter trying to stop you from reading by slapping his sticky hands all over your book. Okay?"

She looked up at me with tear filled eyes and nodded. God, I loved this child with all my heart, as much as if she were my own. I had loved her pretty much from the moment I met her, much the same as I had her father, but the first time she called me 'momma,' I fell even harder. It had been the day of our wedding, here on the ranch, a service held in the pasture, and then a reception in a marquee that Jesse and the boys erected. Jesse and I were having our first dance to Etta James' *'At Last'*, when Addy tugged on Jesse's perfectly tailored suit jacket and said, 'May I have this dance with my momma?'. With both of us crying, Jesse, Addy, and I all danced together and I had never been happier.

"I love you," I whispered, and kissed her head that I was clutching to my chest.

"I love you too, Momma." She lifted her head and beautiful blue eyes stared up at me. "Momma?"

"Yes, Addy," I replied, smoothing down her hair.

"Will you give Clemmie the box of hearts?" she asked. "Tell her what she needs to do."

I nodded and held my breath to hold back the sob.

"Tell her that she needs to be really careful," she said earnestly. "Only give people their heart when she knows it's right. When she knows it's true love."

With more tears, I gave her one final squeeze. "I will, I promise."

I didn't want to let go, but she had to be booked in at the halls of residence by four, and it was already one-thirty. Jesse had asked me to go along, but I thought he needed to be alone with Addy for the two hour drive. They were as close as father and daughter could be, did everything together; rode out on a Sunday morning together, went fishing together, she'd even been known to go out with him during calving season, sometimes at night, too if there had been a difficult birth. That we'd argued about, but Jesse was adamant that his girls should learn everything that he would eventually teach Hunter.

As I let Addy go, Jesse kneeled down in front of her and took hold of her hands.

"Okay?"

She nodded. "Yes, Daddy."

"That's my girl, but remember; if at any time you want to come home, you just pick up a phone and no matter what is happening on this ranch, I will leave and come and get you. You are my precious baby, my first born, and I will always be there for you."

Jesse swallowed hard, pushing Addy's hair away from her face, while I had to swipe away a tear from my cheek.

"I wasn't always the best daddy," he said quietly. "I know that, but I always loved you. You, your sister and brother, and your momma are my life and if anything happened to any of you, my heart would be broken, but I'd carry on for the rest of you. But when Momma Melody died, I forgot that you needed me even more than ever before, and I'll be forever sorry for that. Just know that you're my angel and I adore and love you."

Jesse coughed to hide the emotion in his voice, but he couldn't help but let out a heart wrenching groan when Addy flung her arms around his neck and squeezed him with every bit of strength that she had.

"I know you love me, Daddy, you were just a little bit broken, until Momma came to live with us," she said against his neck.

Now my tears careened as fast as white water falls down my face and I could see that Jesse was struggling to hold it together.

"Yes, Addy, I was a little bit broken, and your momma did heal me, but I should never have let you think that I didn't care about you, and I should never have neglected you the way I did. I guess my head was up my ass for a while."

"Jesse!" I scolded through tearful laughter.

"It's okay, Momma. I know not to say that."

I patted Addy's head and gave Jesse one of my looks that I used on the kids when I was disappointed with them. Jesse, like the kids, just laughed.

"Okay sweetie, you ready?"

Addy nodded and wiped at her face before turning to me.

"I love you Momma, and tell Clemmie and Hunter I'll see them on Thursday."

I nodded, unable to speak. We'd left Clemmie and Hunter with Bella, Trent the foreman's wife, thinking that it would all be too traumatic for them as they wouldn't understand that Addy was actually coming back. Jesse had worked horses for the last five years, as well as having 650 pairs on the ranch, so he needed a foreman and Trent had become invaluable. He and Bella lived in Jesse's old cabin that we had also extended.

Jesse had offered the job to Zak, but with twin boys, a terror of a three year old girl and Sarah to keep check on, he'd turned it down. Sarah still caused havoc when we had girl's night and she was my best friend who I loved like a sister.

"I'll see you in a few hours, honey," Jesse said and leaned forward to take my mouth in a soft kiss. "I love you."

"I love you, too, both of you."

I waved goodbye until I could no longer see the truck, and then stood waiting for a few more minutes. I kind of hoped that they'd come back and Addy would say she'd changed her mind, but they didn't.

When Jesse got home just before dinner, he looked thoroughly washed out; today had been hard on him. What he'd said to Addy was true. After Melody died, he couldn't see past his own grief and pushed away the most precious gift that he'd been given. The one decent thing that Melody had done for him. Thankfully, Addy didn't suffer any long term effects of that time and in some ways, it made her love for Jesse even stronger, and his for her.

"You okay, baby?" I asked as he dropped his forehead to my shoulder, his hands resting on my hips.

"I will be. It was hard, you know."

"I know, but I'll make it better for you."

Jesse lifted his head and grinned.

"You wanna make another baby?" he asked excitedly.

I slapped his chest and gently pushed him away.

"No, I do not. Not yet anyway. But I'd sure love to practice, cowboy."

Jesse dropped his head back and roared with laughter at my attempt on his accent. In all the years since I'd first come here, I still hadn't mastered it.

"God, I love you, Armalita."

"Hey, what've I done wrong? You only call me Armalita when I'm in trouble."

"Nope." he shook his head. "I think you'll find I call you Armalita before I fuck you long and hard and smack that delicious ass of yours."

I thought about it and he was right; I just assumed it was make up sex.

"In that case, Mr Connor, you'd better take me to bed and do what you've got to do."

With a dip of his body, he had me upside down over his shoulder and carried me upstairs, creeping past Clemmie and Hunter's rooms so as not to wake them.

He made good on his promise on fucking me long and hard, but he also gave me a baby, too; you'd think I'd have learned that when Jesse Connor wants something, he usually gets it. So, nine months and ten days later, Ruby Jessica Connor was born completing our family. She was named after a fluffy white rabbit and her great, great aunt who had died the previous fall; and just like her she was loud, sassy and opinionated, but adored by everyone.

A week after Ruby was born, I sent a thank you card to Dean and Ambrose Ricks-Johnson, thanking them for being the best couple I had ever met.

THE END.

BOX OF HEARTS PLAYLIST

Can't Help Falling In Love – Elvis
Is This Love – Bob Marley
Please Don't Go – Joel Adams
Hero – Enrique
Thinking Out Loud – Ed Sheeran
Sunshine – TIEKS ft Dan Harkna
Mercy – Shawn Mendes
At Last – Etta James
Starving – Hailee Steinfeld
Say You Won't Let Go – James Arthur
All of Me – John Legend
Earned It – The Weekend
Treat You Better – Shawn Mendes
Lullaby – Nickleback
Daughters – John Mayer
Let Me Love You – DJ Snake
Fresh Eyes – Andy Grammer
Dancing on My Own – Callum Scott
Tears – Clean Bandit ft Louisa Johnson
English Rose – The Jam
Iris – The Goo Goo Dolls
Better Man – Paolo Nutini
If I Ain't Got You – Alicia Keys

ACKNOWLEDGMENTS

For me this book was an absolute joy to write, the words simply flowed and I loved every minute of it. That being said, writing a contemporary romance instead of a romantic comedy, was scary too. I wasn't sure how it would be received, especially having to get the US dialogue correct-Aleesha Davis to the rescue. Thank you Aleesha for your editing and for ensuring that I used the right words. You made the whole experience a little less daunting.

To JC Clarke of The Graphic Shed, thank you for such a beautiful cover and formatting. I'm excited to be working with you on this series, and I know that there are some beautiful covers to come.

Miranda Bly, thank you for naming my rancher. I can't imagine him as being anything else but Jesse now. You picked a perfect name.

To Caroline James and Victoria Johns, you girls rock. I can't believe just over a year ago, as the song goes 'I just hadn't met you yet'. You both help me so much with plot lines, inspiration and confidence. You're my cheerleaders and have no idea how much that means to me coming from two such talented women.

To my street team-Laura Jackson, Hayley Buckley, Ally Williams,

Nadine Keedy, Laura Nelson, Cal Sleath, Samanth Ann, Nicole Roberts, Colette Locock, Catherine Hayward, Alison Daughtrey-Drew and Stephanie O'Neil. Girls you are the best. Your support is unfailing and you always put a smile on my face.

Patsy Taylor and Sherri Bell, thank you as always for loving my words even in their rawest form.

Laura Barnard, you are Super Woman. I thought I'd got it covered until you started to help me, so a mahoosive thank you for everything.

To my family, I love you more than you'll ever know and I hope that I make you proud.

Finally, as always Mr. A. David, I know I'm always busy typing away in the corner, but my heart is always with you- even if I only join you on the sofa to watch football. Your encouragement and love means the world to me and if it wasn't for you and your vocabulary I'd be a mess.

Much love, as always,
Nikki X

Printed in Great Britain
by Amazon